" 'TIS FORBIDDEN FOR YOU TO TOUCH ME, ALEX,"

Kitt reminded her bodyguard. She felt a stab of alarm when her warning had no effect. But she refused to be the one to back away. Her flashing eyes dared him to come closer. Dared him to try and kiss her.

He gave her a wolfish smile. "You let go first."

She realized her hands were twined in the hair at his nape and snatched them away. "Now you let go," she said.

The feel of his breath on her flesh had already sent an expectant shiver down her spine when he finally stepped back. "You're safe from me, my lady," he said, though his eyes sent a different, dangerous message. "I will keep my promise. No matter how great the temptation."

Kitt could not deny she had wondered what it might be like to kiss him. Perhaps she had even let him see it in her eyes. But she knew better. To succumb to mere physical desire was disaster, plain and simple.

You must get rid of Alex and hire someone else as your bodyguard. Someone safe...

JOAN JOHNSTON

The Bodyguard

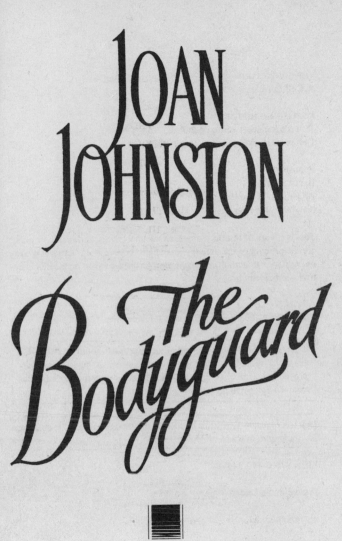

D e l l

THE BODYGUARD
A Dell Book

PUBLISHING HISTORY
Dell mass market edition published April 1998
Dell mass market reissue / March 2008

Published by
Bantam Dell
A Division of Random House, Inc.
New York, New York

Dell is a registered trademark of Random House, Inc., and the colophon
is a trademark of Random House, Inc.

ISBN 978-0-440-24474-5

Printed in the United States of America

www.bantamdell.com

OPM 10 9 8 7 6 5 4 3 2 1

*This book is dedicated to
my writing friends
with thanks
for your love and support.*

Prologue

FROM CHILDHOOD KATHERINE MACKINNON HAD been taught how to reive cattle, how to disappear like mist into the Highlands, and how to hate the English. Even so, she was shocked and appalled by her father's deathbed request.

"You canna mean what you're asking, Father," she said, adjusting her plaid scarf with trembling fingers.

"'Twas the fourth Duke of Blackthorne who struck the mortal blow that killed your grandfather at Culloden," he reminded her. "The fifth of that name enforced the ban against the plaid and the playing of the pipes. And the latest Blackthorne bastard, sixth of his line, has raised the rents to starve us out."

"I know, Father, but—"

"They couldna kill us off," he interrupted her. "They couldna break our spirit. But a man canna watch his bairns starve."

"Father—"

"I'm dying, Kitt. 'Tis up to you to carry on the fight when I am gone. You must do what I ask."

As Kitt looked down at her father's nearly emaciated form, a beam of sunlight danced through the window of the stone-and-thatch cottage where she had spent the whole of her two and twenty years. *The sun should not be shining on such a sad day as this*, she thought.

Suddenly Kitt felt all of the grief and anguish and disbelief anew. Her mother had died shortly after giving birth to her. Now her father was threatening to leave her . . . forever. She refused to accept it.

"Dinna speak of dying, Father," she cajoled. "I'm not ready to let you go."

"I'm done for, lass. I willna live another day. I give you the care of our people. I trust their lives and the future of the clan to you. I name you Chief of Clan MacKinnon and hereditary Laird—Lady, I suppose it must be—of Castle MacKinnon, lately called Blackthorne Hall."

A shudder passed through her as she acknowledged the enormous weight of responsibility her father was laying upon her shoulders. Her father's closest advisor, Duncan Fraser, who stood nearby, gasped in dismay at her father's pronouncement.

"You canna name a woman The MacKinnon, Rob!" Duncan said. "The men willna follow her."

"For my own sake I ask it, Duncan," her father replied. "For the love that Clan MacKinnon bears my father, I demand it."

Kitt's grandfather, Jamie MacKinnon, was revered by his clansmen because, though mortally wounded himself, he had helped Bonnie Prince Charlie escape to Mallaig after the disastrous Battle of Culloden. As a final punishment for his treason against the English king, Castle MacKinnon and the surrounding land had been awarded as a prize of war to the Duke of Blackthorne—"There being no living male heir to The MacKinnon."

Of course, the grant had been in error. But who could blame her grandmother for remaining silent about the child growing in her womb? She would likely have been put to the sword herself. Why take the risk when the child might be female? And she had bitten her tongue when Robert MacKinnon was born, fearing her tiny son would be dispatched by the bloodthirsty duke before his claim could be recognized.

Duncan Fraser had stepped into the breach caused by Jamie's death and had watched out for Robert MacKinnon, making certain that he took his rightful place as The MacKinnon when he was a young man. But no claim had ever been made against the English for the return of the castle or the land.

Now Duncan was bent with age, and her father was dying of it. Someone must lead, and there was no first-born son to follow as chief. Only a daughter.

"'Tis folly to name a woman as chief," Duncan said. "'Tis never been done in my memory. But if you wish it—"

3

"I do," Rob said. "Leave us, Duncan. I have words to speak to my daughter."

Once Duncan had left the bedroom, her father said, "Step closer, lass. There's a way to reclaim the castle and the land, if only you have the courage to follow through with it."

"Shouldna Duncan hear this?" Kitt asked.

"My plan is for your ears alone, lass. Now lean close. I havna much strength to say what must be said."

Kitt bent her head close to her father's, a thick lock of her long dark hair falling over his chest. Quickly, she tucked it behind her ear and knuckled away the womanish tears on her face, masking her fear of the future with a wobbly smile. As her father whispered his plan, the blood drained from her face, leaving her ashen.

"I canna do it!" she cried, stunned at what he'd suggested. "I willna do it!"

Once upon a time, the gnarled hand that grasped her wrist could have crushed her bones, but age and illness had stolen her father's strength. She could easily have pulled away, but respect and love for him held her in place.

"Swear to me you'll do as I ask . . . for the sake of our clansmen."

"You ask too much!" Kitt protested. "There must be some other way." Her blood pounded in her ears like surf against the rocky Scottish coast. "Let me get Duncan—"

"Nay, lass. Duncan willna approve. Nor will the others. 'Tis likely they will hate you for it. But 'tis the only way. Swear," he rasped, his breath rattling in his chest.

If she had hesitated a moment longer, his spirit would have flown, and the promise would not have been made. But Kitt saw the light dying in his eyes and in an effort to keep him with her she blurted, "I swear, on my honor as The MacKinnon, to do what I must to win back the castle and the land."

"That's a good lass." The air soughed from his lungs, but he did not struggle for more. He merely closed his eyes and gave in to death.

"No, Father!" she cried. "Dinna leave me!" A sob welled up like a giant wave inside her and became an ululating cry of pain. "Father! Father, dinna go!"

She felt Duncan's firm hand on her shoulder, urging her away. "He's gone, child. He canna hear you."

Kitt shook off his touch and snarled, "Go away, old man, and leave me be." She stared at him defiantly, The MacKinnon who must be obeyed.

Once Duncan was gone, she threw herself across her father's broad chest, held tight to his neck, and wept like the woman she was. Her ragged, keening moans quieted the mockingbirds and found an echo in the whispering wind from the sea. She wept until her throat was raw and no more sound came out, until there was only an ache in her throat and in the place where her heart should be.

It was dark when her old nurse, Moira, came in and told her it was time to let the women take her father and lay him out. She let herself be led away and sat down at the table near the hearth and stared sightlessly at the bowl of sheep's-head broth with leeks and carrots that Moira put before her.

At long last, she folded her hands, said a prayer for her father's soul, and accepted her fate. She would do as her father had instructed. She would make a claim in both the English and Scottish courts for the castle and the land.

"You must claim the grant is defective because there was indeed a male heir—living in your grandmother's womb," her father had explained. "The duke willna be able to resist coming to Scotland. He will want to see who dares lay claim to what he thinks is his. He will try to buy you off. He will try to frighten you away. You mustn't let yourself be swayed, lass. When he comes, this is what you will do . . ."

Kitt's stomach clenched with dread as she recalled her father's instructions. She was resigned to do what she must, though every proper sense revolted against it.

Father, you ask too much of me.

But what other hope did her people have? When the duke came, she would act. The clan would have its revenge, the land and the castle would once again belong to The MacKinnon, and her people's suffering would end.

She had sworn an oath to her dying father, and no force in heaven or on earth could make her break that vow.

Chapter 1

THE SEA WAS VICIOUS, INTENT ON KILLING HIM, but Alastair Wharton, sixth Duke of Blackthorne, was not ready to die. He was too young—a mere three and thirty years—and had too many sins upon his soul to meet his maker.

"Strike the mainsail!" he shouted. The sound was lost in the howling wind that tore at the canvas, driving his ship, the *Twin Ladies*, toward the rugged coast of Scotland. Or at least, where he supposed the coast to be. There had been no sight of land before the storm had broken at sunset, and the inky darkness was so complete, it was as though the ship lay wallowing in the belly of a whale.

In the light of a swaying lantern, he could make out three sailors clustered together and yelled, "You there! Get that sail down!"

The sailors turned their backs on him, ignoring the order. They were talking heatedly, gesturing wildly,

7

obviously frightened by the storm. It was his own fault that such unreliable seamen were on board. He did not sail often, and it was easier to hire the men he needed, rather than keep a regular crew. Those three were the last to be brought on board in London, and they had been malingerers from the start.

A twenty-foot wave of icy saltwater crashed onto the deck, making it slick as an eel, drenching Alastair and chilling him to the bone. Shivering, teeth chattering, he clung to the ship's wheel, determined not to give in to the sea.

I cannot die now, he raged silently. *Not now.*

It was too great an irony to die now, when he had just taken the first steps to reconcile with his nine-year-old twin daughters, Lady Regina and Lady Rebecca. All those years he had wasted! All those years he could have been loving them, but for Penthia's malevolent declaration that the twins were not his. Alastair had lately had the urge to strangle her. But Penthia, Duchess of Blackthorne, was already three years in her grave from a drunken fall down the stairs of Blackthorne Abbey.

Once upon a time, he had loved her more than life itself. It was hard to remember the naive boy he had been all those years ago when he had wooed Lady Penthia Straith and wed her. He had been two and twenty, without a bit of Town bronze, but determined to have the belle of the Season—the same exotic beauty who had reigned the previous four Seasons.

Lady Penthia Straith had reached the age of one and

twenty without accepting an offer. It was rumored that over the past four years she had refused all the most eligible *partis*. The first time he saw Penthia, Alastair had found her striking blue eyes and alabaster skin and raven-black hair breathtaking. He had found her worldliness and sophistication even more attractive. He had made up his mind on the instant to have her to wife.

His father's untimely death had forced Alastair into a ducal role far sooner than he was ready, and beneath the facade of confidence was a young man unsure he could carry off the part. With Lady Penthia by his side, Alastair knew he could face the *ton* and pretend to be duke until the guise became more natural.

He'd had a great deal to offer her. Besides being a duke, he was as rich as Croesus and handsome as well. Not quite so good-looking as his younger brother Marcus, perhaps. His hair was not so perfectly blond, and his eyes were a troubled gray, not the uncommon blue of his brother's. But there were not many who could match the Beau for looks.

In his pursuit of Lady Penthia, he had concealed his youthful eagerness, his yearning to hold her, his thundering, head-over-heels heart, behind a facade of ducal regality. Alastair could still remember the first time he had managed to get her alone in the garden at Viscount Raleigh's ball.

The night air had been surprisingly warm and heavily perfumed by the viscount's rose garden. He had walked arm in arm with Lady Penthia along a gravel path, unable to breathe, feeling the heat of her gloved hand through his jacket and shirt, the weight and warmth of her breast against his sleeve.

His heart fluttered against his ribs with excitement and fear. He intended to kiss her. He had been planning it for weeks. He had heard enough of his brother's exploits—Marcus was considerably more into the petticoat line than he was—to know what he must do. He stopped near a tall hedge that concealed them from the party inside, released Lady Penthia's arm, and angled himself to face her.

"I—" His voice came out as a croak. He was grateful for the darkness that hid his painful flush. He cleared his throat and tried again. "I find you more beautiful than words."

Somehow she had come a step closer, and he could feel her breasts pressing against his waistcoat. "Do you, Your Grace?" she said in a sultry voice that lifted the hairs on his arms.

He stuck a finger beneath the perfect *trône d'amour* his valet, Stubbins, had tied with his neck cloth, to give himself a little more room to breathe.

She looked up at him shyly from beneath lowered lashes, and his heart skipped once before it began beating frantically within his ribs, like a bird bent on escape from a cage. The blood thundered in his ears, and he spoke too loudly when he said, "May I kiss you?"

Lady Penthia laughed, a gentle sound that nevertheless communicated her amusement.

He should not have asked, he realized too late. A real rake, a true rogue—his brother—would simply have taken the kiss. The humiliating flush once again raced up his throat to sit on his cheeks.

"I should not have asked," he said, meaning he should not have presumed so far.

"But of course you should," she murmured.

To his amazement, she went up on tiptoes and leaned forward and pressed her lips to his. His arms circled round her—hard enough to crush her—because she laughed again and pushed him away and said, "So eager, Your Grace? Let me catch my breath."

He made himself loosen his hold, but he did not let her go. He pressed his mouth against hers and gave back the kiss she had given him. He was tentative at first, having kissed only a few tavern wenches and willing dairymaids when he was at Oxford. A widow in the town of Comarty near Blackthorne Abbey had taught him most of what he knew about satisfying a woman in bed, but his lessons had not included much kissing.

His body trembled when Lady Penthia's hands twined in the hair at his nape. He wanted desperately to taste her, to put his tongue inside her mouth, but he knew that was not the sort of behavior one forced upon one's future wife.

She made a sound in her throat, more pleasure than protest, but Alastair knew he had already held her longer than he should. He felt almost dizzy when he let her go. His body had hardened revealingly so it would have been impossible to go directly back inside, even if that had been his desire. But he was not finished. There was something else he wanted to accomplish.

He opened his mouth to offer for her, but the words got stuck in his throat. It was, quite simply, fear that she would refuse him. "Shall we walk?" he said, practically dragging her beside him as he strode along the gravel path.

He thought he saw a flash of irritation on her face but decided it must be his imagination when she smiled prettily up at him and said, "Will you speak with my father tonight?"

He stopped and stared down at her. Well. He had not needed to say the words after all. She had assumed the proposal. And why not? He had taken her into the dark and kept her there too long—he could hear the music had stopped—and kissed her and held her in his arms.

Except, somewhere inside him a voice said, "The offer should have come from you."

Another voice reminded him that he had what he wanted. She was his. He felt a swell of pride, a feeling of triumph that overrode that other, less certain voice. "I shall call at Straith House tomorrow morning to speak with your father. Shall we go inside now?"

"You will not fail me?" she said, her eyes anxious.

"I shall not fail you."

When Alastair paid his addresses to Lady Penthia in her father's drawing room at the town house on Berkeley Square, he did so knowing that he had her father's delighted approval for the match. Alastair felt certain Lady Penthia must love him as much as he loved her. Why else—after refusing all those other offers—had she chosen him?

She was seated on the sofa when he entered the room to tell her he had her father's permission to wed her. She looked up at him, a smile on her lips, her eyes shining with . . . It was not precisely love, but rather . . . jubilation. And why not? He felt joyful himself.

He dropped to one knee, a flamboyant gesture more appropriate to his brother, but an indication of the depth of his feelings for the woman to whom he was about to propose marriage. To his consternation, his hand, when he reached for hers, was shaking. Her hand was surprisingly cool and dry and calm, with none of the signs of anxiety he found in himself. He hurried to speak, for fear his legs would give out under him.

"I . . . I love you, Lady Penthia. Will you do me the honor of becoming my wife?" he blurted.

"Yes, Your Grace, I will."

His throat tightened with emotion, and he blinked to keep his vision clear. "I will do my best to make you happy."

"I am counting on it, Your Grace," she said with a pleased smile.

It was not quite the answer he had expected. He had been hoping for a declaration of her love in return, but he attributed the lack of one to maidenly modesty. After all, they hardly knew each other. Her declaration would come with time. They had their whole lives to spend together.

He leaned forward to touch her lips with his, but

she turned aside so he brushed her cheek instead. That surprised him, but he could understand her shyness at being kissed in her father's drawing room.

"Until later," he murmured.

"Later," she agreed.

But he never had her alone in the month that followed before they were wed in June at St. George's.

It was not until his wedding night that Alastair realized his bride was not quite so pure as she had led him to believe. He would never have known, except that he had swallowed his pride and gone to the widow in Comarty and asked her what he could do to make the wedding night easier for his bride. Mrs. Jensen had explained in great detail what he must do, and he had followed her instructions explicitly.

Except, there had been no barrier.

His pride had kept him from asking his lady wife who had come before him. But he began to look askance at her when she flirted with other men. And he noticed how often she teased his brother, who returned jibe for jibe, but who was obviously infatuated with her.

The real trouble began when they left London and returned to Blackthorne Abbey, his estate in Kent. There was little in the country to interest Penthia, yet that was where he felt most comfortable. He trusted his neighbors not to steal his wife. And he was not so sure she could not be stolen by another man. It became plain she was dissatisfied with him, that she had none of the feelings for him that he held for her, and that she tolerated his attentions at night because it was her duty.

He rejoiced at learning his wife was expecting a happy event within a year of their nuptials. But the partnership he had envisioned marriage to be was nothing like the actual estrangement from his wife he lived with from day to day.

"There is no need for you to come any longer to my bed," she said at the same time she announced she was with child.

He had been more than willing to return to the widow. She, at least, seemed to enjoy his touch.

He consoled himself with the thought of having a child to love in Penthia's place. He spent time with his brother and his friends and gave his wife the public courtesy that concealed his personal discontent with their relationship. And in fact, his life found new meaning the night his wife was delivered of twin girls, Lady Regina and Lady Rebecca.

Penthia was furious she had not borne him an heir, but Alastair was content that the title go to Marcus if his wife gave him no son. He had taken one look at the two identical little girls with their tiny noses and rosebud mouths, their blue eyes and black hair, and promptly lost his heart.

He had spent far more time in the nursery than any gentleman should. He had delighted in their first smiles, their first teeth, their first unsteady steps. His life would have been perfect if only Penthia had shared his pleasure in the twins. She wanted to return to London for the Season, but he would not leave the girls to go with her, and he did not trust her to go alone.

He had woken one violent, stormy night, with the branches of a giant oak cracking against the window-panes and the wind whistling eerily in the ancient stone Abbey, and thought to look in his wife's room to see if she was frightened by the storm.

A ragged streak of lightning had revealed her empty bed, the sheets tousled, the imprint of her head on the pillow. He had pulled on a pair of buckskins and his Hessians and gone searching for her, unsure what might have happened to her. He looked in the kitchen, in the drawing room, in the library, a sense of foreboding growing in his breast. He had finally gone to the crumbling east wing of the Abbey, where Marcus had his rooms, to enlist his brother's help in searching for his wife.

And found them together in Marcus's bed.

His wife had been naked, her breast glistening in the candlelight where his brother's mouth had just released it. Thunder clapped overhead, a deafening ovation for his foolish love. Alastair would never forget the horrified look on Marcus's face or the defiant glare in Penthia's blue eyes.

"Why?" he had asked, the word torn from his throat.

"I wanted him," she said.

"Marcus?" he rasped.

"Alex, I . . . she . . . I . . ."

He had seen the tears of regret in Marcus's eyes and looked away before he could forgive his brother. It was an unforgivable act. He had turned and left, his Hessians echoing on the stone floor as he escaped the wretched scene.

No one would ever know the effort it had taken to remain civil to his wife and his brother before the world, when inside him burned a rage so hot, a hurt so painful, he was eaten up with it.

Marcus had come to him, his eyes full of misery, wanting to explain, wanting absolution. Alastair had cut him off.

"There will be no discussion of what happened. Ever."

Marcus had left Blackthorne Abbey shortly thereafter to join the army, and Alastair had turned to his daughters for solace. With them he could forget the pain for a little while. Regina and Rebecca were the one bright light in his otherwise bleak existence. He loved them with his whole being, and they returned his love in full measure. He had been able to bear the pain of his failed marriage and his brother's betrayal because he'd had his daughters.

Until Penthia robbed him of even that joy.

She had begun to drink to excess not long after Marcus left Blackthorne Abbey. Alastair had stopped inviting company to the Abbey, because she embarrassed him and herself. He had thought she could do him no further harm, that she could not sink lower, until the night she came to the children's nursery and found him holding one-year-old Regina in his arms, rocking her to sleep, while Rebecca lay in her crib nearby.

"You love those bloody twins more than you do your own wife," she accused in a drunken slur.

"I loved you once, Penthia," he replied.

"I never loved you!" she spat back. "I wanted to be a duchess. And I am. Duchess of Blackthorne. Hah! Duchess of some moldy old abbey. I hate it here! I hate you! And I hate those bloody twins!"

He did not know why she was so intent on hurting him, had not even realized he still could be hurt. "Go away, Penthia," he said, putting Regina up over his shoulder and patting her back to quiet her agitation at her mother's angry voice.

"Put that brat down, Alex, and attend to me," Penthia demanded. "I am your wife."

"You're foxed, Penthia. Get yourself to bed."

"I said get rid of that bloody brat!" She threw her empty crystal wineglass at him but missed, and the splintering glass ricocheted off the stone wall behind the rocker.

Regina let out a howl of pain.

Alastair lurched to his feet and felt his insides clench when he saw blood streaming from the child's lip where a shard of glass had cut it.

His gray eyes glittered dangerously when he raised them to his wife. "Get out, Penthia. Before I put my hands around that lovely neck of yours and squeeze the life out of you."

"The brat's barely scratched!"

"A drop of my daughter's blood means more to me than your whole miserable life."

Penthia's face flushed with rage. "No blood of yours runs through her."

"What?"

"Regina is not your child," she said in a voice laced with malice. "The twins are not yours."

"I don't believe you," he said in a deadly voice.

She hesitated, her eyes narrowing, her features hardening before she said, "No? Then ask your brother."

Alastair gave an agonized cry, as though he had been stabbed, and stared down at the wailing child in his arms. It was not possible that Regina was not his. He had not found Marcus with Penthia until after the twins were born. "You're lying," he said.

She smirked. "Am I? You'll always wonder now. Are they mine? Or not? Look at their eyes, Alastair. Not gray like yours, but blue, like his. Because they're your brother's children."

"Get out of my sight, Penthia. Leave now or I swear I will shut that lying mouth of yours forever."

She lurched drunkenly for the door, shoved it open, and left the room.

Alastair daubed at the blood on Regina's upper lip with a soft, lace-edged muslin handkerchief monogrammed with the letter *B*, for Blackthorne, until the flow stopped, and she had quieted in his arms. He settled back into the rocker and pulled her close and kissed her forehead. He laid his head back against the wooden rocker and felt the sting in his nose and the quiver in his chin. He gritted his teeth, but the moan escaped, squeezed his eyes shut against the threat of tears, but felt the hot wetness on his cheek as one spilled.

Through a blur of tears, he stared down at the drowsy child in his arms and realized the effects of the slow-working poison Penthia had administered.

This child is not flesh of my flesh. My blood does not run in her veins. My wife lay with my brother and created her. She is no part of me.

He stood and laid the child in the crib next to her sister. He could not kill the love inside him for the tiny beings. But his pride would no longer allow him to display it. How could he show love—for all to see—when these children were proof of his wife's betrayal?

From that day forward, he had kept his distance from Regina and Rebecca. He had not stopped loving them. He had merely stopped wearing his heart on his sleeve. From that day forward, a drunken Penthia had delighted in telling anyone who would listen that the duke's children were not his . . . they were his brother's.

He had never confronted Marcus and demanded the truth. He had not wanted to know for sure. But he and his brother had become more and more estranged after Penthia's accusation. And because he refused to deny his brother access to the children—*his* children—"Uncle Marcus" had a relationship with Regina and Rebecca that was far more loving than the one they shared with their "father."

Recently, when they had been in London, the nine-year-old twins had stolen away to go sightseeing and vanished somewhere within the shadowed streets and crooked alleys. Alastair had admitted to himself, when he thought they might be lost to him forever, how foolish he had been. Even if they were not his flesh and blood, they would always be the Duke of Blackthorne's daughters. And he loved them.

When the twins were found unharmed, he had surrendered his pride and held Regina and Rebecca and felt their small arms around his neck and realized he no longer wanted to keep his distance from them.

But his transformation from distant parent to proud papa had occurred only days before he left for Scotland. If he died at sea, their memories of him would more likely be of the stern and unloving father he had been for the past eight years than of the joyful and loving man he had been for the past nine days.

If I survive this storm, I will put the past behind me once and for all. He would be the sort of father he had always planned to be. And he would forgive his brother. If only the sea did not claim him first.

"Land ho!"

In the gray light of dawn, a rocky shore could be seen in the distance. Alastair grinned. He was going to survive. He was going to have a second chance at life.

"The mainmast is giving way!" a sailor shrieked.

A tremendous gust of wind had grabbed the sail and broken the mainmast in two as though it were a twig. The falling mast was headed straight for Alastair, and he dove out of the way as it crashed into the ship's wheel.

There was no way to control the ship now. The wind

and waves were driving them toward the rocks, where the ship would certainly be broken into pieces.

Above the howling wind he heard a man yell, "Git 'im, Danny!"

Alastair instinctively ducked, and the blow that would have brained him landed on his shoulder instead. He whirled to find himself surrounded by the three malingering sailors. "What's this?" he shouted.

"Someone wants you dead," one of the sailors yelled with a grin that displayed his toothless gums.

They attacked him all at once, and although Alastair gave a good account of himself, he had no chance, not with the wooden pin one of them was using to bang away at his head and shoulders. He felt the knot forming on his forehead, felt his eye swelling closed, felt his lip splitting and the blood pouring freely from his flattened nose. Once they had him pinned down on the deck, Gums said, "Let's finish 'im 'ere."

"We was told to throw 'im overboard and let 'im drown," the one called Danny said. "And that's wot we're goin' to do."

"I'll take those fine boots first," Gums said, yanking at Alastair's Hessians. "And that jacket."

"Wot's left for me?" Danny protested.

"Help yourself to that waistcoat with the silvery threads and his shirt and trousers," Gums said.

"But the shirt's all bloody, and them trousers too!"

"Wot do I get?" the third man asked.

"Those are fine stockings," Gums said.

They stripped him to his smalls and tied his hands

and bare feet, "Like a pig for roastin'," Gums said with satisfaction.

"We'll be lucky to outlive 'im," Danny muttered, squinting up at the rain pounding down on them from the cloud-ridden sky.

"Let's get it over with," the third man said.

"Wait!" Alastair yelled over the wind. "Why are you doing this? Who wants me—" He felt a rush of terror as they picked him up and threw him over the side. A scream built in his throat as he started to fall, but the air exploded from his lungs in a grunting *oof!* when he hit the icy surface, and his mouth and nose filled with saltwater as the sea closed over his head.

Alastair experienced a moment of sheer panic before he realized the stupid ruffians had tied his hands in front of him. As he sank farther into the depths, he reached frantically for his feet to untie the knots.

But he had jerked reflexively when he landed, and the ropes had tightened in the water. He could not get free.

When his lungs seemed ready to burst, he broke the surface, gasping for air. A huge wave immediately closed over his head and twisted him back underwater.

Alastair forced himself not to fight the wave, and when it had gone, his body floated back to the surface, but much closer to shore. He had to get his hands and feet free, or he would be dashed against the rocks, where the wind and tide were inexorably taking him.

He took a breath and slid underwater, bringing his feet up where his hands could reach them, making himself work calmly and methodically. It took several tries before he was finally able to loosen the knots. Once his feet were free, Alastair worked on the ropes that bound his hands, but there was no way he could get the knots undone.

Alastair heard a terrible crunching sound and turned to watch his ship sinking far beyond the shoreline. It must have hit some submerged rock farther out in the bay. He saw the three sailors heaving some barrels and a wooden crate over the side and then jumping in after them.

"I hope you make it to shore," he said, teeth chattering with cold. "I'll make sure you hang, along with whoever hired you to kill me."

As he kicked his way toward shore through the choppy, icy sea, his mind kept returning to the question of who wanted him dead. The only person with whom he was in enmity was his brother. He could not believe Marcus . . .

Then it dawned on him who might want him dead.

After the Battle of Culloden, Alastair's grandfather had been rewarded for his valor with Castle MacKinnon and the rich property that surrounded the stone castle in Scotland. The land and the castle, renamed Blackthorne Hall, had belonged to the Dukes of Blackthorne ever since.

Six months ago a young Scotswoman, Lady Katherine MacKinnon, had laid claim to being The MacKinnon of Castle MacKinnon. She had challenged the original patent from the English king to his grandfather on the grounds there had been a living heir to The MacKinnon at the time the "conditional" grant was made. She had made no secret of her hatred for all things English, especially the Dukes of Blackthorne.

Alastair had been contesting the woman's claim through his London solicitor without much success and had decided to go to Scotland himself. He had been on his way to meet the apparent imposter when he was thrown into the sea.

Perhaps Lady Katherine had decided to eliminate him in hopes that his brother would be less likely to fight her claim. If so, she was in for a rude surprise. He had no intention of dying. He would have his revenge on the lady and the three cutthroats who had done her dastardly work for her.

As soon as he saved himself from the sea.

Chapter 2

KITT WAS JUST ABOUT TO FALL ASLEEP AGAIN, after being woken by the howling winds of a storm racing inland from the sea, when she heard the sound of straw crackling. Fearing an intruder, she had placed the seemingly innocent straw on the dirt floor of her bedroom to warn her. It was no comfort to be right. The danger was real, and to her chagrin, she was as frightened as any virgin of what she knew her clansmen intended.

From the moment six months ago when Duncan had announced at a meeting at the kirk that she had been named The MacKinnon, her clansmen had opposed the idea of a woman as chief.

"Rob should have chosen one of us to lead," Ian MacDougal had ranted. "'Tis not proper for a wee bit of a lass to be telling men what to do."

"Aye. She ought to have a husband, and he should be chief," another argued.

"Would you deny my father the right to name his successor?" she challenged.

"He was too old and sick at the end to realize what he was doing," Ian retorted. "You should be married and holding a bairn in your arms, not standing before us giving orders!"

Kitt fought back the grief that threatened to overwhelm her. She was very much aware of her empty arms, empty of the bairns she should have borne with Leith. But her father had refused to let her marry him, and then a tragedy had taken Leith from her. And then she had agreed to carry out her father's foolhardy—and ignoble—scheme.

Kitt saw the mutinous expressions of her clansmen and knew what she said in the next few minutes would make all the difference. She was their only hope, whether they realized it or not. She had not chosen the role of savior; it had been thrust upon her. And she had fought fiercely against her fate.

"I wish to marry Leith," she had said to her father a full year past. "We love each other."

"Pah! Leith cannot save the clan, lass. You must marry Blackthorne. 'Tis the only way to regain what was ours."

"I hate him, Father, as I hate all Englishmen. 'Twas bred into me, and I canna change it. Besides, 'tis a fool's dream that the duke will even look at me."

Her father had searched her face with narrowed eyes, her wide-set green eyes set off by dark, arched brows, her plain, straight nose, the full-lipped mouth above a strong, square chin, and the raven curls that framed it all. "You're every bit as beautiful as your mother. Mark my words, lass. He'll have you."

"But I willna have him!"

"You'll have no one else," he had said.

Kitt had been as proud and stubborn as her father. She had refused to go along with his plan. In turn, he had forbidden her to marry Leith. But Leith had died . . . and she had given in to her father.

"Would you be willing to choose a husband from among your clansmen, Lady Katherine?" Duncan asked.

I will agree to anything temporarily . . . until I can put my father's plan into action.

"Aye," Kitt said, her hands on her hips as she surveyed the motley crowd gathered at the kirk.

"How shall I choose a husband from among you?" she asked. "What qualities should I seek in the man who will become The MacKinnon in my place?"

Most of those gathered were married, but there were enough unattached men to give her a choice. She walked from pew to wooden pew along the aisle of the small stone church, feeling the heat of the Sunday afternoon sun through the colorful leaded glass windows, eyeing each eligible man as though she were evaluating a prime piece of horseflesh.

"Fletcher is the biggest man among you," she said, putting her hands around the enormous biceps of a redheaded, freckled giant.

Fletcher blushed so hard his freckles disappeared, but flexed his muscles. "Aye, that I am."

"But he canna put two thoughts together in a row," someone murmured.

"That's true," Kitt agreed, joining the general laughter. She left Fletcher and crossed to a much smaller, much older man with dark, serious eyes. "Cam is the wisest."

"But he's too old for breeding up an heir," a voice protested.

"A finely aged wine often performs best," Cam countered.

"Also true," Kitt said, giving him an approving smile.

"Cam cannot defend himself against an enemy, much less defend the clan," someone else argued.

"Birk is the best bowman," she said, pointing to a lean young man. She turned to face a middle-aged, heavyset man. "But Angus can wrestle any man to the ground."

Then she focused on a man whose face was scarred from fire. "And Evan is the finest swordsman. How shall I choose between them? And if the choice is for my own sake," she added, "why then, Tavis must be in the running."

Tavis flashed her a devilish grin. He was the most handsome, with thick brown hair and dark brown eyes and legendary experience with women.

The men began looking at each other warily, realizing the choice might not be so easily made.

"What if one of us could win your heart?" Ian said.

Ian MacDougal was not so much clever, as shrewd. He often won his fights, but not always fairly. Kitt recognized him as a dangerous opponent. What he suggested supposedly gave every unattached male in the room a fair shot at becoming chief. But she didn't trust him.

"I am willing to be wooed," she said cautiously.

"Well, then," Ian said. " 'Tis settled. The man who wins the lady's heart—the man she takes to her bed—becomes chief."

The man she takes to her bed. Kitt met Ian's gaze and saw the threat there. *The man who forced her to his bed,* Kitt thought with a shudder of dread.

Nevertheless, Ian's idea had merit. It would keep her clansmen distracted while she settled her business with the Duke of Blackthorne. None could complain because it gave every man an equal chance in the contest. And she was happy because it gave her the final choice of a winner, and she knew she would never choose any of them. Especially not Ian.

"I agree," she said. "Whoever wins my heart becomes laird."

Looking back to that day, Kitt realized it had been a mistake to pit her clansmen against each other. Over the past six months there had been numerous fights, and she had found herself in more than one precarious situation with an unrequited suitor. Her clansmen were increasingly impatient with her failure to choose one of them, and she had begun to fear they would soon take matters into their own hands.

One of them finally had.

The crackling straw had woken her in time to

defend her virtue, but Kitt was frightened by the man's boldness. He had broken into her house in the dead of night for one purpose—to rape her, to impregnate her, and thus win her consent to be his wife. It was a time-honored way of acquiring a Scottish bride.

Easy, lass. You needna panic. You've the means of protecting yourself. The dastard willna succeed.

She had been taught by her father to defend herself as well as any man. But Kitt was all too aware, as she lay huddled in her bed, clutching her grandfather's jeweled sword, Hellbringer, to her chest and listening to the harsh, hushed breaths of the intruder, that she was merely a woman.

Her hands shook beneath the covers and a trickle of sweat stole down between her breasts, despite the cold that created foglike dragon's breath every time she exhaled.

Kitt clutched the ancient broadsword tighter, feeling it slip within her sweaty grasp. Hellbringer had gone to battle many times and killed many enemies. This would be one more.

She had no intention of giving anything away without a fight. Not the castle, not the land, and most certainly not herself.

You willna convince your clansmen of your fitness to be chief by killing one of them, a voice inside warned.

How else am I to protect myself?

Choose a husband from among them, one you can control.

Will the clan respect my choice?

'Tis what is necessary to buy time. Once you have chosen a husband, even if you never intend to marry him, this silliness will cease.

There was nothing silly about the copper taste of fear in her mouth. There was nothing silly about the very real threat of rape.

"Take that ye bandit, ye robber, ye rogue!" someone shouted.

Whap! Whap! Whap! The broom met its mark each time the old hag wielded it, landing on the head and shoulders of the intruder. "Out. Get out!" *Whap! Whap! Whap!*

Kitt sat up in bed, the sword clasped tight in her hand, watching with astonished eyes as her old nurse batted Ian MacDougal toward the door of the small cottage in the gray, predawn light. The giggle came without warning, as much the result of relief as the ridiculousness of the situation. Her laughter soon overlaid the painful grunts of the hulking MacDougal, as he retreated beneath the swats of the broken broom.

"Moira, let him be," Kitt said, grinning. "You've made your point."

"I'll leave no such refuse in the house," the old woman said, intent on forcing Ian from the cottage.

"You need a husband, Katherine MacKinnon," Ian shouted angrily, his large hands held over his head to protect himself from the old woman's broom. "I'm as good a man as any."

Kitt's grin disappeared as she rose from her bed, for the first time revealing the sword in her hand. She watched Ian's eyes go wide as she grasped the clay-more menacingly in both hands.

"What do you plan to do with that?" he demanded.

"Spit you with it."

Ian began backing out the door. "You'll get your comeuppance, lass. If not me, some other man will claim your bed. 'Tisna right for a woman to lead men."

"Whether 'tis right or no, I am chief. Go home, Ian. The choice of husband is mine, and I will never choose you."

"I am the best man, lass. And I am not the only one who thinks to make your mind up for you," he said ominously. " 'Tis time to choose."

"Out, Ian. Get out!" Kitt said.

As Moira latched the cottage door behind the man, she said, "Ian has a point. Though this was no right way to make it."

"Not you, too, Moira," Kitt said with a groan as she backed up far enough to slump onto the bench before the fire. She was grateful for the large shirt—her father's shirt—that hid her knocking knees. She doubted whether Ian would have been so quick to leave if he had known how frightened she was. "Father named me The MacKinnon. I have the right to be chief," she told her nurse.

"Having the right isna the same as it being right, my darling Kitty," Moira said, crossing to take the heavy claymore from Kitt's badly shaking hands. Lacking the strength to lift it onto the brackets over the fireplace where it normally hung, she leaned it against the stone hearth.

"Ye should've expected it," Moira scolded. "Ye didna have to be chief, Kitty. Ye could've refused."

Kitt sighed. Even Moira did not know the truth. She did not want the job; she had not been able to refuse it. "I know everything I need to know to be chief."

"Except how to be a man," Moira retorted. "Ye are as God made ye, Kitty. A woman. 'Tis best ye pick a man to lead and marry him."

Kitt's chin jutted. "I will prove my worth to them. It will simply take time."

But time was running out.

Moira put the broom to use again, this time sweeping the straw from the hard-packed dirt floor in Kitt's bedroom. She opened the cottage door to greet the rising sun as she brushed the last evidence of Kitt's fear out the door. "They think ye're bringing trouble on their heads by going to the English courts. Even yer father didna dare to claim the castle," she pointed out. "'Tis folly, plain and simple. No good can come of it."

"'Tis mine."

"Hush, child," Moira said. "Twasna cowardice that kept The MacKinnon silent before ye, but wisdom of a kind that comes with age and knowledge of his enemy."

"Aye. The enemy. The English. I hate them!"

"'Twas yer own clansmen offered ye harm this day, lass, more's the pity." Moira set down the broom and grasped Kitt's hands between her gnarled fingers. "Look at ye, still shaking, child. 'Tis only a matter of time before they discover the truth."

It was difficult to meet the wise old woman's gaze. Though Moira's skin was stretched tight over her facial bones by age, her gray eyes were still bright and sharp, and she saw far more than Kitt wished. "What truth is that?"

"Dinna bother denying it, lass. I've seen ye pretending, but we both know 'tis only your pride that willna let ye admit—"

"Admit what?" Kitt said in exasperation, yanking her hands free and pulling her feet up onto the bench to hug them to her chest.

"Ye're scared down to yer toenails. When yer father— God rest his soul—was here to protect ye, I didna speak my mind. But I canna keep silent now. Ye need help. Ye need—"

"I willna marry one of them!" Kitt snapped.

"Hush and listen," the old woman commanded. " 'Tis time ye—"

Kitt shoved herself up and bounded toward the front door, her hands covering her ears. "I willna listen—"

"Choose yerself a *gille-coise*."

Kitt whirled and stared. "A bodyguard? You think I should choose a bodyguard?"

"Why not?" Moira retorted. " 'Twould solve so many problems."

Before Culloden, the clan chieftain would have had a household that contained his courtiers, a bard and a seneschal, a piper and a sword-bearer, a quartermaster, a cup-bearer, a warder, and, of course, a personal body-guard who stood fully armed behind the chair of his master.

Those days were gone. The existence of such a house-hold presumed the laird had a castle in which to house them. Castle MacKinnon had become Blackthorne Hall, and the chief's advisors—and the chief herself—now lived in simple stone-and-thatch cottages on land sur-rounding the castle, paying exorbitant rents to the de-testable Duke of Blackthorne, sixth of that name.

Kit found the suggestion tempting. If only there were some man she could trust. She shook her head. "Whoever I chose as my bodyguard would likely open the door to his friends and welcome them in."

" 'Tis worth considering," Moira said. " 'Twould mean the end of night raids on yer bed, at least. And a body could get some sleep."

Kitt laughed. "I see. I need a bodyguard so you can get a full night's rest."

Another knock on the door set Kitt's heart to gal-loping again. She glanced at Moira, who stared at the door in alarm.

"Not another one," Kitt snapped, grabbing the basket-hilted claymore in both hands. "Two in one night is—"

Moira crossed to the window and peered out. "Hold, child. 'Tis only Dara Simpson, Patrick's wife."

Kitt breathed a sigh of relief and lifted the broad-sword as though to set it back in its resting place. She suddenly began to tremble again. Her arms felt so weak she could barely hold the weight of the weapon.

What's wrong with me?

Kitt set the claymore beside the hearth as though that was what she had intended all along and wiped the beads of sweat from her forehead with the sleeve of her father's shirt.

She stared into the fireplace, feeling the acid burn in the pit of her stomach. It was not her kinsmen she feared, but the revenge she must take on the Duke of Blackthorne. Marriage to her bitterest enemy. That was the crux of her father's plan. Kitt wasn't sure she could go through with it. She was afraid that in the end she would fail him . . . and her clan.

Kitt took a shuddery breath and let it out. *I will do what I must, Father. Somehow.*

She went to the door and opened it.

"Come in, Dara," she said with a hard-won smile, reaching for Dara's hand and drawing her inside. "Sit and have a cup of tea."

"I canna stay," Dara said, stepping inside and curtsying. She adjusted the woolen arisard around her shoulders and clutched it beneath her chin, but she was visibly shivering. "Patrick would beat me senseless if he knew I'd come," she whispered. "But I dinna see who else I can ask for help. You're The MacKinnon, whether Patrick likes it or no."

"Come sit by the fire," Kitt urged. While Moira put water on the hob to heat for tea, Kitt pressed the young woman onto the bench by the fire, pleased that at least

Dara had sought her counsel. "Tell me what I can do to help."

"We canna afford to pay the rent and feed the wee ones both. So Patrick has taken to fishing the duke's streams and hunting his forest," Dara blurted.

Moira, who was heating a pot of water for tea, crossed herself and muttered a prayer.

"I'm afraid for him," Dara said, her eyes filling with tears. "But I canna let my bairns go hungry, can I?"

Kitt stared grim-lipped at the despairing woman sitting before her. Dara was not so different from the rest of the clan. They all suffered terribly from rents that had been raised thrice in the past year, so that only enough was left after the rent was paid to put food in the children's mouths and buy more seed to plant.

" 'Tis only a matter of time before Patrick is caught," Dara continued. "He'll be transported . . . or worse. And what will become of my wee bairns then?"

Kitt's stomach clenched with memories of what had happened to Leith. She wanted to tell Dara she had already taken the first steps toward saving them all, but she could not take the chance that word of what she intended would spread to the others.

"I'll speak with the duke's steward," Kitt said, laying a comforting hand on Dara's shoulder. "Surely Mr. Ambleside will give you a temporary reprieve on the rents, at least until the crops are harvested."

"Patrick's already asked. Mr. Ambleside said no."

Kitt felt the knot growing in her stomach. "Perhaps I can be more persuasive."

"Please help us," Dara begged. "Please."

"I'll do what I can. In the meantime, tell Patrick I forbid him to hunt or fish on the duke's property."

At the word *forbid* Moira grunted, but Kitt shot her a look that silenced her.

"What shall I feed my bairns?"

"Moira will give you some smoked haddock and some leeks and carrots and a plum cake she made yesterday." But as Kitt watched Moira gather the meager offerings in a basket for the woman to carry home, she realized it would not be enough to keep Dara's five children fed for very long.

"Have faith," she told the woman. "I will find a way to make all well."

Dara looked doubtful and grateful at the same time. She bobbed a curtsy and said, "Thank you, Lady Katherine."

As Kitt closed the door behind Dara, she turned, took one look at Moira's expression, and said, "Spit it out."

" 'Tisna yer place to forbid a man to feed his family."

"Patrick will surely be caught, Moira. If he's caught, 'tis transportation to Australia for sure. Then what will become of Dara's bairns? 'Twas good advice I gave her."

"Except it comes from a woman."

"What difference does that make?"

"Patrick Simpson must be shamed enough that he canna feed his family. Think what he will feel when his wife tells him ye've *forbidden* him to steal what he canna earn. 'Tis likely to send him right back out the door."

"I canna help it if he acts the fool."

"A poor man hasna much but his pride, Kitty. Will ye take that too?"

"Pride willna do him much good if he's dead!"

Moira held her tongue, but Kitt felt the older woman's censure. She wished she could confide in Moira and seek comfort and advice. But her father had warned her not to tell the old nurse anything. She had never felt so alone.

Kitt quickly put on a cambric dress and her polished leather half boots and wrapped herself in a plaid woolen shawl against the cold of the June morning. She sat near the fire while Moira brushed the tangles from her waist-length black hair before plaiting it and pinning it at her crown. The curls refused to be tamed and several escaped at her temples and nape.

She had risen to leave when Moira said, "Sit and eat, Kitty. 'Tis a long walk to Blackthorne Hall."

The concerned look on Moira's face had her sitting again to eat an oatmeal bannock and drink a cup of tea before she left the cottage.

It was mid-morning by the time she arrived at the entrance to the castle, hot and sweaty from the vigorous trek along the rutted dirt road. She had taken off her shawl, knotting it around her hip. She hailed several crofters working in the wheat fields outside the castle, then crossed the drawbridge that was always down over the drained moat and made her way to the double wooden doors that led into the keep.

In medieval days, the stone castle had guarded against raiders from ships along the coast. She could hear the waves crashing against the rocks at the base of the cliff and smell the tang of salt from the sea. Before she knocked on the thick wooden door, Kitt unknotted the shawl from her waist and resettled the MacKinnon plaid around her shoulders to add what consequence she could to her appearance.

A butler answered the door dressed in red-and-black livery trimmed in gold braid, the cost of which would have fed Dara and Patrick's children for a year.

"Servants to the back door."

His disdainful order in clipped English made her temper flare. She put the flat of her palm on the door before he could shut it. "I am no servant, sir. As you would know if you had lived here long."

The butler raised a supercilious brow as he looked her up and down. "What is your business, miss?"

"Tell Mr. Ambleside that The MacKinnon is here to see him."

The butler looked dubious. "The MacKinnon?"

She took advantage of his lax pose to push the door farther open and to step inside. "I will wait here in the main hall," she said firmly. "While you tell Mr. Ambleside I am here."

The butler hesitated, then did as she bid.

Kitt's father had described Castle MacKinnon to her many times, from tales his mother had told him of the years she had lived there. But her first glimpse of the inside revealed a sort of grandeur she had not expected.

The Great Hall had a forty-foot-high vaulted ceiling and a mammoth stone fireplace guarded by two chain-mail figures. Large tapestries and portraits of the duke's ancestors decorated the walls. Through the door to the drawing room she could see the carved lion's paw legs on a sofa covered with a red velvet so rich she ached to touch it.

The butler returned moments later, out of breath and agitated. "Mr. Ambleside is too upset to see you now," the man said. "There's been an accident, a terrible tragedy."

"I'm sorry to hear it. What's happened?" Kitt asked.

"It's His Grace, miss. His ship was caught in last night's storm and broke up on the rocks. The duke's drowned!"

Kitt felt as though someone had struck a hard blow to her stomach. She couldn't seem to catch her breath.

No. 'Tisna possible. He canna be dead.

She put a hand on the closest stone wall to hold herself upright and was surprised by its roughness. There was nothing elegant about the castle walls. They had been built of stone to house generations of MacKinnons.

But the castle was lost to her now, along with all hope for her people.

"Are you all right, miss?"

"I'm fine." But her voice sounded as though it were echoing from a seabound cave. "I'll return another

43

time," she said, forcing herself to put one foot in front of the other.

She squinted her eyes against the bright sun as the butler ushered her outside. She heard the heavy wooden door close behind her with a groan of hinges and fought not to let her knees buckle.

Kitt had thought nothing could keep her from fulfilling the vow she had made to her father. But neither of them had anticipated this turn of events. The Duke of Blackthorne was dead, drowned in the sea.

Oh, dear God, she thought. *What do I do now?*

Chapter 3

He came awake shivering with cold. His head ached, his throat felt raw, and his body felt battered. He reached toward his throbbing forehead and realized his hands were bound. Blood seeped from a wound at his temple. *I must have hit my head on the rocks as I came ashore.*

He tried to free his hands, but the knots were too tight. The skin around the rough hemp was bloodied, suggesting he had striven in vain to free himself.

Why am I bound? He struggled to remember, but could not.

The sun was barely up, the sky a dreary gray, but there was enough light to show him he lay on a rocky shore, with a cold spray from the sea misting him as the tide came in. The little he wore—sopping-wet smalls—had been torn to shreds by whatever misadventure had befallen him.

Who am I? How did I get here?

He found no answers inside his head. He fought back the fear squeezing his insides and looked around him for something familiar. The barren, craggy rock and the grassy verge beyond meant nothing to him. He tried to sit up, but his ribs protested the movement. He hissed in a breath as he fell back prone on the stabbing rock.

"Bloody hell!"

His voice sounded strange to his ears, bitter and angry.

Bitter about what? he wondered. *Angry with whom?*

Bitter at his obviously meager circumstances, he thought wryly. Angry about being tied up and thrown into the sea. He smiled, then groaned as the upward curve of flesh broke open a cut on his lip.

"Bloody hell!" He barked a laugh at himself. It seemed he had a sense of humor. And a very small vocabulary.

He was also a man of action, because he had the driving urge, despite the pain, to get away from here.

Did someone try to kill me? Or was I the villain? Am I on the run from the law? Is that why I feel the need to get away?

He did not waste time thinking because there were no coherent thoughts to be had, simply gritted his teeth against the agony in his ribs and forced himself upright. It quickly became apparent that the first thing he needed to do was free his hands. The rocks were sharp enough to provide an edge, and after some time, and several more gouges in his flesh, he was free.

"Bloody hell!" he said as he dipped his wounded wrists into the sea to clean off the worst of the sand and blood.

His bare feet were tender, and he winced as he made his way cautiously over the rocks to the grass beyond. The grass was still damp with dew but a welcome relief nevertheless.

"Which way now?" he said aloud.

The surf crashed against the rocks, but otherwise there was no sound, not even a bird's cry. It was as though he were completely alone on some deserted island.

"Not bloody likely," he said, the sound of his own voice reassuring in the silence. "I was headed for ... I was going to ... I had to be ..."

He did not understand why he knew the rocks were rocks and the sea was the sea and the grass was grass, but not who he was or where he was bound or why.

"First things first," he muttered, perusing his pitiful attire. "I need some clothes."

He looked north, then south, unsure which way to walk, since there seemed no sign of life in either direction. He tore some blades of grass and threw them into the air and saw the wind was blowing to the north. "North it is," he said. At least that way he would have the wind to his back.

The sun was well up in the sky when he saw the first sign of human habitation—a simple stone cottage with a thatched roof with smoke coming from the chimney.

He almost hailed those inside, but realized he did not want to be seen in this condition.

I am also a proud man, he deduced. *And apparently unbothered by the prospect of stealing what I need*, he realized as he grabbed a pair of muddy boots from beside the door and stole a shirt and trousers and a length of plaid from oleander bushes where they had been spread out to dry.

The boots were too small for him. That hadn't stopped the previous owner from wearing them, as evidenced by the hole worn through the leather where his big toe now stuck out. He quickly donned the large shirt and even larger trousers, using the rope that had tied his hands, which he'd saved, to bind the too-large trousers around his waist.

His nose pinched at the sharp stench of . . . sheep . . . he thought, identifying the unpleasant smell. He ignored the odor and wrapped the rough plaid around him, blessing the woolen warmth.

"Thank you, kind sir," he murmured, nodding his head to the unseen owner of the cottage. "I will repay you when I can." Did that mean he was not normally a thief? he wondered. Or simply that he was an honorable thief who paid his debts?

He realized the fact that this cottage was here meant there were probably others. He needed something to eat and drink and a bed, preferably a soft one. *A soft bed. Am I used to such luxury, then? Or is it only that I have dreamed of it?*

He had plenty of time to ponder the matter, since

the sun was nearly overhead by the time he reached the outskirts of a village. As he stepped inside the taproom of the Ramshead Inn, he felt almost giddy with relief. *I made it.*

He started to grin, but winced as the cut on his lip split open again. He reached up to dab at the blood with a scratched and filthy hand. *What I would not give for one monogrammed handkerchief.*

The thought was stunning, suggesting as it did that he was a person of some note, at least enough note to have monogrammed handkerchiefs. Whoever he was—had been—right now he was only a man whose jaw ached and whose head throbbed and whose every breath was an agony to his sore ribs. His nose was broken, he thought, and so swollen and tender he walked in measured steps in order not to jolt it.

All he wanted was something wet to soothe his parched throat, a warm bath, and a soft bed, in that order. *A warm bath. Surely that is a luxury, too. I must be a person of distinction. Or a thief with rich tastes*, he thought wryly.

The too-small boots had raised blisters on his heels, and after the morning's walk, he was limping badly. With one eye swollen shut, his balance was none too good, and as he reeled unsteadily into the tavern, the men seated at the tables eyed him as though he were some bumble-witted looby.

And I'm not? He didn't think so. His sense of humor rose again to rescue him. He imagined he must be quite a sight, wearing such ill-fitted clothing and with his face having endured such a beating from the rocks. *Or someone's fists.* He could not discount that possibility.

He sank into a chair at the best table he could find and looked around with his one good eye for the innkeeper. His stomach growled noisily, and embarrassingly, with hunger. He felt certain he could implore the man for what he needed.

A few snickers and more than one blatantly curious look from his fellow patrons brought the innkeeper to his table. "What is it ye want?"

"Good day," he said. The effort suffered somewhat from the night just past, sounding more like a frog than a man. He cleared his throat and continued, "I would appreciate a cup of your best ale."

"I'll see yer coppers first," the innkeeper replied.

"Unfortunately, I have nary a farthing with me."

"No coppers, no ale," the innkeeper said flatly.

How dare he refuse to serve me! The feeling of disbelief that he was not to be served was real enough. But why should he think himself entitled to be served without presenting any coins first? *Who am I?* He realized his hands were shaking beneath the table from a combination of weakness and rage.

He placed his palms flat on the table to push himself upright, but both his head and his ribs protested. He was so exhausted, he gave up the effort and settled for spearing the man with his one good eye. Maybe the fellow recognized him. "Do you know who I am?"

"Ye look like a flat to me," the innkeeper said, "what maybe used to be a sharp."

The patrons in the taproom laughed at the innkeeper's clever play on words.

"I would like some food and drink, please. I will gladly pay you when I have the coin. You see, I seem to have lost track of . . . things." He took a deep breath, hesitated, then plunged in. "To be frank, I cannot remember who I am." He frowned and added, "Except I am quite sure I used to have monogrammed handkerchiefs. That must mean I am a man of some consequence, wouldn't you agree?"

The innkeeper guffawed and slapped him on the shoulder so hard he let out an unwilling moan.

"That's a good one, lad," the innkeeper said. "Yer English accent's not half bad. 'Tis the sand and seaweed in yer hair and the lumps on yer face and o' course them boots with the holes in the toes, that give ye away. Ye need a better costume if ye're going to play the Quality."

"I am not pretending," he said, forcing himself painfully to his feet. His voice hardened. "And I would like a cup of ale. Now."

The innkeeper's faced turned ugly. "Ye've picked the wrong sort to impersonate, lad. I hate the puking English as I hate the plague. If ye were one of 'em, I'd throw ye out on yer arse. So count yer blessings and be on yer way."

He felt the heat of humiliation on his face, felt the anger building along with it, but was not sure how to contend with either emotion. Pride—he seemed to have no end of it—forced him to stand his ground. "You seem to be a fair man," he began.

"Fair?" the innkeeper spat back. "Life isna fair, lad. My only sister and her husband were forced from their home by a greedy English landlord. I've the support of them now and the bairn that's on the way. If ye're English like ye say, ye can rot in hell for all I care. Now get out!"

He opened his mouth to plead at least for a drink of water before he began his journey but shut it again. He would die of thirst before he would beg. It was plain he would get a better reception at an English tavern. "How far to the closest English stronghold from here?"

"That'd be Blackthorne Hall near Mishnish. 'Tis a wee bit of a walk. Ten miles or so, if ye follow the road."

"Ten miles!"

"Ye'd best get started if ye expect to lay yer head on a fine pillow tonight," the innkeeper said.

He considered asking if anyone might be headed in that direction who could give him a ride but decided he would likely be refused. He did not need another humbling. He swayed on his feet and grabbed at chairs along the way to hold himself upright as he struggled toward the door.

When he had nearly reached it, a small voice said, "Sir, here's a cup of ale and a bannock to fill the emptiness inside."

He found himself staring down into the sympathetic blue eyes of a narrow-shouldered boy dressed in a too-small shirt that exposed his wrists and too-short trousers that exposed his bare ankles, which stuck out of a pair of too-large shoes. He guessed the child was nine or ten.

"What're ye doing, brat?" the innkeeper demanded.

The child held out the pewter mug. "Here, sir. Drink it quickly."

He reached for the mug, surprised by the kind gesture from one whose circumstances did not appear to be much better than his own. "Thank you."

The innkeeper crossed quickly, his hand raised to knock the mug aside, but thought better of it when he turned to confront him. Instead, the innkeeper took out his wrath on the boy who had offered succor.

"That's the last of yer defiance I'll suffer," the innkeeper said as his open palm landed on the boy's cheek, leaving a stark red welt. He yanked the bannock out of the boy's hand and crushed it in his fist. The boy cowered as the innkeeper poised his fisted hand for another blow.

"Enough!" he roared, dropping the mug and catching the innkeeper's wrist with a grip strong enough to make the man cry out. He knew he could not hold on for very long. His strength was nearly gone.

The innkeeper was clearly furious at being said nay in his own establishment. "If ye want the care of the lad, then take him," the innkeeper said, easily jerking himself free. "I've no more use of him."

"Oh, please, sir, dinna throw me out," the lad

pleaded, grabbing the innkeeper's apron with both hands and hanging on.

"I'm the one you're angry with," he said, realizing the trouble he had caused. "Don't blame the boy."

"Be gone with the both of ye," the innkeeper said menacingly. "Or I'll have the lads throw ye out."

He looked around the room and saw several of the innkeeper's burly friends rising from their seats. "Come with me, boy," he said.

The boy eyed him askance. "Ye can give me work, sir?"

"I currently find myself traveling without my valet," he said with a wry—and painful—twist of his mouth. *Do I really have a valet somewhere?* he wondered. "Would you care to take service with me?"

"I would, sir," the boy said, a quick grin flashing.

"You will not suffer for your kindness. I promise it."

"Thank ye, sir."

The raucous laughter of the patrons showed what they thought of his job and his promise.

"Ye'll be wantin' food for yer journey," the innkeeper said. "Take this!" He threw the crumbled bannock at the boy, but nearly half the oatmeal biscuit hit the battered stranger in the chest.

Something inside him broke at that final insult.

"Enough," he said in a feral voice. "That is quite enough." He would have attacked the next thing that moved, like some crazed animal, but the boy grabbed his hand and dragged him toward the door.

"Come, sir. 'Tis time we take our leave."

"Ye'll be lucky if ye dinna starve workin' for such as him, Laddie," one of the patrons said. "Here's a little somethin' to help ye on yer way." The man threw the remnants of a lamb chop at the boy, missed, and hit the stranger in the shoulder.

He snarled and would have leapt, but the boy pulled him back. "Please, sir. There are too many of them."

For the boy's sake, he reined the beast inside.

"Ye'll be lucky if they dinna put ye away with that madman," another patron said, hurling a handful of peas.

As they left the inn, he was pelted with all manner of food. Potatoes stuck in his hair, and savory gravies from bones and stews stained his borrowed shirt. The delicious smells wafting from his clothes made his mouth water. He saw a joint of lamb land on the floor at his feet and very nearly stooped to pick it up.

Pride—he seemed to have a damnable lot of it— held him back.

"Come, sir," the boy said, tugging hard on his hand. "Please come."

He stared at the small, grimy fingers that had wrapped themselves around his own filthy hand and allowed himself to be led from the inn, surprised at the boy's unexpected kindness and his belief in his promises. He hoped he would be able to repay the child in some way.

Once they were on the road, the boy let go of his hand and wrapped his arm around his waist to help hold him upright. " 'Tisna necessary to keep up the act with me, sir. I'll not leave ye."

"The act?" he said as he limped along beside the boy, ashamed he had to lean on him, but unable to do otherwise.

"I know ye're not the Quality, sir. If ye'd like to find a ride, 'tis best ye come up with a better disguise. These Highland Scots hate the English—and with good reason."

Just then, a carter with a wagonload of cabbages drew alongside them.

"You there, sir," he said in a voice that sounded condescending even to his own ears. "I would like a ride—"

The carter mumbled something, crossed himself, and applied the whip to his team of oxen, which moved steadily away from them.

"I warned ye, sir. That bird willna sing for ye."

"What?"

"That English nobleman disguise doesna work."

He did not bother explaining the truth. "What would you suggest?"

"Ye might be a shipwrecked sailor. The sand and the seaweed in yer hair will help the story."

"I see," he said.

"And get rid of that English accent," the boy advised. " 'Twould be better if ye spoke like a Scotsman. At least give it a try," the boy said. "There's another wagon coming."

He turned to see two dray horses pulling a wagon.

"Quick, what's yer name?" the boy said.

"Al...Al..." A light flickered and was gone. That was as much as he could remember.

"Alfred? Alan? Alex?" the boy questioned.

The cart was drawing closer. "Alex," he said, choosing the last name the boy had given. It was as good as any. "Alex Wheaton," he said, staring at the bags of wheat on the wagon that was rapidly approaching.

"I'm a sailor home from the sea," he said, trying out a Scottish accent and realizing even as he rolled the *r* on sailor that he knew how to do it. *If I'm Scots, why was I speaking with an English accent? And if I'm English, how do I know how to speak like a Scotsman?*

The boy laughed and clapped. "Yer accent's perfect!" He gave a dignified bow and said in perfect King's English, "Michael O'Malley, at your service, sir."

"That's an Irish name! And what happened to your Scottish accent?"

The boy grinned. "Ye can call me Laddie," he said with a thick Scottish accent. " 'Tis my own disguise."

Why would a boy of Michael O'Malley's age need a disguise? Who was he hiding from so far from Ireland? Alex opened his mouth to ask and closed it again. There would be time enough to discover everything later. It was good to have a name. Alex Wheaton. He needed rest and something to eat and drink. And a ride would not be unwelcome.

"Well, Laddie, let's see if you can charm a ride for us from that farmer."

"Where are we headed, Alex?"

"Blackthorne Hall," he said. Maybe someone in that English stronghold would recognize him.

"Very well." The boy ran alongside the wagon and said, "Please, sir, can ye give my poor brother a ride? His ship was wrecked, and I've come to take him home to our mother. I'll be glad to walk myself."

"Where ye headed, lad?"

"To Mishnish," the boy replied, naming the town closest to Blackthorne Hall. "But we'll be glad of a ride as far as ye can take us."

"The both of ye hop on," the farmer said. "Beau and Belle can take yer weight." He flicked his whip lightly over the rumps of the two huge horses, and they nodded their heads as though in agreement.

Mick shot Alex a triumphant look before helping him onto the moving wagon.

Alex bit his lip to keep from crying out at the pain.

"We're on our way, sir," Mick whispered.

"To Blackthorne Hall?"

"To wherever fortune takes us."

The first thought he had upon waking was that he must have indulged to excess the night before on some very bad port. His second thought was that his feather mattress was in great need of a beating to smooth out the lumps. It felt like he'd been sleeping on a pile of—it *was* straw!

He sat up too quickly and groaned as every wretched ache and irritating pain in his body made itself known.

He remembered he was calling himself Alex Wheaton, but a great deal of the previous day was a blur.

Where am I? How did I get here?

Thankfully, the memories were there. He recalled the farmer had taken them within a few miles of their destination before letting them off. During the day's ride, he had learned a little more about Michael O'Malley.

The boy came from Dublin, where he had two younger brothers and two younger sisters, all with different fathers. "My mother made her living with the gents," Mick said with a too-casual shrug that revealed how very much he had minded. "Having babies was a part of the job. The last one killed her, is all."

Do I have a family of my own? Are they even now missing me? "What happened to the rest of your family?" Alex asked.

"We all went to a home for orphans. But it was more of a workhouse, which I found out pretty quick. I crawled out through the bars in the window one night and ran away. I promised the others I'd make my way in the world and come back to get them."

The boy shrugged again, an insouciant, devil-may-care gesture that made Alex's throat constrict. "How long ago did you leave them?"

Mick looked him in the eye and said, "Two years."

"How old were you then?"

"Ten."

That made the boy twelve. Starvation had kept him small, Alex supposed. He tried to imagine what a child like Mick must have had to do to survive these past two years. He did not like the dire pictures that formed in his mind.

The boy's story had not provided any reason why he would need to disguise himself. Alex did not think the poorhouse spent much time searching for runaways. It should not have been necessary to flee the country to escape detection. Which meant there was more to Mick's story than he had told.

"Why did you help me?" Alex asked the boy. "You must have known you would make trouble for yourself."

Mick shrugged again. "I've been hungry a time or two myself."

The simple but eloquent answer silenced Alex. The youth possessed an excess of courage and kindness, and Alex hoped he would one day be in a position to reward both.

To his shame, Alex slept most of the ride. Mick woke him when the farmer stopped at a crossroad where he planned to turn off.

"End of the line," Mick said.

"How close are we to Mishnish?"

"About two miles. Maybe a little more."

Alex discovered his muscles had tightened while he had been asleep, and he could barely move. It was mortifying to ask for help, but he had no choice. "Can you give me your hand, Laddie?" he said, reaching out to the boy.

Mick extended a small, callused hand and helped him off the wagon, then stood beside him while he caught his balance, waiting for a bend in the road to take the farmer out of sight.

"I'll be leaving ye here," Mick said.

"What? Why not stay together?"

" 'Tis easier for one to find work than two. Besides, I canna take care of ye. I've promises to keep."

"Maybe once we reach Blackthorne Hall—I mean, if I am an Englishman—"

Mick put a hand on his arm—it was intended as comfort, Alex realized—and said gently, " 'Tis plain you canna walk any farther today. My advice, Alex, is to find the nearest barn and sleep until morning. There are farms all up and down this road. You willna have trouble finding one."

The boy took off at a brisk pace on the narrow, rutted road.

"Where are you bound for, Laddie?" Alex called after him. "How can I discover your direction if my circumstances change for the better?" *If I find out who I am...*

"Find a barn, Alex. Rest," Mick called back to him.

"I'm bound for Blackthorne Hall," Alex said. "Ask for me there."

The boy did not stop or turn to acknowledge him.

Alex was too weak to walk very far—certainly not the two miles to Mishnish that Mick apparently intended—and darkness had fallen by the time he slipped inside the first barn he found and shoved a small pile of straw into a bed. Despite his awful thirst, the gnawing hunger, and the discomfort of his lodgings, he had instantly fallen asleep.

Alex stretched to get out the kinks from a night spent on a hay bed. His body ached worse than it had the previous day, but he felt a great deal more hopeful this morning. He was only two miles from Blackthorne Hall. Two miles from an English stronghold where he might very well be recognized. Two miles from the promise of a good claret and any mouthwatering dish he desired. Two miles from the offer of a hot bath and clean clothes.

He was drawn from his musing by the sound of a slap—a hand meeting flesh—and a woman's angry voice outside the barn.

"I thought you learned your lesson yesterday, Ian. But I suppose some are slower than others."

He heard another slap and a woman's outraged cry of pain.

"I learned not to give you warning," a rough male voice replied. "That is what I learned. Your father's sword is no use to you now."

"Stay away!" the woman cried. "Dinna touch me!"

"I intend to have you, Katherine," the man said. "Whether you will or no."

"I think not," Alex said, stepping out of the barn. As knights in shining armor went, he supposed he left a great deal to be desired. But he did not see anyone else stepping in to help.

One look at the woman's attacker made him question whether one of the blows to his head had not left him slightly deranged. The thickset man towered over him and had beefy arms that strained the seams of his shirt. Black hair half-covered his dark eyes, and an unkempt black beard hid the lower half of his face. He held a broadsword in his large-knuckled hand and looked like he knew how to wield it.

When the giant turned to confront him, Alex got his first look at the woman backed up against the stone wall of the barn. If it had not already been parched, his mouth would have gone dry —she was that beautiful. His body tightened viscerally. It was as though they were attached by some invisible cord that vibrated between them, plucking every sensitive nerve in his body.

She looked at him with worried eyes—intriguing eyes, he thought, as green as...as a fresh-hewn lawn...somewhere...Where? Alex frowned as the brief glimpse of a long expanse of manicured green lawn disappeared from his mind's eye.

He could see the white swell of her breasts, where the oaf had torn her muslin blouse—half-concealed by her long, tangled black hair—and the lush curve of her hip, where her brown skirt was bunched in the villain's fist.

Alex's gut tightened.

He wanted her. Might even have taken the villain's place if he had been the sort of man willing to use force on a woman. It seemed he was not.

His eyes met hers and an ancient flare of recognition sparked between them, before the look in her eyes changed to something much less inviting. He could see, even from where he stood, that she wanted nothing to do with him.

But he could not leave her to be raped. He must at least protect her from harm. Chivalry demanded it.

The pair were frozen in a violent tableau, staring at him.

The man recovered first and demanded, "Who are you?"

"A knight in shining armor," Alex replied. "Come to rescue the fair maiden." To his surprise, it had not come out sounding flippant, as he had intended. His parched, gravelly voice was entirely serious.

The brute laughed aloud. "Go away," he said, using the claymore to wave Alex away as though he were a fly on a dung heap.

"Let the lady go," Alex said, his shoulders squaring, his stance widening, as anger lent him strength he had not known he still possessed.

"Or what?" the villain demanded in a menacing voice, brandishing the broadsword in Alex's face.

The whole situation was ludicrous in the extreme, Alex thought, seeing it as though from a distance. A man without any memory of who or what he was, dressed in a shepherd's shirt and trousers and shoes with holes in the toes, was about to fight a ruffian over a bit of fluff who probably gave herself to men for a coin every day of the week.

His glance slid to the growing bruise on the young woman's cheek where the lout had slapped her, and he realized, as the hairs rose on the back of his neck, that if the brute did not release her forthwith he could easily be persuaded to kill him.

"Let her go. Now."

"She's mine," the villain said. "I claim her by right of possession. What do you say to that?"

Alex did not bother to reply. He simply balled one of his bruised and torn hands into a fist and, using every ounce of strength he had left, planted the brute a facer.

It was a lucky hit, and the man crumpled to the ground.

He nearly crumpled himself. He cried out at the agony he'd caused himself with the blow and cradled his wounded hand against his chest.

The woman wrenched the claymore out of the fallen man's hand and stood holding it in both of her own, her back to the stone wall, watching Alex warily. "Stay away," she warned.

Alex decided this was not the time to explain he only wanted to get to Blackthorne Hall in hopes that someone there might recognize him. Considering how the locals felt about the English, she was as likely to spit him on her sword as to thank him for her rescue. It was easier to pretend to be Alex Wheaton.

"I realize I might look fearsome," he said, lightly touching his face. "But I mean you no harm, lass. All I ask is a drink and something to eat, and I'll be on my way."

"I could have saved myself," she said fiercely. "I

didna need your help." To demonstrate her self-sufficiency, she swung the sword and decapitated a nearby scarecrow.

Alex scowled at the demonstration—ladies had no business wielding swords—and yelped when the scab on his lip broke open. "I dinna care if you needed my help or not," he croaked. "All I want is . . ."

Alex felt himself wavering on his feet, the brief spurt of energy having deserted him once the emergency was past. "All I want is something to drink and . . ."

An ancient woman appeared in his line of vision.

"Bring him inside, child," the old woman said. "Canna ye see the man needs yer help?"

"What makes him any different from Ian?" the young woman demanded.

"He didna help Ian," the crone said. "He helped you. Take a good look, Kitty. How tall yer young man is, how brawny. Ye canna deny his courage, facing down Ian and a sword with naught but his fists. Beneath all those bruises, I think ye've found yer bodyguard."

Chapter 4

MR. CEDRIC AMBLESIDE PACED THE LIBRARY floor at Blackthorne Hall in agitation. "So the duke's body has not been found?"

The three louts he had recruited from the London docks bobbed their heads like corks in the sea.

"Yes it was found, or no it was not?" Mr. Ambleside demanded.

"Ain't seen 'ide nor 'air of 'im," the big one said.

"Not since we threw 'im in," the small one added.

"But you can confirm to the authorities that the duke went into the sea and did not come out?" Mr. Ambleside said.

"That we can," the toothless one replied.

Mr. Ambleside stopped his pacing and stared at the three sailors. "Get rid of those clothes. Burn them."

"But these is the duke's—"

"Precisely," Mr. Ambleside said. "If I can recognize them, so can someone else. Burn them."

"But—"

He grabbed a pair of lapels sewn by Weston and pulled the man wearing the finely tailored jacket—now somewhat water-damaged—onto his toes. "You fool. How could you be wearing the duke's clothes unless you had found his body?"

The toothless man gulped.

Mr. Ambleside let the man go with a shake of his head, then crossed to a highly polished Sheraton desk, opened the drawer, and took out a purse. "Here is what I promised you." He threw the purse of coins to the closest sailor, but the other two both grabbed for it, and a free-for-all resulted on the Turkish carpet.

Mr. Ambleside rolled his eyes. That was what came of dealing with the lower elements. One could not trust them not to kill each other as easily as whatever mark one gave them. Mr. Ambleside laid to with his cane on the shoulders of the nearest man, who quickly abandoned the pile.

He applied the same remedy to the other two and they quickly separated. Once they were standing before him again he said, "Get rid of those clothes before you tell your story to the magistrate. Then take yourselves back to the gutters of London from whence you came. If I see you again after today, I will hire someone to do for you what I hired you to do for the duke."

"Throw us into the sea?" one asked stupidly.

"Kill you, sir," Mr. Ambleside replied, lest there be any doubt of his intent. "Farewell, gentlemen."

Three heads bobbed again as they made their exit

from the room. Mr. Ambleside could hear them arguing over the purse by the time they reached the echoing stone hall.

A figure rose from one of the two gold silk-covered wing chairs facing the fireplace. Clay Bannister, Earl of Carlisle, had been invisible to the three louts, and Mr. Ambleside realized, when he perceived the nobleman's ashen face, that perhaps it had not been wise to confirm the manner of the duke's demise in his presence.

"What have you done, Mr. Ambleside?" the Englishman demanded. "What have you done?"

"Merely what had to be done, my lord," Mr. Ambleside replied.

"You had Blackthorne killed?"

"I did."

"But... but... that's murder!"

"Not at all," Mr. Ambleside said, seeing the danger in such language and wishing to avert any consequences that might arise from the earl's regret. "The duke's ship went down during a storm at sea, and he was drowned."

The earl's dark brown eyes reminded him of a mortally wounded deer. Stupid boy. The earl had no notion of what was necessary in this world to survive. That was always a problem with the Quality. No sense of perspective.

Clay Bannister had become the Earl of Carlisle one year before at the age of one and twenty. Before dying, his elder brother, Charles, had gambled away the family fortune and indulged in enough debauchery to ruin the family's reputation in the neighborhood. Mr. Ambleside had visited the new earl to welcome him on the duke's behalf and to take the young man's measure.

"May I congratulate you on your new circumstances, my lord," he had said when the earl invited him to sit in the drawing room at Carlisle Castle. He had shifted subtly to avoid a dip where a hole in the brocade seat of the chair had allowed the horsehair stuffing to escape. "Please let me know if I may be of any help to you."

"No one can help," the earl had said bitterly. "Unless you have a fortune you would like to give away."

"I am afraid not, my lord," Mr. Ambleside replied sympathetically. "I knew Carlisle Castle in your father's day. It was quite magnificent."

"Yes. It was." The young earl turned away, but not before Mr. Ambleside saw the despair in his dark eyes.

The earl clutched a handful of the rotting velvet drapes and stared through a broken, leaded-glass window at a weed-choked lawn. "It seems I have inherited nothing but debt to add to my own. My brother sold all the land that was not entailed—everything but the castle itself—to the Duke of Blackthorne to finance his excesses. I had no idea..."

The earl's voice faded, and Mr. Ambleside saw him swallow hard. "It is my hope one day to buy it all back."

"Buy it back, my lord?"

"The land," Carlisle said. "I will have to buy back the Carlisle land my brother sold to Blackthorne. Do you think the duke might be willing to sell to me on credit?"

With those words Mr. Ambleside had realized how truly naive the young man was. Credit? For an impoverished earl with no assets but an entailed castle? Hardly likely. Mr. Ambleside recognized an opportunity when he saw one, and the angry, embittered, and indebted young man was ripe for the plucking.

"I am afraid the duke is not likely to relinquish the land under any circumstances," Mr. Ambleside said.

"I know I could have managed the estate and made a profit. If only there were an estate to manage."

"Perhaps I might make a suggestion, my lord."

The earl's sharp eyes had focused intently, disconcertingly, on him as Mr. Ambleside set forth a plan by which Carlisle might regain the land he had lost and Blackthorne Hall as well. Of course the scheme had not been entirely honest. Honesty had not gotten Mr. Ambleside what he was entitled to in this life. Cunning and deceit had been much more useful in achieving his ends.

And there he had hit a snag.

It seemed the young man had not yet sufficiently sunk to depths that would allow him to entirely abandon his honor—a quality which Mr. Ambleside knew from personal experience the current earl's elder brother had not possessed in any great quantity.

"I will not stoop to thievery," Carlisle said flatly.

"It is not precisely—"

"It is stealing," Carlisle interrupted.

Mr. Ambleside had kept himself purposefully still, tamping down the temper that threatened to erupt and spoil everything. What did the earl call years of unpaid bills to his tailor and his bootmaker and the tradesmen who supplied him with all manner of goods? He knew how the Quality lived their lives. Bills—except gambling IOUs—were seldom discharged in a timely manner, if at all. If that was not thievery, what did one call it?

Yet, in the Englishman's eyes, by the rules of his class, he had lived honestly, even nobly. Mr. Ambleside revised his course and continued.

"Very well. I will simply rent the Carlisle land your brother sold to the duke back to you."

"I cannot afford it."

"The rent can be deferred, my lord, until you have profits with which to pay it. I can even write in an option to purchase back the Carlisle land, and perhaps whatever Blackthorne land is unentailed, upon the duke's death."

Mr. Ambleside watched hope light up the young man's eyes.

"You can do that?" the earl asked.

"I have absolute authority to manage the estate as I see fit. When you consider how cheaply the duke bought the land from your brother Charles, you might even say he owes you such an accommodation."

Mr. Ambleside watched the young man chew on his lower lip as he thought over that bit of fraudulent reasoning. He had discovered during his years of larceny that any evil could be justified if one came up with a logical enough reason for it.

He had not explained to the young man that in order to make the land available to him he would be raising the rents and forcing the current tenants off the land. And that he planned to make sure Blackthorne died of something other than old age. He was not sure he could trust the earl to see the felicity of such an arrangement. Since he could not trust the earl's sense of fair play not to interfere, he said nothing about such consequences.

Mr. Ambleside had watched the earl's eyes narrow suspiciously and realized the young man might not be quite so reckless and imprudent as he had believed or hoped.

"Why would you be willing to help me? What is it you hope to gain from such a plan?" Carlisle asked.

Mr. Ambleside gave him a slightly colored view of the facts. "I have a debt of my own to settle with the duke. If I decide to rent the land to you, and Blackthorne should later disagree with the terms, that is a matter strictly between His Grace and myself. You are not involved."

"Why not approach the duke directly with your complaint?"

Foolish youth. Carlisle still believed honesty was the best policy. "Blackthorne is a rich and powerful man," Mr. Ambleside explained. "He could destroy me as easily as a ship is dashed to splinters against the cliffs. No, my lord. I prefer to wreak my vengeance without bringing the full weight of His Grace's influence down upon my head. If helping you should cause Blackthorne to suffer in even a small way, be certain you are absolved of all guilt in the matter."

The dear, gullible boy had believed him.

"Never fear, Mr. Ambleside," the young earl said, his face wreathed in a relieved and happy smile. "I will make sure the land provides a profit. Blackthorne will receive payment after the first harvest—with interest. And if I am as successful as I hope to be, I will be in a position, when the time comes, to repurchase the land."

So Mr. Ambleside and the desperate Earl of Carlisle had drawn up papers renting the Carlisle land owned by the duke to Clay Bannister. Of course, Mr. Ambleside had gone a bit further than the young earl had anticipated or intended and given him an option to buy every stitch of Blackthorne land that was not entailed— which happened to include, unbeknownst to the earl, the land on which Blackthorne Hall itself was built.

Mr. Ambleside was trembling inside the day that Carlisle signed the paper setting down their agreement. He had been making plans for so many years, had even made sure the entailment that had previously existed in regard to Blackthorne Hall was not renewed upon the former duke's death. Neither Blackthorne nor his English solicitor had been apprised the land and the castle could be sold. He had cunningly arranged to steal everything Blackthorne owned in Scotland.

"Blackthorne is dead," Mr. Ambleside said calmly, coolly, as he stood facing the earl in the duke's library. "You are the one holding an option to buy his estate in

Scotland upon his death. You are the one with the most to gain from his murder."

"I had no part in what happened! You lied to me. You deceived me."

Mr. Ambleside shrugged. "I'm afraid it was necessary. There is no turning back now. We will proceed as we began. You have an ironclad contract to purchase the duke's land upon his death. You will exercise it with monies I will provide to you."

"I will not!"

Mr. Ambleside stared into the earl's defiant eyes and said, "I do not intend to see my fortunes flounder because you have turned craven."

"Are you calling me a coward, sir?"

Ambleside realized, when he saw the young man's jaw muscles jerk, that he might have gone a hair too far. The Earl of Carlisle was lean and fit and reputed to be quite a swordsman.

"Stand down, my lord," he said. "I am not impugning your courage, merely your fortitude in the face of what may, perhaps, become a nasty investigation."

"Investigation?" the earl said in a strangled voice. "You think the magistrate—"

"I fully expect, since the duke's body has not been recovered, that someone will be sent to find it."

"What if they find the duke trussed and tied as those fools said they left him? Foul play will be suspected."

"I am certain the scavengers in the sea will solve that problem for us by devouring His Grace," Mr. Ambleside said. "I shall, of course, set my own spies to searching for any remains that may drift up on shore."

"I can no longer be a part of this, Mr. Ambleside. I cannot follow through with the purchase of the land—not even what was mine. I cannot bear the thought that I may have been responsible in even a small way for the death—"

"You will live with whatever guilt you feel," Mr. Ambleside said. "Or you will die for it."

"What are you saying?"

"That you are the one who wanted your lands back and plotted with me to get them."

"I signed an agreement to rent land," the earl protested. "I never intended murder!"

"Pardon me, my lord. You and I both know that, but if any suspicion were to fall on me for the duke's death, I should have to tell the magistrate everything, including the fact that you more than once wished the duke to Hades, and that I only helped you to send him there."

Carlisle gripped the nearest wing chair with a trembling hand. "That is monstrous, sir."

"On the contrary," Mr. Ambleside said. "It is merely a matter of self-preservation. Now, perhaps you would like to discuss the next step in our plan."

The earl's face was all sharp angles. A straight nose, and a square chin—and the shadows in the room and the loathing and shame in his eyes—made him look, to Ambleside's surprise, quite dangerous.

"The devil take you, sir!" the Englishman snarled.

"The duke is dead. The house should be in deep mourning. How can you even consider—"

"Excuse me for interrupting again, my lord," Mr. Ambleside said. It really was unfair that a morally upright child like Clay Bannister should become an earl when there were men, such as himself, so much better suited to the role who were overlooked simply because they had been born on the wrong side of the blanket.

"Time is of the essence," Mr. Ambleside said. "Lady Katherine MacKinnon has challenged the duke's right to the land in court and might very well find a friendly ear. Blackthorne Hall might be given back to her even though you have a legal right to buy it from the duke.

"The sooner you are able to win the lady's hand in marriage, the more comfortable I will be with the situation. Once we know the land will stay in the family, so to speak, you are free to lend your voice to hers in acquiring the land from the courts. An exchange of monies might not even be necessary. Would that soothe your wounded pride?"

"I cannot imagine playing suitor at a time like this," the earl protested.

"If you cannot win her hand, and she wins her battle in court, the duke's death has been for naught," Mr. Ambleside said in the sternest tones.

He knew from the tortured expression on the young man's face, he was likely contemplating the lady he had left behind in London when his fortunes had been changed by the sudden death of his brother, an accident Mr. Ambleside had also arranged when Charles was of no further use to him. Carlisle had bemoaned the loss of his one true love more than once while foxed.

"Lady Marjorie is engaged to another," Mr. Ambleside reminded the young man. "Marriage to Lady Katherine restores all you have lost."

"Except the woman I love," the earl said bitterly.

Mr. Ambleside was easily old enough to be the young man's father, and he sometimes played the role for effect. He had learned that manipulating people simply involved saying the right things to achieve the response one wanted.

"What is done is done," he said, crossing and putting a comforting hand on the earl's shoulder. "The duke is dead. Your lady is lost. Lady Katherine is your destiny now." He felt the young man shudder and hurried to say, "Gossip says the foolish female has agreed to marry any man in her clan who can win her heart. If you do not proceed with your courtship immediately, you may find the land stolen from your grasp by some poor Scots farmer."

Mr. Ambleside thought again how unfair life was. It was sheer misfortune that he was a Blackthorne bastard rather than the legitimate firstborn son. Though gossip had long since revealed the secret of his birth to the neighborhood, no Blackthorne had ever publicly acknowledged his relationship to the family.

His mother had been an upstairs maid in the household of Alistair Wharton's grandfather, an innocent when His Grace had taken her to his bed after a drunken party on the eve of his wedding.

His mother had been let go from her position, of course, but in payment for her silence, the duke had given her a cottage and quarterly allowance, and had promised, if the child were a boy, to educate him at the best schools in England. His mother had told him again and again how lucky he was, that if it had not been for the duke's generosity, he might have grown up to be a shepherd or a farmer or a footman.

Cedric Ambleside had not thanked the duke for what he had; he had cursed the duke for what he had been denied: a legitimate birth, a father who acknowledged him, the right to the whole meat pie instead of crumbs from the table. He—not the present duke's father—should have inherited Blackthorne Hall.

It should all have been his: the title, the lands in England and Scotland, the immense Blackthorne fortune.

Under Scottish law, the illegitimate son inherited equally with the legitimate one. At the very least, half of what Alastair Wharton owned in Scotland should have been his. Instead, he had nothing.

Cedric Ambleside was merely a steward for his nephew, the Duke of Blackthorne. Because Mr. Ambleside had always been kind to Alistair Wharton on his visits to Scotland as a child, the grown-up duke believed Mr. Ambleside to be a perfectly trustworthy guardian for his Scottish estates.

Was it any wonder Mr. Ambleside wanted something for himself? Was it any wonder he felt justified in scheming to get it?

"I will woo the girl," the young earl said, interrupting Mr. Ambleside's thoughts. "But after this, I want nothing more to do with you."

"Very well, my lord. Marry the girl and win the castle and the land, and we are quits."

"What is your reward when all is said and done, Mr. Ambleside?" the earl demanded. "I know you well enough by now to understand you give nothing for nothing."

Mr. Ambleside smiled. It was almost as though he had produced a particularly bright child, or an obstinate pupil had finally learned his lesson. He willingly named his prize.

"What do I get? Why Blackthorne Hall, of course."

Chapter 5

 Mick O'Malley shook his head and muttered, "Ye're a nodcock, Laddie. Ye should've let the man go thirsty. Ye should've let him starve. At least then ye wouldna be going hungry yerself."

It wasn't the first time he had gone without supper, although Mick had gotten used to regular meals over the past year, and it was harder to do without. But the years he had spent with his belly gnawing at his back had given him enough in common with the stranger that he had not been able to resist helping. He hoped someone was offering a similar kindness to his brothers and sisters right now.

The last word he had heard from them had come six months ago. His sister Glenna had gone to work in the kitchen of a great house in Dublin, and the housekeeper had offered to write a letter for her. Glenna had taken advantage of the opportunity to send word to him of how they all fared, but he had left the place where he had told her he would be, and following him from place to place, it had taken almost a year for the letter to find him.

Glenna worked long hours, she said, but had plenty to eat and a warm bed at night. The others, she feared, were not faring as well. He took out the letter, which he had read so often it had worn thin along the creases. He pored over the words that were all he had to connect him to his family.

Corey and Egan are chimney sweeps, but so far neither has been badly burnt in an accident. I worry about Corey. His master does not feed him well, in hopes he will stay small enough to fit into the tiniest chimneys. He is dreadfully thin. Egan cleans the great church chimneys. He says he is not afraid to climb to such enormous heights, but I think he only says that to comfort me.

The baby, Blinne, is still at the orphanage. They have put her to work scrubbing floors.

When are you coming home, Mick? I miss you. We all miss you. I visit Blinne on Sundays and tell her about you. How blue your eyes are and how black your hair. How you held me when I was scared and how you promised to come back for all of us.

You have not forgotten us, have you? Egan

thinks he remembers you, but he is not sure. Corey cries when I mention your name.

Come soon, Mick.

All our love,
Glenna

Mick felt the tears well in his eyes and wiped them away, feeling even more sorely the loss of his job at the inn. He had not earned much, but at least it was work. He rocked his arch over the comforting lump in his shoe. He hadn't nearly enough to send for his brothers and sisters. And with all the farmers being forced off their land by the clearances, there were fewer and fewer jobs to be had by a boy like him.

He had known full well the risk he was taking when he helped the unfortunate man at the inn. It was likely to delay his homecoming even longer. But he did not think Glenna would blame him for what he had done.

Come soon, Mick.

Her plea brought a lump to his throat. *Oh, Glenna, I miss you all so much. I wish I could do more. I wish . . .*

Wishing was a waste of time. Mick shoved himself to his feet and dusted the hay from his clothes, determined to do something about his situation. He had walked for a little more than an hour after he had left Alex Wheaton, which had brought him into the town of Mishnish. He had gone from the tavern to the smithy to the cooper without finding work, and then had found himself a soft bed of hay at a farm within sight of town. Surely he could find work in Mishnish today.

Blackthorne Hall is near Mishnish.

"Why not?" he said aloud. "There might be a job for me at such a grand estate. Or at least some scraps to be begged for at the kitchen door. And maybe that poor gentleman really is someone of note, and he'll have found a friend there who'd be willing to help such as me."

Mick practiced a bow and said, " 'Tis me, Laddie, come for my reward—a job, if ye please." He grinned and shook his head. Mick O'Malley knew better than to believe in happily-ever-after endings. They only happened in fairy tales. But luck...Luck was something else altogether.

Mick spotted a hen roosting in a corner of the barn and smiled. "Breakfast." He reached beneath her soft breast into the warmth of the nest and stole an egg from under the hen without so much as ruffling her feathers. He made a tiny hole in the shell with a small knife he carried in his pocket, then sucked out the contents.

It willna be long now, Glenna, he thought as he sneaked out of the barn. He bathed his dirty face in sunshine as he headed down the rutted road toward Mishnish. *All I need is a bit of luck. And today...today I feel lucky.*

Chapter 6

"COME INSIDE," KITT INVITED HER ERSTWHILE knight. "The least I can do is offer you breakfast."

The suggestion brought a delighted curve to her rescuer's lips. He flinched and muttered "Bloody hell!" as he touched his middle finger to his bleeding lip, but the brief smile had been intriguing. She wondered if he was a handsome man. It was hard to tell beneath all the bumps and bruises and the broken nose.

"You've made a powerful enemy today," she said. "The man you just struck down fancies himself the next Laird of Clan MacKinnon."

"I have no intention of challenging him for the honor," the stranger said.

Kitt saw where his eyes had come to rest and pulled her gaping blouse together with her free hand as her face flushed with a combination of anger and embarrassment. She gestured with the sword for the stranger to go ahead of her, and he followed Moira into the cottage.

"Sit down," she said, pulling the bench out from the table near the hearth with the toe of her shoe.

He almost collapsed onto the bench, and Kitt realized for the first time just what bad condition he must be in. Which only made his rescue all the more heroic.

"I'll need some figwort for these bruises, Moira, and some of your goldenrod and valerian salve. And hot water. Lots of it to clean off all this dirt and blood."

She set the claymore by the hearth where she could easily reach it, then turned to face the stranger.

He was staring at her as though he were privy to her innermost secrets, yet she knew they had never met before. She avoided his glance as she removed the plaid from across his shoulder. She leaned over and reached for the hem of his shirt where it was tied by a rope inside his trousers and began pulling it loose.

"What are you doing?" He caught her hands in his, holding her captive until she met his questioning gaze.

She looked into his eyes—at least the one that wasn't swollen shut—and felt her stomach shift sideways. There it was again. That unwanted attraction. She allowed her face to reveal nothing of her inner turmoil. "There's no sense getting your shirt all wet and dirty—dirtier than it is," she amended, wrinkling her nose as she got a whiff of it, "when I'm cleaning your face. Let me take it off."

He let her go and swiped at the front of his shirt. He

made a disgusted face and said, " 'Tis filthy already. And I dinna think I should be undressing—"

The rest of his protest was muffled as she grabbed two handfuls of muslin and pulled the shirt off over his head.

Kitt stifled a gasp when she got a good look at him. Moira had not been wrong. He was brawny, all right. His body looked sculpted, and whoever had done the work had known what he was about. Powerful shoulders, a deep chest whorled with dark blond hair, corded muscle in his naked biceps and forearms, strong thighs visible through trousers snugged tightly over them, and large, capable hands. He was beautiful, if such a word could be applied to a man. Except for the bruises, of course.

Kitt admired the perfect dimensions of the stranger's body as she would a glorious sunset or the sight of purple heather on the hillside. It gave her pleasure to see God's work done so well.

"I need some water," the man said.

"Yes, I know. I'll clean you up," she replied soothingly, brushing caked sand from his forehead and cheeks and picking not only straw, but what looked like seaweed, from his hair. He winced when she accidentally skimmed his broken nose.

He caught her wrist, groaning as his bruised knuckles protested even that much movement. "I need a drink," he clarified. "Water."

Kitt eyed him cautiously. "I'll get it," she said. "If you'll let me go."

"Pardon me," he said, releasing her.

Kitt wondered at the stranger's fine manners as she crossed to the other side of the room, dipped a cup of water into the bucket she had filled that morning, and brought it back to him. "Here. Drink your fill."

Any pretense of fine manners disappeared once he had the water in his hands. He drank as though he had been walking in the desert for days, excess water streaming down either side of his mouth as he gulped thirstily. He emptied the cup and held it out to her with a gusty sigh. "More, please."

"When was the last time you had something to drink?" she asked as she refilled the cup and handed it to him.

He emptied the cup a second time before he said, "Yesterday. At a cottage by the sea."

"Is that where you live?"

"No. I . . . No."

"Where are you from?"

"South of here," he said. "A rather inhospitable place."

Looking at his battered face, she was forced to agree. "Are you a farmer?"

"I've most recently been at sea."

She focused her attention on the work at hand, dabbing at his blood-caked features and his torn knuckles with a warm, wet cloth. "I promised you breakfast," she said. "Are you hungry?"

"A little." He hesitated and said, "Actually, I'm famished."

"Moira, a bowl of oatmeal, a bannock, and some tea for our guest."

He reached for the cloth. "I can do that mysel—Ow!"

"Shh!" she said soothingly, blowing on a cut running through his eyebrow that had opened when she soaked out the sand that was ground into it. There was a knot the size of a goose egg on his forehead. One eye was merely a slit, while the other was surrounded by black-and-blue bruises. His nose was swollen so huge it was hard to tell what size it was intended to be, and if it had once been straight, it was no more. His lower lip was twice its size, and she noticed he licked at a cut on the edge that bled steadily.

"Your face looks as though you've been in a brawl. Did you win?" she asked.

The stranger looked at her through his one good eye, which she suddenly noticed was gray. "I'm alive to tell of it."

"Perhaps you'd make a good bodyguard for The MacKinnon after all."

"Bodyguard?" He sat up straight, then gasped and grabbed at his side.

She frowned. "Do you have broken ribs?"

"Only bruised, I think," he gritted out between teeth clenched against the pain. "Why does The MacKinnon need a bodyguard?"

"Because she's being plagued by all manner of suitors," Moira said, setting a ceramic pot of greasy yellow salve on the table in front of him. "Like that idiot Ian

MacDougal ye chased off this morning. Ever since my darling Kitty said she'd marry the man who could win her heart, we havna had a moment's peace around here."

The stranger stared at Moira for a moment longer, then turned his attention to Kitt. "*You* are The MacKinnon?"

She grinned and made a quick curtsy. "Lady Katherine MacKinnon at your service, sir. And what might your name be?"

He hesitated so long, Kitt wondered if one of the knocks on his head had stolen his senses. "Your name?" she reminded him.

"Alex Wheaton."

"Tell me about yourself, Alex Wheaton," Kitt said as she continued her labors on his bruised face.

"There's not much to tell."

Kitt applied the goldenrod and valerian salve as gently as she could with her fingertips, but he hissed and jerked away at even that slight touch. She realized the wounds must be very fresh, and she put a hand on his shoulder to keep him still. "Easy. It will make all well."

She was curious to know more about this man who Moira thought would make a good bodyguard, especially because he was being so secretive about himself. "Do you have a family, Alex?"

His gaze moved away from hers. "I dinna . . . dinna wish to speak of them."

He was unhappily married, Kitt decided. Or perhaps his wife had died. He wore no ring. Kitt realized the direction of her thoughts and brought herself up short. Surely she had not been entertaining ideas about the stranger as a prospective husband, not with an entire clan to choose from.

"What brings you here?" she asked.

"I . . . decided to do some traveling."

"Why?"

"You ask a lot of questions."

"If I'm to hire you as my bodyguard, I need to know a little bit about you." She smiled and said, "You might be a wolf in sheep's clothing."

She felt his shoulder tense beneath her hand.

"I have no designs on your person, Lady Katherine. I'm willing to be your bodyguard and fight to keep you safe. That's all you need to know."

Moira cackled. "Well, lass, there's yer *gille-coise*."

Kitt had balked at the idea of having someone to protect her. She could take good care of herself. But Ian had come very close to overwhelming her this morning. She did not relish the idea of having her choices taken away by some man's brute strength.

And it was especially important that all her choices be left open now that her father's plan seemed to have come to naught. With the Duke of Blackthorne drowned, she was going to have to find some other way to save her people that did not involve the duke. And soon.

"I canna pay you much," she said.

"A roof and a bed and a meal now and then will be enough."

She eyed him again and wondered why she trusted this stranger on such short acquaintance. It was hard to judge him by his face, which was badly battered, but his ready defense of her that morning, his quiet presence, and his obvious strength had all made a good impression. Whatever his past, whatever troubles had plagued him, he was here now and he was willing to help.

"Very well, Alex Wheaton. I appoint you bodyguard for The MacKinnon. 'Tis an ancient and honorable position. Do your duty well."

He captured her hand in his, looked deep into her eyes, and said, "I shall guard you with my life."

Kitt felt her breath catch as he made the solemn vow. She knew what such a promise might cost him. There was at least one man who would stop at nothing to have her. Alex would earn the meager pay she had offered him. At least with a bodyguard to protect her, she had bought some time to think of another way to save her people.

She set the salve on the table and was about to put the lid back on it when Alex stopped her.

"Wait." He took the salve and dipped a finger into it, then reached up and gently smoothed it across the bruise Ian had put on her cheek. "You have a wound of your own that needs tending."

His fingertip was rough and not precisely clean, but she felt an ache in her throat at his thoughtful gesture.

"There," he said, setting down the pot and wiping

the excess salve off on his trousers. He looked up at her and said, "My first duty as bodyguard completed."

Kitt shivered, but not from the cold. He was watching her again, and she found herself trapped by his gaze, unable to move. The more certain Kitt became that she should look away, the less willing—or able—she was to do so.

"Yer breakfast, Alex," Moira said, breaking the spell.

"Thank you, Moira." He dug in with relish, nearly swallowing the bannock whole. He must have felt Kitt watching him because he looked up abruptly, his cheek bulging with food, and reddened. He swallowed what was in his mouth and said, "I must confess I canna remember a time when I was so hungry. I thank you and your mother for—"

"Moira isna my mother," Kitt interrupted. "She was my nurse. My mother died birthing me."

"Oh. I'm sorry."

"'Twas a tragedy for my father, right enough," Kitt said. "He found his one true love late in life and lost her when I was born. And I was not a son."

"He was blessed to have you," Alex said in a quiet voice.

Kitt wondered what he meant. Her father had never been happy with her. She had borne the double burden all her life of having killed the only woman her father could ever love and not being the son that might have mitigated her mother's death.

Not that she hadn't tried to fill the role. Over the

years, Kitt had stomped out every vestige of what could be described as female behavior. No missish tears. No megrims. No eyelash-batting flirtation.

She had learned to fight with dirk and sword. She had listened as her father explained the art of raiding, preparing herself for the day she would go with him. She had hidden her knock-kneed fear that she would not measure up in battle, so he would not see it.

But however much she learned, she was still a female. She still wore a skirt and suffered her courses each month, as her body prepared itself to bear a child. Ironically, it was in being a woman—who could seduce the duke—that she had finally pleased her father. And she had failed him even in that, because the duke was dead.

Kitt had not wanted a bodyguard, because it meant once again admitting she was only a woman and needed someone stronger to protect her. She consoled herself with the knowledge that even a man needed to be shielded from those enemies devious enough to stab him in the back. And Ian certainly qualified. There was nothing wrong with having necessary weapons—like a bodyguard—at her disposal.

Kitt fought a grin as she watched her bodyguard devouring his bowl of oatmeal as though it were Mother's Eve pudding. He was as hungry as a wolf. And he reminded her of one—wary, watchful. And mysterious. She had to admit she was intrigued by Alex Wheaton. Where had he come from? What was he doing here?

He glanced up and caught her staring.

Kitt felt a thrill—or was it a chill—run down her spine as he searched her face with the one eye that wasn't swollen shut. She was still trying to think of some explanation for her rudeness when someone knocked on the door.

"Not another one," Moira said with a groan.

"I'll see who it is." Kitt opened the door to find a youth she didn't recognize. She felt a presence at her shoulder and realized Alex had left the table—hungry as he was—to stand beside her.

"Who is it?" he said.

The boy's eyes rounded. "Alex! Is that you?"

"Laddie!" Alex exclaimed. "How did you find me?"

"I've come with a message for The MacKinnon," the youth said, holding up a parchment with an embossed wax seal. "From the Earl of Carlisle himself."

"I'll take that," Kitt said.

The boy drew back the parchment and held it clutched against his narrow chest. " 'Tis for The MacKinnon."

"You've found her, Laddie," Alex said. "Lady Katherine is The MacKinnon."

"Well. Ye've landed on yer feet," Mick said with a grin, as he handed over the letter to her.

"You two know each other?" Kitt asked, her eyes narrowing suspiciously as she looked from the boy in ill-fitting clothes to the stranger in equally ill-fitting clothes she had hired to protect her.

Alex realized that Michael O'Malley would spoil everything if he revealed that Alex Wheaton had been an Englishman yesterday. He couldn't imagine that The MacKinnon would be much pleased by the fact she'd hired one of the enemy to defend her against her clansmen.

"This is Laddie," he said before Mick could answer. "We grew up on neighboring farms."

He saw Mick's eyebrows shoot nearly to his hairline and then the slight nod as the boy acknowledged his clanker. "Would you mind if I have a word with the boy?" he said to his new employer.

"Go ahead."

As Kitt crossed inside to the table and sat down to read, Alex quickly ushered Mick outside, far enough away from the front door that they wouldn't be overheard. "I need a favor, Laddie," he began.

"What is it, *neighbor*?" Mick asked. "Nothing havey-cavey, I hope. I've just gotten myself a plum bit of employment, and I'm not anxious to lose it."

"I need you to keep my charade as an Englishman a secret from Lady Katherine."

The boy's mouth cocked up on one side mischievously. "Oh. Is that all?"

"'Tis important, Laddie," Alex said in his best imitation of a Scots accent.

"Sure, Alex. I understand. Ye wouldna want the lady thinking ye're crazy."

"I dinna care if she thinks I'm an idiot, so long as

she doesna know I'm English. By the way, how did you find employment with an earl?"

"I thought ye might go to Blackthorne Hall, so I went there myself. Ye never know with the Quality," he said sheepishly. "Sometimes they're a little dicked in the nob. Ye could have been . . . someone.

"Anyway, I went to the kitchen door to ask for food and to see if you were there, and Cook was wailing that the Duke of Blackthorne was dead, drowned in the sea. 'Twas sheer luck that the earl saw me there as he was leaving the Hall. He asked me if I wanted work and here I am."

Alex had heard nothing after Laddie said, *"The Duke of Blackthorne was dead, drowned in the sea."* His heart began to beat faster. Had he been with the duke? Was that how he had ended up in the sea as well?

"How did the duke drown?" he asked.

"The earl told me the duke's ship went down in a storm off the coast. Everyone drowned except three sailors, who lived to tell the tale."

Three sailors and me? Alex wondered. Something more than a storm had wreaked havoc on that ship, he'd wager. Otherwise he would not be so battered. Otherwise his hands would not have been bound.

"What happened to the three sailors?" Alex asked.

"The earl didna think much of them," Mick said. "He said the 'stupid louts'—his words, not mine—went back to the London docks where they came from."

Alex frowned. Should he try to follow them to

London? Perhaps they knew who he was. Or perhaps they were the ones who had tried to kill him. He would be better off investigating his identity here, he decided, where he had at least one friend in Michael O'Malley. And where he had a roof over his head and food in his belly.

"What does the Earl of Carlisle want with Lady Katherine?" he asked Mick.

"He did a lot of muttering while he was writing, but the long and short of it is, I think he means to woo her, wed her, and bed her."

Alex's jaw dropped. "What?"

Mick pulled Alex close so he could whisper, "The earl kept me standing by his side while he wrote his letter. I couldna help but read it."

"You can read?" Alex asked.

"Certainly," Mick asserted, his chest puffed out. "Canna say I knew every word, but most of them I did. Taught myself. Ye never know when such a skill might come in handy. This time it did."

"So the earl's planning to court The MacKinnon?"

"He's asked her to tea at the castle—Castle Carlisle that is—next week. Do ye think she'll go?"

"I dinna know," Alex said, staring in through the open door at the woman sitting in the shadows. "The earl would be a better catch than any of her clansmen. But the earl's also English. If she's like the rest of the Highlanders, she canna like him simply on that score."

He tried to imagine what an earl had to gain by marrying an impoverished noblewoman, although her beauty was reason enough, he supposed, for any man to desire her. He might have believed that the lady herself was all the young earl wanted, except right now he could not—dared not—trust anyone.

"Alex, would you come here, please?"

Alex stepped back inside the house with Mick on his heels and stood waiting to hear what Lady Katherine had to say.

"Tell the earl I'll be glad to come for tea next week," she told the boy.

Mick touched his forelock and said, "I will, milady." And then, to Alex, "Take care, neighbor," and took his leave of them.

"I've been invited for tea next week at Castle Carlisle," Lady Katherine said. "I'll need you to go with me."

"I'm ready to serve you, my lady," Alex said.

"You'll meet most of my clansmen tomorrow at the kirk." She wrinkled her nose and said, "I think perhaps we had better clean you up a bit first."

Alex flushed as red as a mangel-wurzel. He was aware his clothes stank—how could he not be? They had been a constant offense to his senses. But he had nothing else to wear. "I—"

Lady Katherine rose and put her fingertip to his lips to silence him. His body quivered at the touch. "Dinna feel ashamed, Alex," she said quietly. "The clothes are fine enough, but I canna be wrinkling my nose at the smell of you when I'm telling my clansmen I've hired you as my bodyguard.

"Go to the barn and strip off your trousers so Moira can wash them along with your shirt. She'll fill a tub of water for you to bathe in."

"I . . ." What could he say? He could not protest that this was not how he normally dressed . . . or smelled. He did not know for sure.

He angled down the chin that had shot up in pride and defiance when Lady Katherine had first spoken and said, "As you wish, Lady Katherine."

Alex turned and left the cottage with as much grace as he could manage. It took all the restraint he had not to run the whole way to the barn. Once he got there, he leaned against a wooden stall and lifted one foot to pull off the too-small borrowed boot, then yanked off the other and threw it aside. He untied the rope that held up his too-large trousers and jerked them down, along with the one thing that fit him, his smalls.

It was only then he realized he could not very well hand over his clothes to Moira naked as the day he was born. He looked around for something to cover himself and found a woolen blanket that smelled of horse, though he had seen no horse since his arrival. It was not a large blanket, and it barely covered him in front and not at all in back.

He jerked around when he heard a female gasp.

"I didna think you would already be—"

Alex found himself facing Lady Katherine, her face flushed with the same heat he felt in his own cheeks. He cleared his throat but could think of nothing to say.

"Here," she said, thrusting a stack of things at him.

To take it, he would have had to let go of the blanket. Instead, he asked, "What do you have there?"

"Clean clothes."

"The only clothes I have are lying there," he said, gesturing with his chin at the pile he had dropped on the straw-littered dirt.

"You'll need something to wear while those are drying," she said. "You can wear these. I also brought a pair of shoes that may fit better than your own. And a dirk. You will need a weapon."

He recognized her charity for what it was and wanted to refuse, but remembered his blisters and kept his mouth shut.

She hung the articles she had brought over the top of the wooden stall, set down the shoes and the exquisite blade in its jeweled sheath, stooped to collect his dirty clothes, then stood up and stared at him without speaking.

He stared back. "Is there something else?"

She opened her mouth and closed it without making a sound, but her eyes spoke volumes. The attraction was there.

He watched her fight it. And conquer it.

While he stood like a dolt, both hands clutching the blanket, she crossed past him with the handful of soiled clothes to the corner of the barn and dragged a large wooden tub out into the middle of the dirt floor.

"Moira is heating water now," she said in a rush. "You willna have to wait long."

Then she was gone, as though she had never been there. Alex began to wonder if it had all happened in his imagination. Except, the part of him that was male had reacted quite violently to Lady Katherine's appearance and left visible proof that she had been there.

"Bloody hell."

"Ye needna swear at me. I'm moving as fast as I can," Moira snapped as she entered the barn.

The sight of the old crone carting a heavy bucket of water prodded him into action. "Let me help."

"Best ye hang on to yer dignity," Moira said as he started to let go of the blanket, "and let me handle this."

He reached for the plaid lying across the stall where Lady Katherine had left it and wrapped it around his waist to cover his nakedness. When he turned to face Moira, the old woman gasped. "What's wrong?" he asked.

She stared at him with a trembling hand held over her heart. "I knew she liked ye," Moira said. "I didna realize she trusted ye so much."

She looked almost frightened, and Alex felt himself becoming frightened at the thought the old woman might keel over at any moment. "What is it?" he asked. "What's wrong?"

"She gave ye his things," the old woman said in awed disbelief. "His plaid and his dirk and his belt."

"Whose things?" Alex said, anxious because the crone seemed to regard the clothing as something special.

"Those things she brought for ye to wear..." she said in a reverent voice. "They belonged to her father."

Chapter 7

K<small>ITT HAD OFFERED HER FATHER'S CLOTHES TO</small>
Alex because it was all she had that she
thought might fit him. But she was unprepared for the
sight of him actually standing in her father's shoes.

Unlike her father, Alex was fair-haired, which had
only become apparent after he bathed, and gray-eyed—
Moira had put an herbal compress on his black eye,
which had reduced the swelling so she could more easily make out their color. But his confident bearing reminded her of her father when he had still been a
young and powerful leader of his clan.

Alex looked like a laird should look, his back ram-
rod straight, his shoulders squared impressively, his
chin lifted in a pose that might have seemed arrogant
except she knew he was a simple man who had become
her bodyguard to keep his belly full and a roof over his
head.

"I thank you for the clothes," he said as he stood in

the doorway to the cottage, tugging on the plaid. "Moira said they belonged to your father."

"Yes." She swallowed past the sudden constriction in her throat and crossed to help him adjust the plaid beneath the belt. "Yes, they did."

"Perhaps I shouldna—"

"He would have wanted you to have the use of them," she said, cutting off any further discussion of the subject. "Let's go."

"Where are we going?" he asked, his eyes following her around the room as she made preparations to leave.

"I have visits to make to my people, to see how they're faring." *To admonish them not to poach on the duke's domain, no matter how great the temptation.* Her lips thinned before she added, "And to leave food."

He frowned. "There's hunger here? I walked the road and the ground seemed fertile."

"It is." She had mended her torn blouse while he was bathing and now arranged a woolen plaid around her shoulders against the chilly wind. She froze as he lifted her hair, which she had left down, out from under the shawl and let it fall over her shoulders.

" 'Tis beautiful," he murmured as his fingers brushed the length of it. "Silky as . . . I cannot think of anything to compare it with."

Kitt shivered as his fingers brushed the length of it. "You shouldna be noticing such things," she said, stepping away from him.

His lips flattened, but he gave her a deferential nod. "Aye, my lady."

She picked up the basket Moira had filled with foodstuffs, but he took it away from her and settled it on his arm. Because it would have been silly to argue that she could carry it herself, she let him have it.

Kitt set out at a brisk pace for Patrick Simpson's cottage, worried that he might have ignored her advice, wondering how she could persuade him of the folly of poaching on the duke's land. She was grateful for Alex's silence at first. She had a great deal to contemplate, not the least of which was her meeting next week with the Earl of Carlisle. He had been in the neighborhood for a year and had completely ignored her. Why the sudden interest in her now?

As the minutes passed, Kitt became distracted by the large shadow her bodyguard cast, which led her to examine the corded sinew in the forearm that was curved around the heavy basket he carried, his large hands, and his long, lean fingers.

"I feel like a particularly succulent roast on a platter," he said with obvious humor in his voice.

Her gaze skipped to his face, and she saw the same humor reflected in his eyes and mouth. "I'm sorry."

"I'm not," he said. "Perhaps you'll want a taste later."

The innuendo was there. The male interest. The totally inappropriate interest, considering their respective roles. "You said you had no designs on my person," she reminded him.

"You didna make the same claim, I'm thankful to say."

She stopped in the middle of the worn footpath that edged the duke's land and turned to confront him with her hands on her hips. How he could look so masculine holding a woven basket on his arm? "Even if I found you attractive—"

"Then you do?" he said with a grin meant to charm, and which, she had to admit, was quite charming.

"Even if I found you attractive," she repeated through gritted teeth, "I could not possibly indulge such an interest. I have an obligation to marry where it will best serve my clan."

"Even if you canna like the man?" he said, the grin gone.

"My feelings canna matter," Kitt said. "My father made that plain to me before his death."

"I dinna understand such thinking."

She started walking again, unwilling to endure his disapproving look. "You must see we are a poor clan," she said. "Even more so since the Duke of Blackthorne began raising the rents to force us off our land."

"Greedy, is he?"

"He's raised the rents thrice in a year. Most can barely feed their bairns after they've given the duke his due."

"Have you confronted him and asked for relief?" Alex questioned.

"He wasna here to confront," Kitt retorted. "He lives—lived—far away in the south of England where he couldna see the damage his demands wrought. Now he's dead and heaven only knows what Blackthorne bastard will replace him."

"Perhaps the new duke will be more sympathetic to your plight."

"I'm not counting on it," Kitt said. "I had only one hope of saving my people, and that died with the duke. I tell you, Alex, it has been a very long six months since my father died and named me his successor."

"Why did he pick you to be The MacKinnon? Why not one of your clansmen?" Alex asked.

"I was not his first choice," Kitt admitted with a rueful smile. "He wanted Ian MacDougal to lead after him. But I refused to marry Ian."

"Why?"

"I didna love him." She looked up at him and continued, "My father was too proud to admit he couldna control his own daughter and too stubborn to choose someone else. He named me as chief only because I . . . I finally agreed to marry a husband of his choice."

"So you're to marry Ian MacDougal after all?"

Kitt shook her head. "No. Not Ian. Someone else. An *Englishman*." She could not keep the venom from her voice.

"Is it all Englishmen you hate, or is there someone in particular you loathe?" Alex asked. "I mean, aside from Blackthorne raising the rents, what have the English done to you?"

"There was Culloden," Kitt replied.

"That was more than fifty years ago," Alex said.

"The Scots will never forget . . . or forgive."

"I'll remember that," Alex said. "But tell me, recently, what harm has an Englishman done to you?"

Kitt turned to face him, her eyes bleak. "They killed the man I loved."

"I'm sorry."

"Sympathy willna bring him back," she snarled.

"How did it happen?"

"Leith was caught poaching on Blackthorne land and transported. He died on board ship before he ever reached Australia."

"He was breaking the law," Alex pointed out.

"Leith only sought to feed his starving brothers and sisters," Kitt said. "Starving because the bastard Duke of Blackthorne raised the rents once too often."

"What happened to Leith's brothers and sisters?"

"They moved away to Glasgow. Even so, the two youngest died of hunger. You can see why I canna allow Patrick Simpson to be transported," Kitt said. " 'Tis a death sentence."

"Surely not always."

"I willna take the chance with one of mine," she said.

Alex noticed the possessive *one of mine*. There was nothing false about Katherine MacKinnon's sense of responsibility toward her clan. He wondered how far she was willing to go to gain her ends. "Who did you finally agree to marry?"

Her green eyes were filled with hate as she said, "The bloody Duke of Blackthorne."

"The duke?" Alex asked incredulously.

"I promised my father on his deathbed that I would trick Blackthorne into a handfast marriage, then do my best to get pregnant and bear a son to inherit the land. It doesna matter now. The duke is dead, drowned in the sea."

"If the duke had lived, would you have gone through with it?"

She met Alex's shocked look with determined eyes. "I would do anything I believed would improve the lot of my clansmen. Even sacrifice myself in an Englishman's bed."

"How did you plan to convince the duke to wed an impoverished Scotswoman?"

"My station is not so low," she said. "You forget I'm a lady by birth. Two generations ago, Blackthorne Hall belonged to my family—not his. I am pursuing the matter in the courts, but it would have been easier to marry him."

Alex scowled. "I canna believe you were willing to do such a thing! 'Tis despicable to marry a man for profit."

" 'Twas not for profit! 'Twas for the sake of my people. The land and the castle were stolen from us after Culloden by the English. Blackthorne Hall—Castle MacKinnon—should have been mine. If the duke wasna so cruel, I doubt my father would have suggested anything so desperate."

"Even so, I canna like it."

"*I* didna *like* it!" she spat. "I tell you I had no other choice."

"The courts—"

"Move too slowly," she interrupted. "Bairns are starving. My clansmen are being forced off land their families have farmed for generations, never to return."

"What will you do now that the duke is dead?"

"I dinna know," she admitted with a huge sigh. "I made a vow to my father on his deathbed that I would do whatever was necessary to save the clan. Now that his plan has come to naught, I...I dinna know what to do."

Alex gingerly rubbed at the two-days' growth of beard on his bruised chin, then said, "If you're willing to go so far, I'm surprised you havna thought to steal back a little of what the duke's taken from you."

"'Tis too dangerous."

"Why?"

"If anything went missing, the duke's steward, Mr. Ambleside, would not have to look far to find the obvious suspects."

"You'd have to be caught with the loot."

Kitt searched Alex's face. "Are you seriously suggesting I rob the duke's estate?"

"Think of yourself as a Scottish Robin Hood, stealing from the rich to give to the poor. There's a certain nobility, even justice to the crime, is there not?"

Kitt's brow furrowed uncertainly. "I suppose. You make it sound so easy, but—"

"It is."

"Not so easy as you might think," she argued. "There are soldiers billeted not far from Mishnish to keep the peace. We have few weapons, even fewer horses."

"If you're clever enough, you willna need weapons or horses."

Kitt pondered the idea a moment longer, then shook her head. "It wouldna work."

"Why not?" Alex persisted.

"I dinna believe the men would follow me. And I wouldna send them on such a perilous endeavor without their chief."

"I see," Alex said. "That's a problem right enough."

Kitt could hear weeping through the open windows long before they reached the door to the one-room stone-and-thatch cottage where Patrick and Dara Simpson lived with their five children and Patrick's elderly mother. She hurried her pace, knocking loudly on the wooden door.

"Dara, 'tis Lady Katherine."

The door opened in a rush and a teary-eyed Dara stood before her, a babe in one arm and two small children clinging to her skirt. "Come in. Come in. Disaster has struck!"

Kitt's heart leapt to her throat. "Patrick has been caught poaching?" She heard the answer in Dara's gulping sob, saw the answer in Dara's frightened hazel eyes.

"When I told Patrick what you said, he left the house without even eating any of the supper you gave us. He didna come home last night, and this morning Mr. Ambleside came to tell me Patrick was caught with two rabbits by the gamekeeper. He said—" She grabbed her mouth to hold back a wail of grief, but it did no good. "He said Patrick is to be sent before the magistrate and will surely be transported. He said he knows we canna pay the rent, and that we must leave. Leave!" she cried. "Where can we go?"

"Shh. Shh," Kitt said, pulling Dara, clinging children and all, into her embrace. Her heart was thumping madly. She knew exactly what Dara was feeling. Leith had also been caught poaching . . . and had died on the journey to Australia. "Quiet yourself, Dara. You're frightening the children. I've brought food—"

" 'Twill keep us alive, but for what?" Dara demanded. "If only your father had named someone else as chief. If only—"

"Feed your bairns, Mrs. Simpson," Alex interrupted, handing the distraught woman the basket of foodstuffs.

Dara's reproach tied a knot in Kitt's stomach.

If only your father had named someone else as chief.

Her father's plan had failed. And she had not come up with a better one.

Why not do as Alex suggested? Why not steal from the duke? Why not take back what Blackthorne wrongly took from you?

Kitt kept her thoughts to herself, but for the first time in a long time, she let herself hope that she could avoid an unwanted marriage. It could work. Not that she would risk any of her clansmen in such a dishonest venture. She would do the stealing herself, with Alex's help in planning the ventures. Surely he would be willing. After all, it was his idea.

Kitt helped feed the children, marveling at the way Alex calmed Dara Simpson, at his ease with the smaller boys and girls, even taking the baby, Brynne, from Dara, holding her gently in his strong arms while Dara and Kitt dispensed portions of lamb stew and dried figs to the other children.

"You look comfortable with a bairn in your arms. Do you have children of your own?" Kitt asked.

"'Tis not so difficult when you treat them as little people," he said, supporting the baby's head as he switched it to the other arm in order to help wee Connie reach for a piece of fruit.

"Little people?" Kitt said.

"Smaller versions of ourselves," he said. "Take this little one, for instance. She's looking at me so intently with those blue eyes of hers, I think she must be wanting to tell me something important, if only she could talk."

"Like what?" Kitt asked, intrigued.

He grinned and held Brynne away from his shirt, which had an obvious damp spot. "'I'm wet. Change me.'"

Kitt laughed. It took her a moment to realize he had never answered her question. Did he have children of his own somewhere? And a wife who had borne them? If so, why had he never spoken of them. He would make a good father. Considerate and caring and kind.

You shouldna care, Kitt warned herself. *The likes of*

him is not for you. You've a duty to marry where it will serve your clan. Dinna be thinking of brawny shoulders and a tender heart.

But Alex was undeniably good with children. Kitt watched as he won the confidence of each child in turn, until even the eldest girl, Rhiannon, who had eyed him suspiciously from the moment she saw him, finally gave in and allowed him to put a comforting hand on her shoulder.

When they took their leave Kitt said, "Please dinna worry, Dara. I'll figure out some way to save Patrick, and I'll find a place for all of you."

"Dinna make promises you canna keep," Dara said bitterly.

Kitt felt the sting of her words, but it was Alex who replied, "Trust The MacKinnon, Mrs. Simpson. She will make all well. Never fear."

Kitt found as much reassurance in Alex's speech as Dara Simpson obviously did.

" 'Tis sorry I am for doubting you, Lady Katherine," Dara said, bobbing a curtsy. "We'll be ready when you have a place for us to go."

Kitt waited only until they were far enough from the cottage that she couldn't be overheard before she said, "I'm willing to rob the duke, but I'll do it myself. I willna risk the others."

"We'll do it together," Alex said.

"I'll go alone. You can help me plan—"

He stepped in front of her, cutting her off. His gray eyes were dark with anger.

"I'm your bodyguard. 'Tis my duty to protect you. But even had you decided not to go, I would have gone on my own. Any man so careless of the needs of his tenants deserves to be robbed."

"Thank you, Alex," Kitt said, moved by his offer of support. "I accept your offer of help. But first we must rescue Patrick Simpson and send him and his family away from here."

Alex frowned. "That may be more difficult, and is likely to be more dangerous, than stealing from the duke. Patrick is sure to be well guarded."

"Aye. We can count on it."

"Perhaps this is something you should broach with your clansmen. They may want to help. There are bound to be consequences—searches and the like—afterward. Everyone should be forewarned."

Kitt chewed her lip. "You're right, of course." She feared her clansmen would not follow her if she tried to lead them on such a raid. Alex would see the situation for himself. Even if they would not help, she intended to see Patrick Simpson freed. She would not leave him to suffer the same fate as Leith. "I'll speak with everyone tomorrow before services at the kirk."

"I like this Duke of Blackthorne less and less," Alex said.

"I hate him," Kitt declared simply.

"Yet you would have lain with him? Borne his child?"

Kitt met Alex's angry glance without flinching. "I

would lie down with the devil himself, if it would save my people."

When they reached the kirk the next day and Kitt saw the distrustful faces of her clansmen, who were gathered outside the door, she shifted unwittingly toward the man at her side. She wondered what tale Ian had spun about his encounter with her the previous morning. Nothing close to the truth, she was willing to venture.

"Who is he, and what is he doing here?" Ian demanded, stepping forward out of the crowd.

"Ian MacDougal, meet Alex Wheaton," Kitt said. "My bodyguard."

Ian's swollen jaw dropped. "That misbegotten oaf? Your bodyguard? The devil you say!"

Kitt felt Alex tense, but to her relief he said nothing, did nothing in response to the insult. " 'Tis customary for the chief to have a *gille-coise*," she said.

"But he's not one of us!" Ian protested.

"Of course not." Kitt let her gaze travel over the gathered crowd. "Every bachelor standing here is a possible husband. We canna have the fox guarding the chicken coop, can we?" she said with a winsome smile.

She watched Fletcher, the biggest man among them, exchange a look with Birk the Bowman. Watched Evan the Swordsman nod to Angus the Wrestler. Met Wise Old Cam's eyes and saw them twinkle with laughter. These few, at least, saw the wisdom of what she had done. A few others, most notably Ian, did not.

"He has your father's dirk," Ian said through tight jaws.

"And his shirt and shoes and trousers and plaid," Kitt confirmed. "What of it?"

" 'Tis The MacKinnon's dirk," Ian said.

" 'Twas his dirk," Kitt said softly. " 'Tis mine now. And I've given it to my bodyguard, that he may the better protect me from my enemies."

"From what Ian's told us, we'll be needing protection from him," Tavis the Handsome said, crossing to stand beside Ian.

"What did Ian say happened to him?" Kitt asked, perusing the purple marks Alex's solid hit had left on Ian's chin.

"That this stranger attacked him without warning," Tavis said.

" 'Tis true," Kitt replied. A hush fell, and Kitt felt every eye on her. "You should know that when Alex attacked, Ian was holding me against my barn wall with every intention of taking what I had no desire to give. Alex asked him to release me, but he would not."

Every man there switched his gaze to Ian, whose face reflected his resentment at being shown in the wrong. "We need a leader, Lady Katherine," he said in a cold, hard voice. " 'Tis time you made a choice."

" 'Tis *my* choice to make," Kitt said, her voice as cold as his. "Alex will ensure there are no further attempts to force a decision sooner than I am ready to make it."

"We need a man to speak for us," Tavis said.

"I have a tongue," Kitt snapped back.

"Patrick Simpson was caught poaching on Blackthorne's land yesterday and put in jail," Duncan said. "'Tis needful someone plead on Patrick's behalf for leniency. I dinna think they'll listen to a woman, Lady Katherine."

Kitt had expected the lack of confidence in her ability to lead, but hearing it spoken aloud still left her reeling. She felt a strong hand close over her shoulder.

"Steady," Alex whispered in her ear. "Remember you're The MacKinnon."

She shot a grateful glance over her shoulder, then said, "I think there is more that can be done for Patrick Simpson than simply pleading for leniency."

"What did you have in mind?" Ian said disdainfully. "Inviting the magistrate home to discuss the matter over tea?"

"I had in mind breaking Patrick out of jail and sending him with his family on the next ship bound for America."

"What? Are you mad?" Ian said.

"He's being guarded by soldiers!" another man cried.

"Where will we find the funds to buy passage?" yet another shouted.

Kitt answered the objections to her suggestion in the order they'd been posed. "It makes perfect sense to rescue Patrick, if you consider the alternative," she said. "And since when could a Highlander not outmaneuver one of the king's soldiers? We'll come in under cover of darkness and sneak away without anyone the wiser. As for where to get funds for the passage to America, leave that to me."

"Where will you get such a sum?" Ian demanded.

"That's my business," Kitt said.

"Ian is right. 'Tis a foolhardy idea," Duncan said.

Kitt stared at her father's advisor, trying not to feel betrayed by his failure to support her. If she had been a son . . . but she was not.

" 'Tis more likely a few of us will end up in jail than that Patrick will be freed," Ian said.

"Not if we plan everything carefully in advance," Kitt argued.

" 'Tis a stupid idea, and we'll have no part of it," Ian said.

To Kitt's dismay, it seemed her clansmen were united with Ian in opposition to her plan. If she allowed him to win this battle, she might as well concede the role of chief to him.

"Cowards," she accused.

The word hung in the air like a pestilential smell, causing scowls to form and noses to curl with distaste.

"I am determined to save Patrick Simpson," she said in a quiet voice. "Who is with me?"

Kitt looked at Duncan, willing him to see the necessity of saving Patrick and his family, but Duncan simply lowered his eyes to his toes. She glanced at Cam, at Fletcher, at Evan, at Birk. All of them avoided her gaze. She did not get through the entire clan before a voice behind her said loudly and clearly, "I will go with you."

Kitt turned to stare at Alex. His bruised face was pale, his lips thinned into a flat line.

"Thank you, Alex." She turned back to her clansmen. "I intend to rescue Patrick—with or without your help."

She stared them down, watching them trade shamefaced glances as they realized the trap in which they were caught.

"I canna let you go alone," Duncan said. "Your father would come back to haunt me."

"Thank you, Duncan."

"If Duncan's to go, I'll go," Cam volunteered.

"Count me in, then," said Birk.

"And me," Evan and Angus said together.

"I'll not be left behind," Fletcher said.

"Nor I," Tavis echoed, taking a step away from Ian.

Kitt's heart was thumping madly in her breast. They had all joined her. All but Ian, and the task would be less difficult if she did not have him to contend with.

"I'll come, too," Ian said. "But not because I believe Lady Katherine knows what she is about. I want to be there when disaster strikes and you all come to your senses and admit you'd be better led by—"

"By a naysayer like you?" Kitt said scornfully.

"What you want to do is dangerous and risks the entire clan for the sake of one who was breaking the law," Ian said angrily.

"A bad law," Kitt said, "enforced by a greedy landlord who raised his rents so high he forced his tenant into disobeying it."

" 'Tis a fool's errand," Ian said. "One only a foolish, softhearted woman would suggest."

The accusation hurt more than he could know. "You dinna have to go with us, Ian," Kitt said sharply.

"I'll go," Ian said. "If only to see you fail. Then we'll see what the clan has to say about keeping a woman as The MacKinnon."

Ian stalked off into the church and was followed by her clansmen who, she noticed, kept their eyes averted as they passed by her. The worst part was, she had to walk past all of them again to sit in the very front pew, where The MacKinnon had always sat.

Walking home after the service, she was aware of the silence of the man beside her. She knew Alex had a good baritone voice. She had heard him singing the hymns during the service. But he had not said a word since offering to go with her on the raid.

"Thank you for supporting me, Alex," she said to break the silence between them.

"Ian was right," he said. "A woman has no business leading men. But considering your father named you The MacKinnon—and until you choose one of them to take your place—they owe you their allegiance. To be honest, I felt sorry for you."

Kitt gasped. "*Sorry* for me?"

The man she had made her bodyguard—the stranger she had given the job of guarding her life—stopped in the shade of a willow growing alongside the burn and turned to face her, his lips set in an expression of disapproval he had not let the others see. "You've acted just like a woman where Patrick is concerned—responding to the situation with your heart instead of your head."

"You may be wearing my father's clothes," she snapped. "But you're not my father, so you needn't lecture me."

"I speak as I feel."

"If you think I'm wrong, why did you agree to help me?" she demanded.

"Because I have no doubt you meant what you said about going alone if need be, and I didna want your death on my conscience."

It was devastating to realize he had no more confidence in her ability to carry out what she had promised than Ian, that to him, she was just another *female*. "I can fight as well as any man," she said. "Better than most!"

He grabbed her shoulders and kicked a foot behind her ankles. A moment later she was lying flat on her back on the hard ground with Alex on top of her.

His face was close enough to hers that she could see he had ridiculously long eyelashes, close enough that she could see the dark gray eyes that dared her to fight back.

"It didna take much to get the better of you, Lady Katherine."

"I . . ." He was heavy, and she couldn't seem to catch her breath. "Let me up," she snarled, humiliated by his easy conquest.

"You should defer to those wiser—and stronger—than yourself," he chided, his knuckles brushing against her cheek. "You're a fragile, beautiful—"

She shoved his hand away. "I'm The MacKinnon," she retorted breathlessly. "Not something fragile or beautiful or—"

He clamped her wrists in the cool grass on either side of her head, but it was his eyes that held her captive. "You can be all too easily battered and broken, my lady," he said. " 'Twould be a shame to spoil something so perfect."

Kitt felt . . . female. She had fought long and hard to free herself from susceptibility to such male blather. All Alex had done was speak a few words, and she felt herself turning to mush inside. Well, he would not win her over using such blandishments. She would not allow it.

She bucked wildly against his strength, managing with a sudden move to roll him over so she was on top. Her breasts were pillowed against his hard chest, and her belly nestled between his thighs. She felt heart-stopping heat. She felt his strength and power. And, dear God, she felt the hardness of him.

Kitt realized when Alex made an animal sound in his throat that she had awakened a sleeping dragon. His features were taut, his breathing harsh.

" 'Tis unwise to accuse men of cowardice for exercising good judgment," he said. "Any one of your clansmen could take you in a fight."

"I can defend myself!" she retorted, jerking sideways to get free. She succeeded merely in rolling him over on top of her again.

He hissed in a sharp breath.

She stared at Alex, stricken, as the exquisite heat and hardness of him found a haven between her thighs. His eyes narrowed, his lips were full and rigid, his nostrils flared for the scent of her. Kitt recognized his arousal because she felt—oh, how unwillingly—the same sharp desire.

"Choose a husband, Lady Katherine," he said in a harsh voice. "You should be home raising bairns, not ordering men about."

"Damn you, Alex. 'Tis not your place to—" She bucked again, but her hip came down on a stone. She bit the inside of her cheek to keep from crying out at the pain, but a sound in her throat gave her away.

"What's wrong?" he asked, instantly concerned. "Are you hurt?"

Kitt closed her eyes and turned her head away. It hurt more than a little, but she had no intention of becoming a female watering pot. " 'Tis not your place—"

"I'm your bodyguard, woman," he said, transferring both her wrists to one hand and using the other to grab her chin and force her to face him. " 'Tis my job to guard your body, so tell me where you're hurt."

Too many feelings were rioting inside her. Female feelings. " 'Tis nothing," she insisted.

"Tell me!"

"I've bruised my hip on a stone!"

She felt his hand on her hip, with only her homespun skirt and a petticoat between her flesh and his.

"There?"

"To the left." More heat. A raging fire. "Alex . . ."

His hand reached farther beneath her right buttock. "There?"

"Ah." That was as close to a cry of distress as Kitt was willing to utter. His hand gently massaged the hurt, but Kitt was feeling a great deal more than relief from his touch. She felt her body arching toward his, pressing against the aching hardness.

"Dinna move," he rasped. His arm slid completely around her, and he clasped her tightly against him.

Kitt shivered as her body tightened inside. She looked into Alex's eyes and realized he wanted her. And saw the abrupt change in his features when it became apparent that he had no intention of taking her.

"Enough," he said. "Enough."

He pushed himself onto his feet and reached down to grasp her hands and pull her onto her feet beside him. "No more such games, Lady Katherine," he scolded, as though she were a child and he her tutor. " 'Tis my job to protect you, not seduce you."

"But I—"

"No argument. The matter is closed."

Kitt was incensed. She had done nothing to provoke him. The seduction had been all on his side. She had succumbed to his touch like a filly to a willing handler. What a burden to be female and so susceptible to a man's touch! She must be ever vigilant against such feminine weakness.

"I will lead my clan on that raid," she said defiantly. "And it will succeed. I can do it, Alex. You will see."

"For both our sakes, I hope you're right."

"There's something else we must do first," she said, eyeing him askance.

"What is that?" he asked.

"Steal the cost of passage to America for Patrick and his family from the Duke of Blackthorne."

Chapter 8

THEY HAD WASTED NO TIME IN PLANNING THEIR clandestine trip to Blackthorne Hall to steal from the duke. Even so, it had taken Kitt almost a week to work out all the details of their adventure to the satisfaction of her bodyguard. On the day they'd chosen, she had waited restlessly for evening to come and had waited even longer for most of the evening to pass as well. Moira had long since gone to bed.

The instant she stepped out of her bedroom, Alex took one look at her and laughed. "What is that you're wearing?"

Kitt looked down at the trousers, a pair one of Dara's boys had outgrown that fitted her like a second skin, and said, "What did you expect me to wear on a raid? My best muslin dress?"

"You'll never pass for a lad," Alex assured her, his eyes full of humor—and something more dangerous Kitt preferred to ignore. "That shirt has two obvious bumps in it, and the trousers . . ." He whistled. "I dinna know too many boys with hips made for bearing bairns."

Kitt blushed at such frank speaking. "I havna finished my disguise." She drapped a plaid around her, effectively concealing her figure. "I dare you to say I'll be recognized in the dark."

" 'Twill not be dark at Blackthorne Hall. Not entirely."

"Dark enough," she said. "Let's go."

"Wait," Alex said.

Kitt stood her ground as Alex's hands reached toward her face. He adjusted the man's bonnet—minus the identifying clan badge—she had donned to cover her hair. She shivered as he tucked in a long curl that had escaped at her temple.

He made a *tsk*ing sound. "No lad has such winsome curls, my lady."

"I dinna plan to stop and visit with Mr. Ambleside," Kitt said, knocking his hand aside. Why was he forever touching her? Always making her feel . . . like a woman. "The idea is to sneak into the castle and out again without being seen," she said with asperity.

"I suppose 'twill be easier for you to maneuver without a skirt if we have to make a run for it," he conceded.

"Aye. Let's go."

Alex's legs were long and he walked fast, but Kitt would have died for lack of breath before she asked him to slow down. She stumbled once and would have fallen, except he caught her arm. She was slung around in a circle and slammed right into him, chest first.

Everything would have been fine if she had not grabbed hold of his shoulders to brace herself, and he had not circled his arms around her waist to steady her. But she had grabbed hold, and his strong arms had circled her.

She was still trying to regain her breath when she looked up into Alex's face. The swelling was long gone from his eye, and all that remained of the knot on his forehead was a yellowing bruise. It was impossible to tell that his lower lip had ever been swollen, and she knew now that it was naturally more full than the upper.

Even his nose had resumed a more normal size, though he would always have a bump on the bridge. The realization struck her that by any standards Alex Wheaton was a comely man. Any woman would be tempted to give him a second glance. Or maybe even stare at him in fascination, as she was doing now.

His eyes were intriguing, changing from a light gray when he was happy, to the color of storm clouds when he was angry or upset. Right now his eyes...were examining her face with as much studious detail as she was giving his.

"You're very beautiful," he whispered.

Kitt looked deeply into his dark gray eyes, felt the heat of her own awareness rise on her cheeks, and watched with her heart in her throat as he lowered his head toward her mouth.

" 'Tis forbidden for you to touch me, Alex," she reminded him. She felt a stab of alarm when her warning had no effect. But she refused to be the one to back away. Her flashing eyes dared him to come closer. Dared him to try and kiss her.

He gave her a wolfish smile. "You let go first."

She realized her hands were twined in the hair at his nape and snatched them away. "Now you let go," she said.

The feel of his breath on her flesh had already sent an expectant shiver down her spine, when he finally stepped back.

"You're safe from me, my lady," he said, though his eyes sent a different, dangerous message. "I will keep my promise. No matter how great the temptation."

Kitt could not deny she had wondered what it might be like to kiss him. Perhaps she had even let him see it in her eyes. But she knew better. To succumb to mere physical desire was disaster, plain and simple.

You must get rid of Alex and hire someone else as your bodyguard. Someone safe.

Even that would be an admission that she could not handle the situation. She could control her own behavior, especially toward her bodyguard. And he had promised to keep his distance. "The matter is forgotten," she said to Alex. "We will speak of it no more."

"But—"

"We can enter the castle through the kitchen door," she said, cutting him off. " 'Tis likely to be unlocked."

He opened his mouth as though to continue the discussion but shut it again without speaking. Perhaps he recognized, as she did, that such an involvement could lead to nothing more than disgrace for her and dishonor for him.

"What do we do if the kitchen door is locked?" he said.

"You'll have to help me climb in through a window." She turned and began walking again.

"The windows at Blackthorne Hall are all far above ground and quite small," he pointed out.

"I'm aware of that, which is why I'll have to be the one to go in and come around to unlock the door for you."

They had discovered that Blackthorne Hall was completely unguarded. And why not? Who would dare to steal from the duke? The repercussions would be swift and absolute. Transportation at the very least. If they were caught inside the house, they might even be shot.

Kitt's heart was already racing from her encounter with Alex, and it speeded up so that she could hear her pulse pounding in her ears as they crossed the moat that surrounded Blackthorne Hall. Her father had taught her to move quietly, to attack an enemy with stealth. She had even been taught there was no dishonor in stealing from one's enemies. Reiving cattle was practically a Scottish rite of passage.

She had never actually gone on a raid before.

Kitt had practiced all the necessary arts of war, but that was all she had ever done. Practice. This was the real thing, and she found herself unaccountably frightened by the enormity of what she was doing. She did not want to be transported from the only home she had ever known. She did not want to die.

Given a choice, she would not have chosen to steal. But the duke had left her no choice. Kitt was surprised at the depth of the revulsion she was able to conjure for Blackthorne, even though he was already dead.

A full moon gave them enough light to see where they were going when they reached the grounds on the other side of the moat, but there were no lanterns in any of the upstairs windows they could see to indicate that the occupants were awake. They inched their way around to the back of the castle in the shadows along the wall.

"Ouch!"

"Shh!" Alex warned. "Dinna move. Someone's coming."

Kitt instinctively moved anyway, backing up closer to the wall near the kitchen door. She bit her lip to keep from crying out as she was jabbed in a dozen places by the rosebushes at her back. Whoever heard of roses planted near a kitchen door? She tried easing herself away from the pain, but her clothing, and a great deal of skin, had snagged on the thorns.

Kitt was too frightened to move, even to save herself further pain. She breathed through her mouth, panting almost, and the raspy noise sounded loud in her ears. Would they see her? Would they hear her?

She very nearly gasped aloud when she saw who

was walking past them. It was Mr. Ambleside and the Earl of Carlisle. What were they doing out and about so very late? She and Alex had scheduled their clandestine visit far past bedtime to avoid just such an encounter. Kitt couldn't help overhearing what Mr. Ambleside and the earl were saying.

"I've heard from the duke's brother, his heir," Mr. Ambleside said. "Lord Marcus refuses to honor the contract, because he doesn't believe his brother is dead. He says he will not act at all until he sees his brother's body. He believes His Grace could not have drowned because he is too good a swimmer. Lord Marcus is so certain his brother is alive, that he is sending a detective, a Bow Street Runner, to search for him."

"Is it possible?" Carlisle asked. "Could Blackthorne be alive?"

"Consider the facts, my lord," Mr. Ambleside suggested. "Then tell me if you think it is possible."

"I don't know what to think," the earl said. "Even if he was . . . when he . . . the sea . . ."

Kitt strained to hear the earl's reply but could not make it all out. "Did you hear that?" she whispered to Alex. "The duke may be alive!"

"Whether he is or not, makes no difference to what we must do tonight," Alex said. "Are you all right?"

"I'm stuck on the rosebushes," she admitted. His hand brushed her cheek, then followed the line of her throat to her shoulder, sending a shiver along with it. "I can free myself," she said, anxious to escape his touch.

"Be still," he said, ignoring her protest.

She felt his hands slide carefully over her shoulders and down her back to where the thorns were embedded. Her flesh quivered at his touch. She moaned and he leaned close to her ear and whispered, "Shh."

His warm breath made her shiver again.

"Are you cold?" he asked.

"No. Yes. No." She jerked when he pulled the cloth free and hissed as a thorn tore her flesh.

"Foolish woman. You've hurt yourself." His voice was low and husky and sounded more like a caress than a scold.

She pressed her forehead against his chest and gritted her teeth to keep from crying out as he freed one thorn at a time.

He was breathing as heavily as she was by the time he was done. "You're free."

Tears of pain sparkled in her eyes when she turned her face up to his. "Thank you, Alex."

"I wish I hadna brought you," he said curtly.

"I brought you," she retorted, feeling the frustration that always simmered beneath the surface when anyone suggested she was less capable than she knew herself to be—merely because she was female. "Anyone could have backed up into the roses," she said. "Even a man."

"'Tis a crime to mar something so precious," he said. "You should not be taking such risks."

"I am The MacKinnon, Alex. 'Tis my responsibility to take such risks. Now check the door to see if 'tis unlocked," she ordered.

He hesitated, then turned away from her and moved the few steps to the kitchen door, which opened when he applied pressure to it. " 'Tis open."

She followed him into the quiet kitchen. The fire in the kitchen hearth had been banked for the night but still provided enough light to make sinister shadows. Kitt froze in the doorway, and Alex had to grab her hand to pull her inside and shut the door behind her.

Kitt shook her head in chagrin when she recognized the things that had frightened her. The dark goblins she had seen in the corner turned out to be pots hanging from hooks on the wall. The ghostly silhouettes above her were cooking herbs, rosemary and thyme, hanging from the ceiling.

"If we hurry, we might be able to get in and out before Mr. Ambleside returns," Alex said. "Which way is the study or the library or wherever it is Mr. Ambleside conducts his business affairs?"

"When I was here last, the butler went to find Mr. Ambleside in a room beyond the Great Hall," she replied. "I canna be more specific than that."

"Come on," he urged. "Hurry!"

Kitt followed quickly after Alex, keeping her back to the stone wall and stopping when Alex stopped. He suddenly backed up into her and turned and clapped a hand over her mouth.

She instinctively fought his hold, but he wrapped his free arm around her, using his body to shield her from whatever he had seen. She was aware of his height and the breadth of his chest and, because her nose was pressed against the open throat of his shirt, the masculine smell of him.

It was ridiculous to be noticing such things when she ought to be fearing for her life. But perhaps it was as well that his presence kept her distracted. Otherwise she might have gone running craven from the castle. And proved everything he had ever believed about her feminine frailty.

Kitt's heart pounded in a racketing tattoo from fear ... and from the feel of Alex's body pressed against her own. It was wretched to feel so much, when she did not want to feel anything.

When she heard footsteps moving away, Kitt reached up to push at the hand Alex held against her mouth. "Who was it?" she whispered.

"One of the servants. No wonder there are no guards outside. The place is crawling with people even at this late hour. Come on."

He hurried away without another word, and she followed him down the hall toward a set of heavy doors. He opened one and peered inside. It was obvious from the crystal glasses on the table between the two wing chairs facing the fireplace, that this was where Mr. Ambleside had entertained the earl. The fire crackled cheerfully and noisily, and several lamps had been lit to brighten the room.

Alex headed for the Sheraton desk angled in the corner. "I'll look here. You check for a hidden safe."

"A safe? Where?"

"In the wall behind the pictures, perhaps. Or in the floor."

Kitt did as Alex instructed, pushing aside several framed landscapes, but found nothing behind them but the stone wall. She lifted the corners of the heavy rug and peered underneath, but the stone floor appeared solid.

"Have you found anything?" she asked.

Alex's attention was focused on a document he was reading.

Kitt crossed to him and asked, "What do you have there?"

"I found it on the desk. It appears to be a contract between the Duke of Blackthorne and the Earl of Carlisle, entitling the earl to purchase any or all of Blackthorne's unentailed property in Scotland, including Blackthorne Hall, *upon the duke's death*."

Kitt stared at Alex uncomprehendingly for a moment before she realized the significance of such a document. "That's impossible! Blackthorne Hall is entailed."

"Apparently not," Alex replied. "From what I see here, the castle can be included in the sale."

"Carlisle was left destitute. There's no way he could afford to purchase the land and the castle."

"Apparently credit may be extended. Read it for yourself," Alex said, shoving the paper at her and returning to his examination of the desk drawers.

Kitt was feeling very sick to her stomach. Apparently this was the contract Mr. Ambleside had spoken of outside, the one Blackthorne's brother refused to act on until the duke's body was found. What if Carlisle should manage to persuade Lord Marcus to let him take possession before she was able to win back the land in court? Would she still have a case for ownership if the land had been sold to a third party?

Alex interrupted her thoughts when he held up a leather purse and said, "A small stash of coins. This cannot be all the funds Mr. Ambleside has in the house. We will need to go upstairs and search his bedroom."

"Surely not." Going upstairs would immensely increase their danger of getting caught.

"Have you another suggestion?" Alex said.

"The bookcase," she said, pointing at an entire wall of bookshelves.

Alex frowned. " 'Tis worth a look," he agreed as he began pulling books out, then shoving them back when he did not find anything concealed within them or behind them.

Kitt dropped the unbelievable contract on the desk where Alex had found it and joined in the search. Her heart was stuck in her throat for the next ten minutes. Every moment it seemed Mr. Ambleside must surely return and they would be caught. But they had to find where he had hidden the duke's household funds. It would do no good to save Patrick Simpson if she could not help him escape to America with his wife and family.

"Let's go," Alex said at last.

"Upstairs?" Kitt said in a faint voice.

"Unless you're willing to admit failure."

"We could steal the candelabra," she said.

"Do you know someone willing and able to buy stolen silver?"

Kitt shook her head.

"Neither do I. Upstairs, my lady. Quickly, before Mr. Ambleside returns."

The stone staircase was narrow and wound upward precipitously to the second floor. There was no rail to protect one from falling off the edge. Kitt clung to the stone wall with one hand and held out a candle to light the way, as she led them upstairs. They were terribly vulnerable to discovery at this point, and Kitt made herself hurry despite the narrowness of the stairs.

Kitt paused to wait for Alex at the top. Fortunately, Mr. Ambleside was the only one living on the second floor, where the rooms were intended for the duke and his family. The servants slept in rooms above them on the third floor. "Which way?" Kitt asked.

Alex looked from one end of the long hall to the other, then turned to the left. "Follow me."

Chapter 9

ALEX WALKED ON TIPTOE PAST THE FIRST DOOR and the second. As he did so, a picture flashed in his mind of what was behind the second door. It was disconcerting to say the least. Had he been here before? Did he know the detestable duke? Had they been friends?

He did not think he could have been friends with someone so cruel as the duke seemed to be. A memory of the gaunt faces, the hollow, hopeless eyes of Patrick Simpson's children flashed behind his gray eyes. No. He was not a man who could stand by and watch children starve.

Nevertheless, he could easily picture the room behind the door. It was a nursery, with two small beds, a rocking horse, and two wooden desks side by side. An arched window looked out onto the sea where it crashed against the cliffs below.

He had a glimpse so brief he thought he might have

imagined it of two small, fair-haired boys playing on the floor with painted metal figures of knights on horseback. Who were the children? he wondered. Was one of them himself? Were they mere acquaintances, or someone he knew intimately?

It was the second time tonight he had experienced such bewildering familiarity. Alex thought back to his first moments in the castle, when he had entered the kitchen and encountered the smell of cinnamon and cooked apples. He had searched the sideboard and found a plateful of apple tarts. His mouth had watered at the sight, and he could almost taste the cinnamon and feel the crunch of the pastry. He knew he loved apple tarts, though he had not tasted any such thing since coming out of the sea.

It worried him to think of the two incidents—the familiarity of the smells in the kitchen, and the certain knowledge of what was behind that second door—when he did not know how he fit into such a picture. He had spoken first with an English accent. And he had apparently come off an English ship—very likely the same ship that had sent the duke to a watery grave.

If the duke is indeed dead, he thought. Which was a matter in doubt if he were to believe the conversation between Mr. Ambleside and the earl.

Alex stopped in front of the door at the end of the hall. "I asked my friend Laddie to talk with some of the servants and discover, without raising suspicion, which room is the steward's," he admitted. "Shall we go inside?"

The duke's steward lived very well, Alex thought as he perused the room. No plain wooden furniture, no simple wooden bed. Everything was of the best quality, the finest workmanship, the richest fabric. But why not? The duke could easily afford such luxury, considering what he took from his tenants. He met Kitt's eyes across the silk-canopied bed.

Her lips were curved in a bitter parody of a smile as she set the candle she carried in its pewter dish on the table beside the bed. "It seems the duke is not so parsimonious with his steward as he is with his tenants."

"Apparently not," Alex agreed. "Come, let us begin our search. We havna much time."

A wooden chest sat at the foot of the bed, but that seemed too obvious a hiding place. The funds would be accessible to whatever servants came into the room to attend the steward's needs. A second look revealed a large padlock. "How are you at picking locks?" he asked Lady Katherine.

The unholy grin on her face made him smile.

" 'Twas very nearly the first thing my father taught me," she said.

"I thought the Scots only reived cattle."

"I dinna know that my father ever used the gift," she said. "But he nevertheless taught it to me. He said the day might come when I would need the knowledge."

"And so it has," Alex said.

He watched as she reached under the man's bonnet and took two hairpins from her hair, straightening them to make a lock pick. She chewed on her lower lip the whole time she worked the lock, so it glistened in the candlelight. Alex found himself wishing he was the one nibbling at her lips, tasting her, kissing her.

What was the matter with him? She had made it clear what she thought of his attentions. They were not welcome.

He had tried not to be aware of her as a woman. He did not even know if he was free to want her. What if he had a wife? He rubbed at his ring finger with his thumb. There was no telltale mark where a ring might have been. He did not seem to have the habit of adjusting a ring with his other fingers. But that did not necessarily mean he was free. He simply did not feel married. He laughed inwardly. He knew very little about himself, certainly not enough to be able to discern such a thing for certain one way or the other.

But could he want Lady Katherine so much if, in another life, he was committed to some other woman? Would his heart not yearn for that other person? Perhaps his attraction to her was merely lust. He had no idea how long it had been since he had lain with a woman. Perhaps it had been a very long time. Perhaps his body needed her.

He watched her tongue lick her lower lip and felt his body tighten with need. He desired her. There was no question of that. But it was more than that. He could not help admiring her adventuresome spirit, her courage, and . . . her talent as a lockpick.

As the lock sprang open she turned to him with a

brilliant smile that made his body harden to rock. " 'Tis open!"

"Well done, my lady," he said, bending on one knee beside her to hide the evidence of his arousal. He resisted the urge to take her in his arms and concentrated on removing the lock and opening the lid. At first he was disappointed by what he saw. It seemed the trunk had been locked to protect Mr. Ambleside's personal treasures, not the duke's.

He moved each item aside as he found it: a fine shaving kit with a silver-handled razor, a leather-bound copy of *The Merchant of Venice*, a pair of furlined leather gloves, three enameled snuffboxes, a jar of tobacco that—he sniffed—smelled bitter, a heavy woolen blanket, and a box that, when opened, revealed an exquisite pair of dueling pistols.

"There doesna seem to be anything here," he said, unable to hide his disappointment.

"Look," Kitt said, reaching inside the lid of the trunk. "Look here."

A small flap showed at the corner. She pulled on it, and it flopped open, revealing a secret compartment.

"How did you know that was there?" Alex asked in amazement.

"The trunk looked too shallow."

To Alex's delight, the hidden compartment was filled with crowns and guineas and pound notes. It also held the duke's record books and several other important-looking documents. Alex would have loved to examine them, but he was aware that time must be running out.

He began stuffing sheaves of bills into a cloth bag they had brought along for just such a purpose.

He paused and said, "How much shall we take?"

"Only so much as we will need for the Simpsons' passage to America."

"How much is that?" Alex persisted.

"I dinna know," Kitt admitted. "Take it all, Alex," she said, grabbing a handful of gold and silver coins and dropping them into the bag. "We'll use the rest to feed the hungry."

"Very well, my lady."

The sound of footsteps in the hall was all the warning they got that someone was coming. Alex tried closing the trunk, but the inner lid caught and left a gap. He had no time to replace the lock, not if they were to have any hope of escape. He rose, tying the drawstring bag full of money securely to his belt.

It was then Alex realized there was no way out except the door through which they had come in. And Mr. Ambleside likely stood on the other side of it. Lady Katherine would surely be recognized. And imprisoned.

He met her eyes across the room and saw the terror there. "Blow out the candle!" he ordered. In the dark they might stand a chance. If he could surprise Mr. Ambleside. If the steward did not cry out an alarm to the other servants doubtless sleeping on the floor above them. And if they could flee down the steep flight of stairs without falling to their deaths or being caught at the bottom by waiting minions of the duke.

How were they going to escape?

Alex saw the stream of moonlight through the window and suddenly knew what to do. "Come with me!" he urged, grabbing Lady Katherine's hand, giving her no choice whatsoever about following his command. He headed straight for the window.

"Where are you going? What are you doing?" she whispered anxiously.

"Trust me."

She glanced at the door, where the latch was already moving, and hurried after him when he tugged on her hand. The second floor of the castle was high above the ground. There should have been no escape by that route, not without a great many sheets tied together, at any rate.

But Alex had known, as he had known what was behind the door in the hall, that he would find a ledge outside the window, and that the ledge would lead to a spot where the cliff angled up so that the drop from the second floor was not so steep.

He stepped out confidently onto the ledge, only realizing at the last second that his large feet barely fit on it. He did not remember the ledge being so small.

Or perhaps you were smaller when you stood on it.

He angled his toes sideways to find a better purchase and leaned back, the sweat beading on his brow and above his lip.

I have done this before, he thought. *And been frightened before*, he admitted ruefully. But he had obviously negotiated the escapade successfully, he deduced with a wry smile, or he would not be here to remember it.

"The ledge is quite narrow, Lady Katherine," he said in a calm voice that belied the chaos he felt inside. "Lean back against the wall and dinna look down," he instructed. "A few steps more will bring us to a place where the cliff angles up and the drop to the ground is not so great."

"How did you know, Alex? About the ledge, I mean, and the spot where we can jump off?"

He could not tell her the truth. It would have meant too many questions he could not yet answer even for himself. "Did you never reconnoiter the field of battle, my lady?"

She laughed very softly. "I have never been to battle, Alex. But yes, I was taught to do so. 'Tis fortunate you were so thorough. I will know next time."

"This is it," Alex said, coming to a halt. "The spot I told you about."

"It is farther to the ground than I imagined," she whispered.

"I'll go first," Alex volunteered as he shoved himself away from the wall and into thin air. The drop couldn't have been more than a dozen feet, but it felt like a great deal more. He rolled to break his fall and came up grinning. "Hurry! It canna be long before Mr. Ambleside discovers the theft."

He could see the whites of her eyes in the moonlight. "Dinna be afraid. I'll catch you."

"I dinna need your help. Move out of the way, Alex."

"Jump and let me catch you."

"I can do it myself!"

"Dinna be stubborn," he hissed, his arms extended wide. " 'Tis too great a distance for—"

Mr. Ambleside's furious voice broke the silence. "Robbers! Thieves! Wake up, you fools! Search the house!"

Kitt took a quick step sideways and leapt. She might have landed safely, if Alex hadn't lurched to catch her. He lost his balance and fell, and she plummeted down on top of him.

Kitt knew the instant she rolled to a stop that she had hurt herself. She lay frozen, the breath knocked out of her, afraid to move, her left leg bent back at an awkward angle.

"Kitt?"

" 'Tis Lady Katherine to you," she wheezed.

"How badly are you hurt?" Alex said, untangling himself and kneeling beside her. "Do I dare move you?"

Kitt moaned. "I dinna know. My leg . . ."

His hands followed the course of her twisted leg from thigh to ankle. "I dinna feel any broken bones."

Kitt couldn't speak. Her heart was clogging her throat. Alex's touch had been impersonal, but she had felt heat in each spot where his fingertips grazed her thigh, her knee, her calf, her ankle. She wanted to move, to escape his touch, but her leg wouldn't cooperate. "Help me straighten out my leg," she said.

She had to clench her teeth to keep from sobbing

aloud as he unbent her injured knee. Tears pooled, and when she blinked, one slid from the corner of her eye.

"Why couldn't you just let me catch you?" he muttered, brushing the tear from her cheek with the pad of his thumb. "Would it be so awful to admit you need a man's help?"

Kitt felt a queer tightness in her chest. It was tempting to lay her burdens on Alex's broad shoulders. But self-reliance was so ingrained she did not know how. "You can help me to my feet," she said at last. Even that was a concession, whether he recognized it or not.

He put his hands under her arms from behind and lifted her as easily as a feather. "Can you stand by yourself?"

She tried putting weight on her left leg, but the pain was excruciating. "I dinna think so."

He swept her up into his arms. "And dinna tell me not to be carrying you to safety!"

She felt very small and very feminine in his arms. She put her arm around his neck to support her upper body and felt the hair at his nape. So soft, for a man who was so hard everywhere else. "Do you have any idea where we're going?" she asked.

"'Tis only a short way to the postern door, which leads down a path to the cliffs above the sea. From there, we can make our way back to the cottage."

"You've thought of everything," she said with a sigh of relief. "Thank you, Alex." She tried to keep from leaning her head against him, but after a while, she gave up and leaned her cheek against his throat.

"Am I hurting you?" he asked, once they were a safe distance from the castle.

Her knee did hurt from all the jostling, and not just a little. But she didn't want him to slow down. The sooner she was home, the sooner she would be out of his arms. She liked it much more than she should. "I'll manage," she said. "Just get me home, Alex."

"I suppose Moira will know what to do," he said.

She bit her lip, then said, "I dinna want to wake Moira. I told her we were visiting tenants this evening. I didna want her to know the truth."

"Why not?"

Kitt chuckled ruefully. "She'd nag. I can already hear her. 'Be careful, Kitty. 'Tis too dangerous, Kitty. Let someone else do it, Kitty.' I'd rather keep this business to myself."

She felt Alex stumble before he began walking even faster, jarring her knee with every step. She gasped and clutched at his neck, pressing her face against his throat to stifle her cry of pain.

"Be strong, little one," he murmured. "'Twill not be long before we're home."

Kitt had long since given up being brave by the time Alex laid her on her bed and removed the plaid that had kept her warm in the night air. Once he lit the candle on her bedside table, she had no secrets. Silent tears had dried on her cheeks, and her lower lip was swollen where she had gnawed on it to keep from moaning aloud.

"Let me wake Moira," he pleaded. "You're white as the sheets."

"You can do what must be done," she said.

He stared down at her and said, "I dinna see how I can treat your knee with you in trousers. They'll have to come off. If I leave the room, can you manage it alone?"

Kitt imagined trying to do the bending and lifting of body parts that would be necessary to undress herself and grimaced. "I dinna think so." It was mortifying to think of Alex undressing her, and she saw he wasn't any more comfortable with the idea than she was.

"We could wake Moira and let her—"

"No," she interrupted. "You must do it."

"Now she wants my help," Alex muttered as he unlaced the heavy men's work boots she was wearing and eased each one off.

To her surprise he rubbed her toes.

"Any blisters?" he asked.

Who would have thought a body could feel so much in her toes? She stared at him and he stared back. "No," she said. "No blisters."

"Well, then . . ."

The trousers had to come off, but she was wearing very little beneath them. Maybe she could manage it on her own. Kitt tried to roll to her side and groaned as her knee protested.

"Dinna trouble yourself, my lady," Alex said. "I will undress you." He paused and muttered, "If it kills me."

She felt panicky at the thought of Alex's hands on

her. Even more so at the thought of his eyes seeing what his hands revealed.

He picked up the quilt folded at the foot of the bed and spread it over her. Kitt gaped. Such a simple solution to protect her modesty. She gave a relieved sigh at his thoughtfulness. "Thank you, Alex."

The sigh caught in her throat as he reached right under the covering, his fingertips skimming her belly as he searched for the belt that held up her trousers and unbuckled it. Before she could protest, he grabbed hold of the snug material on either side of her waist and began tugging it down.

" 'Tis a bit like skinning a squirrel," he said with a grin. "Can you lift a little?" A moment later he held up her trousers with a triumphant smile and said, *"Voilà, chérie! C'est fini."*

A look of stunned surprise crossed his face. Perhaps it was the eloquent-sounding French he'd uttered. More likely it was the memory of having done the same thing to some other woman, Kitt thought cynically. At least the worst was over.

"If you sit up, I can pull that shirt off over your head," he said.

"What?" Kitt crossed her arms protectively over her chest. "Why would I want my shirt off?"

"So I can tend the scratches on your back."

"Scratches?"

"From the rose thorns," he reminded her.

"Oh." There was no way she could doctor herself.

And Alex was right. If the scratches weren't cleansed, she might very well end up with an infection.

"But this bonnet needs to come off first." He tugged it off and half of her hair spilled onto her shoulders.

She reached up to pull out the rest of the pins, but he was there before her.

"Let me."

Kitt sat perfectly still as Alex threaded his fingers through her hair searching for pins. She heaved a shuddering sigh when he finally spoke. "There. I think I've got them all."

The sigh came too soon, because his hands sifted through her hair one last time. " 'Tis incredibly soft," he murmured.

"Alex—"

"Now, let's get that shirt off," he said almost gruffly.

He reached for the hem with both hands, and she lifted her arms as the shirt came off over her head, then clutched at the quilt and pulled it up to cover herself. She was wearing a chemise, but it was old and the material had worn thin.

Alex had the misfortune of catching sight of her rosy nipples beneath the thin cloth before they were hidden from view. "Bloody hell," he muttered. His body was stretched taut with need. It was torture being forced to touch her and yet not *touch* her. He had promised to keep his distance. But he had never counted on this.

He kept his eyes riveted on her face as he brushed her hair behind her shoulders. Suddenly, he saw another woman's face, almost as beautiful, but with eyes as cold as ice. As he stared, the woman's face contorted with rage, and flecks of spittle flew from her mouth, as her blue eyes filled with loathing.

"Alex, are you all right?"

Alex realized he had taken a step back from the bed. Who was the woman he had seen in his vision? What was she to him? He shook his head to clear the image from his mind. He nearly gasped at the hurt that had come with the memory. What had he done to the woman to make her hate him so?

"Alex, you're frightening me."

He wanted to leave, to escape his shadowy past—and Kitt's tempting presence. But that clearly was not an option. "What is it I'm to do now?" he said, his voice brusque.

"What?"

"You're the doctor. What should I do?"

She sent him to a cupboard in the kitchen, where she kept her medicinal herbs. When he returned to the bedroom he held a small brown jar in the palm of his left hand and a small red jar in the palm of his right. "Are these the remedies you wanted?"

She nodded. "Hand the brown jar to me. I can do my knee, I think."

He held it away from her. "Lie down and be still. 'Twill be easier for me to do it." He set the jars down on the floor, then sat on the edge of the bed and turned the quilt up to expose her bruised and swollen knee. "I'll try to be gentle," he said, retrieving the brown jar.

He dipped three fingers into the cool salve and

carefully worked it into her flesh, trying not to notice her slender calves and ankles, trying not to think of what lay a few inches above his hand beneath the blanket.

When she moaned, he said, "I'm done. Turn over onto your stomach so I can treat the wounds on your back."

Gingerly, she shifted her position, giving him an unwanted glimpse of a milk-white breast. Sweat broke out on his forehead. He readjusted the blanket to cover her legs, then turned down the top to reveal an expanse of snow-white skin that had been torn in several places by rose thorns.

"There is blood here that should be washed away. I'll be back." He fled the room, but it didn't take long to retrieve a cloth and a bowl of water. He cleansed her wounds with the cloth, but there was no other way to apply the salve except with his fingers. Her skin was incredibly soft.

The thought of some other man—some man who would never appreciate her pride and her courage—having all of this to himself, made him angry. "I canna think much of your father, to ask what he did of you," Alex said half to himself.

She angled her head to look at him. "What?"

"To marry where you do not love. To marry an Englishman, whom you claim to hate. It seems a terrible sacrifice."

He felt her shoulders tense beneath his hands. "I have no choice, Alex. I promised him—"

"Of course you have a choice. You can—"

She pushed herself up on her elbows, once again teasing him with a glimpse of milk-white breast. "Dinna interfere, Alex. You have one job only, and that is to protect me from those who would harm me."

He felt the flush high on his cheekbones at being put in his place—an inferior place. That damnable pride of his reared its head, provoking him to say, "The one you need the most protection from is yourself!"

"Are you finished?" she said, her eyes stark.

"There are two more wounds I havna touched."

"Finish," she said. "And get out."

He had left the two wounds lowest on her back for last. Actually, they were on the swell of her buttocks. He knew he should not touch her, that he was playing with fire.

"You will have to lie down flat again," he said.

She glared at him but did as he asked.

He did not resist the urge to caress the curve of her back and had the satisfaction—and torment—of feeling her arch beneath his hand. He was leaning over, almost finished, when his finger accidentally slipped into the crease of her buttocks.

She bolted upright in bed, ramming into his injured nose. "How dare you!"

Alex yelped in pain and grabbed his nose. "What's wrong with you?"

She gritted her teeth against the pain in her knee and grabbed at the quilt, almost sobbing when her breasts were momentarily exposed. "How dare you take such liberties!"

"Bloody hell, Kitt—"

"Dinna call me that! I'm Lady Katherine to you. Nothing more! Do you hear?"

She looked almost frightened. And very angry. And quite, quite beautiful.

" 'Twas only a touch," he said softly.

She visibly shuddered. " 'Twas a trespass."

Had his touch been so loathsome? He did not think so. She had responded at first with the slight arch of her back, a quiver, enough to let him know she had enjoyed the feel of his hands caressing her. And now she sought to deny it.

"Touching you—"

"Go away, Alex. Go to bed. Our business is done. I'm tired, and I need to rest."

"Our business isna done, my lady," he murmured as he backed out of the room. "But the battle can wait till you're well enough to continue the fray."

Chapter 10

KITT'S PALMS WERE SWEATY. AND ALL BECAUSE of a visit to a stone fortress that looked like Sleeping Beauty's castle—after the hundred years of neglect. The outside walls of Castle Carlisle were overgrown with thorny vines and the expansive lawn was laden with thistles. The path to the door was nearly invisible under a garden of weeds.

No matter how daunting the visit might seem, Kitt had no choice but to go through with it. It had dawned on her, when she considered her clan's desperate situation, that she might yet save them through marriage—to the Earl of Carlisle. He did, after all, have a contract with Blackthorne that allowed him to purchase the duke's holdings in Scotland.

She had mentioned the subject to Alex the morning following their burglary of the duke's estate, while they were on their way to cut more peat for the fire. She had intended to cut the squares herself, when Alex volunteered to help.

She had taken his hands—his strong, but surprisingly uncallused hands—into her own and said, "I dinna think this kind of work is what you're used to, Alex."

He had pulled his hands free and said, "My back is strong enough. Give me the spade."

It quickly became clear that Alex Wheaton had never cut peat in his life. What had he used to heat his home? Kitt wondered.

" 'Tis done like this," she said, when he had tried for the second time, unsuccessfully, to shove the spade into the thick peat. She took the spade from him and used the edge of it to cut a square the size she wanted before easing the spade into the cut below the roots and lifting the peat out of the ground.

It was hard work, and she hadn't managed even that one square before Alex took the spade back from her. He learned quickly, she would grant him that. And he was not afraid of hard work, though from the grimace of pain each time he lifted the spade, he was raising a few blisters.

He had not been working very long before sweat dripped from his brow. He set down the spade and reached for his shirt where it was tucked into his trousers, hesitated, then asked, "May I?"

For an instant Kitt considered saying no. She didn't want another look—a closer look—at Alex Wheaton's body. Not after what had happened between them last night. But it would only have been pointing out her discomfort to forbid him. She nodded.

The shirt came off over his head, revealing the sculpted body she had so admired the first day she had met him. The dark blond hair on his chest glistened with sweat. Muscles in his arms and back flexed as he picked up the spade and went back to work.

Alex moved with surprising grace and amazing strength as he lifted the peat from the ground and piled it into the wheelbarrow she had brought along to haul it home. *He is not unique,* she told herself. *It is only muscle and sinew and bone.*

And yet, watching him made her stomach knot and her throat ache. She could not take her eyes from him. Finally, of course, he became aware of her scrutiny. He paused and raised his gray eyes to meet her own. Kitt's heart was pounding no less hard than his, though she had merely been watching him work.

"Kitt," he said softly.

"'Tis Lady Katherine to you."

"No. I think not, Kitt."

She heard the longing in his voice. The promise. Oh, the promise in that low, grating sound. Of sensual delight. Of undeniable passion. Of dark, forbidden pleasure. She thought of the way he had touched her last night, of the feel of his hands on her flesh.

He had already taken a step toward her when she said, "Remember your place, Alex. And your promise."

He stayed where he was, but he said, "I am as good a man as any."

"That is not the point. You must know my life is not my own. I must think always of what is best for my clan."

"A strong leader is best for them," he said.

"A strong back isna enough. Nor even a strong will. Something more is required."

"What is that?"

"Wealth."

Alex sneered. "Where do you expect to find such a fortune?"

"You are forgetting the Earl of Carlisle," she said into the silence.

"What about him?"

"I can marry him and save my clan."

He scowled, dropped the spade, and took a step toward her. "Surely you jest!"

Kitt took a quick step backward. "'Tis no jest. You saw the contract. I can marry Carlisle and accomplish the same thing I would have done by deceiving the duke."

"You'd marry a man you dinna even know?"

"I will know him before we're married."

"What if he's a drunkard? A gambler? A debaucher of women?"

"No man is perfect."

Alex snorted. "I see you are determined to go through with this harebrained scheme."

"I am."

"Why would you settle for so little?"

"How do you know 'tis so little? I havna even met

the earl. Perhaps he'll be a paragon, handsome and kind and—"

His teeth must have been very tightly clenched, because a muscle in his jaw jerked. "There must be some other way."

"I havna found it."

"You could steal from the duke."

"Not for long. Sooner or later I would be caught. Then what? Carlisle offers some hope, at least, that the land would remain available to my people for farming, rather than be given over to sheep, as the other landlords have begun to do. And as the earl's wife, I would have some influence, I hope, on the rents he charged."

"Or maybe not," Alex said. "In the ordinary course of things, a wife doesna interfere in her husband's business."

"I dinna intend to be an ordinary wife," Kitt retorted.

"How do you know he'll even have you?"

"I'll make him want me."

"You'll trick him into believing you love him, perhaps? As you would have tricked the duke?"

She had the grace to flush. "I am not without some charm," she said with all the dignity she could muster. "And I do have some consequence. I am a lady."

He snorted in disgust. "No lady plays such tricks."

"How would you know, Alex? How could you possibly know what a lady does or doesna do? Name the last *lady* whose company you enjoyed!"

He opened his mouth to answer but frowned instead. "I . . ." He sighed and threw the spade on top of the wheelbarrow full of peat, then retrieved his shirt from the handle of the wheelbarrow where he had left it and pulled it on over his head. Kitt turned away when he loosened her father's belt to tuck in his shirt.

"I think 'tis folly to marry for such a reason," he said. "At least promise me you'll take the earl's measure before you do anything so stupid as to tempt him to propose marriage."

"How dare you—"

He had her by the shoulders before she could finish her sentence. "I dare because I care what happens to you. I dare because marriage to the wrong person can make your life a living hell!"

She stared helplessly up at him, wondering if he spoke from experience. But he seemed startled himself at both what he had said and the vehemence with which he had said it.

"Let me go, Alex," she said quietly.

He seemed to realize suddenly how tightly he was holding her. He let her go and took a step back.

She rubbed her arms where his hands had been. "Your concern is misplaced, Alex. I can take care of myself."

"Can you?"

"Perhaps it would be better if I find another *gillecoise*."

He thrust an agitated hand through his hair. "That willna be necessary. I'll keep my opinions to myself."

"Do I have your promise on it?"

"Aye."

All through that day and the next he had kept his mouth shut, but she had felt his eyes on her. He had been almost sullen this morning when she announced it was time to visit the earl.

"You canna go wearing that," he said.

She looked down at the perfectly appropriate pale green silk morning dress with capped sleeves decorated by a darker green ribbon tied beneath her bosom. "What is wrong with it?"

"That is obvious to anyone with eyes." His gaze focused on the square, low-cut neckline, which revealed a great deal of her bosom.

"'Tis the fashion," she said, nevertheless feeling the blush rise on her cheeks.

"'Tis more like presenting wares for sale."

"Would you have me drape myself in sackcloth? My purpose is to attract the earl's attention."

"That gown should do it. In fact, it will fairly make his mouth water."

"Good," she said, refusing to be disconcerted by his statement—or the avid look in his eyes that had accompanied it. "Then I will have accomplished my purpose." As she pulled on her gloves, she felt him lay her shawl across her shoulders, effectively hiding what had previously been revealed.

"Lest you catch a chill," he said.

Kitt snorted and let the shawl fall away as she turned to examine Alex's appearance. "I must say you will be a credit to me."

He was wearing the only formal garb her father had

owned—a Highland costume that consisted of a doublet of forest-green velvet with lozenge-shaped buttons worn over a white waistcoat and shirt, a plaid kilt, tartan hose with scarlet garters, and buckled black shoes. His accessories included a goatskin sporran, her father's dirk, a long shoulder plaid, and a matching bonnet with the MacKinnon clan badge.

"I feel like an imposter," he said, rearranging the sporran.

Kitt crossed to Alex and adjusted the plaid at his shoulder. "I dinna think my father would begrudge you the use of his things, Alex. 'Tis all part of the image I am presenting to the earl."

"What image is that?" Alex said, raising a dark brow. "Rare bird, ripe for the plucking?"

Kitt laughed. "I certainly have the plumage for it," she said, whirling in a circle for him. "What do you think, Alex? Will I do for an earl's wife?"

"The better question is, will he make a good husband?"

"You promised, Alex," she said with a warning look. "Not another word about the earl."

Alex rode the edge of his promise. He did not speak critically of the earl, but he lambasted the condition of Carlisle's property. Of course, Kitt was forced to admit as they stepped up to the front door of Carlisle Castle, it was in wretched condition.

"The earl needs a gardener," Alex whispered as he knocked on the weathered wooden door.

As the butler opened the door, it fell off its hinges.

"And a carpenter," he muttered.

Kitt glared Alex into silence and said, "Lady Katherine MacKinnon to see the earl."

"This way, milady," the butler said, gesturing her inside.

The butler fitted the door back onto the hinge before closing it, then led them down a dark, narrow hallway to an equally dark room. Not dark so much as dreary, Kitt realized. Dust covered everything, even the windowpanes, and cobwebs had claimed the corners.

The Earl of Carlisle crossed from where he was standing near the fireplace—the one bright spot in the room—to greet her, a warm smile on his face.

Kitt was struck dumb by her first sight of him. *Why, he's handsome! No, not just handsome. Striking.* Chiseled cheekbones, dark, wide-spaced eyes, and a strong nose and chin gave him a face with more character than beauty. His form was as favored as his features. Perhaps it was not going to be such a sacrifice to marry the earl, after all.

He was also charming enough to put her at ease. "I have been meaning for some time to invite you here to congratulate you on being named The MacKinnon, but I have been much occupied with estate matters since my brother's death. Welcome to my home, Lady Katherine."

Kitt curtsied as the earl bowed. "Thank you, my lord. May I introduce my bodyguard, Alex Wheaton."

Kitt saw the astonishment on the earl's face, turned to discover what had put it there, and saw what the earl must have seen—the power, the grace of movement, the absolute authority in Alex's bearing. And, of course, the antagonism on his face.

"Carlisle," Alex said.

Kitt groaned inwardly at the breach of etiquette. The earl, having the greater consequence, should have spoken first.

She was grateful when the earl took no notice of the insult, but merely nodded and said, "Good day, sir."

Alex gave a cursory, condescending nod in return. *As though he were the one with the title and not the earl*, Kitt thought with another inward groan.

As the earl escorted her farther into the drawing room, she took a surreptitious look at the magnificent gilt furniture and plush velvet drapes. An immense carpet that almost reached the edges of the vast room must have come home with some knight from the Crusades.

Further study revealed the room's contents suffered from the same neglect as the outside of the castle. The seat covers had worn thin and the velvet was faded and the carpet was patched in several places.

From all appearances, the earl was rolled up. Which explained the offer of credit in the contract to purchase Blackthorne Hall they had seen on Mr. Ambleside's desk.

"Please make yourself comfortable," Carlisle said, gesturing her toward an elegant Grecian couch covered in faded red velvet. "And you, too, sir," he added in a brusque voice.

"I will stand," she heard Alex reply. He crossed with

her to the couch and stood behind her, vibrating with hostility.

Kitt had anticipated Alex's enmity toward the earl, but she was surprised to see it returned. It was plain the two men disliked each other on sight, but she didn't want Alex aggravating the situation. She would have a word with him later about courtesy to his betters.

Fortunately, Clay Bannister, Earl of Carlisle, did not seem the least intimidated by Alex's bristling posture. He asked a footman to have tea brought to the drawing room and then sat down right beside her on the sofa.

"I did not realize you had a bodyguard," Carlisle said, his glance flicking over her shoulder to Alex.

"I hired Alex only recently," she replied, purposefully not glancing at the man towering over her. Looking at Alex garbed in her father's Highland dress did strange things to her insides.

Not that the Earl of Carlisle's attire did not catch her eye. In fact, she had never seen a more fashionably dressed man. The exquisitely tailored russet jacket conformed to Carlisle's shoulders and tapered to his slim waist, and his buff trousers hugged his flat stomach and muscular thighs like a second skin. His black hair was cut to fall rakishly over his forehead, and his high starched collar and intricately tied neck cloth framed a face with strong, angular features that were admittedly attractive.

Kitt flushed when she realized he had caught her staring. "Pardon me, my lord."

"Look your fill," he said. "So long as I am allowed equal time to indulge in the same pastime." He smiled engagingly as his eyes dipped to her daring décolletage.

Alex growled like a dog whose bone was being threatened.

Kitt shot him a warning look, then smiled back at the earl. "I'm sure you didna invite me here just to look at me."

"What if I had?"

Kitt stared at him, momentarily disconcerted. Ever since the invitation to visit the earl had come, she had wondered if there was some hidden reason why he wanted to see her. It had seemed odd that he would have waited so long if his invitation was simply what he had said when he greeted her: a welcome to the new Chief of Clan MacKinnon. It now seemed it was something more than that. She was afraid to believe in her good fortune.

"I dinna understand your meaning, my lord," she said.

"I think you do," Carlisle replied, his dark eyes focused intently on her.

The look was sensual enough to make her nervous. Maybe this was all going to be much easier than she had dared to hope. "I prefer plain speaking," Kitt said. "What is it you want, my lord?"

"Very well. Plain speaking it is. I would like to court you, Lady Katherine."

Kitt smothered a startled gasp with her fingertips.

Alex grabbed her shoulder so tightly she thought he would crush her bones.

"Alex, you're hurting me," she said quietly.

Carlisle frowned at Alex and said, "I begin to think you may need protection from your bodyguard."

"Not at all. He . . . I . . ."

"I had not thought Mishnish a dangerous place, Lady Katherine," Carlisle said, eyeing Alex. "Why do you need a bodyguard?"

" 'Twill seem silly when I explain," Kitt said, discomfited more than she had thought by the charming smile Carlisle aimed at her.

"Nothing you say could be silly to me," the earl said with a warmth in his voice that she found alluring and which brought another warning growl from the man standing behind her. She dared a glance at Alex and saw his lips had thinned to a straight, disapproving line.

She felt a stab of annoyance. It was not Alex Wheaton's place to judge her actions. And she would lop off his head with her grandfather's claymore if he ruined things for her with Carlisle.

"The truth is," she explained to the earl, "I have been seeking a man to marry, someone who can become The MacKinnon in my place. A few of my clansmen have become a bit anxious to claim the role. I hired a bodyguard to make sure the choice of husband remains mine."

"And will my attentions be welcome, Lady Katherine?"

He started to reach for her hand but paused when Alex shifted a step closer and made a menacing sound deep in his throat. The earl shot Alex a threatening look in return, but Kitt noticed the earl's hand returned to his own side of the couch.

Her clan would hate her marriage to an Englishman. They would be furious to see themselves lorded over by the enemy. But choices had to be made. Better to have an English overlord here, than be forced to emigrate somewhere else.

Kitt was willing to make the ultimate sacrifice of herself, and her own desires, for the good of her clan. It was what she had promised her father on his deathbed. Perhaps this very young nobleman—he was three years younger than she—might be molded to suit her needs very well indeed.

"I am willing to be courted," she said at last.

"Wonderful!" the earl replied with a boyish smile that made him look even younger than his two and twenty years.

Kitt shot a quick, silencing look over her shoulder at Alex, who had shifted behind her. It allowed her to see how little he thought of the earl and his suit.

"Would you like to take a walk with me?" the earl said.

"That would be lovely," Kitt replied.

The earl reached for her gloved hand to help her to her feet, then slipped her arm through his. "We can go out through the French doors onto the balcony and then walk down into the garden."

She glanced over her shoulder and mouthed the words, "Behave yourself!" to Alex as the earl led her outside into the sunshine.

He glowered back.

"The sky is beautiful today," the earl said, as they walked down the steps into the garden. "So blue. Not a cloud in sight."

It quickly became apparent that the sky was the only beautiful thing they would see. The rose garden was choked with weeds.

"I have plans to return all of this to its former glory," the earl explained. "But I will need a wife to help me renovate the house," he added with a twinkle in his eye.

Kitt flushed at the blatant insinuation that she might, if she wished, become that wife. "Castle Carlisle possessed great majesty once upon a time, my lord. I'm sure it will again."

She saw pain flicker briefly in his eyes before he said, "Thank you, Lady Katherine. I try to believe that. I have to believe that, or I think I would go mad."

She was surprised to feel sympathy for him, for what he had lost when his elder brother had sold everything to pay his gambling IOUs. She looked into Carlisle's dark brown eyes and said, "I think Castle Carlisle will become whatever you make of it, my lord."

They had reached the steps that led over the rock wall that surrounded the garden to the pasture beyond.

He eyed the crumbling steps and said, "Shall we walk farther? I could lift you over the top."

"Why not?" Kitt said.

She was anticipating the earl's hands on her waist when she felt two strong hands grasp her waist from behind. From over her shoulder she heard Alex tell the earl, " 'Tis my responsibility to ensure my lady's safety."

"Are you suggesting I would drop her?" the earl said, incensed.

Alex lifted her up and over the stone wall, then vaulted it himself, leaving the earl on the other side. "Why take the risk?"

Kitt saw the earl was furious at being outmaneuvered by Alex, but what could he do? She was already over the fence. The damage was done.

Carlisle vaulted the stone fence—she noticed he accomplished the feat as easily as Alex had—and, staring Alex in the eye, took her gloved hand and once more laid it on his arm. "Shall we walk some more, Lady Katherine?"

Kitt felt immensely encouraged by the earl's clear-headed behavior. Not many men—especially young men—would have acted so rationally in the face of such provocation. She smiled at him and was rewarded with a smile in return. She shrugged Alex's warning hand off her shoulder and said, "I would love to see more, my lord. What is over that hill?"

Carlisle grinned at her. "Honestly? A bit of heather and a great deal more thistle."

She laughed. "I love them both." Because they both were Scotland—its beauty and its pain. "Let's go look."

"My lady—" Alex said.

"You needn't come with us, Alex," Kitt interrupted. "We willna be going far."

" 'Tis my job to guard your back, my lady. 'Tis necessary I stay close enough to do so."

Carlisle made a sound of disgust. "I'm hardly going to harm the lady. I plan to make her my wife."

"She's not your wife yet," Alex said in a formidable voice. "Until she is, 'tis my duty to be sure she remains safe in your company."

Carlisle bristled, but once again forbore to make a scene. "Very well. If you must play watchdog, come along." He turned to Kitt and said, "It must be bothersome having such an annoying puppy on your heels all the time."

Kitt laughed and glanced over her shoulder at Alex. "Sometimes he's fun to play with. And he's very good at fetching."

Alex growled, and she felt the earl's arm tense under her hand.

"Just so long as you can keep him from biting, I'll be happy," Carlisle said. He stopped abruptly and reached down to pick a delicate pink primrose. He held it out to her and said, "For you, my lady."

No man had ever offered her flowers, not even Leith, because she would not have taken them. Flowers were for females. It seemed she had more than a little to learn about the unfamiliar role. "Thank you, my lord."

She brought the blossom to her nose and detected a soft fragrant scent. An instant later she sneezed.

Alex plucked the flower from her hand.

"Alex! What are you doing?"

"That flower clearly did not agree with you." He handed her another flower, a fragile white blossom. "Try this one, instead."

Kitt stared at Alex. Why offer her another flower? If one blossom made her sneeze, chances were the second would do the same. She took it anyway and carefully raised it to her nose. It had a different, lighter scent. She laid the soft petals against her flesh. But she did not sneeze.

She glanced at the earl and saw why Alex had given her the flower. The young man was obviously vexed.

Kitt made a point of twirling the flower Alex had given her, then threw it over her shoulder and put her hand back on the earl's arm. "A nice specimen, to be sure. What I would really love is a bouquet of heather. Shall we continue our walk, my lord?" she said, smiling up at the earl.

Carlisle looked mollified and led her away.

Kitt wished she could have kept the flower Alex had given her, but she had to remember her purpose in coming here was to bring the earl up to scratch. Once she got Alex away from here, she was going to remind him firmly of that fact.

Kitt suspected the rest of the earl's conversation during their walk around the estate was limited by the man shadowing their every step, but she was perfectly willing to talk with Carlisle about farming. The subject was important under the circumstances. To her surprise, Carlisle was not only knowledgeable, he had a great many new ideas he had learned from books.

"If I had enough land, I would put into practice some of the things I have read," he said. "I've been negotiating to buy back all the Carlisle land my brother gave away to Blackthorne, but—"

"Gave away?" Alex interjected.

Kitt had almost forgotten Alex was there, and his interruption struck a nerve with her, as it obviously did with the earl. She shot him a reproving look, but she doubted he saw it because his gaze was focused on the earl, who was glaring back at him.

"Blackthorne as good as stole the land from my brother," the earl said. "He paid so little for it."

"Are you saying the duke acted unscrupulously?" she asked Carlisle.

"I am. Which is why I have—" Carlisle cut himself off. "I did not realize so much time had passed," he said, eyeing the lowering sun over the green hills. "We should turn back to the house."

His touch was warm and firm, but there were no calluses on his hands. He had done a great deal of studying about farming, it seemed, without ever doing much actual work. She wondered if any of the ideas he had discussed with her would actually increase the production of crops.

"Would you care to go riding with me on Thursday

afternoon?" Carlisle asked. "We can take a picnic with us."

Her clansmen were meeting at her home on Thursday morning to plan Patrick Simpson's rescue and might not be gone before the earl arrived. "I canna go Thursday."

"The day after, then," he suggested.

"I had to sell my horse," she admitted.

"I have a mount you might like."

"And one for me, I trust," Alex said.

Kitt could feel the tension radiating between the two men and realized suddenly that the earl had hoped to get her alone by taking her riding. It was equally clear Alex was having no part of that. "Do you ride, Alex?" she asked.

"I'm sure I can manage," he replied, pinning the earl with a baleful stare.

"Very well," Carlisle said, his mouth tight with displeasure. "I will bring two mounts. Shall we walk back to the house?"

Kitt looked around and realized it would be a shorter walk home if they cut across the field, rather than returning to the house. And she didn't relish another confrontation at the stone wall. "Alex and I can go on from here," she said.

"Very well, my lady." In open defiance of her bodyguard, the earl raised her gloved hand to his lips. At the last instant, he turned her hand over and touched his lips—and Lord have mercy, his tongue—to her wrist above her glove in a way that caused her insides to clench.

"*Au revoir*, Lady Katherine."

Kitt was rattled. She had not realized that, on top of his good looks and his charm, the earl could be such a persuasive lover. She had been willing to marry him for the sake of her clan, an arranged marriage to benefit both parties and to fulfill her promise to her father to win back the land. But she had not expected to feel anything, not for one of the enemy.

"Good day, my lord," she said. "I will look forward to our ride."

She was aware of Alex at her side as they began the walk home. He didn't remain silent for long.

"Did you ever stop to wonder why an impoverished earl would wish to marry an impoverished Scotswoman?"

"What?"

"I want to know if you have considered what motive the earl might have for marriage to you," Alex said, taking such large, angry strides that she had to hop-skip to keep up with him.

"His motive can be no worse than mine," she said.

"The man is obviously no farmer."

"He can learn. Or be taught."

"If he doesna gamble away the land first."

She was frightened by the fury in his voice. This was no lapdog, growling at a stranger. This was a feral wolf. Yet she refused to be cowed. "What does it matter to you, Alex? This is my problem, and I will solve it my way."

He put his face so close she could feel his hot breath on her cheek and said, "By seducing the boy? He's barely old enough to be out of leading strings!"

"He wants to court me. You heard him say so."

He grabbed her arms and gave her a shake. "But why, Kitt? Why? It makes no sense!"

"Perhaps he admires me."

"He doesna know you. How can he admire you?"

"You dinna know me, either," she said. "Yet I have seen you look at me as though you would eat me alive. What are your motives, Alex? Why do you want me?"

" 'Tis lust, plain and simple," he snarled at her.

She had not expected him to say he loved her, but his response was a slap in the face. The blood flowed hotly to her cheeks as though he had actually struck her. She looked at him from eyes she hoped did not reveal the extent of the wound he had dealt her.

"I will marry whomever I must to get back the lands and the castle for my people—the Earl of Carlisle or the devil himself. I swore to my father I would do it. And I will!"

He let her go suddenly, as though he had been having some sort of fit and had come to his senses.

She rubbed her arms where he had been holding her, wondering why she did not send him away right now. "I dinna think this will work, Alex. I dinna think I can keep you as my *gille-coise*."

"You need me now more than ever," he replied.

"I plan to let the earl court me, Alex. I plan to marry him, if he will have me."

" 'Tis a dangerous game you're playing."

" 'Tis no game, Alex," she said. "I only want back what belongs to my family—Castle MacKinnon and the land that surrounds it."

"At any price?"

"At whatever price I must pay!"

"I dinna trust Carlisle."

"What makes you think the earl wants anything more from me than a wife to manage his home and provide him an heir?"

"You want something more from him than a husband," Alex pointed out.

"What is it you think he expects to get from me?" she demanded.

"The land."

"Blackthorne's land? 'Tisna mine to give him. I've only made claim to it in the courts."

"A claim that, with his help, might very well succeed. If you were married, he would own the land free and clear without having to buy it on credit—and could sell it for profit."

Kitt stared at Alex, suddenly seeing the truth in his suggestion, suddenly seeing the hidden danger of marrying the earl, thereby confirming his claim on the land, and perhaps putting it entirely in his control without any debt that might require him to keep it.

"I think if you do win the land, Carlisle will take it from you and lose it gambling or mismanage it so badly that things will become even worse for your clansmen than they are now."

Kitt's stomach knotted. "Surely not!"

"His brother had a history of gambling."

"But Carlisle has never gambled more than he had."

"Just everything he had," Alex retorted.

"Perhaps," Kitt conceded. "But he seemed to know a great deal about farming."

"Ideas from books. I doubt Carlisle has worked a day in his life. What makes you think he will turn over a new leaf?"

"I can manage him," Kitt said.

"How?"

"There are ways a woman can control a man," she said, meeting his gaze suggestively.

"A man has the same weapons," he replied, slipping his hand around her nape.

Her heart thumped an extra beat when his thumb brushed the skin beneath her ear. "What is your point, Alex?" she said breathlessly.

"I suspect the earl knows more about such arts than you do, my lady. He will likely have the advantage in any such encounter."

"Perhaps," she said, reaching out to splay her hand across Alex's chest, her forefinger catching in the hollow of his throat. She felt his heart begin to pound beneath her hand. "And perhaps not."

His eyes focused on hers, his lids half-lowered, his gaze filled with wanting.

"Don't worry," she said, releasing him before he managed to seduce her entirely. "I'll be safe from the earl's entreaties."

"How can you be sure?"

She shot him a gamine smile. "You will be there to protect me."

Chapter 11

ALEX WAS FRIGHTENED BY THE CONTINUING void where his memory should be, but he had no inclination to share his fear—or seek comfort for it. He lay curled up to sleep on a pile of straw in Kitt's barn, mindful of the cow chewing her cud and the cat rustling the straw as she hunted down rats, and the animal smells—not all of them pleasant.

He wished he knew where he belonged.

He was no closer to knowing his name now than he had been when he woke up at the edge of the sea two weeks ago. But he had a great deal more insight into who he was. A proud man. One who liked children. A passionate man. And a jealous one.

He could cheerfully have strangled the Earl of Carlisle when Kitt smiled up at him . . . when she laughed for him . . . when she accepted a wildflower from his hand. He had felt an unaccountable rage—completely

187

out of proportion to the earl's behavior—that made him wonder if he'd been in a similar situation in the past.

And yet, while he could not agree with Kitt's methods, he understood the madness that drove her to contemplate marriage to a stranger. The hollow eyes and distended stomachs of starving children provided a goad he felt himself. If only he were a man of some consequence, a man with a valet and monogrammed handkerchiefs, a man who was used to good wine and a comfortable bed, he could offer her another solution to her dilemma than marriage to Carlisle.

He wished there had been time to open that door on the second floor of Blackthorne Hall and see if there really was a nursery behind it. Surely he had been to Blackthorne Hall before, as a child, perhaps. How else could he have known there would be a ledge outside Mr. Ambleside's window and a place to jump down?

Who am I? The question echoed inside his head. But there was no answer.

Perhaps he should go to Blackthorne Hall and introduce himself to Mr. Ambleside, as he had originally intended, and take advantage of the man's hospitality. Perhaps he was a person of some note, maybe even the duke himself!

Alex played with the idea for a moment. What a wonder that would be, to be the richest man in England and Scotland. To own the land and the castle and be able to act the white knight and rescue Kitt and all those starving children.

Alex sighed. If he were the duke, it meant he was

the greedy landlord responsible for all that terrible starvation. He did not want to be that man. Though Kitt had said she would marry even such a man to save her people.

Alex curled his hands into angry fists, but winced when flesh touched flesh. Kitt had put salve on the blisters he'd earned cutting peat last week, but they were still tender. What kind of workingman had no calluses?

A thief. A brigand. A murderer.

More likely, if he showed up at Blackthorne Hall he'd be arrested for some offense he'd committed. Perhaps he'd had some part in the duke's demise. No, he could not go to the Hall and show himself openly. But perhaps he could use Michael O'Malley to investigate further. He trusted the boy not to give him up to the law if he turned out to be an unsavory character.

Meanwhile, he would continue where he was. No telling what Katherine MacKinnon would do if left to her own devices. At least if he stayed with her he could control the situation, if not his own impulses toward the woman.

He had seen her in a great many situations over the past two weeks and had learned as much about Katherine MacKinnon as about himself. Her sense of responsibility toward her tenants, her willingness to personally visit each and every one to dispense food bought with the stolen guineas, even though it meant hobbling around on her sore knee, had earned his admiration and respect.

She could also be impulsive and unpredictable, as

he had discovered one hot summer afternoon this past week. While passing a loch between visits to the tenants, she had stopped, set down her basket, and begun to unbutton her blouse. He had stared at her in shock for a moment before she laughed at him and said, "I thought I'd take a quick dip in the water to cool off. Do you want to join me?"

"I dinna know if I can swim," he said. "I havna tried." *Since I lost my memory.*

"I'll keep you afloat while you find out," she said. "Come and join me."

He mopped the sweat from his brow with his sleeve, glanced up at the hot sun, and said, " 'Tis an invitation I canna refuse."

She stepped behind a bush before her attire became indecent, but his mouth had long since gone dry. For a woman who had been embarrassed by having him tend her wounded knee, she was showing a surprising lack of modesty. "Promise you willna look before I'm in the water," she called out to him.

Standing behind his own bush, he grinned but said, "Only if you'll promise to close your eyes when I come in."

She laughed, and he heard a splash. "I'm in. Your turn."

"Are your eyes closed?" he said.

"What do you think?"

He walked out from behind his bush and found her staring at him, her eyes full of laughter. She was nearly covered by water, but it was apparent she had not taken everything off. He could see the straps of something white over her shoulders. He took his time getting into the water—which was frigidly cold—but to his surprise, she didn't turn away.

"I dinna think I've ever seen a man so beautiful," she said, once the water covered his hips.

"And have you seen a great many like this?" he asked, his lips tilted in amusement.

"Only Leith," she admitted. "Come, let's see if you can swim."

She reached for his hands and he walked forward and gave them to her. She led him farther into the water so that only his toes were touching the silt and rocks at the bottom. "Let me know if you feel afraid."

"I'm not afraid," he said, though his heart was thumping madly.

"Shall we go deeper?"

He nodded and she gave a tug and suddenly there was nothing beneath his feet. He felt a momentary panic but heard her say, "Kick your feet."

He did and realized it was enough to keep him afloat. "I guess I can swim."

"I'll let go of your hands now. If you feel yourself sinking, paddle hard with your hands and your feet."

Alex discovered he was an excellent swimmer, and because she was too, they enjoyed a good half hour of fun in the water. His hands slid across her flesh as often as hers slid across his. They might have been two innocent children playing. But they were not.

She called a halt to it when his hand accidentally

grazed her breast and found her nipple taut with desire. "'Tis enough," she said. "We have more errands to do."

To his surprise, she did not ask him to look away as she left the water. So he did not. And was treated to the enticing sight of her slender back and buttocks through her wet muslin underthings.

She stopped and glanced back at him over her shoulder, her lips curved in a teasing smile, her eyes filled with mischief, and said, "You can come out now."

If he had stood up, she would have seen a great deal more of him than she had seen when he entered the water. "If I come out now, you'll shortly be as naked as I am."

Her eyes had widened in alarm before she turned and ran for the bushes.

He had laughed. And groaned. Her impish sense of humor had nearly done him in—and had left him wanting more.

Alex shifted in his straw bed. He felt a sneeze coming on. He was probably getting a case of the influenza from staying in that damned frigid water too long. He held his breath and stayed very still to fight the sneeze, then gave in with a loud "Achoo!" He rubbed his itchy nose against his sleeve and focused his mind on his situation.

It was not at all a comfortable proposition to think of spending every day with Kitt, but being forbidden to touch her. His body ached for her, and it did not help matters to know she likely wanted him as well but had no intention of indulging either herself or him.

"Bloody hell!"

His body tightened at the thought of holding her, kissing her, putting himself inside her. He ached for her like a foolish boy who has not yet had his first woman. Could he remember his first woman? Alex realized he could not connect a particular face with the act, though he knew he had performed it many times. Enough to know it was one of life's great pleasures.

He could simply seduce her. She was susceptible to him.

Alex grimaced. Whatever he might have been in the past, he did not see himself as a ravisher of women. But it was all he could do to keep from quivering like a stallion near a ready mare whenever she touched him—however innocent it was. The best thing to do would be to leave this place.

Unfortunately, he could not simply abandon her. He had agreed to become her bodyguard because it had seemed expedient to do so, but there was no doubt in his mind that Lady Katherine needed someone to guard her from her own clansmen. Not to mention knaves like Carlisle. The moment she no longer had a bodyguard, Ian MacDougal or one of the others—would force her into marriage.

And Alex shuddered to think what would happen to her on that dangerous and foolhardy raid on the jail if he were not there to protect her from harm. He would make sure Kitt was kept safe from any man whose attentions she did not welcome—including himself.

Alex slept the sleep of the righteous, knowing all

would soon be right again with his world. Or at least, as right as it could be when he intended to deny himself something he wanted very much.

He dreamed of Katherine MacKinnon. In his sleep he made slow, sensual love to her. He did not want to let go of her, but some insect was crawling on his face. He reached up to slap at it, and ran into something more substantial.

"Wake up, sleepyhead."

Alex opened his eyes to find the face that had haunted his dreams so close that a mere few inches separated their mouths. The insect turned out to be a piece of straw Kitt was brushing against his cheek. He was still caught up in the dream and his body felt painfully unsatisfied. He wanted a taste of her. Just a taste.

Don't do it, Alex. Don't. You will only regret it later.

His mouth was on hers before he'd cleared the cobwebs from his mind. He pulled Katherine down on top of him, feeling her breasts pillow against his chest. His hands grasped her buttocks and pressed her firmly against the hardness between his legs.

He knew he had caught her by surprise, because her mouth formed an "Oh!" that left an entrance for his tongue. He thrust inside and moaned when he felt the warm wetness of her mouth. He rolled her over, pinning her beneath him.

All of the innocent touching they had done in the water last week was a prelude to this. He pinched her nipple between his thumb and forefinger and felt her clutch his hair with both hands as her body arched agonizingly into his groin. He reached for her skirt and pulled it up and out of the way, then palmed the heat of her. Oh, God. She was wet, even through the cloth.

His tongue searched her mouth for satisfaction, thrusting in an imitation of the sex act, as his hand searched for a way through the thin muslin. Her body trembled, and she made a wild sound in her throat as he rubbed against her with his thumb. The material gave way with a tearing sound.

And she bit his tongue.

Alex jerked his head away, still caught in a sensual fog, and stared at the woman beneath him.

Her eyes sparkled with tears of rage and humiliation. And awareness and arousal. And perhaps even frustration, though her next words belied any of that.

"You coxcomb! You cabbage-head! You—You clod-pole!"

There was no excuse if his touch had been unwelcome, yet he found himself making one, for both their sakes. "I wasna yet awake," he said. "I thought you were part of my dream."

She shoved him off of her and stood, brushing the straw from her skirt. Her face flamed red, and he realized why when he looked at the front of her blouse. Her nipples were puckered and plainly visible beneath the muslin. She might not have welcomed his attentions, but there was no denying she had been aroused by them.

"That canna happen again, Alex. I must be able to trust you. Would I be better off on my own?"

"I can be trusted—when I'm fully awake." He rose and brushed the straw off of himself. "It willna happen again. Why did you not send Moira to wake me?"

"I . . . I . . ."

He looked into her face and saw the truth. She had wanted to be with him when he woke. She might even have wanted him to touch her—though she ought to have known better. From now on, Alex thought, he would have to protect both of them from themselves.

"The men will be here soon to plan the raid," she said. " 'Tis best you come inside and break your fast before they arrive." She turned and left, but his eyes caught on the sway of her hips and stayed there until she disappeared from sight.

Once she was gone, Alex swore every oath he knew. The cow gave him a look over her shoulder, and the black cat with three white boots left off washing her one black paw to stare. He was filled with terrible regret for what he had done. Because having once tasted Kitt, he only wanted more.

By the time Alex had finger-combed his hair, washed the sleep from his eyes, and swallowed a bannock with some tea, Ian MacDougal and Duncan Fraser had arrived. Before the sun was fully visible all of the MacKinnon clansmen were present. Sitting on the floor, on the benches on either side of the table, and standing along the walls, they filled up the small stone cottage.

Alex stayed by Lady Katherine's side as she greeted the men. He made eye contact with each one, confirming his intent to protect her from danger even if it came from her devoted clansmen.

When Lady Katherine called the meeting to order, Ian interrupted her and said, "Now that all of us are ready to act, I see no reason why The MacKinnon should risk her life on this raid. 'Tis dangerous for a woman—"

"The plan is mine, and I'll see it through," Kitt interrupted.

"I canna allow it," Ian said.

Her eyes went wide and then narrowed as her brows lowered ominously. "Canna allow it? Who are you to say what The MacKinnon will or willna do? I can fend for myself as well as any man."

Ian shook his head. "I canna let you go."

A fierce expression settled on her face. "You dinna tell me what to do. *I* am The MacKinnon."

"She's right," Alex said quietly. "There must be one leader, and one only. Unless you're willing to replace her now, she goes."

Ian looked around the room for support for that alternative, but found none. "She might be killed," Ian protested.

"I'll be there to protect her," Alex said.

Resigned to having Lady Katherine present on the raid, Ian said, " 'Tisna necessary that she throw herself into the fray, is it? She can wait nearby to give whatever aid the wounded might need."

Kitt opened her mouth to object again, but this time Alex agreed. "He's right, Lady Katherine. We may need someone to doctor those who get hurt. You would be most helpful standing by with your herbs to do what you do best."

Kitt looked around to gauge the feelings of her clansmen, and Alex saw the moment she resigned herself to waiting nearby while the others put themselves in the path of danger.

"I dinna want any of you dying, so I'll be there to make sure none of you do," she said at last.

It was a broad enough statement that Alex wondered for a moment if she harbored any thoughts of thrusting herself forward at the last minute. It would be his duty to see that she did not.

"When shall we go?" Ian asked.

"I've learned the soldiers will be on maneuvers and gone from their barracks sometime within the next two weeks," Kitt said. "We can set a watch to learn the day they leave and break Patrick out of jail while they're away."

It was agreed that Kitt would send word to those involved in the raid when the time was right. The planning done, the men left to go about their daily tasks, so there would be no suspicion among the authorities that this day was different from any other.

Once he and Kitt were alone again in the cottage, Alex's thoughts returned to what had happened between them that morning. One look at Kitt's face revealed the same awareness. He was afraid that if he stayed anywhere near her, he might be tempted to do something foolish for which, since he was fully awake, he would have no convenient excuse.

"Fletcher asked if I could give him some help in the fields," he said. "His wife offered supper afterward, so I'll be back late. I'll see you tomorrow morning, when you are to ride with the earl."

"I'd forgotten," Kitt said. "I suppose we'll see if you ride as well as you swim."

"Aye," he said, wondering if she would prove as enticing on horseback as she had in the water. "I suppose we will."

One of the reasons why Kitt hated the Duke of Blackthorne so intensely was because she had been forced to sell her horse, Blanca, to pay the high rents on the land. She had raised the dapple-gray mare herself, and it had nearly broken her heart to part with her two years before. She had not ridden since.

Alex showed up for breakfast looking red-eyed and slightly dissipated. "I had a pint or two with Fletcher," he confessed.

"Can you ride this morning?"

"I can...if I can," he said with a lopsided grin.

As it turned out, Alex was a more than capable rider, something he proved when it became apparent that Carlisle had provided him with a fractious mount. Or, to be more precise, a black Thoroughbred stallion with hellfire in his eyes and hatred in his heart.

Carlisle had already mounted Kitt on a well-mannered Thoroughbred chestnut mare with a white blaze when Alex's friend Laddie showed up driving a cart with the curvetting stallion tied on behind.

"We had a wee bit of trouble getting him saddled," the boy admitted. "Are ye sure ye want to ride him, Alex?"

"Do you have another mount for me?" Alex asked Carlisle.

"You see the extent of my stables, sir," Carlisle replied from atop a solid bay gelding whose bloodlines were somewhat suspect. "If you cannot manage Lucifer, I am afraid we will have to leave you behind."

It was plain to Kitt that Carlisle had planned all along to leave Alex behind. She wasn't sure whether to be sorry or not. These days, the earl seemed less of a threat to her than Alex.

Kitt watched as Alex approached the wide-eyed stallion, its ears laid back flat, speaking to the animal in a soft, calming voice. He waited until the stallion's ears came up before he untied the reins and slipped them over the stallion's bobbing head. In that same singsong voice he said, "Move the cart away, Laddie."

Kitt expected Alex to lead the huge stallion to the same stump Carlisle had used as a mounting block. Instead, he grabbed a handful of black mane and launched himself gracefully onto the horse's back. A second later his boots were lodged in the stirrups and he was ready for whatever antics the stallion might provide.

Lucifer did not disappoint him. The stallion reared and pawed the air. His angry, trumpeting neigh raised gooseflesh on Kitt's arms. She gasped, afraid Alex would slide off the stallion's back. He simply held on to the mane and leaned forward to speak in the stallion's ear, using that same quiet voice. The stallion landed on all four hooves and stood quivering, listening.

Alex looked Carlisle in the eye and said, "Shall we go?"

Carlisle said something under his breath that Kitt didn't catch, but she didn't ask him to repeat it. "This way, Lady Katherine," he said, heading for the hills near Castle Carlisle. He spurred his mount into a trot, glancing back at Alex to see whether he could manage to keep the stallion at such a sedate pace.

In fact, he could not. Lucifer bucked at the restraint, then curvetted. Alex steered the prancing, crow-hopping stallion in a complete circle around Kitt and the earl, who continued in a trot along the road.

"I've been looking forward to this ride ever since I last saw you," the earl said. His eyes registered his pleasure as they moved over her face and form.

"So have I," Kitt said. Though she had been looking forward to the ride itself, not the visit with the earl.

"I suppose you've heard we have a thief in the neighborhood," Carlisle said.

Kitt struggled to keep her face impassive. " 'Tis all anyone talks about. Does Mr. Ambleside have any idea who it might be?"

The earl scowled. "He suspected me, if you can believe it."

"No! Why would he think such a thing?" Kitt said.

"It is no secret my pockets are to let," the earl said.

"But I would never dishonor my family name by stealing from the duke. Though I suppose what I am doing is certainly questionable enough."

"What are you doing?" Kitt asked, her curiosity piqued.

"Mr. Ambleside has agreed to rent me the lands my brother sold to the duke and to defer any payment on the rent until I've seen a profit."

Kitt couldn't believe her ears. Mr. Ambleside had refused to defer Patrick Simpson's rent, and yet he had offered a much greater consideration to the earl. The reason for Mr. Ambleside's generosity quickly struck her. Carlisle was an Englishman. And the duke was an Englishman.

And she had to marry an Englishman and somehow manage to swallow her enmity and live her life with him.

At that moment, Alex crossed in front of her on the curvetting stallion. His eyes burned with a rancor that matched the look in his mount's eyes. Unfortunately, she could not afford to indulge such feelings. She must make conversation. She must win the earl's regard.

She pulled her Thoroughbred back to keep it even with Carlisle's slower mount and said, "Where did you get Lucifer?"

Carlisle shot her a chagrined look and said, "I practically stole him at Tattersall's in London. Or so I thought, until I tried to ride him."

"You mean you have not?" Kitt asked.

Carlisle shook his head. "He threw me every time I

mounted him. Nor has any friend of mine ever been able to ride him." He cocked a brow. "Your bodyguard has the best seat and lightest hands I have ever seen."

Kitt looked closely at Carlisle and saw he meant the compliment sincerely. It took quite a man to be able to admit he had been bested and to do so with grace and charm. She must see the good in the earl and forget he was an Englishman.

"I am amazed myself at how well Alex rides." Kitt turned to the earl with an impish grin and proposed, "Shall we test him to see just how good he is?"

Carlisle shot her a crooked smile that made him look almost boyish. "Why not? If you're sure you're up to it."

Kitt's response was to drive her heels into the mare's flanks. She had missed the feel of the wind whipping in her hair, the feel of a powerful animal beneath her. She hid her face against the mare's neck and let her have her head. It felt like she was flying.

She turned to share her joy with the earl—and found Alex on Lucifer beside her instead. She jerked her head to look for the earl and saw that he was far down the hill behind them, and that his struggling mount was losing ground every minute.

She started to pull up, but Alex grinned and said, "I'll race you to the loch."

She gave the earl one last glance before she grinned back at her bodyguard and said, "You're on!"

Alex would have won handily, except the stallion flushed a covey of quail that sent him leaping sideways a full five feet and nearly caused Alex to lose his seat. She laughed as she passed Alex at a gallop, kicking her lathered mount to even greater speed.

She was sitting on a stone beside the loch, her mare grazing nearby, by the time Alex caught up to her. He slid off the blowing stallion and tied the animal to a tree before he joined her.

"I won," she announced with a smile. "Where's my prize?"

He had already bent to kiss her before she could stop him. It was intended as a quick kiss, a bare meeting of lips, but it turned into something more. Her lips clung to his, and when she pressed her hand against his chest, she could feel his heart beating a rapid tattoo.

She turned her face away, and he straightened abruptly. She touched her fingertips to her damp lips and looked up at him. "Why did you do that?"

" 'Twas what I would have asked if I had won," he said simply. He dropped to the grass in front of the stone where she was sitting as though he had not just turned her world upside down. He leaned back, crossed his hands behind his head, and said, "I dinna know when I've enjoyed anything so much."

Was he referring to the kiss or the ride? Kitt wondered. "I enjoyed it, too," she said. For either one, her answer would have been the same.

They sat in silence for a very long time, the sun beating down on them, warming the stone and the grass and their flesh, until she could hear the wind in the leaves and the lap of water against the shore and the occasional splash of a fish in the loch.

"I wonder where Carlisle ended up," Alex said at last.

"It was awful of us to leave him behind," Kitt said.

Alex looked up at her and grinned. "You could have turned back at any time."

She laughed. "And miss beating you? Never. Where did you learn so much about horses? I thought you were a sailor."

He hesitated, then said, "I was a farmer first." Before she could ask another question, he rose gracefully to his feet. "We'd better go find the earl."

"I suppose we should." She stood and realized the stone she had been sitting on was too high to use for mounting her horse, and there was no stump handy. "I'll need you to help me mount."

"Certainly, my lady."

Kitt was confused by Alex's sudden formality. He had been quick enough to kiss her and happy enough to sit with her, but now he acted as if he couldn't put distance between them quickly enough. What was wrong with him?

One look into his eyes gave her an answer. There was nothing distant about his eyes. They were dark and heavy-lidded. His lips were full, his features taut.

And they were very much alone.

Kitt felt the lure of the forbidden. She had some inkling of what it might be like to make love to Alex, had been overwhelmed, in fact, by the feelings he had inspired when she had woken him in the barn. It was tempting to ask for another touch. Another taste.

But it was folly to expect a wolf to sniff at a piece of succulent meat and then not to swallow it whole.

She said nothing, nor did he, as he threaded his fingers together to make a stand for her foot and boosted her up into the sidesaddle. A moment after that he was in the saddle again, and they were on their way.

The danger had been averted.

An opportunity has been lost, she thought with a surge of regret.

"There you are," the earl said, riding toward her, greeting her with a rueful smile. "I don't blame you for leaving me behind. I hope you had a nice ride."

"I did," she said, returning his smile, grateful that she was to be forgiven for leaving him and glad he had not come upon them a little sooner.

"I looked for you in a different direction," the earl continued. "I should have known you would come to the loch."

" 'Tis beautiful this time of day."

"Not as beautiful as you."

Neither of them looked at Alex. Both of them already knew what they would see on his face.

"Shall we ride again next week?" he asked.

"I would like that," she replied.

Kitt kneed her horse to join Carlisle and never looked back.

* * *

The day the soldiers left for maneuvers, Kitt sent word to her clansmen to come to her cottage after the moon rose that night. Alex felt the tension in the room as each man reviewed his assigned task. Not everyone would go on the raid. Some would stay behind to provide alibis for the others in case there was any question of their involvement later.

"Guard her well," Duncan said as he left the cottage. "She has her father's courage, but a woman's foolish heart."

"Well I know it," Alex replied.

Kitt said nothing in front of Duncan, but she had no intention of standing by while the rescue went on without her. Nevertheless, she pretended to be content with her assigned role and even brought along a small pouch of medicinal herbs in case any of her clansmen got wounded.

"I dinna intend to be left behind, Alex," Kitt said, breathless because she was trying to keep up with his long strides.

"I'll slow down a bit, if you insist."

"'Tis not what I mean, and you know it," she retorted.

"You'll be safer out of range of the soldiers' muskets."

"The soldiers are gone on maneuvers."

"They'll have left a few behind to guard the jail. 'Tis safer for you to wait in the trees and let Ian and the others do what must be done."

Kitt huddled in the copse of trees near the jail with

Alex and seethed as she was forced to watch, rather than lead her clansmen on the raid.

She saw Fletcher and Tavis take down one of the guards in front of the jail with a knock on the head, while Evan and Angus captured, bound, and gagged the other. Then the four of them and Ian headed inside to find and free Patrick Simpson.

She and Alex waited. And waited.

" 'Tis too long since they all went inside," Alex said when perhaps five minutes had passed. "Something's wrong. Wait here while I—"

"I'm no safer here alone than I would be with you," Kitt protested.

"Stay here!" Alex snapped.

Before Kitt could protest again, he was gone. She saw him hesitate, calling out softly to Fletcher and Evan before he disappeared inside the jail.

The instant Alex was out of sight, she followed after him. She was as capable as any man of doing her part, and she intended to prove it once and for all.

Kitt hadn't taken two steps before she heard someone coming through the undergrowth. She froze with her back to a tree until two men—soldiers!—passed by her. They were swaying drunkenly, hanging on to each other, and had apparently been in the bushes relieving themselves. If they got past her, they would likely see the men as they exited the door of the jail and raise an alarm. She realized she had no choice except to try and stop them.

Her heart was pounding with fear and excitement

as she stepped out of her hiding place. "What are two fine fellows like you doing out so late?" she said.

"What's this? What is it you want?" one of the soldiers asked in a drunken voice.

"Only a little company," Kitt said in a sultry voice. She planned to lead the two of them farther into the copse where the door to the jail would not be visible. The soldiers looked so drunk she was certain she could outrun them. "Why not come over here and—"

They both lunged for her at the same time. One grabbed her arms and wrenched them behind her while the other clamped a hand over her mouth so she couldn't scream.

"Well, well," one said to the other. "Shall we keep this treat for ourselves, or share it with the others?"

"I say we should help ourselves first. They can have whatever's left when we're done."

Kitt's eyes went wide with terror. *Alex, where are you? I need you. Come find me, please!*

Chapter 12

ALEX HAD DONE EVERYTHING IN HIS POWER during the planning for the raid to ensure no one would be hurt—either clansmen or soldiers. But as he stepped inside the jail he saw everything had gone wrong. Blood pooled under the body of a soldier who lay next to Fletcher. The Scotsman still had a dirk stuck in his side.

"Fletcher?"

"I'm still here," the big Scotsman whispered. "But that soldier's in a bad way."

Alex laid his fingertips on the wounded soldier's throat and found a weak pulse. He wadded up the man's shirt beneath him and pressed it against the wound to stop the bleeding. With luck the man would live.

Then he knelt beside the wounded Scotsman and whispered, "Can you stand?"

Fletcher grabbed at the hand Alex offered him. "More soldiers than we thought stayed behind."

"How many more?"

"One in back, two more expected soon," Fletcher said.

"Wait here. I'll be back for you. Dinna sit down. When we come out, we'll be moving fast." Alex edged quietly, carefully, farther into the jail, searching for Ian and the others. He heard the English soldier before he saw the four MacKinnon clansmen with their hands held high.

"It won't be long now until my friends return, and then we'll make sure you have a cell of your own," the soldier said.

Alex surveyed the scene, deciding how best to hit the soldier so that his musket would not discharge. He didn't have much time. The soldier was obviously expecting help to arrive soon.

He made eye contact with Ian to let him know what he planned, then leapt at the soldier. He caught him between the shoulder blades and forced him down. The man's head hit the wall with enough force to knock him out. His musket clattered to the floor and Ian quickly retrieved it.

Ian started to bludgeon the soldier with the wooden stock, but Alex grabbed his wrist. "There's been enough harm done this night. Where's Patrick Simpson."

"Patrick!" Ian called. "Where are you, man?"

"Here!" Patrick shouted from the last of the cells along the wall.

Alex took the keys from the waistband of the fallen

soldier and threw them to Tavis. "Hurry! There are more soldiers somewhere nearby."

It took a matter of moments for Ian to free Patrick Simpson. The crofter had apparently caught his foot in a mantrap on the duke's land and broken it. His ankle was still swollen to twice its normal size, and he could barely stand.

"Let's go," Alex said, slipping an arm around Patrick's waist and pulling the crofter's arm over his shoulder.

"We should free the others," Ian said.

" 'Tis not what we came to do," Alex said, standing in Ian's way as he reached out a hand for the key. "The MacKinnon waits. Patrick Simpson is free. We should leave before someone else gets hurt."

"Alex is right, Ian," Tavis said. "We should go. We must take Fletcher home to his wife."

Ian grimaced but nodded his head abruptly in agreement. "Ach. So we'll go."

Tavis helped Angus to haul Fletcher up over his shoulder and then came to stand on the other side of Alex to help support Patrick Simpson's weight.

Ian went first with the musket to look for the English soldiers. " 'Tis clear," he said. "But I dinna know for how long."

Alex's heart was pounding from more than the exertion of carrying Patrick Simpson. One soldier with a bad headache, Fletcher wounded, and another soldier wounded, perhaps seriously. If the soldier died, his comrades would be relentless in their pursuit of those responsible. The sooner Patrick Simpson and his family left Scotland, the better.

By the time they reached the copse of trees where Alex had left Kitt, he was more than a little anxious. If she had been there, he might have taken out his frustration over the disastrous raid on her. But she was not.

"Where is The MacKinnon?" Ian demanded.

"She was here when I left," Alex retorted. He looked over his shoulder toward the jail, wondering if Kitt had snuck in behind them and was in there now. "I'll go find her. Take Patrick and Fletcher and get out of here."

"You may need help," Ian said.

"I can handle it." Alex was headed back toward the jail before Ian could argue further.

They had taken the most direct route, over open land, when they left the jail, but Alex decided to go back through the trees, where he could more easily hide if more soldiers unexpectedly appeared.

He heard Kitt before he saw her. It was plain she was in trouble. He broke into a run, heading toward the sound of her cries.

Kitt kicked one man in the shin and cried out in pain as he slapped her hard across the face. A hand clutched her breast possessively. One soldier pressed his mouth against her cheek, while the other tore at her skirt from behind. A scream of terror was caught in her throat.

The man behind her suddenly went flying. The other lifted his head to find out what had happened but barely had time to yelp before Alex's fist smashed into his mouth. He went down without a sound.

Alex grabbed her hand and started running. "Let's get out of here!"

Kitt took two steps and stumbled, falling forward onto her knees. Alex scooped her up into his arms, and she grasped him around the neck as he took off running again.

"Is Patrick safe?" she asked breathlessly.

"Yes, but Fletcher's been stabbed and one of the soldiers as well."

Kitt drew in a sharp breath. "Will Fletcher—"

"He'll live. This whole business was folly from the start."

" 'Twas no such—"

"Shh," he warned. "We're being followed."

Kitt searched over Alex's shoulder for some sign of pursuit but saw nothing in the moonlit darkness. She listened but all she heard was the sound of Alex's harsh breathing and her own and the crunch of bracken beneath his feet.

Kitt saw a flash of white in the moonlight—the lapel of a soldier's uniform. At the same time, a drunken voice called out, "You, there! Halt, or I'll shoot!"

"This way, Harry," a second drunken voice shouted. "We can cut 'em off."

"They're catching up to us!" Kitt braced herself when she heard a musket being fired, but it was Alex who grunted with pain. "Are you hurt?" she cried.

" 'Tis nothing." He readjusted her weight in his arms and began running again but with a decided limp.

"You're wounded! Put me down," Kitt insisted.

"I think I'll keep you where I know you're safe."

And where any musket balls would hit his body instead of hers, she realized. "Alex, set me down. I can run."

"Look there. Help is on the way," he said.

Sure enough, Kitt saw Ian leading Tavis and Evan back toward them. She breathed a sigh of relief. It would all be over soon. It was unfortunate Fletcher had been wounded. She hoped the soldier did not die, but even if he did, she would not regret the rescue she had ordered. And thanks to Alex, she had suffered no more than a dent to her pride.

The second shot came as Alex stopped to set her down. She stared up into his astonished face a moment before he crumpled to the ground. "Alex!"

She knelt beside him and felt, rather than saw, the blood streaming from the wound in his back. "No! Oh, no. Ian, help!"

Ian shoved her out of the way, hauled Alex over his shoulder, and said, "You two help Lady Katherine. I'll take care of him."

Tavis and Evan each grabbed one of her arms and hurried her toward safety, followed more slowly by Ian. When Kitt heard the third shot fired, she struggled to turn around.

"We canna go back, Lady Katherine," Evan said.

"You must get away from here before the rest of the soldiers wake and begin their search."

"Is everyone else safe?"

"They've all gone home," Tavis replied. "Fletcher is—"

"I know. I'll send Moira to make certain he's well doctored. Who's escorting Patrick and his family to the coast?"

"I'll do that," Ian said from behind them. "And put this one on the ship as well."

"What?" Kitt stopped so abruptly her arms were nearly jerked from their sockets by the two men. "You'll do nothing of the kind. I want Alex taken to my cottage."

"He's sore wounded," Ian said. "Better he should die at sea and his body be slipped overboard than we should have to find a place to bury him."

Kitt felt a spurt of panic. "He isna going to die."

"His shirt and trousers are soaked with blood," Ian said. "Likely he willna survive."

"Take him to my cottage," Kitt said. "Alex saved my life. I'll not let him die alone at sea."

"The soldiers are bound to come searching—"

"Do as I say!" she snapped. It was an order from The MacKinnon, and though Ian grumbled, he did not disobey.

Kitt thanked Tavis and Evan at her door and sent them home to their families.

"What's amiss?" Moira cried in alarm when she saw Kitt with Ian and his burden.

"Alex is hurt. I can care for him, if you'll go to Fletcher. He's been cut and will need stitching."

Moira looked from Kitt to Ian and back, and Kitt saw the question in her eyes. *Will you be safe alone with Ian?* Kitt nodded. She did not think Ian would bother her tonight—especially since the only person who had stood between him and his goal had been removed when Alex was shot.

Once Moira was on her way, Kitt lit a lantern and led Ian to her bedroom. She removed the quilt from her bed, leaving only the sheets.

As Ian dropped Alex onto the stout wooden bed, he said, "Maybe now you'll admit a woman has no business on a raid. If this man dies 'twill be your fault. We're not safe yet. The soldiers will be searching for any who are wounded.

"If fortune favors us, Fletcher will be able to work a little tomorrow, so he'll not be suspect. Choose a husband, Katherine. Choose me and end this foolishness."

Kitt began to shiver as the adrenaline that had sustained her through the raid and their flight from the soldiers began to dissipate. "I dinna like you, Ian. I dinna desire you. I dinna love you. Even more, I dinna trust you."

Ian's face flushed visibly in the candlelight. "Whether you want me or no, whether you trust me or no, I will have you to wife, Katherine. Make up your mind to it."

Ian took a step toward her, but when her determined eyes met his, he changed his mind. "When this stranger is dead and gone, I'll be back to claim what's mine."

Kitt shuddered as he stalked away, then shook off the foreboding she felt at Ian's threats. She hurried through the cottage gathering the things she would need to treat Alex's wounds.

Would it make any difference to Ian if she explained that she planned to marry the Earl of Carlisle to help the clan gain back what they had lost? More likely he would be enraged that she contemplated making an Englishman laird of Clan MacKinnon.

Kitt heard Alex muttering in her bedroom and called out to him, "Be still. I'm coming." She arrived at his bedside moments later carrying a knife, a bowl of water and a cloth, a collection of herbs and salves, and what remained of a bottle of good Scottish whiskey that had been untouched since her father's death.

Alex was moving restlessly on the bed, and she realized he could not be comfortable lying on his wounded back. However, she also needed to treat the wound on his thigh, which she could only do from the front.

The whiskey first, she thought. She held Alex's head up and tipped the bottle against his mouth. "Swallow some of this, Alex."

"What is it?"

"Something to ease the pain."

He swallowed, coughed, and swallowed again. "I've used this before to ease the pain," he said. "It doesna work."

"Drink enough of it," she promised, "and it will."

When she thought he had drunk enough, she let his

head rest on the pillow again and set the near-empty bottle aside. "Lie still," she said soothingly. She brushed back the hair that had fallen over his forehead, loving the feel of it, loving the thought of doing it, wondering why she hadn't done it before.

"Am I going to die?" he asked in a quiet voice.

Kitt couldn't speak. She could not bear the thought of Alex dying. But sometimes the flow of blood from such a wound could not be stopped. Sometimes wounds did not heal at all. And Alex was sorely hurt.

Finally she said, "You've been shot twice, Alex. You have a flesh wound in your thigh that needs tending, and then I must remove the bullet from your back. I'll try not to hurt you any more than I must. Should I tie you down?"

"I'll lie still," he said, then added with a rueful twist of his mouth, "As still as I can."

He lay still even though she was hurting him, and she was only cutting away his trousers to expose the wound on his upper thigh. She heaved a sigh of relief when she realized the bullet had passed completely through the fleshy part of his leg. A few stitches would be enough to close the wound, but she needed to hurry, because Alex was losing blood at an alarming rate.

She quickly gathered needle and thread, worried by Alex's silence. "Alex?" she said softly, peering into his face. His gray eyes were glazed with pain. He had lost so much blood he was chalky white.

"Yes, Kitt, what is it?"

"Lady Kath—" She bit her lip on the correction. If

he lived, there would be time enough to correct him later. "I must stitch the wound on your leg. It will cause you pain."

"Do what you must."

He grasped the bedsheets tightly in both hands but didn't move a hair as she cleansed the wound, making sure there was no cloth from his trousers left inside. She pushed the needle through his flesh as quickly as she could, closing the wound with small, neat stitches, so the remaining scar would not impair his ability to walk or to ride.

Sweat dotted his forehead by the time she was done. Her father had lain still for her ministrations, but he had yelled like a child from the pain. Alex's stoicism was disturbing, almost frightening, because she thought perhaps he was too weak to yell. "I must turn you over now, Alex."

She tried to do it by herself, but he was too heavy. Kitt realized she probably should not have sent Ian away. "Alex, I canna turn you by myself. You must help me."

"I shall try, Kitt. Be patient with me if I cannot do as you ask."

Kitt frowned. The sentence had sounded unlike something Alex would say, but she didn't have time to think about it, because he was trying to turn himself over. He moaned through his teeth as she shoved at his shoulder until at last he was lying on his stomach.

"Thank God that is done. I trust you will be careful when you cut out that ball. I think I shall sleep now, shall I?"

Kitt stared at Alex in alarm. "What happened to your accent, Alex? Alex?"

He had fainted.

Kitt stared at the wounded man lying on her bed. He had spoken like an English nobleman, his voice crisp and condescending.

Maybe I imagined it.

But she had not. She knew she had not. Kitt said the words over in her head. They sounded just as foreign. Alex Wheaton—or whoever he was—was no simple sailor, she realized. Who was he? Why had he come here? And what did he want from her?

Her pulse began to race. If he truly was an Englishman, why had he let them go through with the raid? Perhaps even now the soldiers were on their way to her cottage. Perhaps even now her clansmen were being arrested.

Could Alex really be an Englishman, and thus her enemy? As much as she wanted to deny the possibility, she could not. The clues had all been there from the start, but she had ignored them: the lack of calluses on his hands, the ignorance of how to cut peat, the way he had mastered the unconquerable Thoroughbred stallion. The English arrogance and condescension had even been there when he greeted the Earl of Carlisle.

She knew her father would not have hesitated in making the decision to let Alex die. It would be enough to leave the wound in his back untreated. He would slowly but surely bleed to death if she did nothing.

But I am not my father. Or my father's son. She was

a woman. Who felt a great deal more than she should for an Englishman. Her enemy.

The fact that she could not contemplate killing Alex did not mean she did not recognize the danger he presented to her clansmen. If only she knew whether Alex had told anyone where he was going or what they had intended to do tonight. Was Patrick Simpson even now being recaptured?

Kitt brushed her fingertips across Alex's broken nose. The marks on his face were real. Whoever he was, he had enemies of his own. Perhaps he was fleeing the law in England. Perhaps he was an outlaw. Kitt was torn, uncertain what to do next. He was far too dear to her to be the enemy.

Save his life. Then you can worry about whether to choke the life out of him for keeping his true identity a secret.

She used her knife to cut a slit down the back of her father's shirt to expose a ragged wound that seeped blood. It would not take much to make the blood flow more freely, to make the end come more quickly. She was careful not to let that happen.

Kitt's stomach revolted at the thought of digging for the musket ball in Alex's flesh, and she swallowed back the bile that had risen in her throat. She had no choice. He would die if she did not retrieve the metal ball from his body. She reminded herself that Alex had been wounded saving her life. That she might have been the one who needed surgery if it had not been for him.

The task became easier once she got started. She

removed his bloody trousers, then cut off the remnants of the shirt, glad there was no one present to see her hot flush as she remembered how powerful, how virile Alex had looked walking toward her at the loch. She kept her eyes averted now, but it was impossible not to see glimpses of his flesh. If only he had been a simple sailor. If only he wasn't an Englishman!

By the time Kitt finally dug the ball from Alex's back, her shoulders ached from bending over him. He was conscious enough to feel pain, because he twisted away and moaned when she used a warm cloth to cleanse the wound.

She once more brushed the blond hair from his forehead and said, "Be still. I willna hurt you."

Not yet.

Once she had tended to Alex, Kitt settled herself on a pallet near the warmth of the hearth to wait for Moira's return. But she drifted into sleep.

Kitt was woken by muttering in the next room. To her surprise and alarm, the sky was already lightening with the beginning of day. How could she have fallen asleep! She rose and hurried into the bedroom to see how Alex had fared during the night.

"Where is she?" Alex muttered. "Drunk as she is likely to be . . ."

Kitt wondered who "she" was. She put a hand to his forehead. It was feverishly hot. She should have expected it. She should have stayed awake to watch over him.

Kitt leaned close when Alex began to speak again

and realized that she was hearing that same clipped, upper-class British voice he had used last night.

"My brother...and my wife...together. Please, God, no! Not mine? The twins...not mine?"

Kitt listened, fascinated and appalled.

"Get out before I strangle you...Hate you...hate you both...for deceiving me..."

Kitt could hardly believe what she was hearing. It was easy to piece together a whole from the fragments Alex had given her. It was nothing she would have imagined. Apparently Alex's brother and Alex's wife had lain together and Alex's children—twins?—were not his, but his brother's.

How awful for him.

There was more to the story that she did not wish to contemplate. He hated his wife and his brother. He had threatened to strangle someone. Had Alex murdered his wife or his brother or both? Was he a wanted man in England? Was that why he had come to Scotland and pretended to be someone he obviously was not?

"Who are you?" Kitt looked into his gray eyes, which were open but appeared blank, unseeing.

Alex moved restlessly, wincing and moaning with pain. He stared sightlessly at her.

"Who are you?" she repeated. "Why did you come here?"

"Blackthorne," he whispered. "I am Blackthorne."

Kitt jerked away, stunned. "'Tis not possible. The duke is dead. Drowned in the..."

Alex Wheaton had come from the sea. She had brushed the sand from his face, taken the seaweed from his hair.

Alex Wheaton is the Duke of Blackthorne in disguise.

Kitt shook her head in disbelief at such an incredible idea. Why would Blackthorne pretend to be someone else, especially such an insignificant someone else? Why not return to Blackthorne Hall instead of staying with her? Alex had slept on a bed of straw!

The Alex she knew could not be the detestable duke. He had held Brynne so carefully in his arms. And swum naked in the loch. And downed a pint or two with Fletcher. And kissed her and touched her until she was half in love with him.

Kitt felt like howling. It wasn't possible!

But what if it was true? What if Alex was the duke?

She could not see him committing murder, not even for such a terrible offense as what his brother had done. He would be more likely to hide the truth than to admit he had been cuckolded. Perhaps Alex had run away for a while to lick his wounds and ended up here, acting out a charade for his amusement.

How dare he! To make sport of her and her people, why, it was diabolical! Kitt stared at the man, aghast as she realized she had told him her father's plan.

I planned to seduce Blackthorne and get myself with child.

Kitt groaned. No wonder Alex had been so furious

at her plan to trick the duke. He was the very man she had planned to deceive. Kitt felt her chin quiver and bit down to hold back the tears of anger and frustration and defeat.

Blackthorne knew everything. All was lost.

Unless the Duke of Blackthorne remains dead.

Kitt reached for the knife she had used to save the duke's life, and raised her hand to plunge it into his back. There was no question of murder. The duke was already dead, drowned in the sea. He was her enemy. He and his father and his father's father had stolen the lifeblood from her people and now threatened to starve them off land they had claimed for generations. Justice was on her side.

She gripped the knife with both hands to still her trembling. She must do this. It would be better to end the duke's life and to marry the earl instead.

A picture flashed in her mind of Alex putting his body between her and the soldier's musket, so he had been wounded and she had remained whole.

Surely he deserved mercy for such a sacrifice.

"What are ye doing?"

Kitt started and looked up to find Moira standing in her bedroom doorway. She realized that she was still holding the knife and set it down. "He says he's Blackthorne."

Moira nodded, as though she had thought as much all along.

"You dinna seem surprised."

Moira shrugged. "I knew he was no ordinary man, though I didna suspect he was the duke. What is it ye plan to do now?"

"I dinna know what to do," Kitt said, letting out a gust of trapped air. "Perhaps he will die and save me the trouble of deciding."

Moira stepped closer to check Kitt's work. "This was well done."

Kitt pursed her lips. "I should have let him bleed to death. He's likely to have us all transported."

Moira shook her head. "Wait and see what the man has to say for himself on the morrow, my darling Kitty. If he is Blackthorne and he had wanted to stop the raid, he could have done so. He obviously intended for Patrick to be freed."

Kitt thought about that for a moment. "Maybe you're right. He's weak enough that I can just as easily kill him on the morrow."

"That's looking at the bright side, lass," Moira said with a cackle.

"How is Fletcher?"

"He'll be well enough in a day or two, with a scar to brag about in the tavern."

Kitt closed her eyes and gripped her hands together as though in prayer. "Thank God."

"I'll fix us some breakfast," Moira said as she retreated, leaving Kitt alone with Alex.

Kitt brought the rocker from the corner and put it beside the bed where she could watch her patient closely. As the morning sun hit her eyes from her bedroom window, she reached out her fingertips and laid them on his throat. His pulse was thready, barely there.

"Someone's coming," Moira called from the other room.

Kitt froze. Where could she run? There was no escape from the house except through the door, and no way to hide Alex's presence.

She was already out of the rocker by the time Moira said, " 'Tis the boy. The one who works for Carlisle. Alex's friend Laddie."

The boy had said he knew Alex, that they had grown up on neighboring farms. Was he in on the hoax? Did he know Alex was the duke? Kitt hurried to the door.

"Milady," the boy said, touching his forelock as he greeted her. "The earl has sent me with a note for you."

"Come inside," Kitt said. She did not want the boy to leave before she had the answers she needed. He took only a couple of steps inside before she purposefully closed the door behind him.

She took the note, broke the wax seal, and almost sighed aloud with relief when she read it.

Lady Katherine,

Urgent business calls me to London. I must regretfully break our riding engagement next week. I look forward already to the day I can see you again.

Yours, etc.,
Carlisle

Kitt looked up at Moira and said, "Carlisle is going to London on business. He doesna expect to be back next week to ride with me."

"There's a bit of luck," Moira replied.

The boy suddenly pointed and stuttered, "W-what's happened to Alex?"

Kitt looked where Laddie was pointing and saw the remnants of the shirt and trousers Alex had been wearing. She had left them on the floor beside the hearth because she had not yet decided whether they could be salvaged or whether she should simply burn them.

"Was Alex hurt on the raid?" the boy asked.

Kitt gasped in alarm. "How do you know about the raid?"

"You canna keep such a thing secret, milady. Fletcher's wife's cousin works in the earl's stable. He told me you planned to free Patrick Simpson from jail, and of course if you went, Alex must go too. Is he hurt badly? Can I see him?"

"What is Alex Wheaton to you?" Kitt demanded. "And dinna lie again and tell me you grew up on neighboring farms."

The boy turned toward the door, but Moira was standing in front of it. He shifted from foot to foot until Kitt pinned him in place with her stare.

"I met Alex by chance at the Ramshead Inn," he blurted.

"Why did you lie for him?"

He shrugged. "He was a stranger who needed my help. I gave it to him."

"He's English," Kitt said flatly. What kind of Scotsman willingly aided the English in these terrible days? And trusted him not to betray them.

The boy pursed his lips. " 'Tis true he spoke with an English accent at first."

"Who is he?" Kitt asked. "What is he doing here?"

"I dinna know," the boy replied earnestly. "Truly. I'm not sure he knows himself."

"What do you mean?"

"When Alex first came to the inn, he came as a beggar. He had no coin to buy food or drink. He promised to pay later, when he could, but when he was questioned, he said he didna know who he was, that he couldna remember."

Kitt looked to Moira. "Is such a thing possible?"

" 'Tis possible to lose one's memory," Moira said. "A blow to the head might cause it."

Kitt stared at Moira, remembering how Alex had looked the first time she'd seen him, recalling the cut on his temple and the lump on his forehead. "How long before his memory returns?"

"It could return in a matter of days, or weeks, or mayhap not at all," Moira said.

"Can I see Alex?" the boy pleaded. "Is he all right?"

"Why do you care?" Kitt asked, her eyes narrowing suspiciously. "If he's a stranger to you?"

"I feel responsible," the boy said. "I was the one who suggested he pretend to be a Scotsman. And I left him on the road to fend for himself. Perhaps if I had taken him directly to Blackthorne Hall, as he asked—"

"He was headed for Blackthorne Hall?" Kitt asked, aghast.

"Because he hoped someone there—some Englishman—might know him," the boy explained.

And well they might have, Kitt thought, if he really was the duke.

"Please, can I see him?" the boy repeated.

"Of course," Kitt agreed. "Come with me."

She led him into the bedroom. The sheets were twisted around Alex, revealing his injured back and leg, leaving him barely covered.

Kitt was surprised at the sudden tears in the boy's eyes. There must be more to his relationship with Alex than he'd admitted. "Tears for a stranger?" she questioned.

He met her gaze and said, "I was only thinking how we can never know from one moment to the next what misadventure might turn our lives in another direction. When I helped Alex, I was thinking of my own brothers and sisters. They might be needing a stranger's help someday."

She watched him clench his teeth to keep from breaking down altogether. "Can you tell me anything more about Alex?"

"He could remember having monogrammed handkerchiefs," he said with a half smile. "And he offered me a job as his valet."

"Oh, my God," Kitt whispered. *He must be the duke.* "What?"

"Nothing." She dared not reveal what she knew to

Laddie. He worked for the earl, and he was the duke's friend.

"Did you ever notice that Alex matches the description of the duke?" the boy mused.

"He does?" she said, her heart caught in her throat.

"The Runner described Blackthorne as a tall man with gray eyes, a fine, straight nose, and blond hair."

Kitt stared at Alex. "He fits the description, all right. Except for the nose." *It will never be straight again*, she thought as she eased her finger along the new ridge where it had been broken.

"But he canna be the duke," the boy said, shaking his head.

"Why not?" Kitt asked.

"Who would dare give such a beating to a duke?" the boy wondered aloud. "Who would want him dead?"

Kitt stood stunned for a moment. She had never thought of the duke's situation in those terms. Perhaps he had taken an assumed identity because he was hiding from whoever had tried to kill him the first time. "Perhaps his brother wants him dead. Or his wife."

"The duke is a widower."

She felt a surge of relief. "How do you know?"

"I had it from the underfootman who had it from Cook at Blackthorne Hall. The duchess was foxed and fell down the stairs at Blackthorne Abbey three years ago."

Or was pushed? Kitt thought with a shudder. She stared at the man lying in her bed. No, she would not believe it of him. But what should she do with him?

Did she dare give him back into the hands of whoever might want him dead? She could not leave him so unprotected. But what if he lived, and he really was the duke? What revenge would he be likely to take against her, knowing she had intended to trick him into marriage?

"Is there a place you can keep Alex safe until he's well?" the boy asked.

Kitt met Laddie's worried eyes. "I could take him to a cave in the mountains where my grandfather hid from the English. But I couldna stay there long without raising suspicion."

"I can say you went to visit your aunt Louisa," Moira suggested.

"I suppose that would work," Kitt said, "Since the earl canceled our riding engagement for next week." Now she felt sorry that he had done so. She needed to be married to him before the duke recovered... if he recovered.

"I'll carry messages for you," the boy volunteered, "and bring you whatever supplies you need until Alex is well enough to resume his duties."

"We cannot simply disappear overnight like this," Kitt protested.

"Why not?" Laddie said. "'Twould be the safest thing for both of you. The soldiers are out and about today, looking for whoever broke Patrick Simpson out of jail. They're sure to come searching here eventually, and if they find Alex..."

"How can I move him? I have no horse, no cart—"

"I'll manage that, milady. Give me time enough to return to the earl's stable. Fletcher's wife's cousin will loan me a nag and a cart if I say I have errands to run for his lordship. You be ready to go when I return."

Kitt opened her mouth to protest but thought better of it. Laddie was right. The safest thing to do was to disappear. That way she would be alone with Alex when he regained consciousness. She could find out the truth without anyone there to know what she did when Alex told her who he really was.

She put a hand to Alex's head. "He's burning up with fever."

"Mayhap he'll not last until ye can move him," Moira said.

"He must live!" Kitt said fiercely.

"Why?"

"Because I made a vow to my father. And, one way or another, I intend to keep it."

Chapter 13

"THAT BOW STREET RUNNER WAS ASKING QUES-
tions again," the earl said, pacing the stone
floor of the library at Blackthorne Hall. "I'm sure he
believes there was some foul play involved in the duke's
disappearance. I have canceled my riding engagement
with Lady Katherine. Nothing else holds me here. I believe it would be best if I returned, at least temporarily,
to London."

"The Runner can know nothing for sure," Mr.
Ambleside said from his seat behind the Sheraton desk
in the corner.

"He's heard the stories about The MacKinnon's
bodyguard. The man is a stranger to the neighborhood,
and he matches the duke's description."

"You've seen the bodyguard. You've spoken to him.
Was it the duke?" Mr. Ambleside asked with an arched
brow.

"He was arrogant enough!" Carlisle retorted. He shook his head. "But he sounded like a Scotsman."

"What did he look like?"

"Like he'd been in a mill. He had a bump on his nose and a yellowing bruise around his eye and a scab through his eyebrow. Oh, dear God. Why did I not make the connection sooner? He must have been badly beaten. Those idiots! They did not finish the job. It must be the duke!"

"Now, now," Mr. Ambleside said in a soothing voice. "We must not panic, my lord."

"Panic? I am far beyond panic, sir. I am ready to throw myself on the mercy——"

Mr. Ambleside rose and stepped in front of the earl, who was forced to stop pacing. "The Runner can prove nothing without talking to this mysterious stranger, and the man has disappeared entirely from the neighborhood."

"Along with Lady Katherine," the earl interjected. "Do you not find that suspicious?"

"The Runner could not find them where they said they were going," Mr. Ambleside said calmly. "That does not mean they may not show up here at any moment."

"If the duke is alive, I shall confess everything and——"

Mr. Ambleside had kept the pistol behind his back, not wishing to alarm the earl unduly or prematurely. But sometimes it was necessary to make one's point with something more threatening than words. He brought the pistol out from behind his back and aimed it at the earl's heart. "I would not advise baring your soul to anyone, my lord."

"You would not dare to shoot a peer of the realm. How would you explain yourself?" the earl said contemptuously.

"I would say I had caught the mysterious thief of Blackthorne Hall in the act and was forced to defend myself."

Mr. Ambleside had never seen such a comical expression as the one that appeared on Carlisle's face. Shock, of course. Incredulity. And then such fury that he feared the young man would expire of an apoplexy.

"You could not— You would not—"

"I can and I will," Mr. Ambleside said. "I have planned for too many years, and my goal is too close, to lose everything now. There is no reason why we cannot continue exactly as we planned. Blackthorne is dead. You will insist Lord Marcus honor your contract to purchase the land."

"I won't do it."

Mr. Ambleside bit the inside of his cheek to keep from laughing aloud at the puppy's performance. But he had to admire the lad's bottom. Not many men would shout defiance in the face of a loaded pistol. There was more to Clay Bannister than he had at first thought. Which, he admitted to himself with a sigh, only complicated matters.

"It seems we will have to find the stranger ourselves," he said. "If only to confirm he is not the duke."

He watched hope light the earl's despairing eyes.

"Do you think there is any chance he is *not* the duke?" Carlisle asked.

"I think there is every chance he is merely a stranger who arrived in the neighborhood at a propitious moment," Mr. Ambleside said. "Now, what else can you tell me about him?"

"What was it Lady Katherine said his name was?" the earl muttered. "Walton? Weldon? Warden?"

"Wharton?" Mr. Ambleside said in a hushed voice.

"No, that was not it. Aha! Wheaton. Alex Wheaton."

Mr. Ambleside caught sight of the arrested expression on his own face in the gilded mirror beside the door. A stranger named Alex Wheaton. A duke named Alastair Wharton. Was it merely coincidence? He did not think so. A disguise, then. The duke must have survived. That he had not come directly to Blackthorne Hall must mean he was suspicious of the welcome he would receive.

The quiver that ran through Mr. Ambleside left him feeling more alive than afraid. So. His quarry had escaped.

The hunt was on again.

If Kitt had known how desperately ill Alex would become, she might not have been so willing to disappear with him. His fever worsened, and the things he said in his delirium only confirmed her belief that he was the Duke of Blackthorne.

He spoke of racing curricles. And Oxford. Of his

town house in London. And his beloved Blackthorne Abbey. Of falling in love. And being frightened the lady would not accept him. Of his brother's betrayal. And his daughters, Regina and Rebecca, whom he loved, but from whom he was estranged. It had all poured out of him, the entire history of a man's life.

She wished he had remained mute. At least then she could have held on more tightly to her resentment for all the dastardly duke had done. It was not so easy to hate a man who revealed himself to be a vulnerable lover. Not so easy to hate a man who cried over his brother's betrayal, who adored his children, who had learned to despise his wife, but had nevertheless grieved her death.

There was a great deal more to Alex Wheaton than she had ever imagined. There was a great deal more to the Duke of Blackthorne as well. She could not believe that the mere loss of his memory had changed the duke into an entirely different person. Which meant that when she had been with Alex, she had been with the duke.

It was impossible to reconcile the two men.

It was Blackthorne who had sent Leith away to his death. Blackthorne who had mercilessly raised the rents thrice over the past year. And she did not doubt he had come to Scotland originally, as her father had predicted, to dissuade her from pursuing her claim for Blackthorne Hall in the courts.

How could she have learned to care for such a man? How could she have fallen a little in love with him?

It would have been easier if she did not have all those memories of Alex touching her ... kissing her ... protecting her with his own body. It would have been easier if she had not been forced to lay hands on him, to touch every part of his muscular frame with a cool, damp cloth to bring down his fever. The attraction was there, as much as she wished it were not.

On their tenth day in the cave, Alex's fever had been so fierce, she had been certain he would die. She had not been able to rid herself of the bond of desperation that gripped her chest, the knot of despair that made her throat ache, the tears that fell hot upon her cheeks. Or the guilt of caring so much for the man who was responsible for doing so much harm to her people.

She convinced herself there was an explanation for everything, an excuse for the duke's dastardly behavior, some miracle that would prove Alex innocent of all the cruel deeds Blackthorne had committed. She clung to that hope like a drowning man to a piece of driftwood.

She would have gone mad without Laddie's presence. The boy made the hour-long walk up into the mountains every night after his work for the earl was done. He had held her hand during those long, early morning hours when Alex gasped for breath, when she was certain each one would be his last.

"Talk to me, Laddie," she had pleaded.

"The Runner searching for the duke has been at Blackthorne Hall for two full weeks but is no closer to finding Blackthorne. He's searched the neighborhood twice over and has asked a lot of questions about Alex."

"Do you think he suspects Alex is the duke?"

"I dinna know. But no one helped him, ye may be sure of that. An Englishman and a man of the law— 'twas a combination no one could like," he said with a grin.

"I suppose not. How long is he likely to keep looking?"

"I heard he's giving up the search," Laddie said. "That's he's to go back to London within the week."

"Any word on Patrick Simpson?"

"Only that he and his family got to the coast and took ship for America."

Kitt sighed with relief. "One thing went right, at least."

"The soldiers havna given up searching for him. They suspect it was some of his clansmen who broke him out of jail, but everyone was in the fields working the next morning, so who could they blame?" He grinned and said, "It seems the culprits had their faces concealed, and the two drunken soldiers canna agree whether it was two men or two dozen that attacked them."

"The soldiers didna think it suspicious that I was missing from home?"

"Ye're a woman, milady. No female person would be involved in such a raid."

Kitt smiled ruefully, though a moment before she would have sworn it was impossible to smile.

"The soldiers have also been watching to see if anyone has money to spend," Laddie added with a twinkle in his eye.

"Why is that?"

"They're looking for the mysterious burglar who emptied the duke's coffers at Blackthorne Hall."

"He could surely spare what we took," Kitt said.

"So you and Alex did do it!" the boy crowed. "I thought as much."

Kitt was mortified that she had given them away. Too tired to guard her tongue, she was surely at the boy's mercy now, with him an employee of the earl and freely coming and going.

"Mr. Ambleside has offered a reward for information leading to the capture of the thief."

"If you try to collect it, Laddie," she said in direst tones, "I'll come back and haunt you—"

"I'm sorry to interrupt ye, milady, but I canna believe ye think so little of me. I'd cut off my arm before I'd do anything to harm ye. I've no reason to love the English," he said bitterly. "My own father was English and—But that is a story for another day," he said. "Dinna fash yerself. 'Twill all come right again. Watch and see. Alex will live. He's too strong to die."

Laddie was proved right. But it was almost three weeks before Alex was himself again and another week beyond that before Kitt felt he was strong enough to endure an interrogation. By then, she didn't think she could wait another moment to ask the questions that had been simmering inside her. But wait she did.

She awoke one morning to find Alex sitting up on the pallet she had made for him on the cave floor. It was the first time he had woken before her. She hurried over to crouch beside him. "Can you manage? Do you need help?"

He took the hand she offered to steady himself and carefully sat up, leaning his newly healed back against the stone wall of the cave.

"I must confess I'm a little dizzy, but I feel almost like my old self. How long was I unwell?"

"A long time. You had a fever for nearly three weeks."

He lifted the blanket that covered him and looked beneath it. "Have you been my nurse all this time?"

Kitt felt herself flushing. He was naked now and had been for most of that time, and yes, she was intimately acquainted with every part of his body. "Laddie helped me."

He gently brushed one of her rosy cheeks with his knuckles. "Thank you, Kitt."

" 'Tis Lady—"

He shot her a devilish grin. "Surely, after this, we can dispense with such formality."

Kitt rose and stepped away from his touch. She did not want to be charmed by him. Not when she still had so many questions for him. "You're not really Alex Wheaton, are you?" she blurted.

"Did I say something while I was out of my head that suggested to you that I am someone other than who I said I am."

"You said a great deal."

His eyes looked troubled. "Then you are in a better position to know my identity than I am. I must confess, I dinna know who I am, exactly."

Kitt frowned. "How can you not know who you are?"

His eyes remained locked on hers. "I canna remember," he said simply. "I woke up on the rocks along the coast the day before I met you, with no memory of my past."

If it was true, it explained a great deal that had previously mystified Kitt. No duke would willingly spend the night on a bed of straw or take the job of bodyguard when his only wages were a roof over his head and food to fill his belly. Unless he did not *know* he was a duke.

But Alex *had* known who he was. She had asked him, and he had plainly told her *"I am Blackthorne."*

Except he had been delirious with fever at the time. Was it possible he could have spilled so much information about himself while he was delirious and yet not remember any of it now? Surely he was pretending ignorance.

But she could think of no purpose it would serve. Why would he take such a chance with his life? Surely if he had known he was Blackthorne he would have demanded the services of a proper English doctor.

Which meant it was entirely possible Alex was the Duke of Blackthorne. And that he had lost his memory when he'd been beaten.

Tell him, Kitt. Admit the truth now, before you make the situation any worse than it already is.

"Alex, I . . ." She wanted to confess her deceit. She wanted to tell him who she suspected he was. But there was too much at stake. What if, when his memory returned, he was not Alex, but that unscrupulous Blackthorne bastard?

"What have I told you about myself?" Alex said. "I have a great many holes in my memory."

"I know you're an Englishman."

"Uh-oh. So I'm one of the enemy. I suppose I can give up this Scots accent, then."

"I dinna think that's such a good idea, Alex. Ian and Fletcher and Duncan and the rest willna understand my having an Englishman as a bodyguard. I think you must keep it for a while yet. I mean, so long as you are my *gille-coise*."

"If you think I should, then of course I will. Did you learn anything more about me?"

He looked anxious, worried. She was afraid to tell him too much. "What do you remember about yourself?"

He frowned. "Not much. Except I know I must have been to Blackthorne Hall as a child."

"Why do you say that?"

"When we were stealing from the duke, we passed by a closed door in the upstairs hallway, and I knew what was behind it. I suppose I must have been acquainted with the duke as a child."

"Why did you not go straight to Blackthorne Hall and present yourself to Mr. Ambleside?" she asked.

"I considered doing that, but I wasna sure whether I would be welcome there." He hesitated again, then added, "When I woke up on shore, I'd been stripped and my hands were bound. It seemed to me someone did not want me coming out of the sea. I wasna sure who I could trust."

Kitt stared at Alex with wide eyes. She had seen the marks on his wrists, she simply had not realized the significance of them. *Someone had tried to murder the duke!* Whom had he offended? Who would benefit most from his death?

Certainly the duke was not on good terms with his brother, Lord Marcus. And Lord Marcus had sent a Bow Street Runner to search high and low for any sign of Blackthorne . . . so he could finish the job?

Kitt once again opened her mouth to tell Alex who she believed he was and the danger she believed he was in but closed it again. According to Moira, if Alex had already begun to remember his previous life, it was likely the rest would come to him sooner or later. Before it did, she had an unexpected opportunity.

She could fulfill her promise to her father to trick Blackthorne into a handfast marriage and get herself with child. She had thought long and hard about whether she ought to go through with her father's scheme. But nothing had changed, so far as she could see. The castle and the land still belonged to Blackthorne, and having Blackthorne's son was a more certain way to regain it than relying on the courts.

On the other hand, everything had changed, because she knew the man she was about to deceive. And liked him. She might even have fallen in love with him if the circumstances had been different. And she knew that when he found out, Alex would not only be angry, he would be deeply hurt by her dishonesty.

But she did not believe she had any choice.

She knew Alex found her attractive. At the moment, he was even grateful to her for saving his life. Oh, yes. It would be quite possible to get him to couple with her while he was still unaware that he was Blackthorne.

And to be honest, she desired him as much as she believed he desired her. She could honestly give herself to him in exchange for the seed she would take from him. Perhaps it was not a fair exchange, but it was all she could offer.

Alex caught her staring at him and asked, "Is there something else I should know?"

She took a deep breath and let it out. "I . . . You . . . You had a wife," she said at last. "She died."

When she saw the pain in his eyes, Kitt was sorry she had mentioned his wife. She was playing with fire to tell him even that much. The more she told him, the more he would want to know. He was not a stupid man. If she told him too much, he might figure it all out more quickly. And then . . .

Kitt did not let herself dwell on what would happen when Alex regained his memory and learned what she had done. By then, if she were lucky, his bairn would already be growing inside her. She would lose Alex, but she would have the child who would be the salvation of her people.

"Halloooo!"

Kitt jumped up when she heard the call from the mouth of the cave. It wasn't Laddie, because they had worked out a signal between them. She kicked out the fire and blew out the lantern that sat on the small table nearby. "Shh!" she warned Alex. "Be still. It may be a shepherd has stumbled upon the cave accidentally."

Or it might be the soldiers, who had caught up to them at last.

Kitt's mind was racing to figure out how she could keep the soldiers from entering the cave and discovering Alex. It would seem odd for her to be there by herself, but perhaps she could say she had retreated to the cave on the anniversary of some special date.

Two figures in homespun loomed in the entrance to the cave, one large and one small. Not soldiers, then, but who could have found her here?

"Lady Katherine? Is that you?"

"Duncan!" Kitt felt her eyes mist with tears of relief. "Thank God it is you. Who is with you?"

" 'Tis Ian MacDougal, Lady Katherine."

"Ian." The joy left Kitt's heart as quickly as it had come. "How did you find me?"

"Did you think we would not know where you had gone?" Ian said. "Has he died yet?"

"I'm not likely to die anytime soon, if I can help it," a voice said from the shadows.

Knowing who Alex was, Kitt was not surprised to see the authority in his posture when he stepped into the sunlight at the entrance to the cave. He had draped a MacKinnon plaid around himself to cover his nakedness. Except for the ragged beard on his face and his pale complexion, he looked every bit as powerful as he had before the raid.

He took two more steps forward and put his arm around her waist in a gesture that was not only protective, but possessive. "This was worth getting out of bed for," he said, smiling down at her.

"You've taken her to bed?" Ian said angrily. "I should have known better than to leave you two alone for so long. We should have come two weeks ago, Duncan, when I first asked."

"You know the Runner would have followed us," Duncan said. "We couldna take the chance of coming here before he was gone."

"See what your delay has wrought?" Ian said. "She's given herself to him!" He turned on Alex and said, "I should kill you—"

" 'Twas my choice to make!" Kitt interrupted. She was furious with Ian for jumping to conclusions, and angry enough to let him believe the lie for a little longer. "If I chose to lie with Alex, to make him my husband, 'twas because I believe he will make a better chief than any other man."

"Is that true, Alex?" Duncan said. "Have you taken her to wife?"

Kitt's mouth was open to explain the lie, when Alex replied, "If Kitt says we are man and wife, then 'tis true."

Kitt's heart skipped a beat.

Ian turned purple with rage.

Duncan seemed unaffected by Alex's momentous announcement. He merely said, "I wish you both happy. Congratulations, Alex." He extended his hand, and as Kitt looked on in mute disbelief, Alex shook it.

"I'll not wish you well," Ian said. "I hope the fever comes back and kills you. And if it does not, then mayhap I will."

"I dinna think I care for your threats, Ian," Alex said.

"Anytime you want to make a fight of it, I'm ready," Ian said.

"That pleasure will have to wait. My wife and I are still enjoying our honeymoon."

Alex leaned over and kissed Kitt on the mouth. She stared up at him, dazed by his audacity, wondering what kind of courage—or idiocy—it took to provoke a wild animal like Ian MacDougal.

"When will you be returning home?" Duncan asked.

"Soon," Kitt managed to reply.

"Not too soon," Alex contradicted, his hand sliding down to her waist as he pulled her closely against him, his eyes meeting hers with a look that was avid enough to curl her toes. "You're free to leave, Ian, now that you've learned what you came to find out."

"Who are you to be giving orders!" Ian snarled.

"The MacKinnon," Alex said in a quiet voice.

Kitt would never forget the surprise on Ian's face. Or the rage that quickly followed. If Duncan had not been there to lead him away, Ian might very well have attacked Alex. And since he was shaky on his feet, Kitt wasn't at all sure Alex would have come away the winner.

Once Ian and Duncan were gone, Alex wrapped his arm tightly around her waist and sagged against her. "Help me back to bed, Kitt, before I fall down where I am."

"Why did you provoke Ian?" she asked as she helped him stagger back into the cave and settled him once again on the pallet. "You should have let me handle him."

" 'Twas worth the lie to see the look on his face when he heard me say we were husband and wife," he said with a grin. " 'Twas a good joke, Kitt. I hope there'll be no trouble when we return, and you tell everyone the truth."

Alex sat down on the pallet, his shoulder angled against the wall so his wounded back did not touch it. Kitt sat beside him, their hands still clasped.

Kitt was caught in a trap she had set herself.

She could tell Alex who he was and set him free of the vow he had unknowingly made. Or she could perpetrate the fraud that would ultimately give her the power and position to save her clan.

Tell him the truth. Tell him that in Scotland, when a woman declares she is married to a man and he confirms it before witnesses, 'tis as binding as vows in the kirk.

Kitt leaned her head against his shoulder. "Alex ... what if I didna want it to be a lie? What if I wanted us to be husband and wife?" She turned her face up to his, waiting for his reply.

He smiled at her and lowered his mouth to kiss her gently on the lips. "Let's pretend for a while longer, then, shall we?"

Chapter 14

 As they settled onto the pallet that had been Alex's bed, their backs braced against the stone wall of the cave, Kitt found it hard to resist Alex's kisses. She had been attracted to him from the start, but what she had wanted for herself had always been in conflict with what was necessary to save her people. Now that she had her heart's desire, the man in question had turned out to be her bitterest enemy! How strange life was. How very ironic.

It seemed somehow wrong to enjoy herself so much when she was deceiving Alex. And yet Kitt could not seem to stop herself from touching him. She was like a child who had been denied a treat for too long. She ran her fingers through his hair, and for the first time it was her tongue that went searching in his mouth.

Alex made a guttural sound in his throat and their tongues dueled as his hands went seeking the places where she was most vulnerable. She would have coupled with him then and there if he had not murmured, "I'm afraid I'm not being a very good bodyguard, Kitt. I'm supposed to protect you from importunate gentlemen."

She smiled against his lips. "What if I dinna want to be protected?"

"What about your plans to marry the earl?"

Kitt had not expected Alex to be so suspicious, or so unwilling to take what he had once said he wanted. She nibbled on his lower lip, as she had imagined doing a dozen times, to divert him.

He groaned, then caught her shoulders and pushed her away. "I need an answer, Kitt."

She looked into eyes that had darkened with arousal, searching for an answer that would satisfy him. She found the only truth she knew. "When you were so ill with the fever, when I thought you might die, I had a chance to imagine what my life would be without you. I did not like what I saw."

She saw the hope and yearning in his gray eyes, saw that he was tempted to believe her. But he did not. Not yet.

"What about your clan? They have always come first with you."

"I didna lie when I told Ian you would make a good laird for Clan MacKinnon," she said. "And though I canna like how slowly the courts move, the chances are good I can eventually recover the land and the castle by legal means."

"And until then?"

"We will do as the Scots have always done," she said with a smile. "We will reive."

"I canna say I dinna want you, Kitt," he said. "You know very well I do."

Hearing him speak the words with a Scots burr touched her somewhere deep inside. She could almost believe he was a Scot and not the detestable Englishman she knew he was.

"Then be my husband, Alex."

"How can I, when I dinna even know who I am?"

She laid her palm tenderly against his cheek and looked into his eyes. "I know everything I need to know about you, Alex." And so much more than he realized.

She saw the moment when he threw caution to the wind. When he let the carnal beast inside have what it wanted.

"Very well, Kitt. I willna spit in fate's eye. If you are meant to be mine, then so be it."

His mouth came down on hers in a kiss of claiming, a kiss that took and took before it gave and gave. As his arms closed tightly around her, Kitt felt a sob welling inside. She fought it back, pressing her face hard against his shoulder and accidentally forcing his back against the wall.

"Ah."

It was a small sound, but enough to make her aware of his pain. "Your back must be hurting," she said in a voice muffled against his chest.

" 'Tis my head that worries me," he murmured.

A quiver of fear shot through her. "You've been re-membering?"

"I see things in my head. A green lawn. The room behind the door I told you about."

"Do you remember names? Faces?" she asked anx-iously.

He shook his head. "Nothing that makes any sense."

"I dinna want to wait to say words in the kirk, Alex." He might regain his memory before that could happen. "Make love to me now, please."

She must make love to him as often as she could be-fore his memory returned, to breed an heir to Black-thorne Hall.

Kitt looked deep into Alex's eyes, hoping that he would forgive her when all was said and done. She had never before noticed the spray of age lines at the cor-ners of his eyes. How old was the duke, she wondered? She did not know even that small fact. Blackthorne was and always would be a stranger to her. But what kind of monster might he turn out to be when he was once again himself?

Kitt shivered and Alex pulled her close.

"Are you cold?"

"A little." Deep inside she felt a coldness that had nothing to do with the temperature.

The man holding me in his arms is not the duke. It is Alex. Alex is another person altogether, one I can like and admire.

It was a fiction, but one Kitt needed to believe in to keep her guilt and fear at bay. She clenched her teeth to stop her chin from trembling. She fought back the terror that gripped her insides when she imagined what revenge the duke would take when he found out how she had tricked him.

His eyes were heavy-lidded, his lips full. She kept her eyes locked with his as she reached up with shaking hands to remove the pins from her hair. As he watched, she released her braids until her hair fell free over her shoulders. Then she eased herself back onto the pallet, feeling like nothing so much as a lamb ready for slaughter.

She flinched when Alex reached for her, and it was all she could do not to burst into tears.

"I'll not hurt you, Kitt," he said. "You canna know how much I've wanted you." He smiled down at her as his hands tangled in her hair. "'Tis so soft and silky." He lowered his head, closed his eyes, and breathed deeply. "What perfume is that I smell?"

"'Tis nothing but good Scottish soap."

"I shall never forget it, Kitt. 'Twill always remind me of you."

Kitt closed her eyes and felt Alex's kisses on her eyelids. His lips caressed her cheeks, her nose, her chin, and finally the edge of her mouth. "Alex, I can't—"

His mouth closed over hers, cutting off her confession. And then it was too late. His tongue slid inside, hot and wet and invasive. She heard an animal sound of pleasure and realized it had come from her own throat.

She had never realized how powerful a kiss could be. Her body curled inside as though a drawstring had been pulled tight. Her hips arched toward him with a will of their own. Her arms closed around his shoulders, and her fingernails dug into his flesh.

"Easy," he said. "Easy."

He tugged on her hair to angle her head and slanted his mouth over hers for another penetrating kiss. "I need to be inside you." He lifted her and hugged her close, his breathing harsh in her ear. "Oh, God, Kitt. I dinna want to hurt you. At the loch you said you had seen Leith. Did you— Did he—"

"I am untouched, Alex," she said. " 'Twas my greatest regret when I learned Leith was dead."

"I canna be sorry for it," he said, his voice rough. "I canna be sorry you're to be mine and only mine."

As he undressed her, he worshiped her body. The reverence of his touch and the awe in his eyes made her feel cherished when she was at last naked before him.

He was not wearing much by that time himself. She had returned pleasure for pleasure, touching what she revealed, his chest, his muscular belly, and the part of him she had seen before . . . but not like this.

"You will split me in two," she said in a frightened voice.

"No, Kitt. We are made for each other. You will see."

"But—"

"Come, kiss me again. Let me touch you. And if you will, touch me."

There was so much pleasure in feeling the hardness of muscle and sinew beneath his skin. So much pleasure in running her fingers through the curls on his chest, the salty taste of his shoulder, the satisfied, masculine sounds he made in his throat when she nibbled on his ear.

And there was so much pleasure in what he did to her. His callused hand brushing across her hipbone. His mouth and tongue playing with her breasts and sucking hard enough to draw her insides up tight. His hand moving downward, and then his finger sliding inside her, a sudden exciting, frightening invasion.

He distracted her with more kisses, deep, penetrating kisses, as his fingers caressed her. Kitt began to writhe beneath his touch. She didn't know what to do with her hands, and finally put them around Alex, her fingernails scraping across his skin as the sensations increased to unbearable pleasure.

"Tell me what to do, Alex," she pleaded. "I want to please you." She let her hands slide down the length of his back to his taut buttocks and felt him surge against her. She sought his mouth with hers and thrust her tongue deep inside, returning the torment and delight he was bringing her.

Then his hand was gone and something hard was pushing against her flesh. She felt a moment of panic, remembering the size of him, but his mouth was against hers whispering reassurances. He pinched her breast, and the pain of that distracted her from the instant of greater pain as he breached her.

"Ah!" She tensed her body, fearing more pain. But it did not come. She felt full with him inside her. But it no longer hurt.

He held himself still, but she could feel the tension in his shoulders and back.

" 'Tis done, my love," he said.

"You're done?" she said, surprised and a little disappointed.

He chuckled. "No. I said 'tis done." His voice changed, the humor gone, as he put his hands to either side of her face and forced her to look at him. "You're mine now. Forever."

Kitt felt a shiver of foreboding. She opened her mouth to confess the truth—but never got the chance. His mouth captured hers as his body began to work inside her, the friction creating surprising, exquisitely pleasurable sensations. Before very long, her body joined his in a dance as old as the ages.

Kitt had never dreamed one person could become so much a part of another. Had never expected the surge of emotion that claimed her as Alex spilled his seed inside her. Never imagined the devastating consequences of giving her body to him . . . and discovering she had lost her soul.

'Tis done. I've kept my promise, Father. The duke's seed is planted. May it grow into a fine MacKinnon son.

Alex was sucking air to keep moving. His shirt was stuck to him with sweat, and he had to resist the urge to sit down right where he was. Bloody hell. His body would give only so much and no more.

"Sit down, Alex, before ye fall down," Mick advised.

He was not far from a boulder beneath an alder tree, and Alex forced himself to walk the few steps to reach it. "I need to get my strength back," he said as he sank onto the stone.

Mick plopped down in the grass at his feet, shifted his rump away from a thistle, and plucked out a left-over barb. "Ye've been walking for hours, uphill and down. A well man could barely manage it," the boy said. "Why are ye pushing yerself so hard?"

"When I come down out of the mountains and marry Lady Katherine, I'll be The MacKinnon," Alex said. "I must be ready for whatever challenges are thrown my way."

"In other words, ye've got to be ready to fight Ian MacDougal."

Alex laughed aloud. "That's plain speaking, Laddie. It may not come to that, but I'm not taking any chances."

"I dinna understand why ye insist on marrying when ye dinna know who ye are," Mick muttered.

"We've been through this before. I'm sure 'tis only coincidence that I bear some resemblance to the duke. If I were such a grand personage I wouldna be likely to enjoy your company, now would I? 'Tis just as likely I'm a nobody from nowhere." Alex thought it was entirely possible he was a thief. He seemed to have some skill at the trade. "Mayhap when my memory does return, I'll wish it to Hades."

"Shouldn't ye at least go to Blackthorne Hall and let the steward get a look at you?" Mick said. "Then ye'd know for certain one way or the other."

"I'll see Mr. Ambleside once I'm The MacKinnon," Alex said in a hard voice. "To tell him what I think of the bloody Duke of Blackthorne. Any man who could ignore the plight of his tenants is a greedy bastard, and I intend to say so."

"There you are!"

"Here I am," Alex said with a smile, holding out a hand to Kitt, who had just come over a rise and was headed straight for him. She was dressed in a simple skirt and blouse and had a woolen shawl wrapped around her shoulders for warmth. A gust of wind rustled her skirt and treated him to a glimpse of her trim ankles. Her coal-black hair whipped wildly around her face, and it was all he could do not to reach out and grasp a handful of it.

Her delicate black brows were set in a worried frown. "I've been looking everywhere for you."

"I've been walking." Before Kitt could drop to the ground beside Mick, he grasped her hand and pulled her into his lap. "This will be more comfortable than the hard ground," he assured her.

"Alex, you canna be acting like this in front of Laddie," she protested.

"I'll be taking myself off," Mick said, jumping to his feet.

"Dinna go," Alex said. "I want to hear the latest news about Carlisle. Kitt doesna really mind, do you, Kitt?"

Alex watched the boy look to Kitt for permission to stay, then drop back onto his haunches. "What is it ye want to know, Alex?"

"Is it true the earl's gone to London to see the duke's solicitor about purchasing Blackthorne Hall?"

Alex felt Kitt tense in his lap. They both knew the chance she'd taken when she committed herself to him instead of the earl. All might be lost, if Carlisle was successful.

"Aye," Mick said. "But I dinna think even the earl expects his journey will end in success, milady." Mick said. "He scowled something fierce when he got the last correspondence from Lord Marcus. It seems the duke's brother was badly wounded at Waterloo and has gone into seclusion. Lord Marcus said he would do nothing for a year at least."

"There, you see? You have no worries, for a year at least," Alex said to Kitt.

She wriggled in his lap, angling herself to face him, and he suddenly wished he hadn't encouraged Mick to stay. He clamped a hand on her thigh to keep her still.

"What if Lord Marcus has authorized his solicitor to act in his stead?" she asked. "What if Carlisle convinces the solicitor that the contract is valid and should be honored?"

"Then we have a problem," Alex conceded. "How is your lawsuit against the duke faring? When was the last time you heard from your solicitor?"

"Two months ago, at least," Kitt said.

"Then perhaps 'tis time the laird of Clan MacKinnon and his lady paid him a visit to see what is causing the delay."

"You mean go all the way to London ourselves?" Kitt said.

"Why not?" Alex said. "We can leave as soon as we're married."

"That means three weeks for the banns to be read," Kitt reminded him.

"So be it. In three weeks we'll be off for London."

"We canna afford such a trip," Kitt said.

"The lord provides for those in need," Alex replied with a grin.

"You're planning to play Robin Hood again."

"Can I come with you?" Mick asked, his blue eyes sparkling with excitement.

"To London?" Alex asked.

"No, to rob the duke!"

Alex laughed. "Down, Laddie. This time I'm not even taking Kitt with me."

"You canna leave me behind," Kitt protested. "I am—" She cut herself off and met his eyes. She was no longer The MacKinnon. She no longer needed to jump into the fray. Alex was there to lead. He was there to serve her every need. Especially her most urgent need to provide an heir who could inherit Blackthorne Hall.

Kitt looked so disappointed that Alex almost offered to include her. But that was foolish. He knew his way around the castle now, and it was bound to be more dangerous since the house was alerted to the possibility of a thief in the night.

"What if Mr. Ambleside is no longer keeping the duke's funds in the same place?" Kitt said.

Alex stroked his chin. "Perhaps you can be of some use to me, Laddie."

"What can I do?" Mick asked.

"Who's most likely, besides Mr. Ambleside himself, to know where the duke's funds are kept?"

"The duke's steward would not bother hiding his business from the maid-of-all-work, since she's of no account to him. And 'tis likely she does some work in every part of the house. She may know," Mick said.

"Shall we see how charming you can be with the young lady?" Alex said with a teasing smile.

Mick flushed. "I'm—" His voice broke and the flush intensified to something like a scarlet rash on his face. "I'm up to the task."

"Good," Alex said. "As soon as you find out where the funds are hidden, let me know. Off with you now."

Mick bounced to his feet as though they were loaded with springs. Alex couldn't even imagine that kind of energy.

"The next time I see you will be at the bottom of the mountain," Alex said. "We'll be leaving here tomorrow."

"Are you sure ye're well enough?" Mick asked.

"I'm well enough."

Once Mick was gone, Alex turned his attention to the woman in his arms. "You're awfully quiet."

"I'm thinking."

"I'm afraid to ask," he said with a smile. "But I will. What's on your mind?"

"I'm thinking I canna wait to make love to you

until we get back to the cave," Kitt said, caressing the hair at his nape.

Alex felt a jolt of sexual awareness. It seemed he was not as tired from his morning walk as he'd thought. "There's no privacy here, lass," he said in a husky voice.

She slid off his lap, took his hand, and pulled him down onto the cool grass beside her. " 'Tis shaded from the sun here. The grass is soft. Ouch! Mostly soft," she corrected, as she laid her shawl over an offending this-tle. "And the stone will hide us from prying eyes."

She placed his hand on her breast so Alex could feel the pebbled tip against his palm.

"If we keep this up, 'tis likely we'll have people counting on their fingers when our first child comes," he said with a grin.

"I dinna care."

" 'Tis only three weeks to have the banns—"

"I canna wait even three hours, Alex. I want you now."

There was no more argument, no more teasing de-lay. Over the past few days, Kitt had had cause to wish there was a way she could detach her mind from her body so she could allow Alex to use her body without the rest of her being present. But body and soul—a very anguished soul—lay beneath him now.

It seemed she could hate everything Blackthorne was and still want Alex. The problem was, this idyllic interlude could not last forever. Eventually his memory would come back, or someone would recognize him.

And then she would have to pay the price for the pleasure she took now.

Kitt kept her eyes closed, but it was impossible not to feel the heat of Alex's body as he spread her legs with his knees and settled himself between her thighs.

"Am I too heavy?" he asked.

"No." It felt good. Wonderful. She did not feel like the martyr she had expected to become. She forced herself to relax, to welcome Alex's touches, to feel them and respond. She did not have to try very hard.

The duke was a very good lover.

Apparently there were some things that were not forgotten even when one's memory was for all intents and purposes gone. Alex had told her he couldn't remember being with another woman. But he must have known the exquisite sensations she would feel when his mouth closed over her breast, when his teeth nipped and his tongue teased. He must have known that if he suckled her throat, her insides would draw up tight in such an exquisitely lovely way.

Kit moaned, an animal sound of rage and frustration and desire. She felt too much. Wanted too much. And despised herself more every moment because of it. "Hurry, Alex," she begged.

"Patience, love," he said, his voice roughened by desire.

She gripped him tightly at the waist as he lowered his head, kissing his way down her stomach. She felt his silky hair against her thighs before his mouth closed over her, his lips and tongue creating new and unbearably exquisite feelings.

"Alex," she gasped. "What are you doing?"

"Loving you."

Oh, dinna love me. Dinna add that guilt to all the rest. Dinna add that wrong to all the others I will have to pay for.

She planted her feet and arched her body high, higher, until she thought her back would break, reaching for satisfaction that seemed beyond her grasp.

And then the waves broke over her, painful and wonderful. "Alex," she cried. "Oh, Alex."

Alex exulted in the rapture he saw on Kitt's face. He had been afraid of offending her, but he had wanted to taste her, and it had been as wonderful as . . .

He remembered wanting to do this with a woman, but he could never remember doing it. Perhaps he had not. Perhaps this was the first time. Any other time could not have been as exciting, could not have brought him this much joy and pleasure. A man could not feel more than he was feeling right now, could he?

Alex had waited to take his own pleasure, waited to put himself inside her. He could wait no longer. She was still slick when he slid inside her. He saw the surprise in her eyes and said, "There is more pleasure to be had. Much more." He withdrew and thrust again. And again.

He watched Kitt's face as she began to arch into him, press against him, thrust with him. He knew there must be a way to slow everything down, to give her more pleasure and take more himself, but he could not think what it was. His body had taken over and was driving toward relief. He drew his head back and gave a cry of triumph and joy as he spilled his seed within her.

He slid to her side and pulled her into his arms and held her close. "You're shivering," he said. "Are you all right?" He was sinking into sleep when she finally whispered a reply.

"I'm fine, Alex," she said. As fine as any woman could be when she was deceiving a man who loved her.

Chapter 15

MR. AMBLESIDE HEARD THE LIBRARY DOOR OPEN, but didn't look up from the account books he was perusing. He had told Harper he didn't want to be disturbed. He waited a full two minutes, but when the butler didn't remove himself, he heaved a sigh and said, "I said no interruptions, Harper."

"There's a man at the door claiming he's soon to be the new laird of Clan MacKinnon," the butler replied.

Mr. Ambleside didn't reveal by so much as a twitch how astonishing he found this announcement. Before the earl had left for London, he had assured Mr. Ambleside that Lady Katherine seemed amenable to his suit. It seemed Carlisle had been wrong.

Mr. Ambleside chided himself for being so complacent. The lady had delayed so long in making her choice, he had assumed she found no particular man among her clansmen to her liking. He would need to take the man's measure, and if he was going to be trouble, the situation would need to be handled immediately.

The actual meaning of Harper's words dawned on him then: "Soon to be laird." The wedding was still in the future, which meant all was not lost.

"Show him in, Harper." Mr. Ambleside dipped his pen in the crystal inkwell and marked a notation in one of the columns of figures. He intended to let this Scotsman stand and wait to be recognized, much as he had done with Harper. It would put the man in his place without having to say a word. He heard the library door open and close but didn't look up to see his newest nemesis.

"I'm Alex Wheaton."

Mr. Ambleside recognized the name and immediately made the connection. *Alex Wheaton. Alastair Wharton.* Good God. Was it the duke?

He looked up and found himself staring into the merciless gray eyes of the Duke of Blackthorne. He came out of his chair as though he'd discovered his ass was perched on an anthill.

"Your—" He couldn't even get out the words *Your Grace.* He had to stop to swallow down the vomit that was threatening to erupt from his belly. Acid burned the back of his throat. He had not seen Blackthorne since the duke's marriage, eleven years ago. But it was not a face one forgot. "Your visit is a surprise," he managed to say.

"I expect so," the duke replied.

Blackthorne's eyes were cold and unfriendly, and

Mr. Ambleside summoned all of his inner strength to keep from visibly trembling.

"I've come to speak with you about the rents."

"The rents?" Mr. Ambleside didn't recognize his own voice. It was the constriction in his throat, of course, that made it sound like the squeal of a mouse being crushed in a cat's jaws.

"They're too high," the duke said. "Much too high."

"I can explain that."

"I'm listening."

"Would you like to sit down?" Mr. Ambleside asked, gesturing toward the two wing chairs before the fire. Perhaps His Grace would look less intimidating if he wasn't towering over him by a full head.

"No," the duke replied. "This isna a social visit."

For the first time, Mr. Ambleside noticed the accent. He had been too frightened at first to hear much of anything but the pounding of his own blood in his ears. But English dukes did not go around saying *isna*. His brain was scrambling for an explanation for that oddity when it dawned on him that the duke had announced himself as *Alex Wheaton*, not *Alastair Wharton*, or even *Blackthorne*.

Mr. Ambleside stared hard at the man standing before him. Maybe it was not the duke. Maybe it was someone with a similar name who looked a great deal like him. Enough like him to be his twin, except for the broken nose and the scar through his right eyebrow and the clothes. He wore belted trousers and a blousy shirt and a dirk, and had wrapped himself in the MacKinnon plaid.

But the duke had been severely beaten, and his own clothes, as Mr. Ambleside had cause to know, had been stolen. And the name, Alex Wheaton, so very close to Alastair Wharton? No. There were too many coincidences. The man had to be the duke.

But if so, where had he been all this time? Why hadn't the Bow Street Runner found him? And why arrive at Blackthorne Hall speaking like a Scotsman and calling himself Alex Wheaton and claiming to be the new laird of Clan MacKinnon? A game played by a bored aristocrat? Or something more sinister. A trick to make his steward betray himself?

Mr. Ambleside didn't understand what was going on, but decided he might as well err on the side of caution and delay pleading for mercy until he had asked a few more questions.

"I'm waiting," the duke said.

For an explanation of the high rents, Mr. Ambleside realized. Well, he might as well cover his tracks now as later. He reached into the fob pocket of his waistcoat and retrieved a key on a short chain, then crossed to the bookcase closest to the windows. He pushed a lever on the inside of the third shelf and the entire bookcase moved outward. He pulled it fully away from the wall, revealing a false wall that contained a tall iron safe.

He used the key to open the safe and pulled out a sheaf of papers from one of the shelves, letters he'd previously forged with the duke's signature in the event anyone, including the duke himself, ever inquired about the exorbitant rents. If questioned, he planned to plead his strict obedience to duty. They were very good forgeries.

He methodically closed and relocked the safe, then realigned the bookcase and turned to the duke. "Here are the letters I received authorizing the latest increases," he said, handing the letters to the man standing before him.

He watched the duke page through the letters one by one, his features becoming more and more fierce.

The game is up, Mr. Ambleside realized. *He knows the signatures are forged. Even if I escape responsibility for the forgeries, he's going to want an accounting of the extra rent money. At least I've kept that in the library safe. I can say I never forwarded the money because I intended to make improvements.*

He had come so close to having it all! Mr. Ambleside clamped his jaws tight to keep from giving away his rage and frustration. He had learned in all those miserable English boarding schools where he had studied hard to become a proper Englishman, how to keep his feelings hidden, how to look serene and unruffled, when inside his heart ached and bled.

"So the duke authorized the increases. You had nothing to do with it yourself?"

Why doesn't he recognize the letters as forgeries? Mr. Ambleside wondered. *Why does he refer to the duke as though he were someone else?* "I'm merely the steward here," he said. "I merely follow orders."

"How can I get a message to the new duke?"

Mr. Ambleside's knees nearly gave him away. They buckled quite without warning, and if he hadn't been close enough to brace himself on the desk, he would have landed in a heap on the floor. He stared hard at the man before him. It *was* the duke. He was sure of it. But the man genuinely did not seem to know he was the duke.

Amnesia? Perhaps from the beating he was given? It was the only answer that made sense.

"You may leave a message with me. I will see that it reaches His Grace," Mr. Ambleside said in a voice that trembled with excitement.

"Tell the new duke that Alex Wheaton will be wed to Lady Katherine MacKinnon in three weeks, after the banns are read. Tell him we willna be waiting here anymore like sheep for the slaughter, that we'll be going to London to fight him in court. Tell him he'd better come get what's his from Blackthorne Hall and take it back to England. Because before the year is out, the new Laird of Clan MacKinnon will also be Laird of Blackthorne Hall."

It was a bold speech, Mr. Ambleside conceded as he watched the duke stalk out of the library, and proved once and for all that Alex Wheaton had no idea who he was. It was a well-known fact that, after his first disastrous marriage, Blackthorne had vowed never to marry again.

Could Katherine MacKinnon have realized, as he had, that Alex Wheaton and Alastair Wharton were the

same person? He did not think so. He based this con-
clusion on the level of hatred she and her father had always exhibited toward the English. She would never
marry the enemy. And yet, it was a sure way to gain
Blackthorne Hall.

Such speculation left Mr. Ambleside with a great
deal of food for thought. How long would the duke's
amnesia last? Hours? Days? Weeks?

He could not afford to waste any time. He needed
Blackthorne dead before Katherine MacKinnon married him in the kirk and got pregnant with his child. To
be on the safe side, he might as well take care of Lady
Katherine at the same time. An accident perhaps. He
would find someone who could do the job right this
time.

Alex had waited with bated breath for Mr. Ambleside
to look up from his desk and had watched closely for
any sign of recognition in the man's eyes. There had
been none. Alex had come and gone from the library
without the slightest sign from the duke's steward that
he was anyone other than the stranger he had claimed
to be.

However, Alex had experienced another one of
those damned flashbacks, one in which Mr. Ambleside
appeared. Only, the steward was a much younger man.
He'd had a full head of hair, instead of being almost
bald, and it was dark brown, instead of streaked with
gray. And Mr. Ambleside must have thickened in the

middle as he'd aged, because in the vision he looked more fit.

Alex had been a child of perhaps six or seven.

The brief glimpse of the past had come and gone so quickly, Alex hadn't noticed what the two of them were doing together. The instant the library door closed behind him, he brought the memory back into focus to examine it further.

Mr. Ambleside was handing him something. A wooden box with a brass clasp. He opened the box and found . . . knights on horseback. He smiled with pleasure, then turned to show them to . . .

Nothing.

Alex blinked his eyes as though that would make the scene continue, but the image stopped as though he had come to a stone wall.

Who am I? What connection do I have to this house? Why did Mr. Ambleside pretend he didn't know me, when obviously we have met before?

Perhaps he had been a guest and the present had been sent by someone else and delivered to him by Mr. Ambleside. Maybe it had been a brief encounter a long time ago, and Mr. Ambleside didn't recognize him as an adult. What other possible reason could the steward have for not admitting the connection?

Alex had no answers for his questions, but any thoughts he might have entertained about being the duke were cast in serious doubt. There was no reason he could see for the duke's steward not to welcome the duke with gladness.

Unless the steward had recognized him as Blackthorne, realized he did not know who he was, and had chosen not to enlighten him for nefarious reasons of his own. But that scenario struck him as farfetched, based on Mr. Ambleside's lack of agitation in their recent meeting, and he discounted it.

Who am I? The answer was not forthcoming.

At least the trip had not been wasted. Alex had seen for himself the letters from the duke authorizing the increased rents. They were testimony to the duke's ruthlessness. It was apparent Blackthorne had intended the tenants to be driven off the land and didn't care how much harm he caused in the process. Alex was going to take great pleasure in taking Blackthorne Hall away from such a monster.

As an unexpected dividend of his visit, Alex had discovered where Mr. Ambleside kept the duke's money. He had carefully noted where the hidden lever was located when Mr. Ambleside moved the bookcase to reveal the secret compartment. All he had to do was figure out a way to steal the key to the safe from Mr. Ambleside, and there would be funds enough to feed the entire MacKinnon clan until the courts returned Blackthorne Hall to its rightful owner.

Alex was walking to the front door of the castle when he smelled apple and cinnamon and pastry. His mouth began to water, and he saw another vision.

Himself as that same small child. Cook slapping his hand with a spoon as he reached for an apple tart fresh from the oven. Cook warning him he'd burn his fingers if he didn't let it cool first.

Alex reversed course and headed for the back of the house, following the delicious aromas to the kitchen. The door was open, and the moment he crossed the threshold, the heat hit him like a wave. He inhaled deeply and experienced a vivid memory of the kitchen. He knew exactly where the tarts would have been laid to cool—on the windowsill. The room was sweltering hot, and his muslin shirt stuck to his back as he took another step forward.

He looked toward the open window, but the tarts weren't there. He glanced back toward the stove and saw an ample rear end bent over the oven. A young girl stood nearby, ready to help.

"See, Alice? Just right," Cook said. "Now we let them cool over here by the window—"

As Cook turned, her mittened hands holding a hot tray of tarts, Alex came into her line of sight.

"—and they'll taste—" Cook froze as her eyes lighted on him. Her mouth opened and closed like a fish out of water before her eyes rolled up into her head and she fainted dead away.

Alex leapt toward her, catching the tray of tarts before it fell on her and burned her. The metal was hot enough to blister his fingertips, and he yelped and slung the tray onto the wooden counter beneath the window.

He knelt beside Cook and lifted her head. "Help me!" he ordered the kitchen maid who was staring at him, horrified.

"What can I do?"

"Get me that cloth to put under Cook's head," he said, gesturing toward a drying towel. Given some instruction, the girl was able to move. As Alex settled Cook's head on the towel, he said, "And some water."

Instead of a glass of water to revive the cook, the girl brought him an entire bucket. He took advantage of the opportunity to dip in his hand and cool off his burned fingers, then used them to flick water into Cook's face.

The splashing liquid brought her around, and she began to moan piteously.

"What's wrong with her?" Alex asked. "Is she sick?"

"I dinna think so, sir," the girl said.

"Why did she faint like that?"

"I dinna know, sir."

Alex thought he did. She had recognized him. All he had to do was get her to take another look and tell him who he was.

Her eyes flickered open, then widened. She began to moan. "Oh! Oh! Oh!"

"Easy, now. Easy," Alex said. "Do you know who I am?"

"Came back for the tarts, ye did. Out of the sea. Oh, dear Jesus, save me."

Alex frowned. "What?" He turned to the girl. "Can you make out what she's saying?"

The girl shook her head and backed up a step.

"Tell me who I am," Alex demanded.

"A ghost, come back to haunt me," Cook said in a feeble voice.

"Whose ghost?" Alex demanded, leaning close so he could hear her quavery voice.

"His Grace," the Cook whispered. "His Grace, the Duke of Blackthorne, that drowned in the sea."

Alex felt the blood leave his head. He thought he might faint himself. "You're mistaken," he told Cook. " 'Tis a resemblance only."

She looked at him from wary eyes. "Ye're as like him as can be. Except fer the bump on yer nose." She reached out with a shaking hand but did not quite touch his face. "Ye canna be real," she whispered.

He grabbed the counter to pull himself upright. "Take care of her," he ordered the girl.

He felt as if iron weights were attached to his legs, and he had to drag them to make them move to the kitchen door. He squinted as he let himself out into the sunlight.

He felt the heat from the sun and the cool breeze from the sea and heard the seagulls that fought over the offal thrown down from the cliffs. The world had not stopped.

But he felt dead inside.

He could not be the bloody Duke of Blackthorne. He could not be that ruthless, rapacious man! Yet why would the old woman lie? What purpose would it serve?

Perhaps she was mistaken.

Perhaps she was not.

He felt like walking right back inside and demanding that Mr. Ambleside tell him whether he was Blackthorne. But if the man had denied him once already, he had done so for no good purpose.

Alex remembered the raw wounds on his wrists where his hands had been bound. Remembered the beating he had suffered. Someone had thrown him into the sea. Someone had wanted him dead.

But if the steward was involved, why hadn't he looked more frightened to see Alex alive and well in the duke's library? Why hadn't he thrown up his hands and demanded mercy when Alex came through the door?

Because he's a clever man.

It was smarter—safer—Alex decided, to leave and lick his wounds in private. If he was this despicable duke—and he wasn't ready yet to concede that he was—then he had some decisions to make. He wished he had not seen the letters. The letters were proof of the duke's guilt. Otherwise, he might have been able to blame the high rents on someone else. But the letters had been signed by Blackthorne. By him, if he was the duke.

He would make amends somehow.

He could not bring Kitt's Leith back from the dead. And Patrick Simpson and his family were long gone to America. But he could lower the rents. And feed the starving children.

Alex wondered if perhaps there was a reason he had

forgotten his past. Perhaps he did not want to remember it. What other harm had he caused? What other deaths were on his conscience?

Good God. If he was Blackthorne, he had a brother... Lord Marcus. He remembered from the conversation between Carlisle and Mr. Ambleside that Lord Marcus had not believed the duke was dead because he was too good a swimmer to drown. Well, he had not drowned, in fact, though his hands had been tied. Perhaps he should count that as one more tally in favor of him being the duke.

He had to find out more about himself—Blackthorne, that is. But how could he do that without raising suspicion? Mick, of course. Mick could ask all the questions that needed to be asked.

That was one bright spot, at least, Alex thought. If he was Blackthorne, he would be able to help the boy and his family. Assuming Michael O'Malley would take help from him, considering what a bastard he seemed to be.

If only he could remember. If only the past would come back to him. He supposed he could leave here and return to England and find the answers he needed there.

But what if it was someone in England who wanted him dead? He might be putting himself right into the hands of his enemies.

At least he had friends here. Mick. And Kitt.

Bloody hell. Did Kitt know who he was? Was that why she had suddenly been so anxious to marry him?

Had he told her who he was when he was delirious with fever?

It was something he had to consider. Alex remembered the desperation in her green eyes the day she had said, *"I would have married the devil himself to save my people."*

He remembered how she had planned to seduce the duke and get herself with child. He had made love to her more than once. The deed might already be done.

Alex felt sick inside.

Please let it not be true. Please let me be anybody but that bastard Blackthorne.

Chapter 16

KITT HAD TRIED TO TALK ALEX OUT OF SEEING Mr. Ambleside, but without success. She was sure the man—or someone else at Blackthorne Hall—would recognize him as the duke. She paced the floor of the cottage waiting for Alex, half-believing that he would not return.

Finally, Moira took pity on her and said, "Stir this syrup of holly bark while I go outside and gather some ivy leaves."

Kitt sat on the bench before the hearth and took out her frustration by stirring the cough remedy that was brewing over the fire.

"Anybody home?"

"Alex! Thank God, you're back!" Kitt dropped the wooden spoon into the pot and threw herself into Alex's arms. They closed tightly around her.

"What's wrong?" he asked. "Has anyone dared—"

She kissed him to silence him. He had no way of

knowing how dangerous the venture had been, and there was no way to explain either her anxiety or her relief without revealing her deception. But a woman could greet her man with a welcome-home kiss.

Kitt got a great deal more than she bargained for. Alex raked his hands through her hair, scattering the pins that held it in a knot at her crown and pulling her head back so he could kiss her more deeply. His tongue invaded her mouth and ravaged it. He drove her back against the wall, knifing his knee between her legs to spread them wide and shoving his hips against her belly. He was ready for her.

Kitt was reeling from the attack. Although that seemed the wrong word to use, since she and Alex were handfast and he had the right to take her.

But not like this. Not with violence.

She jerked her mouth free and said, "Alex, no!"

He groped her hair, drawing her head back at a painful angle, and stared down at her. "I thought you wanted this."

His gray eyes were dark with arousal, but his lips were set in a grim expression.

"Why are you so angry?"

It was a dangerous question to ask, but Kitt was glad she had when he shuddered, then loosened his hold on her hair and rubbed her scalp soothingly. His hips remained between her thighs but the pressure eased.

That caused a different sort of problem. He was barely brushing against her, but it was enough to tease her body into wanting him. Kitt resisted the temptation to brush against him, but she was like a bit of dry moss on the edge of a very hot fire, and it would not take much for her to go up in flames.

She pressed her face against Alex's chest and kept her arms around his shoulders. What had gone wrong? Something, she was sure. Had Mr. Ambleside recognized him? Was he aware now of how she had deceived him? She felt her stomach clench with fear and with dread.

But Alex was holding her gently now, as tenderly as a lover would. He was nibbling on her earlobe and kissing her neck. He was trying to seduce her.

Kitt felt like crying. Strange as it seemed, it was her duty to lose this battle. She must couple with Blackthorne as often as she could until she knew she was with child. She should not have stopped him.

And she must encourage him now.

She lifted her face just enough so her lips rested against Alex's throat. He tasted salty. She kissed her way up his neck to nibble on his ear, as he had done with her. He made a feral sound, and his arms tightened around her. He pressed his hips against her, nudging her body, urging her to shift closer.

He did not have to do much urging.

Kitt slid her hands into the thick, silky hair at Alex's nape and encouraged him to kiss her by turning her face up to his. She kept her lips slightly apart, wanting him to taste her, wanting to taste him. He tasted of the blackberry tea she had made for him before he'd left to visit Blackthorne Hall.

His hands left her hair and slid around to cup her breasts. She arched her body toward him, offering herself to him. "Alex."

Just his name. A prayer for relief from the torment of wanting him . . . wanting the enemy.

He lifted her skirt and tore at her underclothes, then freed himself from his trousers and thrust into her. Standing up. Against the wall. It took only a few thrusts before he threw his head back, an expression of agony and ecstasy on his face, and spilled his seed inside her.

Kitt was left unsatisfied. She was glad. It was some small penance for the pleasure she normally took. *Loving him should not be so easy*, she thought. She should be enduring the act only for the sake of the child that he would plant in her womb.

She made the mistake of looking into Blackthorne's eyes and saw his regret for what he had done. She did not want him remorseful. She did not want another reason to like him.

"I left you behind," he said, between panting breaths. He reached down between her legs and touched her in a place that made her body quiver in response.

She grabbed his wrist, but he shook his head and said, "Let me touch you."

She turned her face away, unable to look at him, and let her hands drop to her sides. She tried to absent herself from her body, which responded as a violin to a master fiddler's bow. Her throaty cries of pleasure, provided a gravelly counterpoint as her body made beautiful music for him.

He teased her mouth open and thrust his tongue inside in time with the movement of his hand below, until the pleasure became rapturous pain. And she sang for him, a grating sound of satisfaction that became a wail of despair. He had brought her joy, and she could repay him only with more deception.

Her knees buckled, and Kitt would have fallen if Alex hadn't slipped his arms around her to hold her upright. She leaned her head against his shoulder to hide her eyes because she was afraid they would tell him too much.

"Are you all right?" he asked.

She could hear the concern in his voice. "Well enough," she answered, trying to smile.

He looked around and said, "Where's Moira?"

"She's gone to look for some herbs."

"So she could be back at any moment," Alex said.

"Yes."

"Let me help you dress—"

She pulled away from him. She didn't want him to be so considerate; it only made her feel more guilty. It took a great deal of effort to keep her voice even as she said, "I can take care of myself. You should tuck in your shirt."

He turned to unbuckle her father's belt and to readjust himself in her father's trousers. By the time he turned back, she had retied her underclothes and had bent down to search for the hairpins that had fallen to the floor.

He picked one up and handed it to her. "You should leave your hair down."

"It gets tangled in the wind."

" 'Tis beautiful when 'tis tangled."

She didn't want him to make love to her with words, either. It was even worse than when he touched her. She crossed to stir the pot on the fire and asked, "What kept you so long?"

"I ran into Fletcher on the way back."

Kitt tensed. "Is he well?"

"Very well. He thanked me for saving his life... and congratulated me on becoming The MacKinnon. I told him I was not The MacKinnon yet, that the banns had not been read at the church."

Kitt bit her lower lip. She had been foolish to think Alex would not find out the truth, but she had hoped she would have a bit longer before he did. "What did Fletcher say?"

"He was surprised to hear we planned to stand before the preacher, but he was glad of it, because he said there were sometimes problems when children were born of a handfast marriage."

"What did you say?" Kitt asked warily.

"I asked him how he'd learned we were handfast."

"And?" Kitt asked, her body knotted with tension, her eyed focused on the bubbling brew.

"He said Ian had announced it to the clan. How he and Duncan had visited us at the cave. How you told them I was your husband, and I confirmed it before witnesses. It seems that is all it takes for a couple to be wed in Scotland. No preacher is necessary."

Kitt said nothing, but she felt Alex's eyes boring into her. And she realized his Scottish accent was gone.

"And no child of ours would ever have anyone counting the months on his fingers, since we have been wed from the first time I took you."

Kitt looked at Alex from beneath lowered lashes. His gray eyes looked dangerous. His hands stayed by his sides, though they were balled into fists.

"So, my darling wife," he said in a quiet voice. "When were you planning to tell me about our hand-fast marriage."

"I didna think it would matter to you, since 'tis only a Scottish custom."

"And I am English?"

"Well, you are." She lifted her chin and added, "A handfast marriage isna legal in England."

"I see. And you wanted to make sure our union would be legal in both Scotland and England. Why is that, Kitt?"

Kitt tried to think of a logical reason and blurted the first thing that came to mind. "If your memory ever returns, you may want to return to England. I'd want to go with you as your wife."

"I see," he said in that same enigmatic, very English tone of voice. "So you would be willing to leave your clan and come home with me to—wherever home is?"

Kitt swallowed hard. "For a visit anyway."

"I see."

Kitt was afraid he saw entirely too much.

"Perhaps it would be best if I wait until my memory returns before I marry you in the kirk," he said.

"You mean postpone the wedding?" Kitt asked, aghast.

"I mean precisely that."

"But you canna do that!"

"Why not? A handfast marriage is perfectly legal in Scotland. I have no plans at present to leave the country. Do you?"

"You know I dinna. But what if you should get me with child?"

"When the time comes, we can have the banns read. If 'tis still what we both want."

"But—"

"We're handfast," he said, his voice suddenly hard. "That will have to do for now."

There was not much Kitt could say to that.

Alex had been caught off guard by his anger at Kitt. From the moment he realized how she had tricked him into the handfast marriage, some sleeping black dragon had awoken inside him, determined to devour the not-so-innocent maiden.

He wished he knew more about himself. It had been disturbing to feel the urge to hurt someone weaker than himself. And yet, despite his feelings of betrayal, he had managed not to raise his hand to her. He was not, in fact, a savage beast without control of his impulses.

"How did your visit go with Mr. Ambleside?" Kitt asked.

"Better than I could have hoped," Alex said. He had no intention of telling her that he had learned where Mr. Ambleside kept Blackthorne's Scottish fortune. If he really was Blackthorne, he would be giving her the information she needed to steal from him.

Alex sighed in frustration. If only he knew who to trust. He had thought he could trust Kitt, but he had been proved woefully wrong. And Mr. Ambleside was clearly suspect, since he had pretended not to recognize him. The best policy was clearly not to trust anyone. Except perhaps Michael O'Malley, whom he had met by accident and who had already proved his good-hearted nature by helping Alex when he had seemed to be a nobody from nowhere.

"I need to see Laddie," he said, "and find out what he's been able to discover about the location of the duke's funds."

Alex was out the door before his wife had a chance to protest or complain. It was a fair walk to Castle Carlisle, and as Alex approached the crumbling castle overgrown with vines he had another vision—of a three-story edifice with mullioned windows overgrown with ivy.

My home.

But where was it? If he was Blackthorne, then it was in Kent. He could simply go there . . .

What if it was his brother who wanted him dead? Were they friends? Did they like each other? He tried hard to remember but was frustrated by the blackness where his memories should be.

"Alex! What brings you here?" Mick asked.

Alex realized he had walked directly to the stable, where Mick worked mucking out the stalls. "Is anyone else here?"

Mick gestured with the pitchfork toward the two Thoroughbreds. "Just me and what's left of the earl's cattle."

"Good, then I can speak freely." It felt good to abandon the Scottish accent. "I need to talk privately with you."

"I've not found out the location of the duke's money, Alex." He flushed. "Though Jane, the maid, said she would tell me if she knew it."

"That holds no interest for me right now," Alex said. "I want to concentrate on finding out as much as I can about Blackthorne."

"Why?"

"I believe I am Blackthorne," Alex announced with a wry twist of his mouth.

Michael O'Malley leaned his elbow on his pitchfork and grimaced. "Ye're not going to pretend to be the Quality again, are ye, Alex?"

"I was recognized by someone at Blackthorne Hall."

"What? Who?"

"Cook fainted when she laid eyes on me. Said I was the spitting image of the duke." Alex reached up to touch the bump on his nose. "Except for this. And there is more I haven't told you. I found myself cast up on shore the same night the duke's ship was lost at sea. And I have been to Blackthorne Hall before. I've had visions—memories, I suppose they must be—of myself playing as a child in a room upstairs and of myself with Mr. Ambleside.

"And just now as I was walking up to Castle Carlisle, I saw in my mind's eye another stone house, much grander than this one, which I think must be my home in England."

Mick shook his head. "I canna believe it, Alex. I mean, no duke consorts with the likes of me."

"I suppose not," Alex said with a rueful smile. "But I think I must be the duke, Laddie. There was a moment, at the Ramshead Inn, when the innkeeper refused to serve me, that I considered his behavior insolent. Would a common sailor expect such deference?

"And look at my hands." Despite the newly made calluses, his fingers were long and fine. "Are these the hands of a sailor? Or a Corinthian?

"And I have more than once found myself plagued by an excess of pride. That is something a duke would have a great deal of, wouldn't you say? And my English accent wasn't faked, Laddie. It is far more natural to me than the Scots burr."

"But you speak as though you were born to it."

"I think I must have spent time at Blackthorne Hall as a child. I must have learned the speech then."

"If you are the duke, why not just present yourself at Blackthorne Hall, and see if Mr. Ambleside recognizes you?" Mick said.

"I was at the Hall this morning. Mr. Ambleside pretended not to know me."

"Pretended?"

"I'm sure we've met before, when I was a child," Alex said, rubbing the smooth, graying jaw of the cart mare who'd stuck her head over a stall door. "According to Cook, I'm the spitting image of the duke. Shouldn't Mr. Ambleside at least have remarked on the similarity?"

Mick pursed his lips. "Maybe Cook was mistaken."

"I don't think so, Laddie. The problem is, I don't know who to trust. It's obvious someone tried to have me killed. The question is, who wanted me dead? And why?"

"Are ye asking for suggestions?" Mick said.

Alex thrust a hand through his hair. "I suppose I am."

"I think it must have been someone in England," Mick said. "The attack came on board ship before ye ever got to Scotland. The duke has a brother—"

"If Lord Marcus wanted me dead, why would he send a Runner to search for me?"

"Maybe the Runner came to make sure the job was done right," Mick said. "Maybe he came to make sure ye were never found."

"Perhaps. There is someone else who has something very definite to gain by my—by the duke's—death."

"And who might that be?" Mick asked.

"Carlisle."

"I dinna understand," Mick said. "What does Carlisle have to do with the duke?"

"Carlisle has a contract to buy Blackthorne Hall and the land surrounding it, which he can exercise only when the duke is dead."

"The devil you say!"

"It's true. I've seen for myself how anxious Carlisle is to recover the lands his brother sold to the duke. And he's gone to London to see the new duke's solicitor—" Alex stopped himself because another thought had occurred to him. A rather unpalatable thought.

"What are ye thinking, Alex?" Mick asked.

"I'm thinking that perhaps Carlisle made a deal with my brother. I'm thinking they planned my demise, each for his own reasons. My brother inherits the title, and Carlisle gets the Blackthorne land in Scotland."

"Do ye really think so?"

"Anything is possible," Alex said irritably. "The question is how to prove it one way or the other. I need to find out what my relationship was with my brother, whether we were close."

"Ye dinna know?"

"I cannot remember," Alex said.

"Is there anything that can be done to help ye remember?"

"Now there's a good question. I suppose I must ask Moira if she has any remedies that might work."

"Alex . . . I mean, Your Grace . . ."

Alex put a hand on Mick's shoulder. "I must always be Alex to you, Laddie. If it hadn't been for you, I might have found myself jailed as a madman or starving in the street. When I'm able to take my rightful place as the duke, I intend to reward you—"

"I didna help ye to help myself, Alex," Mick said, freeing himself from Alex's grasp by forking a load of dung into a nearby wheelbarrow. "Ye dinna owe me anything."

"Laddie, I—"

"I'll visit the kitchen at Blackthorne Hall this evening and talk to Cook. She has a soft spot for me," Mick said with a crooked grin. "I'll ask her what she knows of Blackthorne. Will that help?"

"It's a good start," Alex said. "Perhaps something she says will jog my memory."

"Are ye sure about all this, Alex?" Mick asked, his brow furrowed.

"I must be Blackthorne, Laddie. Everything points to it. Like it or not, I am the richest man in Scotland and England."

"Oh, Lord!" Mick exclaimed. "What is Lady Katherine going to say when she finds out she's marrying the bloody Duke of Blackthorne?"

Alex frowned. "There is a chance she already knows."

"What?"

"I think she suspected who I was and tricked me into a handfast marriage."

"Why?"

"To conceive a child to inherit Blackthorne Hall."

"A handfast marriage can be broken anytime within a year and a day of its beginning. Will ye deny her?"

"I don't know, Laddie. I haven't decided yet what I want to do."

"Do ye love her, Alex?"

Alex looked sharply at the boy, but did not answer.

"Do ye like her?"

"I cannot help it," Alex admitted. "I started liking her before I knew to protect myself from such feelings."

"Well, dinna wait too long to make up your mind whether to keep her," Mick advised. " 'Tis not fair."

"Fair to whom?" Alex demanded.

"Fair to the bairn that may be born," Mick said softly. " 'Tis no easy thing to go through life as a bastard."

Chapter 17

KITT STARED AT THE MAN SLEEPING BESIDE HER, wondering how a few bumps on the head could have turned the detestable Duke of Blackthorne into an entirely different person. Everything she knew about the duke suggested he was a despicable character. And yet, the man she had been living handfast with for the past six months could not bear the sight of starving children. The man she knew had bent his back to work beside the crofters. The man she knew was a successful reiver who cheerfully shared his ill-gotten gains with her people.

Ever since the day Alex had confronted her about her deception, he had seemed perfectly content to live with her, to share her bed and her life. But he hadn't renewed his suggestion that they travel to London to discuss her claim with a solicitor. He hadn't suggested they be married in the kirk. And he hadn't hinted by word or deed that he remembered anything more of his past.

And yet, some nights when they sat by the fire together, his brow would furrow and his gray eyes would get a distant look and he would go away from her, even though he was sitting very close. It had happened again last night.

She had touched his chin and turned his face toward hers and said, "Alex, where are you?"

"Hmm?" It took a moment for his clouded gray eyes to focus, and when they did, he seemed surprised to see her.

"Where were you?" she asked.

"I was thinking . . . about whether some modern machinery might improve the yield on the farms."

He was lying. Not that Alex had not suggested changes to her clansmen to modernize their farming methods. But Kitt felt sure that was not what had put the troubled frown on his brow. Only, how could she confront him without admitting that she knew more about his past than he seemed to know himself?

Curiosity was a powerful prod, and she found herself saying, "I dinna believe you, Alex. Tell me the truth."

"What makes you think—"

She smoothed his brow. "I dinna think farm machinery put these lines here."

He sighed and tightened his hold around her shoulder. "Did you ever wish you could live your life over and do everything right the second time around?"

It was an odd question, but perhaps not, if he had been remembering who he was. That thought frightened her, but Kitt put it aside and addressed herself to his question. "How could one know whether a different choice might not turn out just as badly?"

"Surely some bad outcomes could be avoided," he insisted.

"If I had known what would happen to Leith," she murmured, "I might have—" Kitt flushed when she realized what she had almost said, but to her surprise, Alex looked understanding, rather than jealous or angry. "The point is, we dinna have second chances," she said. "Once the damage is done, 'tis done."

Leith could not be brought back from the dead. And she had found pleasure lying with the man who had caused his death.

"Some wrongs cannot be undone," he conceded. "It must be equally true that some bad choices have led to good results that one might not wish undone."

Kitt wondered if Alex was remembering the wife who had betrayed him but given him twin daughters. She could not believe he knew that much. Otherwise, why would he still be here with her? "Did you have some particular example in mind?" she asked.

"No," he said. "Nothing in particular."

At least, nothing he wished to share with her, Kitt thought. Which made her even more suspicious that he might be remembering more of his past than he was willing to admit. She had been ready to quiz him further, when he had silenced her by lowering his mouth to cover her own. She had caught fire, as she always did when he touched her, and by the time she was capable of coherent thought again, the subject had been forgotten.

Kitt reached across the pillow to brush a wisp of hair from Alex's forehead and felt an ache in her chest. She had tried hard to keep herself from falling in love with him all these months, but she was losing the battle. If only he had gotten her with child, she could have kept her distance from him—at least physically.

But she had not been lucky enough to conceive in the first month, or the second, or any of the months after that. She had recently ended the courses that meant she had not conceived for the sixth month since they had become handfast.

Kitt felt the tickle at the back of her throat and the burning in her nose. She closed her stinging eyes to keep the tears from falling. The worst part was, she wasn't sure whether they were tears of regret or relief. Regret was understandable. The longer she went without conceiving, the more dangerous was her position and that of her clan. Feelings of relief were purely selfish. Quite simply, she didn't want the closeness she and Alex shared to end.

She was a fool to let herself feel anything for him, especially when she feared he felt nothing in return. Oh, Alex enjoyed holding her and touching her and putting himself inside her, right enough. But he was careful not to offer her anything more of himself. She had tried to keep her soul apart from her self, but even in that she had waged a futile war. When Alex made love to her, it was all of herself that lay beneath him.

He frowned and moved restlessly in his sleep, something he did more and more lately. He must be remembering. It could not be long now before the end came. She reached out to lay her palm on his bristly cheek.

He thrust her away forcefully and said "No!" His eyes flew open, and she glimpsed a look of horror on his face before he turned away. His breathing was choppy and his face bore a sheen of sweat.

"Who did you think I was?"

"Another woman," he said. "One whose touch I did not like half so much." He tried to smile, but failed woefully.

This time she was the one who frowned. He reached out to smooth her forehead with his thumb. "It is nothing to worry you, Kitt."

"You're remembering," she said.

"Yes. A few things."

"Do you know where you come from? Do you know who you are?"

He sighed and sat up, revealing a powerful chest and shoulders that had only gotten broader as he worked in the fields beside her clansmen. She resisted when he tried to draw her into his arms, but not for long. She pressed her nose against his burnished flesh, inhaling the scents of hardworking man and good Scottish soap. She could feel time running out.

Kitt wanted Alex to make love to her, but it would

have been only for the pleasure of it. She must deny both of them until the time was right again for her to conceive. " 'Tis not the right time, Alex," she murmured against his throat.

"Not the right time for a kiss?" he said, suiting word to deed.

Kitt felt her blood begin to thrum and threaded her fingers into the rough curls on Alex's chest, as she had been yearning to do ever since he had sat up. "We shouldna do this, Alex."

"Why not?" he murmured against her throat. "It will bring pleasure to us both." His strong hands, long since callused by the hard work he did in the fields, roamed over her body, bringing pleasure with every rough, but gentle, touch.

"Carlisle has invited us to tea this morning. We havna time—"

It was the last thing she said for a very long while.

Alex had stayed in Scotland long beyond the time when he was certain of who he was. He should have gone home to Blackthorne Abbey. There were reasons why he had not.

First, he had wanted to prove to himself and to the Scots that Blackthorne was not the unfeeling bastard everyone thought he was. While there must have been a reason why he had raised the rents thrice in a year, he had not yet remembered it. He had done his best over the past months to ensure the harvest was more fruitful than it had ever been, and he had stolen from his own coffers what was needed to ensure there was no more starvation.

He had made friends of the Scots by bending his back to work alongside them, by sharing their joys and trials and tribulations—including their hatred for the English duke who had brought them to such a pass. He only hoped when the truth was known they would remember his present help and not the harm he had done in the past.

He also stayed because he still had no recollection of the circumstances under which he had left his home and family to take ship, nor any idea of how or why he had been beaten up and thrown into the sea. It was courting danger to take himself home before he knew for certain what awaited him there.

More and more his dreams were filled with painful incidents from his past that suggested his life in England had been one he might very much have wished to escape.

His brother had betrayed him.

His daughters were not his own.

And it was possible he had murdered his wife.

In the dream from which he had just woken, Alex had stood in the candlelit shadows of a marble stairway arguing with Penthia in hushed tones, trying not to wake the rest of the household. She was drunk, her eyes unfocused, her words slurred. She had reached for him with hands curled into claws, screeching at him like a bird of prey. When he threw her arm aside, she lost her balance . . . and fell.

He saw her tumbling in his mind's eye, her body flailing as she tried to stop her descent. She was raging at him, shrieking in fury, until she cracked her head against the marble stair at the bottom and the sound abruptly stopped.

To his shame, for one instant, he had hoped she was dead, so that once and for all the pain would end.

For seemingly endless moments, the only sound was his own harsh breath heaving in and out of his chest. Then doors began to slam, and he heard footsteps on the upper wooden floors.

He had seen the pity in the eyes of his servants as they passed by him like ants on a mission to retrieve a doomed insect and carry it back to their nest. They knew what his wife had been. He could have strangled Penthia long ago, and they would not have said a word. They rallied round him now, calling for the doctor and carrying Penthia's broken body to her room.

" 'Twas a terrible accident," his valet Stubbins said as he urged him to his bedroom. "Her Grace must have lost her footing in the dark."

They were not even going to say she was drunk, he had realized. They were going to spare him even that small humiliation. He had not argued. He had sunk into the chair by his bedroom window and turned his face against the wing cushion to muffle his sobs of grief.

He had not cried for his wife, but for what might have been. If she had loved him even a little. If she had not tempted his brother. If she had borne him children who were his own.

He understood now why Kitt's deception hurt him so much. He had already been betrayed by one woman who had married him for profit. And he understood now why he had found himself so unwilling to speak of his feelings to Kitt. Quite simply, he did not trust her to love him back.

Alex had brief glimpses of his children that might have tempted him to go home. Reggie defying him, her half boots scuffed, her hair ribbon missing. Becky looking to him for approval, her ribbon perfectly tied and her half boots shined. The two of them tightly holding hands, a united front against the world—and him. When he returned, he was determined to be a better father.

But there was a third compelling reason to stay where he was: Someone was trying to kill him.

He was safer here, where there were fewer places for an assassin to hide, than he would be back in England. So far, there had been two "accidents" in which he had narrowly escaped serious injury. The first had nearly killed Kitt as well.

They had been hunting deer in the hills when a shale rockslide had buried them. Kitt bore the brunt of the falling stone, and she would have suffocated had Birk not been with him to help dig her free. He had realized as he brushed the dust from her pale cheeks, and she opened her eyes to look up at him, that he could not bear to lose her.

During the second attempt, he had barely averted being stabbed when Cam had shouted a warning against a sneak-thief at a traveling fair. He had a scar along his ribs to show for it. It was only later that he noticed that Kitt's shawl had a jagged tear in it.

Alex had begun to think perhaps someone wanted them both dead. Except an accident only yesterday had been a more obvious attempt to kill him and only him.

He had bought mounts for himself and Kitt with some of the money he had stolen from the duke's treasure, and they rode together each morning. Someone had cut his stirrups nearly through, so that when he took a jump, he had gone flying and nearly broken his neck.

It was impossible to place blame without catching the villain in the act. Ian was too openly hostile to be engaged in such underhanded attempts on his life, Alex thought, though he certainly would benefit from Kitt's death. And Mr. Ambleside had nothing to gain from the duke's death that Alex could see.

He felt sure Carlisle was the real culprit, since he would benefit most directly from the duke's death by exercising the contract that allowed him to purchase the duke's property. It was only a matter of time before Alex obtained the evidence he needed to bring charges against the earl in the House of Lords.

Last but not least among his reasons for staying in Scotland was his wife.

Alex had been too young and inexperienced to avoid falling in love with Penthia. He knew better now. He understood the pitfalls of giving a woman that kind of power over him. Especially when he suspected Katherine MacKinnon had married him for reasons as underhanded as any that might have occurred to Penthia before she became Duchess of Blackthorne.

What he found so reprehensible in Kitt's behavior was her pretense of caring. At least Penthia's dislike had been open and obvious from the moment they were married. Perhaps Kitt pretended to care for him because she needed him to couple with her to get the one thing she truly wanted from him—a child to inherit Blackthorne Hall.

Alex understood quite well that once Kitt had gotten herself with child, she would reject him. After all, Penthia had rejected him once she became duchess. But he had not been able to keep from putting himself inside her. He had told himself he could easily walk away when it was over. And it would be over once she was pregnant. He knew that.

But she would gain nothing from her deceit. He was determined to keep her from using his child to gain Blackthorne Hall.

There was one slight glitch in his plan: He had fallen deeply, irrevocably in love with her.

Alex glanced at Kitt, as they walked the last half mile to Carlisle Castle to take tea with the earl, and wondered when liking had turned to love.

It might have been at the fair in July. He had been stripped to the waist and greased like a pig to wrestle Angus, while Kitt stood by and cheered him on, her face flushed with delight as she shouted, "Hold him, Alex! Dinna let him get you down!"

When he had won the prize, a pretty yellow hair

ribbon, he had crossed to her, dirt and grass still clinging to his sweaty flesh, and tied the satin into her long
black hair, fumbling with the bow as though he had
never tied one before. It was a public way of staking his
claim on her, and as she stood trembling in his shadow,
he had felt both possessive and protective.

She had surprised him by kissing him on the mouth
in front of everybody. Her clansmen had cheered them
both—The MacKinnon and his blushing handfast bride.

Or it might have been on the day the last sheaf of
wheat was cut. It was unlucky to be the one to cut the
last sheaf, so all the shearers lined up and threw their
sickles at the same time. Kitt had explained that since
the harvest had come early this year, the last sheaf was
called a maiden sheaf. Part of it would be kept until the
first horse foaled to ensure fertility in the coming year.

"You might want to keep it under your pillow," he'd
whispered.

She had blushed a fiery red and run away.

He had watched as she and the other women dressed
up the sheaf of wheat as a maiden with ribbons and fin-
ery and put it at the head table during the Clyack, or
little winter feast. He had stood up midway through
the meal and drunk a toast to the Maiden, as was the
custom.

He had been looking at Kitt when he said, "May the
crops be plentiful, and the bairns be healthy."

She had kept her lashes lowered and bit her lower lip.
It was the only sign of guilty knowledge—of the wrong
she was doing him—he had ever seen on her face.

Or it might have happened during kirn, the celebration of the harvest that followed the cutting of the last sheaf. Cam had challenged him to retrieve the brass ring that had been dropped, along with a useless button and a more useful sixpence and other odd trinkets, into a bowl containing an intoxicating punch called "meal and ale." As Alex soon discovered, as he performed an act similar to bobbing for apples, one swallowed a great deal of the lethal brew in order to find the prize.

He had worn a grin as silly as any schoolboy when he came up, face dripping, and turned to Kitt with the ring in his teeth. She had blushed like the veriest maiden as he had marched over to her, grabbed her hand, and placed the ring on her bare ring finger.

The grin had faded from his face, and from hers, as he realized the import of the symbolic gesture. They were handfast, it was true, but setting a ring on her finger had made their union all the more real.

He might have lost his heart to her later that same evening, when she danced for him. He had sat at the head table, his eyes mated with hers, as she moved with nimble grace to the music of the pipes. He had been swept up by the mournful sound and had seen in her elegant carriage the pride of a people unconquered despite Culloden. A fine sheen of perspiration had glowed on her brow, reflected by the bonfire around which she danced.

He had taken her hand before the pipes had died and walked with her into the shadows, as other couples had done.

And made love to her.

It was then that he knew his heart could be broken again.

If he'd had any doubt at all of what a dangerous game he was playing, it was gone after St. Bride's day, which was celebrated the first day of February with various rituals beseeching St. Bride to bring the earth back to life after the barren winter.

He had been entranced at the sight of Kitt sitting beside the hearth rocking an empty cradle and singing a lullaby. It was an obvious prayer to St. Bride to help a seed take root in her own barren womb.

"Do you really think that will work?" he'd asked skeptically.

"'Tis the custom," she replied.

"Does it work?"

"I dinna know," she whispered.

But it was plain she was willing to try anything. Because they had been together for a great many months, and while many others had conceived since the fall, she had not.

He had let her finish the lullaby, enjoying the soft, lilting melody, before he reached out his hand and said, "We shouldn't let your efforts go to waste."

She had stared at his hand but didn't reach out to take it. "Sometimes I think 'twill never happen because . . ."

Because she had tricked him into marriage. Because the couplings were done for a corrupt reason.

He could have spoken the thoughts aloud, brought

everything out into the open, and yet he had not. He had fought back the rage inside him. Bit back the accusations he wanted to utter.

She doesn't care who gets hurt, so long as she gets what she wants. How is that any different from Blackthorne's ruthlessness?

Maybe God was punishing her. And him. Because so long as she did not conceive, he would keep coming to her bed. And this marriage of utter inconvenience would go on.

Chapter 18

"GIVE UP, MR. AMBLESIDE. CONCEDE DEFEAT IN this matter and save us both from ruin."

Mr. Ambleside clucked his tongue at the earl. "My dear boy, it is true our efforts have not—"

"*Our* efforts?" the earl said in a choked voice. "My only crime has been a silence I yearn to break. I was never a willing party to murder. You know that. Some higher power must be protecting the duke. There can be no other explanation for his continued existence. How many of your attempts on his life have fallen short of the mark?"

"Actually, it is only four, and I do not think he can be aware of more than three."

The earl groaned. "Three. It might as well be seventy and three! The damage is done. I tell you, he suspects *me*. And I am innocent!"

"Not entirely." Mr. Ambleside sat in a lumpy wing

chair watching the young man pace in the drawing room at Castle Carlisle.

The earl stopped before Mr. Ambleside. "You are right. I am not entirely innocent, because I have remained silent in order to save myself from your threatened accusations of complicity. But no longer. Do you hear me? I will have your word that these attempts on the duke's life will end, or I will—"

Mr. Ambleside moved like a snake, rising from his chair and backhanding the young man, his ring biting into Carlisle's right cheek and drawing blood. "Coward. Fool. Idiot. I will not have my plans ruined because you don't have the courage to keep your mouth shut."

Mr. Ambleside immediately regretted losing his temper, but he could feel the clock ticking on his life-long dream. Time was running out. It was nothing short of amazing that Blackthorne had not regained his memory in all these months. His luck was bound to end sooner or later, but he did not intend to give up until it did.

The earl was gripped by a fit of trembling, but Mr. Ambleside determined it was only the result of rage, and not fear, when the young man grasped him by the throat and began to squeeze. At which point, Mr. Ambleside conceded he had stepped seriously amiss with the earl.

While Mr. Ambleside had been able to impose upon Clay Bannister's youth and inexperience to place him in a compromising position, it seemed the young man had no intention of remaining a pawn forever in the treacherous game they played. In fact, it seemed if he were not allowed to withdraw, he would soon declare himself the winner by eliminating the other party to the contest.

"I . . . can . . . not . . . breathe," Mr. Ambleside managed to gasp, both hands clawing at the earl's implacable one-handed grip.

Another moment and he would have blacked out. A moment beyond that and he would have been dead. A knock on the door was all that spared him.

The loud, abrupt noise brought the earl to his senses. A look of horror and disgust crossed Carlisle's face before his fingers loosened.

Mr. Ambleside gasped a desperate breath and grabbed at his bruised throat. "I will not impose further upon you," he rasped through his crushed vocal chords.

He had already started for the door when Carlisle said, "Come," to whoever had knocked.

The door squeaked open and the butler announced, "The MacKinnon and his wife are here to see you, my lord."

Unfortunately, the butler had not left them waiting in the front hall. As the door swung farther open, Mr. Ambleside found himself face-to-face with his nemesis.

It was too much to hope that Blackthorne would not divine what had just occurred. Mr. Ambleside still had both hands at his throat, while blood dripped from Carlisle's cheek, where Mr. Ambleside's gold-and-emerald ring—the sole gift from his father—had sliced into the earl's flesh.

"I see you already have company," Blackthorne said to the earl. "Perhaps we should return—"

"Stay," Carlisle said. "I've been wanting to speak with you about—"

Mr. Ambleside had no choice. If he didn't act, the earl's honesty would sink them both. He turned and pointed at Carlisle, thereby revealing half of his bruised throat, and cried, "Miscreant! Villain! Thief!"

The earl stared at him, stunned.

Mr. Ambleside took advantage of Carlisle's shock to turn back to Blackthorne. "I've just confronted the earl with evidence that he forged documents I thought were from the duke, requiring me to raise his tenants' rents. Oh, the suffering he's caused! And that is not the full extent of his perfidy.

"He's also forged a contract allowing him to buy Blackthorne Hall and all the surrounding lands *on credit*. I was suspicious from the first, but the documents looked so authentic! You may see for yourself what his reply was to my accusations." Mr. Ambleside removed his other hand to reveal further evidence of Carlisle's attempt to strangle him.

"He's lying!" Carlisle shouted. "He's the one who forged the documents. He's the one who's trying to kill you!"

Mr. Ambleside put a shocked expression on his face. "Have there been attempts on your life, Mr. Wheaton?"

"Mr. Wheaton?" The sound exploded from Carlisle. "Mr. Wheaton? You know very well Alex Wheaton is the Duke of Blackthorne. You hired three sailors from the London docks to attack him on his own ship and throw him into the sea. And you've made four other attempts to kill him, so you can have Blackthorne Hall for yourself!"

Mr. Ambleside observed Blackthorne from the corner of his eye to see whether he believed Carlisle. The duke's eyes had narrowed suspiciously.

"I am all amazement!" Mr. Ambleside exclaimed, putting a hand to his chest as though such an accusation had caused his heart to lurch. "Mr. Wheaton, the duke? You must be mistaken! The duke is dead, drowned in the sea."

"He's standing right in front of you," Carlisle raved. "Are you blind?"

"Well, actually . . ." Mr. Ambleside reached into his vest pocket, pulled out a pair of spectacles, and carefully donned them. "I don't see as well as I might. And I am vain enough not to wear my spectacles in company." He made a point of looking owlishly through the bottled lenses at the man and woman in the doorway.

Mr. Ambleside gave a loud gasp. "Your Grace. It *is* you! How is this possible? I interviewed Alex Wheaton myself. He did not sound a bit like Your Grace!"

"But you recognize me now?" Blackthorne asked, raising a brow in arrogant condescension.

"Of course I recognize Your Grace. I was at your

wedding, if you will recall. Is it possible you have been Alex Wheaton all these months?"

"As it turns out, Mr. Ambleside, I have."

Mr. Ambleside experienced a moment of sheer terror. For how long had the duke known who he was? Why hadn't His Grace come to the Hall for succor, unless he suspected Mr. Ambleside of wrongdoing? "Your Grace—"

"Be still."

Mr. Ambleside was grateful for the interruption, because he had been about to throw himself on the duke's mercy. So long as he had not been accused, there was still hope.

Blackthorne focused his piercing gaze on Carlisle and said, "I find it interesting that you know the details of the shipboard assault on my person, if you were not involved."

The earl looked stricken. "Mr. Ambleside told them to me."

"You have the most to gain from my death."

"Mr. Ambleside—"

"Yes, yes, I know. It would take a very clever man to have conceived my demise, to obtain forged documents, to write the contract to purchase Blackthorne Hall. I do not think you capable of it."

The earl flushed.

Mr. Ambleside gaped. "Your Grace—"

The duke rounded on him, his eyes dark and dangerous. "I might have shown mercy, sir, if it was only my life you had tried to take. But for threatening my wife, and for your utter disregard for the welfare of my tenants, I will see you spend your life in chains. As for you, Carlisle—"

"I am innocent," the earl protested.

"I think not," Blackthorne said, his voice implacable.

"You cannot prove—"

"I have friends in the House of Lords who will believe me when I tell them how you had me stripped and beaten, bound, and thrown into the sea."

"You're making a mistake!" the earl insisted.

"No, my lord. You're the one who has made the mistake by aligning yourself with my dishonest steward. And you'll pay dearly for it. By the time I'm through, you'll find yourself chained hand and foot, like the felon you are, and transported to Australia alongside my steward."

The blood drained from Carlisle's face. "You cannot possibly get them to sentence a lord of the realm to such a fate!"

"Watch me."

Mr. Ambleside had not waited to hear the end of Blackthorne's terrible declaration of vengeance. He had edged his way over to the French doors that opened onto the balcony, intent on making his escape. He had already eased the door open, when the duke's voice stopped him.

"There is nowhere you can run, Mr. Ambleside. Nowhere you can hide that I will not find you."

"Perhaps, Your Grace," he said. "Perhaps. But I am willing to take my chances."

He slipped through the door and ran. He had not expected the duke to run after him. And he did not. He had no doubt Blackthorne believed what he had said. But bitter as he found the prospect of failure, Mr. Ambleside had not made plans all these years without establishing an escape route for himself. He would disappear as completely as a morning mist on the Highland hills.

But not before he had engaged someone to rid the world of Blackthorne once and for all.

Kitt was still in shock. It was obvious to her that Alex had known for quite some time that he was Blackthorne. Why had he continued the charade? She wasn't sure whether to pretend she was learning his identity for the first time, or whether to admit she had known all along. It was plain the game was at an end. All that remained was to see what Alex—or rather, Blackthorne—would do.

Alex reached for her hand and said, "Come with me."

"Where?"

"To Blackthorne Hall."

"Why there?"

All pretense of a Scottish burr disappeared as he said, "It's my home."

She reluctantly took his hand and followed him out of Castle Carlisle. He helped her to mount her horse, then mounted his own, and headed at a walk across the greening hills that led to Blackthorne Hall.

"You don't seem surprised to find out I'm Blackthorne, my dear. Why is that?" Alex said in clipped English.

"How long have you known who you are?"

"For a great many months, my dear."

"Why the pretense, Alex?"

"I could ask you the same question," he said. "But in your case, we both already know the answer."

"And what is that?"

"You wanted the castle and the land." He met her gaze and said, "You aren't going to get it."

"I'll fight you in court."

"Don't waste your time."

"I canna believe you would let us starve, knowing all of us as you do."

"Once I've hired a new steward, the rents will be returned to a fair rate. You don't need to own—"

"Castle MacKinnon—Blackthorne Hall—belongs to my family. I want it back."

Alex sneered. "What will you give me for it? Will you offer yourself as barter again? I might be tempted."

Kitt flushed. They had crossed the dry moat and entered the bailey at Blackthorne Hall. The shadow of the keep fell across them, shutting out the sun. She shivered with foreboding. Grooms came to take their mounts. Kitt would have slid off her horse, but Alex was there to help her down. She felt the heat of his hands even through her riding clothes.

She noticed he didn't bother to knock on the thick wooden door that led inside the keep, simply opened it and stepped inside beneath the forty-foot-high vaulted ceiling as though he belonged there. The two knights still stood guard beside the mammoth fireplace built of stone that had been gathered by her ancestors.

"Excuse me, sir," the butler protested.

"I am Blackthorne," Alex announced.

"But—"

He stepped past the gape-mouthed servant and headed down the hall toward the library with Kitt in tow. "I don't want to be disturbed."

It would have been useless to make a scene. She had no allies here. Kitt's heart began to race when the library door closed behind her with a heavy thud.

"Well, my dear. What do you have to say for yourself?"

She clasped her hands in front of her to hide the fact they were shaking. She looked around her at the Sheraton desk, at the portraits in gold-painted frames, the mahogany shelves filled with leather-bound tomes, at the wealth and comfort to which he had been born and to which—because of Culloden—she had not. "I'm not sorry for anything I've done."

"I expected as much," he said bitterly.

"I made a vow to my father on his deathbed. I only did what I had to do."

"As I recall, you would have married the devil himself, if necessary. In fact, you married an Englishman. It must have been difficult to convince your clansmen to go along with the ruse."

"They were never a part of it, Alex. 'Twas my father's plan that I should have Blackthorne's child."

"So the child could inherit along with my legitimate heirs under Scottish law."

She nodded.

"What if the babe was female?"

She shrugged. "The gamble would have been lost."

"As it turned out, you never got pregnant. Too bad, my dear."

"Not for want of trying!" she snapped.

"No. You were ever willing. Perhaps you would like to give it one last try."

"What?"

"I am returning to England as soon as I can. To-morrow morning, if at all possible. To put it plainly, my dear, our marriage is at an end."

Kitt felt several things at once. Rage that he could dismiss her so carelessly. Despair that she had failed her clan. And desperation. It was the last of these that led her to accept his offer.

"Very well," she said, letting out a shuddering breath. "I will lie with you one last time."

Alex was stunned. He hadn't expected Kitt to take him up on his offer, and now that she had, he wasn't sure whether he wanted to take such a chance. What if, this time, his seed took root?

But it had not for many months, and he would be a fool to deny himself the pleasure of bedding her one last time. Alex knew he had been lucky so far. That he was playing with fire. But he wanted her. And this way he would be able to get his fill of her before he left.

Her callous acceptance of his offer made it obvious

to him that Kitt had no feelings for him, that during their time together she had displayed only what fondness was necessary to deceive him into coupling with her.

"Come with me," Alex said, taking her by the hand.

"You want to couple here? *Now*?"

"Right now. In my bed upstairs."

Alex had a flashback to a time when he had dragged Penthia up the stairs, demanding that she lie with him. By then, he had known she cared nothing for him. He had appealed to the only reason he could think of to persuade her into his bed.

"It is your duty to give me an heir."

He had been more than a little foxed, but he had managed to bed her, much to her disgust. The next morning he had been ashamed of his behavior.

His marriage had been miserable and filled with deceit. He would never have let Kitt get so close to him if he had remembered it sooner. He would never have put himself in a position to endure that sort of pain again. But Kitt had deceived him when he was most vulnerable. He had let himself love her. Even though he knew she did not love him back.

It was too late to avoid the pain, which seemed somehow worse this second time. To his shame, he still wanted his Scots wife. Even worse, he still loved her.

It was small comfort to feel Kitt's frightened hand trembling in his, as he escorted her up the stairs. He was weak in the knees. Alex knew exactly where he was going. He opened the first door to the right on the second floor and found the master suite. The canopied bed was much larger than he remembered, but he had been a child of ten when he was last here.

He closed the door behind Kitt and watched as she looked around the room. "I believe these are the original furnishings. My grandfather saw no need to replace such a splendid bed."

Her eyes looked enormous in her pale face. "Alex, I..."

"No apologies are necessary, my dear," he said as he unbuckled the belt that held up his trousers. "Just undress yourself and lie down."

He had wanted to hurt her, and he saw from the fleeting look on her face that he had. Her chin tilted up in defiance. Her lips firmed in determination. And her eyes narrowed with scorn.

"I see you have decided to show your true feelings at last, my dear."

"I will hate you for this, Alex."

"It is only one more sin to add to the list you have long since laid at my door."

"What do you expect from me?" she spat. "You murdered Leith."

"The only man you could ever love, as I recall."

"When I said that, I believed I would never love again. I didna know I could. But I did fall in love again, Alex. With you. I couldna help it. It just happened!"

"You need not pretend with me, Kitt. You've already told me all your secrets. How you hate the English, especially Blackthorne. Come. Lay yourself down for your enemy one last time, my dear. Make the great sacrifice for your people."

Every movement was filled with pride and defiance as she undressed herself before him in broad daylight. Alex's breath caught in his chest. His heart was pounding like the drums on St. Bride's day as she exposed her high, firm breasts, her narrow waist and flat belly, her broad, childbearing hips, and the lithe legs that had more than once been wrapped around his waist.

It was only when his eyes returned to her face that he saw her hunger. And something else that might have been regret.

Alex pulled his shirt off over his head and yanked off boots and socks before stripping off his trousers and smalls, leaving him as naked as she. When he looked up again, he found that her gaze was as avid as his. She might hate him, but by God, she wanted him.

Good, he thought. *Let her suffer as I do.*

"Come here," he said in a dangerously soft voice.

"No, you come here," she replied, tipping her chin an inch higher.

He could afford to be generous. He had what he wanted. She was his, if only for one more day. Alex took the three steps that put them body to body and brushed her hair back over her shoulders to fully expose her breasts. He leaned down and kissed her breast, then sucked the nipple into his mouth. She made an angry sound as her hands clutched at his hair.

But she did not force him away. She held him where he was. Alex released her and looked into her deep green eyes. The defiance was gone. What he saw was pain.

He should have stopped then. He knew what he was doing to them both. Some demon drove him to pick her up in his arms and carry her to the bed and lay her down.

He did not tarry with her, afraid he would change his mind and send her away. He slipped his hands beneath her buttocks, spread her legs with his knees, and thrust inside. She was hot and wet and ready for him. He met her gaze as he stroked inside her and saw the guilt. Because she wanted him. Despite who and what she knew him to be.

He closed his eyes to shut out what he could not change and drove toward his climax inside her. All the time he was aware of keeping himself—his inner self—from her. He did not kiss her. He did not touch her, except as his body surged into hers. This was not an act of love. It was an act of anger.

Filled with self-loathing, Alex withdrew before spilling his seed, anxious to remove himself from a situation he could no longer control.

Kitt's legs encircled his thighs to keep him from retreating. "No! You promised! One last time!"

He sank back inside her, but grasped her chin with his hand to force her to look at him. "You hate me, and yet you want this?"

He watched her swallow hard. "I want a child, Alex. Our child. I never meant to hurt you. I wanted to tell you the truth so many times, but I was afraid. Because I love—"

"Bloody hell!" he raged, cutting off the lie before she could speak it. "Very well, madam. We will finish it."

When she tried to close her eyes, he said, "Look at me. I want to see your face when I do this."

He looked at her but he didn't see her, because a red rage had clouded his vision. He preferred anger over the pain that threatened to overwhelm him and make it impossible for him to do what she wished. Why did she profess to love him? Why perpetuate the lie?

Oh, God, he wished he could believe her! But he could not. He was a fool to take the chance of getting her pregnant. He should stop this now, while there was still time.

When he hesitated, she reached out and touched him in a sensitive spot she knew would arouse him, then pulled his head down to hers and kissed him full on the mouth.

He kissed her back, their tongues dueling as their bodies skirmished. Her hands moved over him, touching and scratching and arousing him to unbearable heights, while he caressed her satiny skin, loving the softness, the uniqueness of her.

Because he had prolonged the coupling, the moment of climax was all the more powerful when it came. As he spilled his seed, he heard her cry of joy and for one single instant he wished he were not leaving on the morrow. More than that, he wished . . . for a fairy tale. For happily ever after.

He sank on top of her, loving her curves, her warmth, the texture of her skin. He forced himself to withdraw from her heat and rolled over onto his back, then covered his eyes with his forearm.

"You can leave," he said.

"What?"

"I said get out."

He could feel her hesitation, her disbelief, her humiliation. She deserved it, didn't she? Hadn't she deceived him? Tricked him into a handfast marriage? Had carnal relations with him for a reason other than love or even mutual pleasure?

He sat up and met her stricken eyes and said, "Are you deaf? I said get out!"

She was proud even in defeat. Unhurriedly she slipped off the bed and dressed herself while he watched her, wanting her, and God help him, aching with love for her.

There was no mistaking her loathing for him when she said, "When your son is born I will be back to claim what's mine."

A moment later the door closed behind her and she was gone.

Chapter 19

THE AFTERNOON SUN WAS GONE BY THE TIME Alex dressed himself and went downstairs to the library to examine his accounts. He decided to appoint a young man who worked at Blackthorne Abbey as his new steward and wrote a letter asking him if he would accept the position. He then wrote to his solicitor authorizing him to pay amounts back to each and every tenant equal to the rent increases Mr. Ambleside had charged them.

By the end of the day he had written three additional missives. One to arrange for the Bow Street Runners to find and arrest Mr. Cedric Ambleside, a second to begin the criminal proceedings against Carlisle, and a third to inform his brother that he was alive and would be returning home with all possible speed.

He collected the missives and sought out his butler.

"Please have these posted immediately. I'll be leaving for London tomorrow morning."

"You might consider carrying the letters yourself, Your Grace," Harper suggested. "If you intend to leave so soon."

"I have at least two stops to make that may delay my journey." He needed to repay someone for the loan of a shirt and trousers and a pair of shoes. And he wanted to offer a position to Michael O'Malley, the one person who had offered him assistance when he was plain Alex Wheaton.

"But perhaps I'll take this one with me." He plucked out the letter to his solicitor authorizing the refunds to his tenants. If he carried it himself, he would be certain it arrived. "You can take the others."

"You've hardly been here a day, Your Grace."

"I've been in Scotland long enough," Alex said. "I have two daughters I'm anxious to see again."

In that instant, Alex saw himself in the library at Blackthorne Abbey the morning he had taken leave of his daughters before traveling to Scotland. He was stunned to discover himself smiling at them, since every previous memory of himself with the twin girls had involved him behaving like a stiff-legged, pompous ass.

This memory made him ache to hold the twins in his arms.

He was playfully swinging nine-year-old Rebecca high above him. He heard her shriek with mock fright before he pulled her close, then felt her small, cold nose pressed against his throat. She had always been the more timid of the twins, and the more forgiving. He hugged her for a long time, long enough to smell the lilac-scented soap she used, then set her down beside a somber-looking Regina.

He could hardly blame Regina for looking so wary. He had kept his distance from her for a very long time. When he picked her up, she stared him right in the eye, defiant as always. Feeling her resistance, he merely braced her against his chest with his arm around her hips.

He willed her to trust him, to give him a chance. As though she had heard his unspoken plea, she laid her head against his shoulder. He held her tight, rocking her back and forth, and felt her hands steal around his neck to hug him tight.

He had needed to tug Regina's arms free to set her down, and when he did, he watched as her chin wobbled, then firmed. He had not seen her cry since she was old enough to know it was a weakness, and she didn't then, because Rebecca saw her distress and took her hand. The two of them stood united, waiting for him to admonish them, as he always did before he left.

"Be good," he said.

It was all he had ever said, but this time he had wanted to say so much more. *I love you both. When I come back things will be so very different. We'll spend more time together, and I'll be a real father to you.*

Only, he had not come back. It had been a year since he had left them. A year in which they had believed him dead. A year in which Marcus had been their father. Perhaps it was too late. Perhaps they had attached themselves to Marcus and would never learn to care for him the way they did for his brother.

But whether he had sired them or not, he was their father. And he loved them.

Alex felt a tickle at the back of his throat. *I want to be home. I need to be home.*

There was love waiting for him there.

"The roads in Scotland are dreadful at any time of year, but absolutely beastly in the spring," Harper said. "You can expect rain every day and impossibly muddy, almost impassable roads. You might find the sea more hospitable, Your Grace."

"How long before the next ship arrives?"

"A few weeks, a month. One never knows."

"Overland, then." He had to get home. There was a reason to go—joy to be found. And a reason to leave—unbearable pain to escape.

It was no surprise to Alex that he had trouble falling asleep that night. The bed in the master suite, with its three feather mattresses, was far too soft.

The fine brandy he had drunk after supper should have acted as a soporific, but he hadn't indulged in enough of it to dent the anticipation of his happy reunion with his daughters.

And, of course, there was his wife.

Alex wasn't sure what the procedure was to renounce a handfast wife, but he had done nothing, and surely nothing was not enough. There was the chance he had gotten her with child during that final coupling. If she was with child, he would have to do something. He was not sure what. If she was with child . . .

But that was putting the cart before the horse. Nothing was certain yet, except that he knew who he was and who had tried to kill him and he was going home. On that thought, Alex closed his eyes.

In his dream, he was suffocating.

Alex fought the smothering cloth over his nose and mouth, clawing at his face with his hands. His eyes were open, but he could see nothing in the darkness. His wrists were caught in a viselike grip, so he kicked out with his feet. He heard someone cry out in pain, but by then he was gasping for breath and finding none.

"I thought you said this would put him to sleep!" a hushed male voice complained.

"He's stronger than I thought," a female voice whispered in reply.

That lying bitch! She's making sure I don't renounce the marriage. By God, Kitt, you'll pay for this!

It was his last thought before he drifted into blackness.

Alex never saw his captors. He awoke in a small stone cell wearing the nightshirt he had slept in. A heavy chain had been clamped on one ankle and was attached to a ring on the stone wall. The chain allowed him to roam the cell, even to reach the door, which had a single barred window. He could hear the surf beating against the rocks, so he knew he was near the sea. And it smelled musty, as if water had once upon a time seeped through the walls and grown a slimy mold, even though the hard-packed dirt floor was dry.

He did not know how long he had been unconscious before he awoke to a darkness so complete he could not see his hand before his face. He yelled until he was hoarse, but no one heard. Or, at least, no one answered his cries for help.

Alex suddenly remembered being in another dark cell. He was twelve years old, and he had snuck into the passageways that honeycombed the walls of Blackthorne Abbey. He had been drawn into the dungeon by the intriguing sight of a skeleton—and the door to the dungeon had slid closed and locked him inside.

He had yelled until he was hoarse for help that never came. He had soiled himself from fear when he tripped over the skeleton in the dark. He had long since given up hope of rescue when his father found him. He had been ashamed to be seen in such a condition, but his father had nevertheless picked him up and held him and loved him.

Years later, he could feel the tears on his face, and the warmth of his father's arms. Alex realized that it was his determination never to be seen at such a disadvantage again that had made him such a proud man.

It was sobering to think he might not be rescued this time. That he might become just a skeleton in a dungeon. The thirst got so bad his tongue swelled, filling his mouth, and the hunger made his belly ache.

She must hate him very much, he thought, to end his life so cruelly.

His butler would likely believe he had arisen early and left for London. No one would think to look for him until the letter reached his brother saying that he was alive.

By then he would be a collection of bones.

Alex paced the confines of the cell, which was empty except for a slop bucket in the corner. He was cheered by the thought that he was expected to live long enough to need it. He searched for an avenue of escape, a means of overpowering his captors, but found nothing to aid him.

Despair was his enemy. The darkness was frightening, the isolation even more so. He fought the fear by focusing on his revenge. He went over everything in his head. Every lie his wife had told him. Every deceit she had committed. He used his hate to keep himself from giving up hope. He had to live, if only to have vengeance.

He wondered why Kitt had not killed him outright but realized she had probably kept him alive in case she had not conceived during their last coupling. How long before she would know? Long enough to miss her courses. A couple of weeks. Then someone must bring him water, he realized. And food.

Alex planned how he would attack his captor, finding the outline of the door in the wall, imagining how it would open, imagining how he would wrap the length of chain around his jailer's throat and squeeze until he died.

Who had been her accomplice? he wondered. He tried to imagine any of her clansmen helping her to murder him so foully and felt sick inside. Had his efforts over the past months meant nothing to Fletcher or Evan or Birk? To Angus or Cam or Duncan? Was he to be always and only the damnable Duke of Blackthorne?

He missed his daughters. He thought of all the times he could have held them and loved them and had not.

He wished he had forgiven his brother. Marcus had been so very young. And so very sorry.

On the third day, someone brought bread and water. The door never opened. The water-soaked bread was slid under the door on a tin plate.

Alex pounded on the wooden door with what little strength he had left and rasped, "Who's there? Tell me who's there!"

No one answered.

"Tell her I'll come back from the grave to haunt her," he grated past his parched throat. "Tell her my ghost will never let her rest."

He heard nothing. He might as well have been talking to the wind.

The bread and water came regularly after that, once a day, with a piece of fruit once a week. It was obvious he was being kept alive—barely. But for what purpose?

He kept track of the passing days by scratching a mark in the stone wall with the sharp edge of one of the chain links. He made himself walk the distances from corner to corner to keep up his strength, but it was the hate in his heart that gave him the will to keep going.

When he had been confined for twenty-two days, and the food was still coming, he figured she would come to him at last. Surely she had need of his seed. Otherwise, why keep him alive?

But she did not come. It was a week more before the door opened for the first time since he had been imprisoned. He was too weak to attack. He was barely strong enough to stand. The lantern blinded him momentarily. When his eyes finally adjusted, he was not surprised by what he saw.

"Ian! I should have known. What is the plan? To put your bastard in her belly and call it mine?"

"Good morning, Your Grace. I must say you're not looking at all well."

"I have found the food and the accommodations not to my taste."

Ian laughed. It was not a pleasant sound. "You'll have to put up with them a little longer. Unless you would prefer I end it here and now."

"Given that alternative, I will manage," he said. "When will I see my wife?"

"If you mean Lady Katherine, she's to be mine, and the land, as well."

"You'll never get away with this, Ian. I've sent a

letter to my brother, telling him I'm alive. He'll come looking—"

"I'm afraid those letters of yours never got beyond Mishnish. Couldna have the Runners nosing around now, could we, looking for a duke that's already dead, or asking about contracts for land that'll be coming to The MacKinnon."

Alex struck out like the trapped animal he was. His fisted hands struck Ian in the jaw and the stomach before Ian's powerful fist slammed into the side of his head, knocking him down.

Ian kicked him hard in the ribs. "Next time, I'll kill you."

He backed out of the cell, and Alex heard the key turning in the lock. He almost wished Ian had killed him. It was agonizing to live with the pain of Kitt's betrayal.

"Alex, are ye in there?"

Alex thought he imagined the friendly voice, because he had so often wished for it. "Who's there?"

"Alex? 'Tis Laddie. Are ye all right?"

Alex laughed, but the sound never got beyond his chest. "Oh, yes, I'm fit as a fiddle. Can you get me out of here?"

"I'll have to find a way to jimmy the lock."

"Watch out for Ian," Alex warned.

"Dinna fash yerself. He's gone."

Alex tried to get up onto his feet. He didn't want Mick to see him lying on the floor. But he couldn't do it. Ian must have cracked one of his ribs.

"Alex, I canna get the lock open," Mick cried. "I'll need to go away and come back."

"Where am I, Laddie? Do you have to go far?"

"Ye're in the caves at the base of the cliff below Castle Carlisle."

Castle Carlisle? Was it possible Kitt had not had him imprisoned? Was it possible Carlisle was the villain who had arranged to have Ian put him here? "How did you know to look for me here, Laddie?"

"To be honest, I wasna looking for ye. The word from Blackthorne Hall was ye left for England a full month ago. I only wondered what Ian MacDougal was doing sneaking around down here. I thought maybe 'twas some buried treasure he had hidden."

"I would have been buried soon enough, if you had not found me," Alex muttered.

"I have to leave ye now, Alex, to get something to pick this lock."

"Laddie—" Alex heard the panic in his voice and took a deep breath to calm himself. "Don't forget where you left me."

He heard the boy's voice muffled against the door. "Are ye truly all right, Alex? Do ye need anything?"

"If you cannot get me out of here right away, I could use some food and water. And a weapon, if you can find one."

"Sure, Alex. Dinna fear. I'll send word to your wife where you are."

"No!"

"But, Alex—"

"I think she may have put me here."

"Surely not. She loves ye, Alex."

Alex would have laughed, if it hadn't been too painful to do so. "Do as I say, Laddie. Don't speak with anyone."

"All right, Alex. But I think ye're making a mistake."

"Someone wants me dead, and they nearly succeeded this time. I'm sure Ian is only a part of it. I want a chance to find out who is giving him orders."

"Would you like me to follow him, Alex, to see where he goes? I can do that?"

Alex was torn. He was fairly certain Kitt had collaborated with Ian to have him imprisoned. But a part of him didn't want to believe it. A part of him hoped Ian might have joined forces with Carlisle. That made some sense. Or with Mr. Ambleside, if he had not fled the environs. Though Alex believed he was long gone.

"If you can do it without getting caught, Laddie, go ahead and follow Ian. But be careful. I don't want you to end up in here with me."

"Dinna worry, Alex. I can take care of myself. I'll be back as quick as I can."

Alex listened until Michael O'Malley's footsteps succumbed to the sound of the surf. He was suddenly afraid that something would happen to Mick, that Ian would discover him and throw him over the cliffs into the sea or a horse in the stable would kick him in the head or he would eat a poisoned mushroom and die without ever returning. He should have told Mick to tell someone else where he was. Just in case.

"Laddie!" he shouted. "Laddie!" His voice was too weak to carry over the sound of the crashing waves. He would have to hope Mick returned before Ian came back to finish him.

Chapter 20

"HE LIED TO ME," KITT SAID AS SHE GROUND herbs in a mortar at the table before the hearth. "He said he would reduce the rents before he left, but they are as high as ever. Fletcher's youngest has sickened and may die."

"What do ye expect?" Moira said. "Ye didna exactly deal with the duke honestly."

"He promised."

"Ach. He's long gone to England, my darling Kitty, and has forgotten all of us."

"He'll not forget us for long."

"Now, Kitty, what is that look I see in your eye?"

Kitt smiled bitterly. "I am with child, Moira. I will bear Blackthorne's son."

"A son is it? And when did ye begin seeing the future?"

Kitt looked down at her still-flat stomach and put a gentle hand to her belly. "I know it, Moira. God would not have planted this seed if he did not want us to have back what was ours."

"Sometimes God plays games," Moira muttered. "What if the duke denies ye?"

"Denies we are handfast? There are too many witnesses."

"What if he says ye deceived him and lay with another."

Kitt's face blanched. "He wouldna dare."

"He has nothing to lose and everything to gain. How would you prove yer faith, especially when ye lied to him about everything."

"I had no choice," Kitt insisted. "I swore an oath to my father—"

"Some oaths are meant to be broken," Moira said. " 'Twas a sorry thing ye did, Kitty, lying to get a husband."

"I'm sorry for the hurt I caused him, but I would do it again," she said. " 'Twas worth it to have a means of saving us all."

A knock on the door kept Kitt from arguing further with Moira. She rose to answer it, wondering what trouble was waiting there for her.

Speak of the devil, and he arrived. It was Ian MacDougal.

Kitt did not invite him inside. "What do you want, Ian?" she asked, keeping the door between them.

"It seems you've been abandoned, Lady Katherine. You need another husband."

"Go away, Ian." She tried closing the door in his

face, but he pushed past her. She backed up toward the hearth, where her father's claymore hung over the mantel.

"You'll not be needing that," Ian said watching the direction of her eyes. "I've come to make you an offer. The clan needs a chief. Your father always wanted me, and now I've come to claim what's mine."

In the month since Alex Wheaton had confirmed in Carlisle's drawing room that he was the Duke of Blackthorne, rumors had run rampant. Her clansmen had been aghast to discover the snake they had taken to their bosom and had not been surprised that, as soon as he had recovered his memory, the dreadful duke had beat a hasty retreat for England.

"I would spit on him, if he were here now," Duncan had said.

"Even after all he's done to help over the past year?" Kitt asked.

"He caused the want in the first place," Duncan said. "And I dinna see the rents are lower, now that he's got his memory back."

There had been no defense she could make. Apparently, the Alex Wheaton she had known and come to love, and the Alastair Wharton who owned the land and the castle, were two completely different people. And she was married to them both.

"I have a husband, Ian," she said.

"Oh, really?" Ian sniggered in a deadly voice. "When was the last time you saw the duke alive? The last time anybody saw him alive?"

"The night before he left for England."

"No one's seen or heard from him since."

"Of course not. He—" Kitt caught a flicker of something sinister in Ian's eye. "What have you done, Ian?"

"Nothing that your father wouldna have done if he were here."

"You killed him?" she said, her heart caught in her throat.

Ian's lips curled maliciously. "Not yet. But I've got him in chains somewhere he'll never be found."

"Dear God." Kitt launched herself at Ian. Her fingernails raked his cheeks once, leaving ragged furrows, before he could capture her wrists.

"Damn you, woman! What's got into you? 'Tis the bloody duke, who killed your Leith, I'm for killing. Why do you care if he dies?"

"I'm to bear his child!"

Ian stared at her as though she had blasphemed.

"Dinna you see?" she cried. "'Tis the salvation of our clan. It doesna matter what the courts say now, the bairn will have a right to claim it all. 'Tisna necessary to kill him, Ian. We've won."

Ian made a sound of disgust in his throat. "What makes you think he'll accept the bairn as his own? He's already accused me of lying down with you. He'll think you mean to trick him."

"What?"

"I tell you, he willna believe the child is his."

"We were handfast—"

"What good will a handfast marriage do you in an English court?" Ian said. "Besides, Mr. Ambleside made me a better offer."

"Mr. Ambleside has disappeared."

"I'm sure he has. The night he came to visit me he was leaving the country. He offered me money to settle a score for him with the duke."

"Surely you didna take it!"

"His money only sweetened the pie. I wanted the duke dead for my own sake. And for yours."

"No. Oh, no, Ian. You must let Blackthorne go free!"

" 'Tis much too late for that. He's seen me. He knows I was responsible for kidnapping him and holding him prisoner."

Kitt moaned. "Surely he will bargain for his life."

"I canna take the chance he'll change his mind once he's free."

"Then flee, and let me free him. I'll plead for mercy on your behalf. You canna murder the duke, Ian."

"Dinna you see? So far as anyone knows in England, he's dead already."

"But people here know he's alive. Carlisle—"

"Will keep his mouth shut for his own sake. And the Scots will not betray me. Blackthorne must die. For the sake of the clan. You must see that."

Kitt shook her head. "The bairn will inherit— "

"No one will believe the child is his, not when you didn't conceive all these months you were handfast. Our best chance to survive is to deal with—"

A hard knock on the door interrupted him. Kitt brushed past him and found Laddie on her doorstep.

"What do you want?" Kitt demanded irritably.

Mick took one look inside the cottage and felt his heart sink. Alex was right. His wife had conspired to have him killed. Here she was conniving with Ian before his very eyes.

Following his gut instinct, he had come to enlist her assistance in freeing Alex and had just learned a terrifying lesson. His instincts were not always right.

Mick had believed they were in love with each other and both too stubborn to admit it. He had seen the look in Lady Katherine's eyes when she thought Alex wasn't watching her. And he had seen Alex gaze adoringly at his wife. It amazed him how well he had been fooled.

It was plain he could say nothing to Lady Katherine with Ian standing right there listening. He was quick-witted enough to say, "I wondered if you had heard anything from Alex?"

"No, Laddie. Nothing."

"Oh. Well. He promised me a reward for helping him, you know. I thought he might have said something before he left."

"He lied to all of us, Laddie," she said. "I'm sorry."

She looked so miserable, Mick wondered for a moment if he had misconstrued Ian's presence. But Ian crossed to stand at her shoulder and said, "If 'tis help you need, you may look to me. I'll be chief—"

"Is there anything else, Laddie?" Lady Katherine asked, interrupting Ian.

"No," Laddie said. "I've found out all I need to know."

He headed back to Carlisle Castle on the run. It had been several days since he had discovered Alex's whereabouts, but he'd been unable to pick the lock on the door. He had passed Alex a dirk he had stolen from a wall full of ancient weapons in Carlisle Castle and had provided enough food and water for Alex to begin to regain his strength.

But he worried that Ian might return and kill Alex before he had gained sufficient strength to defend himself. "Please let me tell Lady Katherine," he'd begged. "I know she—"

"I forbid it. I would rather die than have her see me reduced to such a state."

" 'Tis only yer pride—"

" 'Tis all I have left."

But Mick hadn't been willing to let his friend die for the sake of a little pride. He had decided to speak with Lady Katherine after all.

And found her conniving with Ian MacDougal.

He arrived at the dungeon door breathless and panting. "Ye were right, Alex," he said through the bars.

"About what, Laddie?"

"Your wife . . . and Ian. He's to be the next MacKinnon." Mick waited for Alex's reaction, but heard nothing behind the solid door. He leaned his cheek against the rough wood. "I'm that sorry, Alex."

"Save your sympathy for my wife," he spat. "She'll need it when I get out of here."

"Perhaps Ian never means to open the door again," Mick said.

"He will," Alex said. "I've been waiting only until I had my strength back to provoke him to it."

"Will it be soon, do ye think?"

"Tonight," Alex replied. "I will be free from this prison tonight."

"Shall I stay nearby, Alex? To help?"

Alex knew better than to say he wanted Michael O'Malley out of the path of danger. The boy would have been insulted at the suggestion he could not defend himself, even against such a brute as Ian MacDougal. "I need you to do something else for me, Laddie."

"Anything, Alex."

"I need you to put together enough supplies to keep me until I can make my way home. Put them in the cave in the mountains where I stayed before. Could you do that?"

"Aye. Gladly. But Alex—"

"I am counting on you, Laddie. The success of my journey to England depends on you."

"I willna fail ye, Alex. And Alex . . . Godspeed."

"Goodbye, Laddie. I'll send for you if—when— I can."

He thought the boy had left when he heard, "Alex . . ."

"What is it, Laddie?"

"I wouldna ask it for myself, ye understand. But

if ye can find work for my family on yer estate in England—"

"You did not need to ask, Laddie. It was always in my mind to offer what help I could. Wait to hear from me."

"Fare thee well, Alex."

If there is a God, he will save me so that I can repay you someday, Alex thought as he listened to the boy's footsteps fade away. He would manage to escape tonight, if for no other reason than to keep his promise to Michael O'Malley. The boy and his family deserved a chance at a better life.

It was hard waiting for night to fall. Harder still to keep his nerves in check. Alex was stronger than he had been a few days before, but he was still no match for Ian MacDougal in a fair fight. But he had no intention of giving Ian a chance to kill him.

He leapt to his feet when he heard the tin plate rattle under the door. "You'll never be The MacKinnon, Ian," he said in a deceptively weak voice.

"She'll have me," Ian replied. "Once you're dead."

"I'm near dead now," Alex replied. "Why not finish the job and be done with it? Or are you too much a coward to kill me when you're looking me in the face?"

Alex heard the key rattle in the lock. It had not been so difficult to provoke the beast. He stood waiting in the dark beside the door, dirk in hand, to confront him.

The instant the door was open, Alex launched himself, blade first, at Ian's bulk. He felt the knife sink deep, heard Ian's grunt of pain, then felt himself being slammed against the stone wall as Ian's giant paw swept across his chest.

The air was knocked out of him, and he thought he heard his barely healed rib crack again. He was totally helpless, totally defenseless. He had failed.

The lantern stood on the floor where Ian had dropped it, and his face remained in the shadows. Alex watched as Ian pulled the knife free from his chest and took a step toward him. "Where did you . . . get a . . . dirk?"

"From a friend."

Ian laughed, a macabre sound. "I didna think you had any." He took a stumbling step toward Alex, then crumpled to his knees and fell forward onto his face.

It took Alex a moment to realize he was dead.

He had never killed a man before. He felt nauseated, and spat to get the rancid taste from his mouth. A wave of regret swept over him. There should have been another way. But there had been no other way. Ian would have killed him. Had been, in fact, starving him to death. Alex fought the urge to vomit.

This sin, too, he would lay at Kitt's door. He was glad she was nowhere nearby. He might have sinned again.

He leaned over to pick up the keys Ian had dropped and unshackled his ankle. Then he tugged the dirk from Ian's clutched fist and winced, pressing a hand to his sore rib. It was not broken, thank God. He wiped the dirk clean against Ian's shirt, then shoved his way up the rough wall onto his bare feet.

He should have taken Ian's trousers and shoes, but

he found the thought of wearing a dead man's clothes too offensive to bear. No one would see him in the dark. And he could get clothes where he was going. Her father's clothes.

There were no other passages than the one that led from his cell to the opening of the sea cave. He set down the lantern on a rock and knelt to splash his face with cold saltwater. He was alive. He was free. He could go to Blackthorne Hall for clothes. He never needed to see her again.

But when he lifted the lantern, it was toward her cottage that he strode, unmindful of the sharp stones cutting his feet or the sharp wind off the sea chilling him to the bone. His anger kept him unheeding of any hurt.

The cottage was dark, but he didn't need a light to find his way to her bedroom. It was easy to sneak in and close the door behind him. In the scant moonlight from the window, he could see the shape of her on the bed. She was lying on her back, her arms outstretched over her head, the blanket barely covering her legs.

He was struck with a lust so strong it made him quiver.

Alex covered her mouth with his hand before he covered her body with his own. He watched her eyes flash open.

"Do not speak. Do not even breathe too loudly, or I will ensure you breathe no more. Will you be silent?"

She nodded once.

He released her mouth and captured both her wrists in one powerful hand. "Your lover is dead, madam."

Her eyes went wide with horror and fright. "My lover?"

"Ian MacDougal."

"Ian was never—"

"Don't bother denying it. He said as much."

"You killed Ian?" she gasped.

"He would have killed me. That was what you intended, was it not?"

"Alex, let me explain—"

"How could I ever have thought I loved you?" he said, looking into a face that seemed so very innocent, but which he knew concealed deceit. "This marriage is at an end. I'll make sure of it when I get home to England. Don't try to pawn off any bastard of Ian's as my child. I'll have you jailed if you do."

"Alex, please—"

He was shivering violently, quivering with hatred. He had just killed a man, and he could easily have killed the woman lying beneath him. He put his hand to her throat and squeezed.

She stared back at him but did not fight him.

"Are you willing to die, then? Shall I murder you and have that on my conscience, too?"

"I love you, Alex."

The pain was enormous, as though he had been stabbed in the heart. He was off of her an instant later and moving toward the chest across the room where she kept her father's things. He could find no trousers, only the kilt he had worn on their visit to Castle Carlisle.

He was too frightened of what he might do to her if he took the time to search further, so he grabbed what he could find, including the borrowed shoes with holes in the toes that sat in the corner of the room. He was running by the time he reached the front door, but her cries reached out to him.

"Alex, wait! I'm innocent. The child is yours. Alex, please. You must believe me!"

Climbing far up in the hills, he could still hear her ululating wails of despair.

Chapter 21

By the time the stone outline of Blackthorne Abbey came into view, Alex had
traversed the breadth of Scotland and England as a
pauper. It should have been a simple matter to throw
himself on the mercy of his friends, or to send a letter
to his valet and wait for Stubbins to bring proper clothing and funds for the return trip. But he had changed a
great deal in the months he had been gone. His pride
was not as important as getting home to his family.

So he had hitched rides and walked and traveled almost as fast as if he had come in a coach and four. He
glanced down at himself and grinned. He looked like a
Highland reiver, dressed in the kilt he had worn for the
past few weeks of muddy travel. He hadn't shaved and
his hair was too long, but he had never felt more fit in
his life.

He wanted to see his children. And Marcus. He
must speak with his brother and offer the forgiveness

he had wrongly withheld. Life was too uncertain. And love was too precious to lose in such a way.

To Alex's amazement, there was not a soul to greet him when he banged the iron ring on the immense front door of Blackthorne Abbey. Most unusual. Where was Fenwick, his butler? He finally opened the door himself and walked in. He started to call out, but decided he would take himself to his brother's rooms in the East Wing of the Abbey, where he was sure to find the answers he sought.

As he walked the shadow-ridden corridor that led from the main portion of the house to the crumbled remains that his brother had claimed, Alex discovered the cobwebs were gone, along with the moth-eaten curtains and the tattered rugs. Had Marcus continued the restoration that had stopped when he had gone into the army?

Alex turned a corner and ran into his butler.

"Yer Grace? Is that really yerself?" Fenwick exclaimed.

He smiled at the little man who had left Scotland to become his father's butler so many years ago. "Yes, Fenwick. 'Tis I."

"We thought ye were drowned!"

"I was not," he said, gripping the shoulders of the tearful old man to reassure him he was real.

Fenwick seemed to recover himself and looked with a frown of alarm at the hands on his shoulders. "Are ye well, Yer Grace?"

Alex realized he had never before touched one of

his servants, not even Fenwick, whom he had taken a liking to all those years ago when he was a boy at Blackthorne Hall. Well, that was going to change. He patted Fenwick's shoulder once more and smiled. "I am perfectly fine, Fenwick. Where are my children? And my brother?"

"Oh, my, Yer Grace. What a basket we are in! What can I tell you, but—"

Alex felt a quiver of alarm. "Is something wrong, Fenwick?"

"Well, not exactly, Yer Grace. But His Grace—that is, yer brother . . . I mean—"

A female voice interrupted him. "Who is that you're talking with, Fenwick? You should be—"

Alex watched as his housekeeper's jaw dropped and her eyes widened in shock.

"Your Grace!" she exclaimed. "Fenwick, it's His Grace! In a kilt!"

Another voice joined the fray. "I say, Your Grace. I had no idea you were home!"

Alex turned to find Sergeant Griggs, his brother's batman. He had lost an arm and was out of uniform, Alex noticed, but otherwise seemed the same. A white-haired, elderly woman, a lady judging by her attire, held fast to his one remaining arm.

"This is Lady Lavinia, Your Grace," Griggs said, making the introduction. "It's Blackthorne, my lady. Home from Scotland."

The elderly lady held out a hand, but Alex was a good foot distant from where she had aimed it. It took him a moment to realize she was blind. He stepped forward and bent over her hand. "So nice to meet you, Lady Lavinia."

"This is wonderful! This is perfect," Lady Lavinia said. "His Grace returned alive and well. If that doesn't beat all. I don't mean to be a rattle-box, Your Grace. I mean a prattle-rate. Or is it a prattle-rattle? Oh, dear, where is that girl when I need her? Take me to my room please, Griggs."

The elderly woman looked upset. Alex was ready to follow after her to inquire if he could be of some assistance, when he saw his brother standing in the East Wing drawing room.

"What is all the commotion?" Marcus said. "Have you found them?"

"Good news, Your Grace—I mean, your lordship," Griggs corrected himself with a grin. "Your brother's home. His Grace, I mean."

Alex stared at his younger brother, the infamous Beau, and saw that his looks were not what they once had been. One side of his face had been terribly scarred. Alex crossed the hall and stepped into the drawing room with Marcus, shutting the door behind them.

"Well, laddie, your big brother is home. How about a fond greeting?"

The tears in his brother's eyes reassured him he had been missed and brought a lump to his own throat. When he saw Marcus was going to shake his hand, he realized it was up to him to close the gap that lay between them. He opened his arms wide. And Marcus stepped into them.

He hugged his brother hard and realized it must have been a hundred years—well, twenty at least—since he had held him thus. He could not keep the grin off his face when he at last released him.

"Where have you been?" Marcus choked out. "We were told you had drowned."

He spread his arms wide. "Here I am. Alive and well."

"Why did you not come home?"

The smile disappeared as he thought of Kitt, but he forced himself to speak lightly. "A cunning lass held me captive through trickery." When Marcus would have interrupted, he held up a hand. "She'll repay the debt she owes me in full. Never doubt it. As for where I have been . . . why, seeing to my lands in Scotland."

"Are you the mysterious laird of Clan MacKinnon?"

"The laird," he said with a thick Scottish burr. "And married to its lady."

Marcus gasped. "You are married, Alex?"

He smiled cynically. "The witch would tell you so. I say it is for the courts to settle."

"What witch?"

"My wife. But Katherine is not a fit topic for discussion. Where are my children, Marcus?"

"I hesitate to say."

Alex frowned. Marcus's worried look, combined with Fenwick's distress, suggested things were not as they should be. He felt a chill of alarm. "I trust they are well."

"As far as I know." Marcus swallowed hard and said, "I seem to have lost them."

"Again?" The twins' last adventure had ended with them being found none the worse for wear in London. If they were lost somewhere on the property, they would show up soon, stockings torn and ribbons flying. He grinned, put an arm around Marcus's shoulder in a bear hug, and said, "You really must be more careful."

"You are so different, Alex. What has changed?"

It was true. Whatever wall had existed between him and the rest of the world had come down during his sojourn in Scotland. He guessed that meant he was no longer afraid to let the people in his life get close to him. He owed that to Kitt, he supposed. She was the one who had taught him to love again. And how precious life could be when one believed one would not have much more of it to live.

"I have realized how short life can be, Marcus," he said. "I am no longer willing to let doubts keep me from loving my children. Or let acrimony separate me from my only kin."

He watched the smile form on his brother's face, saw how the scar drew his lips up slightly on one side. Marcus was no longer perfect. But then, Alex no longer wanted or needed perfection from his brother.

"Scotland is good for you, Alex. You should go there more often," Marcus said.

"Perhaps I will take the twins to see Blackthorne Hall next summer." He smiled and added, "If we can find them."

"I believe they are somewhere in the hidden passageways within the Abbey. Are you familiar with them?"

Alex nodded. He had good reason to remember his near-fatal visit to the dungeon of Blackthorne Abbey. His anxiety increased at the thought of his daughters lost amid the dark passageways. Some of them were quite dangerous. "There's an entrance to the passageways in your bedroom, Marcus. We can start looking there."

They were deep within the honeycombed passageways when Marcus said, "There is something I have been meaning to say for a long time."

"Can it wait?" Alex asked.

"I have waited too long already."

Alex had always suspected that his brother could have told him at any time whether the twins were his children or not. He had never wanted to know for sure. Now, it didn't matter. He would love them whether they were his or not. Still, he held his breath as he waited for Marcus to speak.

"I never lay with Penthia, Alex, except that one time you founded us together. I never put myself inside her. Reggie and Becky are your daughters, not mine."

Alex released a shuddering sigh. "It's good to know the truth at last, Marcus. But before I left, I had made up my mind to love them no matter whose children they were. And I made up my mind to forgive you."

"Thank you, Alex."

Alex thought he heard someone calling Marcus's name somewhere in the passageway. "Do you hear that?"

"It sounds like—It is! Eliza!"

"Who is Eliza?" Alex asked.

"Elizabeth Sheringham, now Elizabeth Wharton," Marcus said. "My wife."

"It seems I have been gone a great deal too long. The Beau has accepted a leg-shackle?" Alex studied his brother in the glow of the lantern he held and realized Marcus looked different, too. Less attractive. But more content.

"It is a long story, Alex," Marcus said. "Suffice it to say I did *not* act honorably toward the lady, that my friend Julian Sheringham—before he was killed at Waterloo—engaged himself to her, and that after a period of mourning, she has recently become my wife."

"Miss Sheringham did not care that your looks were spoiled?"

"No, Alex. She is concerned only that I love her."

Alex felt a stab of envy. "It is a love match then?"

"It is on my side. It was for her, I think, in the beginning. But there have been problems."

Alex smiled ruefully. "With women, there usually are."

They separated then, Marcus to hunt for his wife,

who had also disappeared, and Alex to continue the search for Regina and Rebecca. He headed in the direction of the dungeon where he had been locked as a boy. He could hear Becky long before he got there.

"Is anybody there? We are locked in the dungeon and cannot get out. Help, someone! We are locked—"

He lifted the lantern to the hole in the dungeon door and said, "I can hear you, Becky." *I'm home. I love you both. I promise to be a better father. Please be all right!*

"Father, is that you? You're home? We are locked in!"

What if he had not hurried home? What if he had stopped to wait on his valet? They might have died of thirst. If memory served, the skeleton was still there. His father had said it had always been there, and he would not be the one to remove it. The twins must be terrified to be locked in with it.

"There is a key," he replied in a choked voice. "I will be back with it shortly." His knees threatened to buckle as he moved along the passageway to a crevice where a skeleton key hung on a hook. When at last he shoved the dungeon door open, he saw Regina lying on the floor with her head wrapped in what looked like a makeshift bandage, with Rebecca kneeling at her side.

For several moments he couldn't speak past the constriction of fear in his throat. At last he managed to say, "Reggie, Becky, are you all right?"

"Reggie is hurt, Father. She fell and cut her head."

He crossed hurriedly and sank down onto one knee

beside his injured daughter, setting the lamp where the circle of light lit both their faces. He was alarmed to feel the stickiness of blood in Regina's hair.

"Who put this bandage on?" he asked.

"I did," Becky said in a faint voice. "I tried to stop the bleeding."

He lifted Reggie into his arms and pulled her against his breast. His eyes closed as he felt the warmth of her, smelled the lilac soap that both twins used. "Reggie," he murmured. *Thank you, God.* "I'm so glad you're alive."

He looked down at the second twin, the one who had always been afraid of blood, and said, "Thank you, Becky. I think your nursing may have saved your sister's life."

Alex's vision was blurred with tears, but he reached out a hand to Becky and when she took it, he pulled her close, holding both girls snugly against him.

He wanted to tell them how much they meant to him. He wanted to tell them how much he loved them. He wanted to start over and be the kind of father he should have been from the very beginning. What should he say? How could he make them understand?

"Papa is home," he said, his breath warm against Becky's brow.

"I love you, Papa," Becky whispered in his ear.

"I love you, too," he whispered back.

Over the following year Alex dedicated himself to being a good father. And to prosecuting the Earl of

Carlisle in the House of Lords. He had to be content with punishing Carlisle, because despite the best efforts of the Bow Street Runners to locate him, it seemed Mr. Ambleside had disappeared from the face of the earth.

Alex was sitting in his carriage on the dock the day the Earl of Carlisle stood waiting in line to board a ship bound for Australia, chained hand and foot.

"You've convicted an innocent man," Carlisle said. "You haven't wanted to know the truth. You've believed what you wanted to believe."

"I saw enough to convince me you're guilty of attempted murder," Alex said. "You deserve every year of the seven you've been sentenced to serve in bondage."

"One day I'll come back to England," the young man vowed. "And when I do, I'll ruin your life, as you've ruined mine!"

"You've no one to blame but yourself," Alex said. "Take your punishment and learn from it."

There was no time for more words. The line of chained men began to move up the gangplank. Carlisle refused to budge. "I'm a lord of the realm," he cried out. "I don't belong here!"

Alex winced as a cat-o'-nine was applied to the earl's bare back.

Carlisle howled with pain.

"Shut yer trap," the sailor with the cat ordered. "Unless ye want more."

The earl looked at Blackthorne with hate-filled eyes.

"I'll be back," he cried, as he was inexorably pulled up the gangplank. "Seven years is not forever."

The sailor laid on with the cat, and the earl screamed.

Alex tapped on the roof of his carriage, and it moved away before he lost his nerve and offered the man mercy.

"Maybe he's right, Your Grace."

Alex looked across the seat at Michael O'Malley. He had taken the boy into his home as a guest, insisting that Mick needed an education if he was to be of any use to him in the future. The boy had absorbed information the way a parched landscape drinks the rain. The thirteen-year-old had grown inches in the past year. With the fashionable clothing Alex had insisted on purchasing for him, and with his ability to mimic accents, he could easily pass for one of the Quality.

Alex had wanted to have Mick's whole family as guests, but the boy had protested. "We'll not be taking charity, Your Grace. I'll agree to the schooling, because I can see I might be of more use to you as an educated employee, but positions must be found for Glenna and Corey and Egan."

Alex's offer of help had come too late to save Mick's youngest sister, Blinne. She had been sold to persons unknown a week before Mick came to get her. Alex had hired the Runners to look for her, but he did not hold out much hope. He knew Mick blamed himself for not coming to her rescue sooner.

"I'm surprised at you, Mick," Alex said. "How can you, of all people, take the earl's side?"

"I think sometimes things are not always what they seem."

Alex thought of Kitt's protestations of love. Was that a case of things not being what they seemed? "I'm not mistaken about Carlisle."

"A man's life is at stake, Alex. Isn't it worth at least investigating the possibility that the earl might be Mr. Ambleside's innocent dupe, as he's always claimed. Especially since Mr. Ambleside, who might have proved him innocent, has escaped entirely."

"I'm not wrong. But I will follow up on the matter." He couldn't be wrong. Otherwise, he had ruined an innocent man's life.

When Alex returned home with Mick, he found his brother and his brother's new wife, Eliza, in the drawing room having tea.

"I cannot believe you could be so cruel as to send that poor young man to Australia," Eliza said as she poured a cup of tea for Mick and handed it to him.

Alex slapped his gloves against his free hand. He was feeling too uncertain at the moment to accept such criticism gracefully. "He would have murdered me for a piece of property," he snapped back.

"Are you certain he was guilty? He did not look like—"

"Looks can be deceiving." Alex was in a position to know. Kitt had lied to him with eyes that promised love. "I don't wish to discuss the matter further."

"Very well," Eliza said. "I will be glad to change the subject."

Alex picked up the cup of tea Eliza had poured for him and lowered himself into a wing chair as far from Eliza Wharton as he could get. He had discovered the woman was a positive bulldog when she wanted something.

He had just taken a sip of tea when she said, "I thought I might invite your wife to come here to Blackthorne Abbey for a visit."

Alex choked on his tea. After clearing his throat he replied, "I have no wife."

"Have you repudiated your handfast wife then, Alex?" his brother asked.

"No."

"Then you are still married," Eliza pointed out. "Surely you must want to see your wife."

"I have no desire at all to see her," Alex said flatly.

"Is there any chance she might have been carrying your child when you left?" Eliza asked.

"None at—" Alex cut himself off. He had completely blocked out the memory of his last night in Scotland. It was entirely too painful. He had not believed Kitt when she said she loved him. Nor had he believed the other statement she had made.

The child is yours.

Dear God. It had been more than nine months since he had left Scotland. Was it possible she had borne him a child? Surely she would have contacted him by now.

"I've changed my mind," Alex said, standing abruptly and setting down his tea.

"Then I can invite your wife to visit, after all?" Eliza confirmed with a delighted smile.

"There's no need to invite my wife to Blackthorne Abbey," he said. "I'll be leaving tomorrow to visit her in Scotland."

Chapter 22

THE DUKE OF BLACKTHORNE WAS BACK IN Scotland.

The word had spread in angry whispers until it had finally reached Kitt's ears.

She sat in her bedroom rocking the black-haired, gray-eyed child who nursed at her breast. Gareth was the one good thing that had come from her encounter with the duke. And now Blackthorne was determined to take him from her.

As he had taken her inheritance. He had spent a great deal of money making sure she lost her claim to Blackthorne Hall in court. And then offered her a way to have it back. All she had to do was give him her son. His son.

"Ye should leave here, I tell ye, and take Gareth with ye," Moira advised as she swept a perfectly clean floor for the second time. "When the boy is grown will be soon enough to demand what his father owes him."

"Mayhap by then Blackthorne will no longer wish to acknowledge him," Kitt said quietly. "I think I must give him up to his father, Moira. It was why he was born, you know. To save us all."

"Blackthorne will take him away," Moira said. "He'll be as English as Yorkshire pudding by the time ye set eyes on him again."

"That's a chance I'll have to take."

"What makes ye think the duke will keep his promise to give over the land and the castle?" Moira said.

"'Tis all to be written down in a contract," Kitt said. "Gareth in exchange for—" Kitt's throat choked closed, making it impossible to speak. It had a habit of doing that lately, whenever she contemplated the impossible conditions Blackthorne had laid down for acknowledging Gareth as his heir.

She swallowed down the painful constriction and tried again. "Gareth in exchange for everything Grandfather lost to the English at Culloden."

"'Tis the work of the devil," Moira muttered. "Whoever heard of selling bairns for—"

"Enough!" Kitt's sharp voice frightened Gareth, who let out a wail. "There, there, my sweet," Kitt cooed to him as she settled him on her shoulder. "I'm sorry for scaring you away from your supper."

"When do you see Blackthorne again?" Moira asked.

"I'm to have supper with him tonight."

"Will you take Gareth with you?"

"I must, since he's not yet weaned."

Moira snorted. "What's the duke to say when you get up from the table to leave and feed your son?"

"You're excused?" Kitt said wryly.

"'Tis no laughing matter, Kitty. Blackthorne means to break your heart and punish you for things you never did."

"I lied to him, Moira. I deceived him."

"You never lied about loving him," Moira retorted.

Kitt laid her head back and rocked her son. "How could he believe that I loved him, when I lied to him about all else?"

"He should have known better," Moira said. "He should have felt the truth in his heart."

Kitt closed her eyes. "His first wife deceived him also, Moira. He did not trust his feelings." Besides, how could Alex have known how much she loved him, when she had not known herself until he was gone? It was only then she had realized he was the other half of her.

Though Alex was lost to her forever, she had been willing to share their son. She had simply never imagined he would demand that Gareth live with him in England. It would be the death of her to give them both up.

Kitt turned her face and brushed her nose against Gareth's fine baby hair, breathing in the sweet scent of him. She had labored a night and a day to bring forth Blackthorne's heir. She had almost died. But the joy of having Gareth had been worth the pain. Love for her son had filled the empty places inside her. Now Blackthorne wanted to take him from her.

Alex had said that he would send a carriage for her, and Kitt's heart clutched when she heard the jingle of harness, the rattle of the carriage, and the clop of hooves coming up the lane.

"Dinna go!" Moira cried. "Dinna put yerself in the devil's hands. Run away, my darling Kitty!"

Kitt knew Moira wanted to spare her the pain that lay ahead. But there was no way of avoiding what must be done. "I have no choice, Moira."

"Ye always have a choice. Ye dinna have to do this. No one would blame ye if ye thumbed yer nose at him."

"How can I watch my clansmen lose all they hold dear, while I keep my own child safe in my arms?" Kitt said. "Gareth will want for nothing with his father."

"Except a mother's love."

"Please, Moira," Kitt said, her voice breaking. "Dinna punish me so."

"You could ask to go with yer son to England," Moira said. "Have ye thought of that?"

To her shame, she had. "Alex says I am welcome to come and nurse the child."

"Well, there's yer answer then," Moira said. "Dinna send yer son away with the duke. Go with him and make yerselves a family."

Kitt gave a helpless laugh. "It isna so easy as you make it sound."

"Why not?" Moira demanded. "Ye made him love ye once. Ye can do it again."

Kitt sighed as she readjusted the bodice of her dress, burped Gareth, then laid him on the bed while she placed a shawl around her shoulders. "Fine. I'll go to England. And I'll wiggle my tail in front of the duke until he's fairly caught. Are you satisfied?"

Moira cackled with glee. "Now that's more like the Kitty I know. The poor man hasna a chance."

Kitt hugged her nurse. "I dinna know what I would do without you, Moira."

" 'Tis time ye found out," the old woman said.

Kitt wrapped Gareth in a warm blanket, placed him in a fur-lined basket, and carried him out the door.

Kitt handed the basket containing her son into the hands that reached out for it, then lifted her skirts to step up into the elegant carriage.

Only, the door closed first.

Kitt stared up at the open carriage window, surprised and alarmed.

Mr. Ambleside stuck his head out and said, "I am afraid there has been a change in plans. Tell the duke I will trade him back his heir for the sum of ten thousand pounds."

Kitt watched in horrified disbelief as the driver whipped the carriage horses into a gallop. She ran after the coach shouting, "Stop! Come back!"

But Blackthorne's steward was long gone.

Chapter 23

THE ENTIRE JOURNEY TO SCOTLAND ALEX HAD
let himself hope that Kitt had not wanted
him, lain with him, loved him, simply to have the land.
He had not trusted his own feelings, so he had come up
with a test: Blackthorne Hall in exchange for his son.

She had failed it. What woman would give up her
child, the son of the man she loved, for a piece of land?

Alex had let himself hope, and now that hope was
gone. Kitt had never loved him. Her interest had always
and only been a desire to have back what the English
had stolen from her grandfather at Culloden. Well, she
could have the castle and the land. And good riddance.

He was still coming to grips with the fact that he
had a son. Gareth Alexander Wharton, Viscount Hazlitt,
had been born nine months, nearly to the day, from his
last coupling with his handfast wife. Kitt had been
very lucky. Actually, the luck had been his. He had a
son and heir.

Under the terms of their agreement, he would remain married to her, though they would live apart. It was not what he had wished for, but it seemed he was to be twice mistaken in his choice of a woman to love.

Alex had made more than one serious mistake during his previous visit to Scotland.

He had condemned an innocent man. At Mick's urging, Alex had searched the taverns around the London docks and finally, at the Whistle and Pen, found the three sailors who had attacked him on board ship. According to the three miscreants, it was Mr. Ambleside, not Carlisle, who had tried to have him killed.

Unfortunately, it was an irretrievable wrong. The ship on which Carlisle had sailed for the penal colony in Australia had never reached port, and all on board were presumed to have perished. He had held out some hope for a while that a miracle had occurred, and Carlisle had been thrown onto some foreign shore. But no word had been heard from him by anyone in England.

It was another wrong to lay at Mr. Ambleside's door.

It had become abundantly clear to Alex, once he was not blinded by rage, that Mr. Ambleside had lied to him about everything. It was easy to recognize, once he was looking for them, the sly glances, the dissatisfied looks, the disingenuous remarks. He wondered how long his steward had been cheating him. He had hired the Bow Street Runners to find his uncle, but so far, Mr. Ambleside had remained elusive.

Alex shoved the papers around on his desk. He had

sent a carriage to pick up his wife and child. Soon he would make the exchange. This stone building for his son and heir.

"Alex! Where are you? He's taken Gareth! Alex!" Kitt careened through the library doors and directly into his arms, which he had instinctively opened to her. His gut tightened when he saw the torment in her green eyes and the tears streaking her face.

"Who's taken Gareth?" he asked.

"A carriage arrived and I thought you had sent it, so when someone reached out for Gareth, I handed him inside. But, Alex, it was Mr. Ambleside who took him from my arms. He said he wants ten thousand pounds in exchange for Gareth!"

Alex felt his blood run cold as he thought of his son in the clutches of a man who had thought nothing of hiring men to murder his own nephew. He curled his shaking hands into fists. "Did Mr. Ambleside say where and when we are to meet him to recover Gareth?"

Kitt stared blankly up at him. "No. I . . . I was too frightened even to think of asking. I ran all the way, straight here to you. How will he feed Gareth, Alex? What if he starts to cry?"

"We'll have Gareth back long before he's hungry again. For ten thousand pounds, I am sure Mr. Ambleside will endure a little wailing."

"I'm frightened, Alex."

"So am I," he admitted in a quiet voice. He tipped her chin up with his forefinger and said, "Don't despair, my dear. All will be well."

He watched her realize suddenly that she was standing in his embrace. That she had come to him for succor. And that he had given it.

She stepped back and the hands that had been around his neck were knotted in front of her. "I hope you are right. I pray you are right."

"Have you any notion where Mr. Ambleside might have gone?"

"How could I know? Do you?"

Alex was afraid he did. "There is a dungeon beneath Castle Carlisle."

"Surely he would not take a tiny babe to such a place," Kitt said.

"Where else could he hide? He has no friends here. And Castle Carlisle has been abandoned since the earl was transported. I think it very likely Ambleside has gone there."

"We should go after him."

"I'll go after him. After all, Gareth is to be mine."

Kitt shook her head. "I've changed my mind, Alex."

"It's too late. You've already agreed—"

"I'll leave Scotland and go to England with you, if you wish," she cried. "But I canna—I willna—give up my child."

"Such devotion," Alex said, his lips twisting cynically. "Are you sure you won't change your mind again?"

"I was wrong, Alex. There, I've admitted it. Wrong to lie to you in the first place. Wrong to trick you into marriage. Wrong to make a promise to my father that I knew in my heart was dishonorable. I only did it be-cause I loved him, and I wanted him to love me. Ful-filling his last request was a way to prove myself worthy of receiving his love.

"Can you understand what 'tis like to want love so much you'd do anything—*anything*—to get it?"

Oh, yes, he understood all too well. All he had ever wanted was to love and to be loved.

"I would have loved you, Kitt. I would have trea-sured you all the days of your life."

He watched the tears pool in her green eyes.

"I wish we could start all over again," she said. "I wish you and I and Gareth—"

"Save your wishes for later. When Gareth is safe in your arms."

"You willna make me wait here, will you, Alex? You'll take me with you? I canna bear to stay behind."

He knew he should leave her where she was safe. Especially since he felt a kind of hope he hadn't felt since he'd left Scotland nearly a year ago. That he and his son were more important to her than her clan. That he and Kitt might make a life together.

"Very well," he said. "Come with me if you must."

Chapter 24

DESPITE THE DAMP COLD INSIDE THE DUNGEON at Castle Carlisle, Mr. Ambleside was perspiring. Amazing how pulling one tiny loose thread could unravel everything. He should never have involved Carlisle. He could have managed on his own, but he had not been able to resist manipulating the young man for his amusement.

Blackthorne was another matter entirely.

Mr. Ambleside was tired of dodging the Runners the duke had sent after him. Stealing the duke's son had been an act of desperation. His situation now was precarious, to say the least.

The basket containing Gareth Alexander Wharton sat in the corner of the cramped cell. Mr. Ambleside held up the lantern so he could see into the child's face. It looked like every other infant he had ever seen—large eyes, button nose, rosebud lips. But through an accident of birth, this child would one day be the richest man in Scotland and England.

It simply was not fair.

He felt a sudden murderous rage, a desire to slam the child against the stone wall. When Blackthorne came he would see how little good all the wealth of his dukedom had done him, when a mere steward could destroy his son and heir for the pure pleasure of thwarting him.

It was a delicious thought.

But Mr. Ambleside had never indulged such whims in the past. And he did not do so now. Cold, calculated murder was much more to his taste. And before he was through, the child and its father would both be dead.

"Mr. Ambleside, I know you are in there."

He felt a chill run down his spine as Blackthorne's voice echoed down the passageway from the sea. He was not really surprised the duke had found him. After all, where else could he have gone?

"Have you brought the ransom for your son?" he called out.

"Is the babe alive and well?" Blackthorne replied.

A malicious grin curved Mr. Ambleside's lips. "I'm afraid there has been a slight accident."

"He's killed Gareth!" Kitt cried. "Alex, he's murdered our son!"

"Be still!" Alex hissed. "He's not that stupid."

"Then why would he say such a thing?" Kitt demanded, lowering her voice to match Alex's harsh whisper.

"To spur me to a killing rage," Alex said. "To make me careless enough to come charging down that passageway, where I am sure he is waiting with a loaded pistol to put a period to my existence."

"What?"

"Don't you see? I am the one who ruined all his plans to have Blackthorne Hall for himself. I am the one he wants dead, not Gareth." Alex believed Gareth would not long survive him, if his uncle managed to kill him, but he didn't want to worry Kitt by admitting as much.

"We should have brought help," Kitt said, wringing her hands. "We shouldna have come alone."

"He's one man, Kitt. And better dealt with alone."

"What can I do to help, Alex? I must be allowed to help."

He understood her plea. If he loved her, he should be willing to trust her; and if he wanted her love, he must give her his trust. It was a hard thing to do when everyone he had ever loved—including Kitt—had let him down. But unless he was willing to give up on love entirely—and he was not—he had to risk being hurt again. It was frightening, but not so frightening as the prospect of spending the rest of his life without her.

"Together, I believe we can thwart him. Here is what you must do...."

* * *

Kitt felt an ache in the back of her throat.

Thank you, Alex, for giving me a second chance. I willna disappoint you this time. I promise you that.

As she listened, Kitt's eyebrows rose all the way to her hairline. Alex's plan sounded dangerous. A second chance would not mean much if he were dead. "Alex, is there no other way?"

"He must believe he has won," Alex said. "I cannot be armed when I confront him. I don't think he'll expect you to have a weapon. You'll have to use your own judgment when and whether to make your move."

"What if I judge wrongly?"

"Then you'll be the Dowager Duchess of Blackthorne," he said with a rueful smile. "And will have to raise our son on your own."

"Dinna make fun, Alex. I'm scared. I dinna want to lose you. Not when I have a hope ... not when we may . . ." She looked up at him and saw all the love she felt for him reflected back threefold in his gray eyes.

Kitt wasn't sure which of them moved first but a moment later she was in his arms and Alex was holding her tight. She pressed her cheek against his chest and heard his heart pounding.

Why, he is afraid, she thought. *And yet he trusts me to save us all.*

"I'll not fail you again, Alex," she said. "Never again."

"'Tis time for the play to begin," he said, reluctantly releasing her. "Remember to stay at least a half dozen steps behind me when you come down the passageway."

In a loud voice Alex said, "Damn you, woman! I said to wait here. I cannot have you hanging on to me when I confront the man."

"Please, Alex!" she said in a tearful voice. "Take me with you!"

"I said let go!" Alex slapped her hard, loud enough to be heard down the passageway, hard enough to bring tears to her eyes and make her jaw ache.

He gave her one last, grim look before he turned and ran toward the cell where Mr. Ambleside was holding their son. As he headed down the passageway, Alex called out in a crazed, furious voice, "If you've harmed a hair on my son's head, I'll strangle you with my bare hands."

Kitt counted to ten in her head, as Alex had instructed, then started after him. The setting sun provided a garish pink light in the passageway, but Kitt's gaze was focused on the harsh yellow lantern light emanating from the cell into which Alex had disappeared.

"You'll hang for murder, if you do," she heard Alex reply to something Mr. Ambleside must have said.

She hurried along the passageway, staying close to the wall. When she reached the cell door, she peeked around the corner and saw that Mr. Ambleside was holding one of his exquisite dueling pistols against Alex's right temple and had the other aimed at Gareth, who lay in his basket in the corner.

She took a step back, rested her head against the stone passageway, and moaned softly. Dear God. If she shot Mr. Ambleside, one or both of his pistols would surely discharge and kill those she loved most. But if she waited, she would lose the distraction Alex and Gareth provided. And once they were dead, Mr. Ambleside would not leave her alive to tell of his part in it.

Kitt took a deep breath and let it out. Alex trusted her to play her part as he had written it, and she had promised she would not fail him. Time was running out. She must act.

Kitt took the three steps that put her in the doorway beside Alex, the pistol hidden in the folds of her skirt.

"Oh, God!" she cried, pretending a distress that was part of the act, but which felt entirely real. "Please, God."

Alex's right hand slid behind his back, and she passed the gun to him while Mr. Ambleside's eyes were focused on her. As Alex had predicted, the pistol being aimed at Gareth swung around to point at her.

"You fiend!" she snarled. "Cur! Blackguard!"

During the diversion provided by her verbal attack on Mr. Ambleside, Alex brought his arm up and fired a ball into the monster's heart.

Not one, but both of Mr. Ambleside's pistols discharged, filling the cell with smoke and noise, before he crumpled to the ground. Gareth screamed and kept on crying.

Kitt stood frozen in horror, afraid to look, afraid to see Alex's blood and brains all over the wall.

"Kitt, are you shot? Are you all right?"

Suddenly Alex was standing before her. She put her hands to his face—his whole, wonderful, worried face—and pulled his head down to kiss him. "I'm fine now, my love."

His kissed her back, his mouth pressed reassuringly hard against hers. "I believe your son needs attention, my dear."

He walked her to the corner where Gareth lay in his basket. Keeping himself between her and Mr. Ambleside's body, Alex retrieved the basket with the howling baby inside it.

Kitt lifted Gareth out of the basket and laid him on her shoulder to quiet him. "All is well, Gareth. As your father promised. All is well."

Kitt stared down at the man who'd been the source of so many problems. "Will you have someone come bury him?" she asked.

"I think not," Alex said, his eyes cold. "He is where he belongs. His bones will bother no one here." He put his arm around her waist with one hand and slid the baby's basket over the other. "Let's go," he said.

"Where are we going, Alex?"

"Home," he replied. "We're going home."

"Where is that, Alex?" Kitt asked, her heart in her throat. "Back to Blackthorne Hall? Or to Blackthorne Abbey in England?"

"Wherever you are, Kitt," he said. "That will be home to me. You see, I love you. I've never stopped loving you."

Kitt laughed, a bubbly, delicious, delightful sound. "I love you too, Alex. Oh, I do love you."

Alex grinned back at her. "I expect you to keep saying that for at least the next fifty years."

"I will," she promised. "I will."

A Note to Readers

Dear Readers,

For those of you searching for *Blackthorne's Bride*, this is it! While I was writing the novel, Alex persuaded me to change the title to *The Bodyguard*. Enjoy!

If you are following my Captive Hearts series (*Captive, After the Kiss, The Bodyguard*), you'll be pleased to know my next novel matches those fiesty Blackthorne twins, Lady Regina and Lady Rebecca, with two wonderful characters you've met in *The Bodyguard*—Clay Bannister, the vengeful Earl of Carlisle, and the Irish pauper Michael O'Malley, who turns out to be the grandson of an English marquess!

Watch for my new suspense novel, *A Stranger's Game*, in stores March 2008.

As always, I appreciate hearing your opinions and find inspiration in your questions, comments, and suggestions.

You can reach me at my Web site, www.joanjohnston.com. I personally read and answer my mail, though, as some of you know, a reply might be delayed if I have a writing deadline.

Best always,
Joan Johnston

September 18, 2007

About the Author

JOAN JOHNSTON is the *New York Times* bestselling author of forty-seven novels and novellas, with over ten million copies of her books in print. She received an M.A. in theater from the University of Illinois and was graduated with honors from the University of Texas at Austin School of Law. Joan writes full-time and splits her time between homes in Florida and Colorado. You can reach Joan through her Web site at www.joanjohnston.com.